"Put the cuffs on, Durant . . . now."

Durant slumped. "I had to catch up to you, Ranger. Can't you understand?"

"You understand this," the Ranger said. "There's no time to take you back to town. And make no mistake, Durant . . . if you get in the way of my hunting these men, I'll kill you graveyard dead. Fair enough?"

Durant settled into his saddle, clicking the cuffs on. He stared hard at the Ranger.

"Fair enough," he said. "All I want is to catch up with them and kill the men who murdered my family. After that, I'll take whatever I've got coming."

Burrack looked at Durant's face in the early morning light and squinted. "You really are convinced they're the ones?"

"I'm betting my life on it," Durant said.

The Ranger considered it for a second and replied gravely, "That you are. . . ."

BORDER DOGS

Ralph Cotton

A SIGNET BOOK

SIGNET
Published by New American Library, a division of
Penguin Group (USA) Inc., 375 Hudson Street,
New York, New York 10014, U.S.A.
Penguin Books Ltd, 80 Strand,
London WC2R 0RL, England
Penguin Books Australia Ltd, 250 Camberwell Road,
Camberwell, Victoria 3124, Australia
Penguin Books Canada Ltd, 10 Alcorn Avenue,
Toronto, Ontario, Canada M4V 3B2
Penguin Books (N.Z.) Ltd, Cnr Rosedale and Airborne Roads,
Albany, Auckland 1310, New Zealand

Penguin Books Ltd, Registered Offices:
80 Strand, London WC2R 0RL, England

First published by Signet, an imprint of New American Library,
a division of Penguin Group (USA) Inc.

First Printing, September 1999
 20 19 18 17 16 15 14 13 12 11

Printed in the United States of America

For Mary Lynn . . . of course

Prologue

The heat of midafternoon pressed heavy on the sloping stretch of rocky land and on the wide stretch of wavering sand flats beneath it. In this fiery basin, all lesser creatures of the desert floor had vanished, taken to whatever thin slices of black shade they found among jagged rock crevices or beneath the bleached and brittle remnants of deadfall pinyon and juniper.

A scorpion had ventured out for reasons only a scorpion would know, and after a few short circles with its pincers up as if raising a plea to the blazing heavens, it skirted across the hot sand and back inside the pale white skull of some larger ill-fated creature whose mortal reckoning had come years past.

For a while, a hawk had floated overhead on an updraft of dry, scorched air, but finding nothing of interest moving about in the wavering heat below, the big bird had soon ceased its hunt and drifted away across the crest of the basin toward less harsh terrain, shedding the scalding sun for some darkened rocky loft. Now the only creatures remaining in the arid inferno at this time of day were men—men with guns. And little else to sustain them.

A dry canteen lay at the foot of the rocky slope near the body of a dead horse. A blood trail, now turned black and dry, led upward into the rocks to the body of an old bank robber named Doc Septon, whose dead eyes stared up into the burning sun, and whose dust-matted hair swayed on a slow hot breeze. Twenty yards higher into the rocks, three riflemen made a break from behind a split boulder and struggled upward toward the crest of the hill. When one of them, a young gunman named Wandering Joe Gully, heard no sound of rifle fire behind them, he looked back down the slopes, staggering in place. His eyes searched through the white glare of sunlight and wavering heat. He called out to the black man who'd gone ahead of him, "I think they're dead, Durant. Wait up. Doc must've shot them both."

But Willis Durant neither slowed nor looked back. He knew better. That blasted ranger was still there, still coming, still set on hunting them down and killing them, the same as he'd done to the other three members of their gang over the past four days. This was no time for guessing, or for wishful thinking. When Billy Dig slowed down in front of him, Willis Durant pushed him on. "Keep moving, Billy. Wandering Joe's give out on us." Sweat shined on Durant's forehead. He wiped a shirtsleeve across his face and kept climbing, his breath heaving in his chest.

"But what if he's right?" Billy Dig's voice was a choking rasp. "What if Doc did kill them?"

"Damn it!" Now Durant poked him forward with the tip of his rifle barrel. "Do you really believe that? Hunh? Do you?" He glared into Billy Dig's eyes, goading him on.

"Jesus!" Billy Dig struggled, nearly dropping his rifle as Durant pressed him upward. "Is this ever going to end?"

Durant glanced back, still moving upward on the shifting sand and loose rock. Wandering Joe had given up—that's what this amounted to, he thought. Did the man want to trick his mind into believing the Ranger was gone, that he had the upper hand here? Well, let him. Durant pressed on, his rifle feeling slippery in his wet hand.

Behind him, Durant heard Wandering Joe call out over the rocky slope, "Damn you, Ranger! Are you down there? Can't you see when you're licked? We've won fair and square—we *outlasted yas*! You'll die down there! Why don't you go on home?"

A tense silence passed, then near the base of the slope, the Ranger, Sam Burrack, called up to him, "You know we can't do that, Joe. We've got to finish this, one way or the other. If you want to give up, now's the time to do it. We've got your water. We've got your horses. All you've got left is a hard climb to nowhere."

A shot rang out from the rifle in Wandering Joe's hand as he sidled over into cover behind a rock. "But we've got bullets, Ranger, and you *don't*! We can hold out! Get on out of here . . . who'll know the difference? What do you say, Ranger? Call it a draw? Maybe finish it some other time? This don't make no sense, out here in the heat!"

The Ranger didn't answer. Instead, he slumped against the rock and looked at Sheriff Boyd Tackett. "Get ready. Wandering Joe's had it. He's talking himself into making one last big play on us."

"Wish he'd done it an hour ago." Tackett raised his hat brim and wiped a hand across his brow. "Four days we've been fighting these boys across the basin. Maybe Joe is right. I'm ready to pack it in myself while our horses can still make it to a water hole. What about you?"

"Nope. Not until the job's done. You shouldn't have asked me to come along if you weren't serious." There was a bit of snap to the Ranger's voice.

Weren't serious? Sheriff Tackett stared at the Ranger. They were both dried out and spent. Tackett knew it. White streaks of salt lined their dusty shirts, under their arms, down the middle of their backs. Tackett could have sworn he'd seen heat waver up off the Ranger's shoulders. "I swear, Sam. You don't have to be so testy with me. I've stuck right with you, haven't I?"

A moment of dry, hot silence passed. Then Tackett said, "Tell the truth, Sam. You miss her, don't ya? You miss that little lady of yours." Another silence passed as the Ranger raised his sweat-darkened sombrero, then lowered it and adjusted it on his forehead. As Tackett spoke, he'd hugged close to the rock beside the Ranger when another rifle shot exploded, kicking up a sharp spray of sandstone dust.

The little lady? Miss her? The Ranger thought about it for a second and murmured something under his breath. He shook his head, broke open the big Swiss rifle, flipped out the spent cartridge, and popped a new round in its place. He snapped the rifle shut. At his waist, his big .45 caliber pistol sat empty in his holster—his cartridge belt empty as well. "You beat all I've ever seen, Tackett, asking something like that, at a time like this." The Ranger glanced around the rock long enough to catch a glimpse of Wandering Joe moving down toward them, out from behind the rock now, staggering back and forth behind a tangle of deadfall.

"Well"—Tackett took his last four bullets from his holster belt—"it's gonna be a few more minutes before Joe makes his move. I'm just curious what your feelings are toward the little lady."

The Ranger winced. "Her name is Maria. You wouldn't want her to hear you call her little lady. Believe me."

"Why?" Tackett shrugged. A bullet ricochet whined off the rock above their heads. "She is a lady . . . she ain't all that big?"

"She's just real touchy about names like that." The Ranger

laid the big .58 caliber Swiss rifle across his lap, leaned back against the rock, and let Wandering Joe fire his rifles empty. When he stopped and reloaded, the Ranger swung the big rifle around the edge of the rock and fired a shot. The powerful blast seemed to shake the mountainside loose from the rest of the world for a second as chunks of wood blew out of the tangled deadfall.

Wandering Joe cried out *"Lord God"* at the sound and the impact of the big rifle. The Ranger leaned against the rock, rubbed his shoulder, and took out one of the four remaining rifle cartridges. "That ought to jar him into making up his mind." He pushed up the dusty brim on his pearl gray sombrero. "As far as missing her . . . sure I do. She's a good woman. She saved my life. Hadn't been for her I'd never have killed Montana Red Hollis last summer."

"Where'd you get such a god-awful firearm as that?" Sheriff Tackett asked, looking up from loading his old .36 caliber Navy Colt. He rounded a fingertip inside his ear. "I'm surprised it ain't made ya stone deaf." When the Ranger didn't answer, Tackett finished reloading his pistol, then asked in a lowered tone, "Do ya love her, Sam? Tell the truth now. It's just you and me here."

"That's a very personal thing for you to ask, Tackett. I'd never ask how you feel about the Widow Morris." The Ranger felt his face redden in annoyance, and he looked away, around the rock, seeing Wandering Joe lunge behind a tall cactus, moving down.

"But you could ask if you wanted to. I wouldn't get mad over it. If I was in love with Widow Morris, I wouldn't deny it none."

"Come out and fight in the open, you yellow lawdogs! Fight like men!" Wandering Joe leaned around the side of the cactus, fired three shots in a row, then pulled back out of sight.

"I don't know about *love* . . . Maria and I get along. We know when to step close and when to step away. We understand one another. A man in this business can't ask for more than that now, can he?"

The Ranger placed two rifle cartridges between the gloved fingers of his right hand, leaving his trigger finger free. "Here we go." He raised up slightly, dusting the seat of his trousers. "Looks like Wandering Joe's running out of sweat—fixin' to do something."

"Good. It's about dang time."

The Ranger called out to Wandering Joe, raising his voice to include Durant and Billy Dig higher up the slope. "Any time you're ready, boys."

"They're gone, Ranger," Wandering Joe called out. "It's just me left. Come up and get me!"

The Ranger crouched down a bit and looked at Tackett. "It might be best if you take Wandering Joe down. I'll circle up and catch the other two."

"Uh-uh." Tackett shook his head. "You don't want to get Durant cornered up there by yourself. He's a handful."

"You worried about taking Wandering Joe?" The Ranger stared at him. "Because if you can't handle him, I'll just—"

Tackett flared. "You know better than that, dang it!"

"Well . . . ?" The Ranger hesitated.   ·

"All right then, go on. I'll take care of him." Tackett stood up with a deep grunt. "How long has she been gone now?"

"What? Who?" The Ranger stopped and gave him a glance. Fifteen yards away, Wandering Joe moved forward down the narrow foot path, his rifle up and ready.

"Maria . . . how long has she been gone? Eight weeks? Ten?"

"Pay attention here, Tackett." The Ranger scanned a long rock spill to their left. "Didn't you shoot Buck Whelan awhile ago? I thought I just caught a glimpse of his shotgun barrel over there."

"I can't remember . . ." Tackett started to turn his gaze over to their left.

"Don't look over there," the Ranger hissed in a low tone. "Just take care of Wandering Joe when he makes his move. If Buck's still alive, I'll get him on my way up." He gazed ahead in silence for a second, watching Wandering Joe stalk forward. Then he said to Tackett in a quiet voice, "Twelve weeks tomorrow."

"Huh?"

"Maria. She's been gone twelve weeks. Should be back in Humbly sometime this weekend though . . . I hope."

"All right, lawdogs," Wandering Joe called out to them, "you've hounded me as far as you're going to!"

"That's a long time, Sam, twelve weeks." Tackett held his pistol poised at his side. "I reckon that's why you've been so cross and irritable."

"Have I?" the Ranger asked without turning to him. "I hadn't noticed. Are you ready yet?"

"Yeah, get on out of here," Tackett said in a whisper.

"Watch out for ole Buck's shotgun until I can get around behind him," the Ranger warned him.

Willis Durant gazed out across the deep ravine, then slumped against the wall of rock behind him. A draft of hot air swirled around him. "I thought you knew this country," he said to Billy Dig beside him. Beneath them stood a sheer drop of nearly five hundred feet. At the bottom a thin stream snaked its way among jagged upthrusts of rock.

Billy Dig took a deep breath and let it out, shaking his

sweaty head. "I . . . I do. It's just that today it all looks alike for some reason." He glanced left and right along the jagged, cutaway edge of the ridge. "I've been on this hill a hundred times . . . I thought, anyway."

"Billy, this is not a hill. This is only *half* a hill." Durant felt his breath leveling now, catching up to him. "The other half is a mile across this canyon." He gazed back and forth, his fingers opening and closing on his rifle stock. "We're stuck here."

"Buck's still down there. Joe too," Billy Dig said. "Maybe one of them will do us some good."

"Don't count on it, Billy." Durant stared out across the canyon.

Behind them, down the slope of rock and sand, the sound of Buck Whelan's shotgun exploded, followed by the louder explosion of the big Swiss rifle. "Well, there went Buck," Durant said. In a second, three more rifle shots resounded, not sounding as powerful as the first. Wandering Joe's voice came up to them in a loud, painful cry; then there was silence.

"And there goes Joe." Durant ran a hand across his forehead. "Looks like we'll have the Ranger down our shirts here in a minute."

"Any ideas?" Billy Dig stepped forward an inch, looked down, then jerked back, his face ash white beneath the sheen of dust and sweat.

Ideas . . . Durant just stared at him. Then he looked down into the yawning ravine, and when he lifted his eyes back to Billy Dig, he said, "Yeah, Billy . . . I'm turning myself in when the Ranger gets here. What about you?"

Billy swallowed a dry knot in his throat. He ventured forward then pulled back once more. "I can't go to prison," he said, gazing down. "It just ain't in me. You've been there. What'd you think of it?"

"I won't lie to ya, Billy. It's the worse thing ever. Nobody ought to have to go through it." Durant's voice had gone low, almost a whisper. "Some men can do it . . . some can't. You have to decide for yourself." His dark eyes swept over the ravine, then back to Billy Dig. "Whatever you do, you better do it quick. They'll be here any minute."

"Well . . . I don't want to let you down, Durant. You've been square with me all along. I could stick, make one last play, if you want."

"Naw, Billy, we're all out of plays. You've never let me down. My pistol's gone, and I got two shots in my rifle. How do you stand?"

Billy Dig stepped forward without answering right away. He leaned his rifle between them, gazed down the sheer rock wall, then up at the wide blue sky. When he did speak, his voice had lost all expression. The voice of a dead man, Durant thought, looking at him.

"Here's my pistol," Billy said, raising it from his holster and passing it to Durant without facing him.

"Are you sure about this, Billy?"

"I'm sure." Billy's hands trembled. "So long, pal."

Aw, Jesus. Durant tightened his hand around the pistol and watched Billy Dig lean forward, Billy's arms spreading wide like a man relaxing in a cool sparkling stream. It was simple and quick, and Billy was gone. There was no sound except for the low whir of hot rising wind. Durant stared straight across the open hole in the earth until a full minute had passed. All right, Billy made his choice. Not a bad one at that, all things considered, he thought, reaching behind his back and shoving the pistol into his waistband.

He'd told Billy Dig straight. Prison would have been no

place for that boy—better that he died right here right now. Death wasn't always the worst thing that could happen to a man. Durant had lived long enough to know that much. But ending his own life wasn't something *he* could do. Not just yet anyway. He had too strong a reason to stay alive. He'd get past the Ranger, somehow, someway. And even if he didn't get away right now, he'd bide his time—wait it out, look for his chance. There was still something Willis Durant had to do; something more important to him than life or death.

There were men down along the border he still had to find. These were men who'd murdered his wife and son. And Willis Durant had made up his mind a year ago, the day he'd laid their broken bodies in the cold, hard ground. There was nothing between heaven and hell that would keep him from finding those men and killing them in turn, like the dogs they were. . . .

PART 1

Chapter 1

A hot wind licked at the brim of the Ranger's gray sombrero. He tugged the hat down with his free hand and glanced across the deep canyon. On the far side, in the angry swirl of heat and sand, a lone dust devil rose on the desert floor and careened away, bending low stands of brittle mesquite into brief submission and leaving them swaying twisted in its wake.

"Never counted on you giving yourself up, Durant," the Ranger said, letting out a long breath, but staying alert, still watching the man's eyes. "Figured the next ride you'd make would be facedown across the saddle."

"Sorry to disappoint ya, Ranger." Willis Durant stood with his hands raised chest high, the Ranger moving closer along the thin ledge, the big rifle covering him. "I'm not dead—not even wounded."

The Ranger stepped closer to Willis Durant, looking him up and down. "I'm never disappointed when I don't have to kill a man, Durant. That was just speculation on my part." He glanced out over the ledge, then back at Willis Durant. "Is Billy Dig down there?"

"Yep, he done himself over." Durant's eyes said nothing, staring caged at the Ranger.

"That makes no sense at all." The Ranger shook his head.

"His first time up . . . he'd only have done a few years hard labor. Now you, that's a different story. You'll be getting around on a walking cane by the time you finish this stretch. Seems like you'd been the one to take the plunge, if anybody was going to."

"But, I didn't." Durant bit his words off. A thin lizard crept out from beneath a rock at Durant's feet. He nudged it back with the toe of his boot. "Why don't we get down from here before we get et up by rattlesnakes."

No, he sure didn't. The Ranger offered a thin smile, wondering why Willis Durant, for all his grit and daring, had suddenly decided to turn himself in. Well, there could be only one reason, the Ranger thought. Willis Durant had a plan of some sort in mind. He wasn't giving up this easy.

On an outside chance, the Ranger said, "I suppose you don't mind lifting that pistol from behind your back with one finger and flipping it out there over the edge? It'd make me feel a lot better."

Durant stared at him for a moment longer, his breath closed in his chest, thinking about it, weighing his odds. *No, too risky.* If he died here and now, this whole past year would have been for nothing. He let out a breath, slumped a bit, and said, "How'd you know about it, Ranger?"

The Ranger shrugged, his gloved finger held steady across the rifle trigger. "What's the difference? I just knew about it. Now raise it up and pitch it away." He wasn't about to tell Durant that it had only been a guess—that was bad poker. Let the man wonder about it.

Durant raised the pistol on one finger, held it out to the side, and flipped it away, it clattered, bouncing and scraping down the long rock wall.

"If you've got any other hardware I oughta to know

about, now's a good time to declare it," the Ranger said, gesturing Durant forward.

"No, that's it, Ranger. I'm clean." He held his hands out before him, his wrists close together, seeing the Ranger reach around and take a pair of handcuffs from his back pocket. Durant sighed. "I guess you killed Buck and Wandering Joe on your way up here?"

"Yep. I had to shoot Buck . . . he didn't know when to quit. Sheriff Tackett got Wandering Joe."

"That's what I figured," Durant said.

"So, you're the last of the bunch, Willis Durant." The Ranger snapped the cuffs on Durant's wrists and pulled him forward, backing along the ledge path until the ground widened beneath their feet. Then he stepped behind Durant and nudged him forward. "What was you thinking anyway, riding with the likes of Wandering Joe and that bunch? Robbing banks of all things. Wandering Joe Gully never pulled off a good job in his life."

"He was hiring. I needed the money." Durant stared straight ahead.

"Oh . . . you needed the money," the Ranger said in a flat tone. He shook his head. "I thought you'd learned your lesson and settled down. Last I heard of you, you had a family somewhere down near—"

"Leave my family out of this, Ranger," Durant said, cutting him off. "I just needed the money. Let it go at that. I've got nothing more to say to you."

Down the path, behind a rock, Sheriff Tackett had waited for the past twenty minutes, listening for the sound of the Ranger's big rifle. When the sound didn't come as he'd expected, he'd grown more and more concerned that something had gone wrong. Now, as Durant stepped into sight around a turn in the steep rock path, Tackett almost raised up and shot him before seeing the sunlight glitter on the steel handcuffs.

"Hold your fire down there, Tackett," the Ranger called out behind Durant, seeing the sheriff standing up with his pistol cocked and pointed. "Billy Dig took a plunge off the edge of the cliff. Mister Durant here has decided to give himself up. Can you believe that?"

"I see it, but naw-sir, I don't believe it," Tackett said, lowering his pistol and stepping out from behind the rock. "I was just about to come up looking for you, Sam. Why didn't you let me know what was going on up there? You could have fired a shot or something."

"Couldn't waste a bullet," the Ranger said. "We've run out of everything on this trip." He and Durant stopped a few feet from Tackett. "But here's your prisoner, Sheriff . . . last of the Gully Gang."

"Yeah." Tackett eyed Willis Durant up and down. "And I oughta bust your dang head, robbing my town, causing us all this trouble." As Tackett spoke, he stepped closer, his pistol drawing back for a swipe at Durant's head. But Willis Durant didn't back an inch. He stood eye to eye with Tackett as if daring him.

"Easy now," the Ranger said to Tackett, pulling Willis Durant to the side. "He's your prisoner now. Show some manners."

"Manners my aching arse," Tackett said. "If I did what I felt like doing, we'd leave him stretching hemp out here."

The Ranger shoved Willis Durant over against a rock and said to him, "Sit down there. Catch your breath, Durant. We've got a three-day ride back to town. Just as well eat some jerked beef and have some tea before we start out." He turned his gaze from Durant to Tackett as he spoke. "What do you say, Tackett? Looks like you could use something to settle you down."

"It's too danged hot for tea, Sam," Tackett said, staring at Durant. "I want this snake to tell me why he done me this way. There's a dozen other towns he could've pulled this in . . . all of them with bigger banks."

"Call it the luck of the draw, Sheriff," Durant said. He slumped a bit, looking at Tackett.

"Luck of the draw?" Tackett lunged forward a step. "Why you rotten—!"

"Settle down, Tackett. It wasn't nothing personal." The Ranger managed to move in between the two of them. "He said he just needed the money."

Durant pulled back a step, then sat down and leaned against the rock, still staring up at Tackett. "That's right. I needed the money."

"Oh? Well, I reckon anybody who's ever robbed a bank could say that, couldn't they?" Tackett eased down a bit himself and slid his pistol back into his holster. "But it didn't have to be *my* town . . . *my* bank." He ran a hand across his sweaty forehead and let out a breath. "Where's the money, Durant? It wasn't on none of the others."

Durant hesitated for a second, then said, "Wandering Joe stuck it under some boards, back at that old copper mine where you gulched us the other day." He looked up at the Ranger. "I'll take you to it on the way back."

"That's *real* nice of ya, Durant," Tackett said with a sarcastic snap, bristling up once more. "For two cents I'd—"

The Ranger cut him off, seeing his hands ball into fists. "Why don't you go bring the horses up, Tackett? I'm having myself some tea before we leave here."

"Dang it all . . ." A tense second passed. Tackett shot a glance back and forth between them. Then, grumbling under his breath, he turned and started down the path to the flat-lands.

"He shouldn't get himself so worked up in this kind of heat," the Ranger said, watching Tackett move out of sight. He turned back to Durant, raising the dusty brim of his sombrero. "Can't say I blame him though. Tackett always treated you right." The Ranger glanced at the body of Wandering Joe Gully on the ground ten feet away. Thirty feet farther down lay Doc Septon, brown dust collecting in his wide open eyes and on his dirty gray hair. "Why *did* it have to be Tackett's town? Don't tell me luck of the draw, or I might crack your head myself."

Durant studied the Ranger's wary eyes. "All right, Ranger, it wasn't just about the money." He reached up with his cuffed hands and blotted his forehead on the sleeve of his dusty shirt. "There was more to it. Wandering Joe Gully knew some things . . . some things I needed to find out about." Durant stopped and stared away, southward, out through the wavering heat. His expression turned closed.

"And?" the Ranger asked, coaxing him on. "Did you ever find out?"

"Yeah, he told me some of it." Durant lowered his eyes, letting the Ranger know he had nothing more to say.

The Ranger moved over to the rock and leaned against it, his big rifle cradled in his arms. "Well, whatever it was, I hope it was worth it to you. You're facing many long years on the rock pile over this."

"Damn right it was worth it," Durant murmured under his breath. He stared at the cuffs on his wrists, working his hands back and forth against the hard steel, as if testing his strength against the strength of the metal. "It was worth every year of it."

                    *   *   *

At noon the following day, they rode down to the old copper mine. Inside the darkness of a dusty shaft, they turned over a pile of loose walk boards and lifted the bulging saddlebags full of stolen bank money. Dust streamed off the saddlebags as Tackett raised them and hefted them in his hands. "I won't count it just now," he said, glaring up at Durant, who sat on the sweat-streaked dun beside the Ranger. "But you better hope to heaven every last dollar of it's here."

"Don't worry, Sheriff, it's all there," Durant said. "I watched Wandering Joe hide it. We were gonna meet later, split it up, after we shook you two off our trail."

The Ranger had taken note of Durant's tense, resolute attitude ever since the man had given himself up. Something wasn't right about him. Durant was only partly here, the Ranger thought. A larger part of him seemed to be off somewhere in the distance, not cuffed and facing years in a sweaty prison, but out across the badlands, searching for something in the swirling heat, taking care of important business of some sort. Dark business, whatever it was, the Ranger thought.

After Tackett secured the saddlebags behind his saddle and stepped up into his stirrups, the Ranger let Durant move his horse forward of them a few yards and drew Tackett back beside him with a subtle gesture.

"What's up, Sam?" Tackett asked in a lowered voice, checking his horse down close to the Ranger. Durant's horse walked on ahead of them, its damp tail hanging limp. Durant slumped a bit in his saddle, the back of his shirt darkened with sweat.

"How long since you'd seen this man before they robbed the bank?" the Ranger asked Tackett in a quiet tone.

Sheriff Tackett led the string of tired horses with the dead outlaws' bodies tied across their saddles. He too gazed ahead at Durant, considering it for a second. "Oh . . . five years, six maybe. He's been laying up with a Ute woman over near the Little Red. He's got a son by her, from what I heard. Why are you asking?"

"Just wondering, is all." The Ranger rubbed his stubbled chin, gazing ahead. "He's got something stuck in his craw. Don't know what it is, but it's sure working him. He'll make a break for the badlands if we ain't careful."

"He ain't going nowhere, Sam. I promise you that much. Not after all the trouble we had catching him this last time. I'll drop a bullet in him before I go through all this again. I'm worn plumb down to my toes on him and that whole Wandering Joe Gully bunch."

The Ranger looked at him. "I didn't say he'd get away. I just said he'd try. Usually by now a prisoner's lost all the shine in their eyes. Not him. He hasn't given up, he's just going along. There's something eating at him . . . some unfinished business. I'm just curious what it is." He heeled his white barb forward calling it by name, "Come on, Blackeye," not letting Durant get too far ahead.

That evening they made camp on the edge of the sand flats, beneath a wide dome of starlight. They ate dried beef jerky, some scraps of biscuits Tackett had left over from two days before, and washed it down with hot tea. After the three of them had eaten, the Ranger held his rifle trained on Durant while Tackett unlocked the handcuffs and recuffed them behind Durant's back. Only when Tackett had secured the prisoner and sat him down on a blanket did the Ranger lower his rifle and sit down on a flat rock on the other side of the low fire.

"So, tell us, Durant," the Ranger said, sipping his Duttwieler's tea from a battered tin cup, "how'd you come to hook up with Wandering Joe and his gang of hard cases? I always knew you to be a loner."

Willis Durant leaned back against the saddle on the ground behind him. He seemed to measure his words before saying them. "Billy Dig was already riding with me. We caught up with Wandering Joe and his bunch outside of Wakely. I knew Wandering Joe years back, back before he took to bank robbing."

Caught up with? Not met, or ran into, but caught up with . . . The Ranger took note of the phrase as Durant went on. "You know how Billy was . . . he'd go along with anything. Wandering Joe said him and the others had planned on robbing the bank the day a big mine payroll came in." Durant shrugged. "Wandering Joe said they were short two men to do the job . . . Billy Dig wanted to throw with them. So we did."

"Yeah, you did," Tackett huffed, "knowing danged well it was in *my* town."

Willis Durant lifted his dark eyes to Tackett. "You can't get past that, can ya, Tackett? I told you it was nothing against you. I just went along with Billy Dig on it. Couldn't talk him out of it."

The Ranger listened, putting it together in his mind, not believing a word of it. Billy Dig never had an idea in his life that didn't come from somebody else. There wasn't a way in the world he could have talked Willis Durant into doing anything Durant didn't want to do. Why was Durant playing it this way? The Ranger wanted to know more about it, but he knew if he pressed too hard, Willis Durant would only cut him off again.

The Ranger waited, sipped his tea, and after a moment said, as if passing it off, "Well, I suppose it don't matter now, does it?"

"No," Willis Durant said under his breath, "I suppose it doesn't."

The Ranger stood up, slung the last drops of tea from his tin cup, and dusted the seat of his trousers. "But I can't help wondering about your woman, Durant—the Ute woman? What's she gonna think when she hears about all this?"

Durant's jaw tightened. "I told you before, leave my family out of it."

"All right then." The Ranger stood and looked down at him, the flicker of low flames shining in Durant's dark eyes. "I'm just wondering what I oughta tell that son of yours, if I ever run into him. He's just a little boy now, I reckon. But he'll be grown before you get out of prison. He'll want to know about his daddy, won't he?" He watched Durant's eyes for any kind of sign as he spoke. "I wouldn't want him coming around and holding any grudges on me."

"He won't," Durant said. Even Tackett noticed the finality in the man's voice. He turned his face slightly toward Durant and listened, quiet now, seeing the Ranger was getting close to something here, touching on a raw nerve.

"What makes you so sure of it?" The Ranger rounded a finger inside the tin cup, looking down into it, taking his time, inspecting it. He added in a lowered tone, "I've had that sort of thing happen before. A boy grows up some, gets to wondering about his pa . . . thinking about the man that put his daddy in jail." The Ranger shook his head in concern. "You never know what might come of it."

A silence passed as Durant gazed away, then back into the crackling low flames. His eyes turned deep and lost for a moment. He seemed to shiver. Then he said in a tight tone, "My son is dead, Ranger. There. Are you satisfied?"

The Ranger and Sheriff Tackett let Durant's words sink in. Somewhere a lone coyote cried out from the desert floor.

"I'm sorry to hear that, Willis," the Ranger said at last, lowering his voice even more. "I truly am. . . ."

A cool night breeze moved in across the sand flats, smelling of scorched earth and dry juniper. Again the coyote called out, its voice lingering high up in the darkness. The Ranger stepped over Willis and put his tin cup inside his saddlebags, thinking about all that Durant had said, trying to imagine what was going on in his head. Had he been hunting for Wandering Joe? If so, why? He'd said Wandering Joe had some information he needed. What sort of information was it?

The Ranger moved nearer to Willis Durant. He looked down at Durant's bowed head, and, playing a dark hunch, he asked in a soft voice, "And the boy's ma? The Ute woman? She's dead too, isn't she?"

Durant didn't answer. He lifted his face and only stared up into the Ranger's eyes.

"Isn't she, Willis?" The Ranger stared back until Durant's dark eyes could take no more.

Durant turned his face away. "Go to hell, Ranger!" A muscle twitched in his tight jaw. "Yes, she's dead too! What of it? It's no business of yours."

The Ranger slid his glance over to Tackett, then back to Durant.

"Jesus," Tackett whispered. Then he sat quiet, watching, listening, seeing how far the Ranger could push the man, how much he could get Willis Durant to give up.

The Ranger went on in a quiet, relentless tone. "Your woman's dead. Your boy's dead. And here you are on your way to prison, to have to think about it the rest of your life. Don't tell me Wandering Joe had something to do with killing them? What kind of low, lousy animal would be riding with the man who killed his family—?"

"He didn't kill them! All right?" Durant flashed a smoldering glance at the Ranger. "Wandering Joe had nothing to do with it!"

"But he knew who did, didn't he?" the Ranger pried. "That's the information he had, right?"

Durant only stared straight ahead, but the expression in his eyes said the Ranger was right.

"Who are they, Durant? Tell me their names," the Ranger said, still in a quiet tone.

"I'm not telling you! Now get out of my shirt about it! I'm warning ya!"

Warning . . . ? The Ranger watched Durant struggle forward, trying to rise onto his feet, his hands cuffed behind him, hampering him, slowing him down.

"That's enough, Durant. Take it easy." The Ranger reached out with his dusty boot toe and shoved him back against the saddle on the ground. "You don't have to say no more about it. If you want the ones who killed your woman and son to go free, I reckon it's your choice."

"Damn you, Ranger!" Willis Durant trembled in rage. "I see what you're trying to do. But that's all you're getting from me. I'll kill the ones who did it. They're my business! My business alone! Not yours or anybody else's!"

"Ordinarily I'd agree with you on a thing like that." The Ranger stooped before him, still speaking in a low, calm tone. "But the fact is, you're not going anywhere, Willis Durant. So put escaping out of your mind. Either you tell me who killed them, right here and now, or they'll go free. How's that going to feel to you . . . seeing their faces night after night, all them long years in prison?" Across the desert floor, the coyote called out once more through the darkness, its voice raised as if in protest against the stark land and the endless sky above it.

"How do you think it would feel to me, Ranger," Durant said under his breath.

By noon the following day they were halfway back to town. They'd run out of water, and their horses had begun moving in shorter, more labored steps. They pulled off the trail and stopped at the sun-bleached adobe of an old Mexican goat herder who made his home at the edge of the desolate sand flats. The weathered adobe stood where a steep natural cut bank rose up forty feet and the land spread back on a higher level, covered with sparse clumps of grass and scattered mesquite brush.

The goat herder had spotted them from atop his rise of land and stood waiting for them with a gourd full of freshwater as they made their way up to him. Lank goats had gathered about him as the riders came forward, but now they moved away, seeming to shy from the sight and smell of death on the string of tired horses walking behind the Ranger's white barb.

By the time the three riders had checked their horses down in front of the old Mexican, the goats had drifted back into a black angle of shade beside the adobe. They watched from there with their heads lowered, twitching their scraggly ears.

"Aw, Ranger," the old man said smiling, handing up the water gourd. "I see so many riders pass here five days ago on the flat lands . . . and I ask myself, why would these *loco gringos* be out on the land in this kind of heat?" His smile widened. He stepped around, looking at the bloated bodies beneath a shiny swirl of blowflies. "But now I see why. It is never too hot for the law, and the lawless, eh?"

"Yep, that's a fact." The Ranger drank from the gourd, then stepped down, handing the old man the lead rope to the grizzly string of sweaty horses with their bundles of sour swollen flesh atop them. "They hit the bank back in town last week. I've been riding with Sheriff Tackett here . . . tracking them down across the desert." He brushed a hand up and down his sleeve, and dust billowed. "Can you put us up for the night? Our horses are blown pretty bad."

"*Sí,* of course I put you up . . . for the price of your story." He fanned a hand back and forth, wincing at the terrible smell of death. "Go water your horses first. I'll bring these dead *desperados* in when you are finished." He squinted one eye shut and pointed his finger at the bodies as if it were a pistol, clicking his thumb up and down.

Tackett and Willis Durant stepped down from their stirrups and followed the Ranger as he led his white barb toward the low stone wall of a water reservoir beneath a cottonwood tree. Recognizing Willis Durant beneath the layer of grimy sweat and thick dust on his face, the old Mexican called out to him, shaking his head, "*Santa Madre!* I do not believe my eyes! Willis Durant! What have you done, *mi amigo?* Surely you have not gone back to your *desperado* ways?"

"Don't concern yourself about it, old man," Durant said without turning around.

Ten feet from the stone reservoir, a small burro walked in a slow languid circle, turning the long pole that ran from its back to a squeaking waterwheel. Gourd after gourd of muddy water rose from a dark hole in the ground. The water poured into an overhead trough and ran over and down into the stone reservoir. The Ranger pulled up a wet plank that stood damming the trough and allowed water to run out into another trough, this one on the ground at their feet. The three tired horses stepped in and lowered their muzzles into the muddy water, drawing long and deep.

"Seems like everybody's as surprised as we are, Durant."
The Ranger passed him the gourd full of clean water.
"Reckon you've let a lot of folks down."

"I did what any man would do," Durant said. He raised a
drink of water with his cuffed hands. When he let them
down, he stared into the Ranger's eyes. "I've heard you've
got a woman yourself, Ranger. Tell me what you would have
done . . . under the same circumstances."

"Well . . ." The Ranger considered it for a second. "I
wouldn't go rob a bank, that's for certain. Can't see how
breaking the law would solve anything."

Durant didn't answer right away. Instead, he passed the
gourd on to Tackett, who took it, drank from it, then dipped
his bandanna in it. Tackett pressed the wet bandanna against
his brow, up under his dusty hat brim.

"The law is the last thing on a man's mind when something like that happens," Durant said, once he'd thought
about it and let out a breath. "What man gives a damn about
the law when his family's been butchered like animals?"

The Ranger could see Durant was still boiling inside with
rage. But at least Durant had let down a little. He'd began
talking about it. That helped. Now that Durant had started
talking, the Ranger needed to keep him talking, get the
whole story out of him somehow.

"You stepped way out of line, Durant," the Ranger said,
just to keep the conversation going. "No man has a right to
go against the law, to settle things for himself, no matter
how bad he's been wronged. Had you used your head, the
law would have been after your family's killers right away.
Instead, you put yourself outside the law . . . got yourself in
more trouble than you can get out of."

"All I knew is that I had to get to these men," Durant said.

"Had to find them any way I could. Wandering Joe Gully knew where they were."

"Oh? And did he tell you?"

"No, he didn't. I . . . I never got the chance to ask him." Durant stalled before he answered—just long enough that the Ranger could tell he was lying. "I still don't know where they are, Ranger. That's the truth."

"Then I reckon you never will know," the Ranger said, not wanting to push too hard all at once. That was enough for now. *Give the man time . . . he'd come around.* He'd given up a lot already.

The Ranger pulled the white barb back from the trough. The big horse slung muddy water from its muzzle and shook out its damp mane. "If you ever change your mind, decide to tell me who they are . . . I'll listen. Otherwise, you'll just have to live with it from now on."

The Ranger hitched the white barb in the shade of the cottonwood tree, walked over to the old Mexican, and took the lead rope from him. Flies swirled. Durant stood watching the Ranger through caged eyes while the Ranger and the Mexican watered the rest of the horses and led them off away from the others to loosen the bodies from their backs and drop them on the ground.

When an hour had passed, and Tackett had seated Durant against the cottonwood tree, stepping back to keep him covered with his pistol, Durant still stared after the Ranger, watching him talk with the old Mexican. The two of them walked to the black spot on the ground with their arms loaded with mesquite and sun-bleached twigs and kindling. The Ranger caught a glimpse of Durant staring at him now and again as he and the old man laid out the makings for a cook fire.

"Willis Durant is a serious *hombre*," the old goat tender

said. "I would not want to face him with a pistol in his hand." He looked over at Durant, thirty feet away. "I think he does not plan on you taking him back to town."

The Ranger only nodded. But the old Mexican was wrong, he thought. Durant would make a break for it if he could—sure he would. But making his getaway was not what he was thinking about right now. Durant had something more to say . . . maybe not about where the men were who'd killed his family. Not just yet. But he had to say something. Right now he just needed to talk about what had happened. The Ranger had a notion that Durant hadn't talked about this with anybody. Now that he'd talked about it a little, maybe he needed to get the whole story out—to keep it from driving himself crazy.

That evening when the air began to cool and a cook fire licked up at the rack of sizzling goat meat, the Ranger sliced off a blackened piece of rump onto a tin plate, took it over to where Durant sat with his cuffed hands on his lap, and set the plate beside him. Without looking Durant in the eye, he said in a quiet tone, "Here you are, Willis. Eat that and I'll bring you some more."

Without another word, the Ranger had straightened up and started to turn away when Durant said in a shaky voice, "They . . . they took turns with her, Ranger . . . before they killed her. Hear what I'm saying?"

The Ranger stopped and lifted his hat brim, but still did not look into his eyes. "Yeah, I hear you."

"The boy came in . . . tried to stop them. They . . ." His voice stopped and could not finish.

"Eat your dinner, Durant," the Ranger said, stepping back and putting the man off for now. "I'll bring you some coffee."

But before the Ranger had walked away another step, Durant said, raising his voice, "They were friends, Ranger. Hear me? They were supposed to be my friends . . . those two."

"Oh?" The Ranger only stopped, still not turning toward him. "Try not to think about it right now, Willis. It ain't helping you none."

He walked back to the fire and carved off a slice of meat for himself onto another tin plate. Tackett and the old Mexican goat tender stepped in beside him, carving off meat onto their own plates. Grease dripped and sizzled in the low flames. "I heard what he just told you, Sam," Tackett said, shaking his head as he sucked grease drippings from the tip of his thumb. "Reckon he'll give it all up?"

"We'll have to wait and see," the Ranger said. "He's one tough knot, that's for sure. But it's eating at him pretty hard. He might spill it before we get back to town."

"I hope he does." Tackett spoke through a mouthful of meat. "Whoever the men are, I'd hate to see them get away with something like that."

"Me too," the Ranger said, lifting a piece of meat from his plate. "But I can't crowd him about it, I've seen that. It's all up to him."

Tackett worked a fingernail between his front teeth and spit out a fleck of gristle. "It's a terrible thing, a man losing his family. I reckon I'd feel the same way he does . . . wouldn't want somebody else to kill them, not if I could get to them first. Would you?"

"I don't like thinking about things like that, Tackett." The Ranger took a bite of meat and glanced around the endless darkening land. He resented Tackett asking him such a thing. He had no idea what he would do in such a situation. So why even think about it? From beneath the cottonwood tree, Willis Durant stared at him, his dark eyes seeming to smolder—shining deep and determined in the coming darkness.

Chapter 2

There were fourteen riders in all atop the ridge, but now four of them turned their horses and rounded out of sight, into a long dry wash, headed down toward the rails below. A few yards above the flatlands, these four riders took positions back out of sight, above the spot where they could leap out on top of the freight cars without being seen. Their horses stepped back and forth on restless hooves, sensing, knowing something through the tension of the reins—through the feel of the men on their backs.

The ten other riders sat on their horses, strung out atop the stony ridge at a point where they could spot the train as it came out from between the high buttes, leaving behind its billowing wake of wood smoke and steam.

The men could see the train, yet no one on the train could spot them—not from here. Major Martin Zell had sent two riders all the way to the high buttes a thousand yards away to make sure of it before taking this position. Major Zell knew his business. He should—he'd been at it long enough. Behind the line of riders sat a gray-bearded old man in an empty tandem freight wagon. His name was Dirkson, and he watched the others through steely eyes.

The mood and manner of the riders was somber and quiet—no play among these men. They attuned themselves to the work at hand and had no questions about their part in it. When Major Zell robbed a train or raided a town, he did so with military precision. Each man atop the stony ridge knew his job to the letter. Once they hit this train, there would be little talk, and no time wasted.

They'd come here to rob the army munitions car near the rear of the train—nothing else. They would break the coupling and send the rest of the train forward. The four Union soldiers guarding the munitions car would have to be killed. Then Zell and his men would have plenty of time to load their wagon, disappear across the sand flats, and on across the border.

The operation would go as expected, same as always, Major Zell thought, watching the train below them come out of the long curve where it had reduced its speed. He checked the watch in his hand—*right on time*—then flipped the watch shut and stuck it into the pocket of his low-cut Mexican vest. "Barnes, prepare your men to descend onto the left flank."

"Yes, sir, Major," a younger man's voice called out. Part of the line broke away, four horsemen in a row, falling their animals back a step, turning them, and then moving quickly and quietly off toward a narrow trail. When the last of the four had moved out of sight, Major Zell turned and nodded to one of the men on his other side. "Parker, you and your three men take position."

"Yes, sir." Payton Parker shot the major a caged glance and turned his horse, three men dressed in Mexican attire turning with him. When the four had moved off along another trail in the opposite direction, old man Dirkson in the freight wagon adjusted his loose-fitting straw sombrero down on his head, slapped reins to the backs of the four

mules, and moved the heavy tandem wagon out behind
them.

"I'll trouble you for a chew now, Mr. Bowes." Major Zell
held out a gloved hand.

Liam Bowes laid the twist of tobacco into Zell's hand
with a crisp snap and spread a straight, tight grin. He sat
with his ornate Mexican sombrero back off his head and
resting across his squared shoulders, held by a hat string
around his neck. His iron-gray hair lifted on a hot breeze.
When Major Zell had taken a bite from the twist of tobacco
and handed it back, Bowes took a bite himself and put the
tobacco away. "How's the arm, Major?"

"Fit as ever, Mr. Bowes." Zell slapped his right hand
against his left shoulder. "Let us proceed." Zell backed his
horse a step, then looking around as if to make sure no one
was watching, he spoke in a lowered voice, one hand resting
on the cavalry saber on his hip. "Watch your backside,
Liam. If all goes well, this should be our last raid on American soil. You know the superstition about a soldier in his
last battle."

"I'll be careful, sir. And you do the same." Together they
heeled their horses off along the narrow downward trail, the
dust of the other riders still drifting around them.

On the sand flats below, Payton Parker had sent two of his
men to take position farther up along the tracks; their job
would be to cover the engineer and oiler once the train was
brought to a stop. Payton's task, with his brother Leo, was to
take a look-out position a few yards down the steep slope
and watch for any sign of trouble back along the rails.
They'd gone over halfway down the slope before Payton finally reined his horse in a spray of sand and turned to his
brother, who did the same beside him. "This will do for now,
Leo."

Leo looked both ways along the rails, seeing only the tip of the distant engine stack rising above the roll of the land. "I think we're down too far." He stood in his stirrups and craned his neck upward for a view of the distant buttes. "It's hard to see anything from here."

"I don't want us caught high up away from the others if something goes wrong," Payton replied. "This was Zell's mistake to begin with. I say we play it safe and let him clean up his own mess."

"But the sooner we get the ammunition and get out of here, the quicker we get our share of the gold." Leo looked his brother up and down. "It ain't like you to go slacking off on a job. What gives?"

"I'm getting sick of taking orders from Zell and Bowes, that's all. They're old men, still fighting a lost cause. It's time we make what we can from this bunch and move on to better things. To hell with the south rising again. Zell and Bowes has been too lucky too long. But it's running out on them." He spit. "Hadn't been for them messing up last time out, we wouldn't be here stealing ammunition today."

"It weren't their fault we didn't get everything we needed last time. How was Zell supposed to know there was no ammunition on that load—"

Payton cut his brother off. "Listen to me, Leo. The *federales* pay for guns and bullets, not for excuses. They've got the weapons. That took two dozen men and a half dozen wagons. But it won't take that many to haul this ammunition across the border once it's loaded. I've talked to Delbert and McCord. They'll go along with me. We can deliver this load ourselves and only split the money four ways. Think about that . . . it comes to nearly fourteen thousand dollars apiece . . . all in gold!"

"But, Payton, our pa died in that war. That oughta mean

something. Besides, we got a crazy Negro gunning for us this side of the border. We best lay low and go along with things. That's why we joined Zell in the first place, ain't it?"

"It don't matter one lick to me how our pa died. As for Durant gunning for us, he might not even know we killed that squaw and his little half-breed buck. I'm sick of laying low like a couple of whipped dogs. I bet ole Wandering Joe Gully is kicking up his heels somewhere right now . . . having a gay old time. We should've stuck with him."

"Maybe you ain't worried about Durant, but I am. He knows we kilt his wife and kid—he's bound to. Think he'd just walk right past us on the street, forget what we done? Naw, sir. Him or us is going to die."

"To hell with Willis Durant. If it happens, it happens. All we need right now is that Mexican gold—bunches of it." Payton grinned, rubbing his thumb and finger together in the universal sign of greed.

"You're the oldest, Payton. But gee, I don't know." Leo raised a hand beneath the brim of his Mexican sombrero and scratched his head.

Payton glanced up the narrow trail, seeing Zell and Bowes move down past them. "Just keep quiet and stay covered here. Go along with me on things, Leo. If I see a move coming that will better us both, I'm taking it."

On the train below, Maria had all of Prudence Vanderman she could take. She'd met Prudence only a few hours earlier when the train had taken on water at Circle Wells. The porter had seated Prudence Vanderman across from her and made the introduction, explaining that there were sand lizards in Prudence's private car, but for Miss Vanderman not to worry, he'd have them lizards out and killed in no time. Yeees, ma'am, he would! But so far he hadn't.

No sooner than Prudence Vanderman had taken a seat, Maria began to see it was going to be a long, annoying ride. The first words out of Miss Vanderman's mouth had been in reference to Maria's accent. "Oh, you must be Mexican." Then before Maria had a chance to say that no she was not Mexican, but Spanish, Prudence had gone on to mention how well behaved the Mexican house servants were on her father's estate, and that they were such quaint and lovely people, the Mexicans.

At that, Maria had only settled back and let out a breath—*sí,* she was Mexican. She'd noticed the way Prudence's eyes had gone up and down her, taking in Maria's denim riding skirt, her leather vest, her scuffed high-topped boots, the leather riding gloves folded down into her waist belt. In the seat beside Maria, lay her Winchester rifle, the stock scarred and sweat-stained. *Nothing in common here . . .*

For the next two and a half hours, Maria had only nodded her head now and then and listened to Prudence Vanderman complain. Her trip had been terrible . . . she never should have left Denver . . . it was her personal misfortune that her travel secretary, Miss Mosley, had come down with a near terminal case of dysentery.

It was unthinkable that she, the daughter of industrialist tycoon Jameson D. Vanderman, should be traveling alone now all the way to California. Wasn't it terrible the sort of people you met traveling by rail these days? And so on it went, until Maria found herself thinking how good it might feel to pick up her rifle and shoot this Prudence Vanderman in her foot—Prudence with her oh so soft and luxurious blond hair and her monotonous, singsong voice, which sounded more like some strange and pampered bird, Maria thought.

At this point, lest she actually feel compelled to follow

through on her dark fantasy, Maria had gotten up, excused herself, and walked out onto the rear platform for a breath of air. She spent nearly a half hour out on the platform, thinking about Sam, missing him.

Now Maria swayed in the aisle, coming back to her seat as the train came out of its long turn between two shadowed buttes and into the pressing heat of the sand flats. She sat down in her seat, looked across into the bubbly blue eyes of Prudence Vanderman, and reminded herself to stay calm.

"Goodness, you seem to have brought a herd of buffalo back with you." Prudence Vanderman fanned a white lace handkerchief in front of her face and smiled condescendingly at Maria. Seeing the low, smoldering fire flicker in Maria's dark eyes, Prudence added quickly, "Of course I realize it isn't your fault, you understand. No, indeed not." She wagged a dainty finger for emphasis. "I'm afraid the terrible smell of wild beasts is simply one more hardship imposed on us by this wretched wilderness."

"*Sí,* I understand." Maria stared at her and spoke in a flat tone. "You are saying that I stink." Throughout the long, hot trip Prudence Vanderman had insisted that everything about the train, the passengers, and the land itself smelled of buffalo musk. Maria hadn't felt like telling her it had been years since buffalo herds of any significant number had been seen south of the high American desert.

"Weeeell"—Prudence squeezed out the word, wrinkling her petite nose, again with the condescending smile—"I find the word 'stink' to be rather a crude descriptive. But I think it *is* only fair to say that either of us could stand to freshen up a bit."

Maria stared at her in silence for a moment, both of their heads bobbing slightly with the pitch of the rails beneath them. Then, as the engine struggled to regain its speed,

Maria leaned slightly forward and asked Prudence if she
didn't think it was perhaps time to check with the porter
once more and see if he'd yet managed to get rid of those
dreadful sand lizards? Prudence pressed a finger to her lips
and gazed out across the sand flats. "Yes, perhaps I should.
It will be getting dark before long. . . ."

"*Sí,* and believe me, you will not be comfortable, or safe,
out here overnight," Maria pointed out. "Hot leather seats?
An open public car? No private facilities?" Maria leaned
even closer, glancing across row after row of empty seats to
the four scruffy-looking old miners farther up the aisle. "And
at night! *Santa Madre!*" Maria crossed herself quickly. "You
would not believe what animals these men become."

"Where is that porter?" Prudence Vanderman's voice took
on a sharp, nervous edge as she half rose from her seat and
glanced across the nearly empty car. One of the old miners
looked back and spread a toothless grin. Maria smiled to
herself and gazed out through the dusty window. But her
smile faded as she spotted the sidelong sheet of dust kicked
up by the three riders cresting a low rise of sand. *Mexicans?
Vaqueros?* She didn't think so, not in this part of the country. And at that moment she realized that once more the train
began slowing down—slowing when it should be building
up speed.

"I suppose I'll simply have to go find—"

"Stay down!" Maria grabbed Prudence by her forearm
and jerked her down into their seat.

"Now, see here!"

"Shhh, be quiet." Maria spoke to her without taking her
eyes off the three riders until they'd heeled forward out of
sight toward the front of the slowing train. Then she shot a
glance to the four old miners and saw them stir, as curious
now as she was about the train slowing to a stop. "Keep your

heads inside," she shouted as one of them reached over to raise the window higher.

"What on earth?" Prudence collected herself on the hot leather seat.

Maria looked at the small purse on Prudence's forearm. "Do you have a mirror in there?"

"A mirror? Why yes, but whatever for?"

"Give it to me!" Before Prudence had a chance to respond, Maria snatched the purse open and rummaged through it.

"How dare you!" Prudence slapped at Maria's wrist as Maria yanked the small mirror from the purse. Now the train had made a lingering halt as the sound of metal groaned beneath them.

"Get down in your seat and sit still. The train is being robbed." Maria raised the dusty window a couple of inches and eased the mirror out, holding it in a way to give herself a narrow view of the three riders stopping alongside the engine with their pistols drawn and pointed upward.

"Being robbed!" Prudence's eyes widened. Up the aisle, the old miners dropped down onto the floor. Maria moved over beside Prudence, snatching up the rifle as she went. She held the mirror out once more and took a view toward the rear of the train. Three cars back she spotted two more riders as they stepped in between two cars. The screech of metal against metal resounded—the coupling being pulled, she thought. What was back there? The express car? The army flat car? One of those, of course. But there were soldiers guarding the flat car. Hadn't they seen anything, she wondered. Why wasn't there gunfire coming from back there?

"Get on the floor, quickly!" Maria dropped down, yanking Prudence with her. "If we are lucky, they will take what they came for and let us be. Lie still until it is over." She jacked a round up into her rifle chamber and listened.

Outside on the rear of the flat car, the two remaining soldiers stood with their hands raised high. At the front end, the other two soldiers lay in dark pools of blood, their throats sliced, their rifles still leaning against the canvas-draped cargo boxes where they'd stood while they'd smoked their cigarettes.

Without a word, Barnes stood in his stirrups, holding the reins to another horse beside him, and waved his arm back and forth, signaling for the old man to bring the tandem wagon up across the low rise of sand. Dirkson stood in his wagon seat and, upon seeing the signal, slapped reins to the mules' backs.

While the wagon lumbered up over the rise, down at the flat car, Barnes scanned the high slope on the other side of the train. In a low voice he spoke to the young man coming off the side of the flat car and onto the horse Barnes held by its reins. "Do you see Parker up there anywhere? He's supposed to be guarding our rear."

"Haven't seen him or his men either." The young man wiped a knife blade across his dusty trouser leg and slipped the big knife down into his boot well. "He best be on his toes though. We've got a long blind spot back between those buttes." The men looked at the black hole of shade slicing into the high wall of rust-colored earth, and they said no more as their eyes searched back along the rail cars.

Nothing stirred. The train sat silent except for the low steady pulse of the idling steam engine. Barnes caught a sharp flash of light up along a passenger car. His hand had snapped instinctively to the pistol on his hip. But then he gave a faint smile and settled, catching a glimpse of a lady's pocket mirror as Maria jerked it back inside the window. *No problem there . . .*

"I think he saw me." Maria huddled down between the seats beside Prudence Vanderman. Seeing the look of terror on Prudence's face, she shook her head slowly. "But he will not bother with us. These men seem very professional in their work."

"How can you tell—?"

"Because it is my business to know such things."

"Oh." Once again Prudence Vanderman looked Maria up and down, getting a different picture now of this woman in her faded riding skirt and her scuffed high-topped boots. Along the aisle, the old miners came crawling to them. One of them carried an old single-barrel shotgun strapped to his back.

"You women all right back here?" the first one whispered, wiping a long wisp of hair across his bald head.

"We are all right. You men stay down." She glanced along the backs of the miners as they raised their faces to her. "Is that the only gun any of you have?"

The third man rose slightly and rummaged a hand inside his dirty shirt. "I got this little two shooter here . . . it wouldn't knock a fart out of a bullfrog." His cheeks reddened as he saw the look on Prudence's face. "Pardoning my language, please."

Before Maria could turn down his offer, he'd brought out the derringer and pitched it to her. *"Gracias."* She glanced at it and shoved it down into her boot well. "But it is best we lie still unless they come in here."

"You're absolutely right, ma'am," the first one said, looking up at her with worried eyes. "Let them Mexicans do what they came for and skin out'n here is what I says."

Mexicans . . . ? For some reason Maria didn't think so.

Why not? They dressed like Mexicans . . . like *vaqueros.*
What was it? Something gnawed at Maria. Was it the way
the three men rode? The way they sat their saddles? *Maybe.*
She put the question aside, turned, and once more slipped
the mirror an inch outside the window. Above them, quiet
footsteps moved along the top of the car, heading back.

Major Zell and Liam Bowes rode up at the same time as
the old man rolled the tandem wagon up close to the flat car.
Bowes had put on his wide sombrero and tugged it low on
his forehead, his face blackened out in darkness against the
harsh glare of sunlight. Two of the other men who'd first
dropped onto the train came slipping down from atop a
freight car and gave the old man a hand as he stepped up
from his wagon seat.

"Where are the Parkers?" Bowes asked in a lowered
voice, scanning the high slope. When no one answered, he
drew his horse back a step and moved it toward the rear of
the train, looking into the distance at the high, shadowed
buttes. When he turned his gaze up onto the slope, he saw a
quick flash of light glisten on Payton Parker's rifle barrel.
What was going on up there? Payton's signal was supposed
to be *three* long flashes off his rifle barrel. What was this?

At the flat car, hands worked deftly, cutting tie-down
ropes from the canvas covers, snatching crate after crate of
rifle ammunition, boxes of black powder, cannon shot. Two
of Parker's men, Delbert and McCord, had rode back and
swung over their saddles onto the flat cars. They hefted and
pitched crates from the car to the tandem wagon. Old man
Dirkson asked them in a near whisper through his scraggly
gray beard, "Where the hell is Parker and his brother?"

"They're up there," McCord answered. "Don't worry
about it." Yet, even as he spoke, his eyes turned to the high
slope, searching for Payton Parker's signal. Nothing there.

Major Zell had raised his hand, ready to signal toward the engine and send the rest of the train forward. But with his hand raised and ready to drop, Zell saw the concerned look on Bowes's face as Bowes turned his horse to cross the tracks and rode up. Zell waited. The two men at the engine stared back with their pistols covering the engineer and oiler, one gunman on the ground, the other in the engine. "What's the hold-up?" the one in the engine whispered down. A dark gleam came into the eyes of the gunman on the ground.

Just as Liam Bowes started to step his horse up onto the thin trail, a rifle shot cracked the silence of the land. Payton Parker yelled down, "Train coming!"

Old man Dirkson spit, pitching crates onto the wagon. "Hope Parker ain't let us down." He quickened his pace, loading the wagon.

"Hold that engine!" Zell shouted to the two men up front. It was the first words spoken aloud, and inside the passenger car Maria took note of the voice. *Uh-huh . . . not Mexicans.* She drew the mirror back inside, knowing something had gone wrong for them.

Halfway up the high slope, Payton and Leo Parker saw the engine nose forward from the darkness between the buttes. At first they'd seen a faint curl of steam rise up farther back. That was when Payton had started paying attention, and had fired the warning shot. Now both the Parkers backed their horses a step, seeing the second train start to approach from a thousand yards away.

"We got trouble, Leo. Let's go."

At the flat car, Major Zell saw the train emerge from the buttes and draw to a stop. "Keep loading," he called out to the men on the flat car. "Get as many crates off as you can."

Liam Bowes slid his horse to a halt before Zell. "Parker

wasn't paying attention, sir. They've slipped in through our back door."

"Never mind that now." Zell drew the long rifle from his saddle scabbard. "You know what to do, Mr. Bowes."

"Right, sir." Bowes kicked his horse forward to the front of the train. As he reined his horse down, the two gunmen had already acted on their own, the one inside shoving the engineer and the oiler out onto the ground, the one on the ground shoving them away from the train. The gunman in the engine turned and jammed the steel lever into reverse and opened the throttle. "Get it done," Liam Bowes called to them.

The engine hissed and groaned and began jarring backward, the couplings of each car jamming in turn until the whole line of cars rocked into motion. The gunman leaped down from the engine as two sharp cracks of pistol fire from the other gunman's pistol sent the railroad men slumping onto the hot sand. At the flat car, old man Dirkson jumped into the wagon with one last crate of ammunition in his arms. In a second, the wagon rolled away from the train in a flurry of dust, the mules braying beneath the slap of the reins.

Feeling the backward lurch of rail cars, Maria rose from the floor, steadying herself against the back of a seat. "Get ready, we're getting off!"

"Oh, Lord," one of the miners groaned, all four of them struggling to their feet. "They've sent us all to hell, I reckon."

"Come with me." Maria grabbed Prudence by her forearm and pulled her up. "You have to make a jump for it."

"For . . . for what?" Prudence Vanderman's eyes were wide and terror-stricken.

"For your life! Now come on." Dragging Prudence with

her as the train struggled to pick up speed, Maria looked at the four miners. "Jump out on this side and make for the rocks and brush."

"But they'll shoot us," one miner called out.

"Come on . . . it's your only chance." Maria kicked open the door and shoved Prudence Vanderman away from the train. Prudence landed and rolled in a spray of dust, her pantaloons showing white and frilly as her dress spun upward. Her white lace handkerchief flew free of her hand and tossed and fluttered in the hot, dry air.

"Lord-a-mercy!" The first miner hesitated in the open door. "I never seen a train speed up so fast."

"Go!" Maria placed a boot in his back and shot him forward, out into the hot air, the train picking up momentum. "It will only go faster, the longer you wait!" she yelled into the faces of the other miners. They understood and scurried one after the other, until looking back, Maria saw them scrambling through the dust and dried brush, scattered like a covey of running quail. But Prudence Vanderman sat slumped in the dirt with a hand to her forehead, looking dazed.

There was nothing Maria could do for Prudence Vanderman at the moment. She swung out of the car door onto the steel rungs leading up the side of the car. Right now, Maria had a train to stop.

Chapter 3

Atop the train, Maria crouched down and moved forward, struggling to keep her balance in the hot wind. Beneath her, the cars rocked and swayed, gaining speed. Looking back over her shoulder, she'd caught a glimpse of the other train. It had stopped now, out from between the buttes and less than five hundred yards back. From a stock car, a loading plank fell to the ground with a puff of dust. Off to her left, the wagon sped away across the pitch of sandy earth, old man Dirkson's straw sombrero flying off his head and spinning in the air behind him.

"It's a woman! Get her!" Payton Parker and his brother Leo had slowed down now, joining the others. Payton's rifle went up to his shoulder, taking aim.

Maria heard voices calling out on the ground as she leaped from one car to the next, heading for the engine. A shot rang out, and she heard the bullet thump against the side of the train. Then another shot fired, this time the bullet whistling past the back of her head. She hurried on, her rifle in hand.

On the ground, Zell spun his horse around, raising a hand as the other riders moved in and formed up around him. "You two, go with the wagon." His gloved finger pointed, and two riders turned and headed out between the wagon tracks. "Mr. Bowes, form an assault formation."

"Yes, sir!" Liam Bowes waved his arm, and the men gathered their horses in around him. He raised a hand and shoved Payton Parker's rifle barrel away as Parker was about to shoot again toward Maria atop the train.

"Damn it, Bowes! I had her!"

"Forget her, Parker." Liam Bowes's eyes caught Parker's for just a second, but long enough for Parker to see the question there. Why had Payton waited so long before giving his signal, or before firing the warning shot, Bowes thought. Payton turned from him and joined the others.

Back at the other train, soldiers led their horses down the loading plank, dust stirring beneath the horses' hooves as the soldiers mounted and formed abreast on the ground. The runaway train moved backward toward them, gaining speed. Maria looked down into Zell's face as the train rumbled past him. She slid down into the wood box and scrambled across cord upon cord of dried firewood, and on toward the engine.

"Blast it," Zell said under his breath. But he had no time to waste on her. He turned to Bowes and the others. The men had hastily formed into an assault position, waiting for him to lead the charge. "All right, you know what to do, men! We hit as the trains collide!" His voice rose above the roar of the train and the clacking of the rails.

At the troop train, a barrel-chested sergeant moved quickly among the forming men, shoving them, cursing and shouting orders at the top of his lungs. He kept one eye on the other train coming ever faster toward them. "Move your arses, men! Lively now!" A young private came down the plank, leading two horses, and the sergeant snatched the reins to one horse from his hands. "Fall in on the lieutenant! Quickly, men! Let's go, *let's go!*" He looked up into the stock car, seeing the jam of men and horses forcing their way out through the door. "Get those men and horses out of there! For God-sakes!"

Maria, sliding down into the cab of the engine now, glanced around at the controls. *Now what?* She had no idea what it took to stop a train. Pitching her rifle to the side, she pulled the first handle she came to, hoping it was the throttle. The loud roar of the engine spun down. She had guessed right, but the momentum of the train only lessened slightly, the thrust of the other cars pulling it on.

Overhead, she grabbed a long drooping chain and yanked it. But—*Santa Madre!*—it had nothing to do with the brake!

A long, deep steam whistle screamed out. Still holding on to the chain, she grabbed the long steel rod sticking up from the floor and pulled back on it with all her strength. A loud screech of steel against steel sounded beneath her. *Thank God!* She held fast, feeling the train rack and bump as car after car stretched against their coupling.

Outside, Zell drew his long saber, racing forward, leading his men toward the forming soldiers. Ahead, the young soldiers saw the advancing attack and prepared to meet it head-long. The helpless troop train idled beside them. The stock car still rumbled with the sound of frightened men and horses struggling to get out of it.

Zell saw the runaway train beside him grinding down, long trails of sparks swirling up from the locked steel wheels of the engine. Inside the engine, Maria held fast, not knowing how to lock the brake. She'd turned the overhead chain loose and now lay back against the brake lever with both hands wrapped around it, feeling the train slow down, but knowing it wasn't enough. Any second this train would plunge into the train behind it. Then what?

She braced and whispered a prayer under her breath, the

steel wheels screaming beneath her, the sound of gunfire starting to explode along the track. Through the smoky window of the engine, she caught sight of Prudence Vanderman alongside the rails, Prudence staggering in place with a hand to her head, her dress torn down one side, a strand of blond hair dangling down her face.

In the fraction of a second before the collision, Maria thought how ridiculous Prudence looked out there, wandering around amid all this madness. Then the world tilted back and forth as the caboose peeled away in a spray of splinters and strips of steel, plowing into the engine of the train behind it.

"Holy Joseph, Mary, and George," the cavalry sergeant whispered, turning his horse. The soldiers' horses shied away from the spectacle as their riders struggled to keep them under control.

Except for three young soldiers and their horses, all the troopers had managed to scramble down out of the stock car. Now these three remaining unfortunates were hurled forward in a tangle of hooves and limbs. The sergeant could only wince and turn away. "Stand fast, men! Prepare to engage the enemy!"

Even as he spoke, the sergeant watched the military bearing of the riders coming at him. *Sombreros? Vaquero clothing? Who were these men trying to fool?* These were not Mexican bandits. They rode abreast like a well-trained fighting unit, yet the sergeant could tell by their pace that they would soon break into an assault wedge. He'd bet that the point of that wedge would drive through his troops and force their line open. He'd seen this a hundred times. Mexican bandits didn't fight this way.

The engine of the second train withstood the impact of the caboose, the cattle catcher plow splitting the car from one end to the other in a high spray of shattered wood and metal, until the heavy steel coupling of the next car raised the engine enough to let the thrust of the entire colliding train get beneath it.

As broken pieces of board and metal showered down from the hot air above, the big engine rode up ten feet in the air, scooting backward, the cars behind it racking and pitching sidelong off the rails. Blinding sheets of sand leaped upward from beneath skidding rail cars. The line of troops broke away from the crash. Like some large wounded creature making its death cry in battle, the risen engine gave off a last billowing blast of steam and crashed onto its side as Zell and his men veered around it into the scattering soldiers.

"Hold fast, men! Give them a fight!" the young lieutenant shouted, jockeying his horse in front of the nervous troops. "Hold this line and push them back! We shan't let this border trash have their way with us."

Holy, merciful . . . ! The sergeant righted his horse and gigged it toward the lieutenant. *Couldn't this fool see what was coming at them?* "Lieutenant Howell, sir," he bellowed, "let them through our line . . . form a gauntlet of fire! Give them chase! Don't try fighting them at a standstill—" His words fell short beneath a volley of gunfire.

Lieutenant Howell heard the sergeant, but he would have none of it. He glanced at the line of worried troops as they shied to one side at the sound of the sergeant's voice. "As you were, men! Steady as they come!" Lieutenant Howell raised his drawn saber toward the coming riders. "Prepare to fire . . . !"

"My God, Sergeant Baines, what's he doing?" a young corporal shouted as the sergeant slid his horse in beside him, breaking into the line. "He'll get us killed!"

"No, he won't!" The sergeant grabbed the corporal's horse by its reins. He glanced around and saw the advancing riders already starting to break into a wedge, ready to sweep through them. "Take this half of the line forward ten yards. Catch the head of that wedge and fall alongside it . . . flank it! Break it up!" Now the thunder of oncoming hooves shook the ground beneath them.

The corporal shot a dark glance toward the lieutenant. "Damn his pompous—"

"Get it done, Corporal!" The sergeant shoved his horse away. Shots came in from the advancing riders beneath a loud war cry. Clumps of dirt exploded up at the hooves of the frightened army horses.

The corporal spun his horse, widening a break in the line. "You men, spread apart. Advance ten yards, fall into a flanking position!"

The sergeant broke his horse into a run toward the lieutenant as the corporal moved the men forward.

"What's the corporal doing, Sergeant?" The lieutenant craned upward in his stirrups, seeing half the line bolt forward and move away to one side. A shot whistled past his head.

"Sir! Be careful, sir!" The sergeant ducked slightly, ignoring the lieutenant's question.

"Sergeant, he's moved half of our line away! What in God's name is he doing?"

"I wouldn't know, sir! But we can't sit out here at half strength. Let me take these troops to the side, or they'll be cut to pieces!"

"Very well, Sergeant." The lieutenant jerked his frightened horse sideways, giving the sergeant room. "Someone will answer for this!"

"Yes, sir," the sergeant answered quickly, then called out

to the troops. "All right, men, move out along their left flank. Fire at will! Break them up!"

The wedge of Zell's riders rushed forward in their own raised dust, their serapes and sombreros flapping in the scorching wind. At the center of the wedge, Zell saw the cavalry troops before him break away into two lines, one line forward of the other, staggered into a flanking pattern that would give off more rifle fire than they would have to take. Young lieutenants were seldom this battle savvy.

Zell had planned to break through them in his assault wedge, taking out half their ranks on his way. It would have crushed them and left them stunned. But that wasn't going to happen now, he saw. They formed into two lines that would cover his men from both sides, staggered just enough to keep the cavalry troops from firing on one another. *Blast it!* Now this was going to cost him men, good men that he couldn't afford to lose. Who was that lieutenant? Smart, whoever he was . . .

The sound of rifle fire lifted into a relentless swell above the surge of dust and powder smoke. Behind Zell and Bowes, horses screamed, tumbling end over end, their riders thrown into the sand like broken dolls. The assault pushed on. Troopers fell from their rearing horses, man and animal locked in a death waltz. A mist of blood permeated the hot, dusty air. The troops held their flanking lines; and as the assault force charged through them, both lines closed around behind it, giving it chase now, Zell's men being put upon by heavy fire behind them.

"All right, lads!" Sergeant Baines yelled above the clamor of the melee. "Ride them down."

At the head of the assault wedge, Zell veered off to the right, leading his men toward the low rocky hills. He wasn't going to let this turn into a rout. His men needed cover now, a place to regroup, out of the heavy rifle fire. Once in the rock cover, he would split his forces and leave half of his men firing from behind the rocks while he moved the rest of them higher up the hillside. There they would take position and cover for the others as they moved up. His men were good—they could work in this kind of fighting pattern for a long time.

The young lieutenant would have to see this as a costly proposition. Would this cause him to pull his troops back? Zell hoped so. If not, they were in for a long, bloody battle. Behind him, his men saw what he had in mind. They swung hard right with him, giving themselves more of a sidelong firing position now instead of defending their rear. Immediately, the cavalry troops had to draw back a bit and lessen the heat of the chase.

"Fall back, men," Sergeant Baines bellowed, racing to the front of the chase. "Stay at their rear. Don't give them targets!" The troops who heard him swung wide, staying behind Zell's men. The ones who couldn't hear the sergeant soon got the message, seeing others swerve out of the line of fire while they themselves still felt the brunt of it.

"What in the name of God are you doing, Sergeant?" Lieutenant Howell yelled in a rage, reining his horse up beside Sergeant Baines as Baines turned his horse toward his troops. "We had them on the run! Stay on them, man!"

"No, sir! I knew you would see they've taken to the rocks. You'd have wanted me to pull the men back, right, sir? If not, our boys will be sitting ducks . . . out in the open on the sand flats below them!"

The lieutenant looked around, confused for a second, but then getting the picture. "Yes, right then. Carry on!"

Back at the crash site, where a heavy blanket of steam and wood smoke blanketed the earth, Payton Parker and his brother Leo had managed to duck away, up the side of the hill into the cover of scrub juniper as Zell and Bowes formed the men and made the charge. Now, with the fighting over five hundred yards away and moving upward into the rocks, Payton ventured down to where the two women lay coughing beside the rails.

"Well, look here," Parker said. "The little woman who caused all the trouble." He walked into the smoke, holding his bandanna up over his nose and mouth. On the ground, Maria lay stunned but conscious, hovering over Prudence Vanderman as if protecting her. Payton Parker reached out with the toe of his boot and pushed her aside. He laughed, then called out through the smoke. "Get over here, Leo, look what we've got." Blood trickled from the large knot on Maria's forehead. She reeled in the dirt, unable to make sense of anything.

Leo's voice called back to him. "There's four old men slipping up into the rocks."

"Forget them. Here's the woman who slowed the train down and screwed everything up. She's going with us."

Leo stepped in, fanning a hand back and forth, and looked down at the two women. "I don't know, Payton . . . maybe we oughta leave them be. We've got enough problems." In the distance the battle raged.

"Are you crazy? She caused our problems. Hadn't been for her slowing the train down there'd be dead soldiers packed inside that troop car right now." He reached down, grabbed Maria's arm, and yanked her up. "She's going with us . . . they both are. Get the other one. We'll go high, circle around, and meet Zell on the other side, after the shooting stops." He grinned.

"This ain't a good idea." Even as Leo spoke, he stooped and gathered Prudence Vanderman in his arms. "I think we best get away from here while we can. Bowes acted pretty steamed about us not doing our job. He'll really be hot when he sees we didn't make the charge—"

"Shut up, Leo! We're not going anywhere until we get our hands on that Mexican gold. We take these gals to Zell, tell him we couldn't make the charge because we found these two. What was we supposed to do, leave them there, after this one messed everything up?" He turned and yanked Maria along behind him.

Leo followed with Prudence in his arms. "I hope you know what you're doing here. I can't see why we don't just do like everybody else . . . get our job done and draw our share."

"Because that's not the way to get ahead, Leo. You just go along with me. I'll make us rich." Payton Parker grinned, coughing as he led his brother out of the smoke and up into the cover of rocks along the hillside.

Chapter 4

A fly buzzed somewhere . . . but it seemed far off in the distance, Maria thought, until it landed on her nose and caused her to stir and try to raise a hand to brush it away. But her hands would not move. She batted her eyes, and through a lifting gray veil she saw the long shadows of evening stretched across the men and horses around her. Her hands were tied. For just a second she couldn't remember why. Then it came back to her as her mind fashioned a glimpse of what had happened—the train, the gun battle, the deafening crash. She remembered flying backward, her hands coming off the brake lever. She remembered a great fog engulfing her as she somehow managed to make her way to Prudence Vanderman, who lay on the ground alongside the tracks. Then what . . . ?

"She's coming around, Bowes," a voice said; and looking up from the ground, Maria saw the grizzled, bearded face hover near her and felt the wet bandanna press against her forehead. "Easy there," old man Dirkson warned when she tried to struggle. "We've had all the fight out of you we're gonna take for one day."

Payton Parker stood over her, looking down with his hand on his pistol butt. "I say put a bullet through her head, after all the trouble she's caused. That's why we brought her to the major. Thought he'd want to kill her himself."

"Oh, you did, huh?" Old man Dirkson glared at him.

"That's right, I did." Payton Parker gazed around at the others, seeing how well his story would set with them. "If he don't want to, I will."

Now Maria struggled upward onto her knees, lashing out at him with her tied hands.

"Why don't you just shut up, Parker." Old man Dirkson grabbed Maria and pulled her back. He glared up at Payton Parker. "You don't want to start discussing *who* caused all the trouble back there."

"What's that supposed to mean?" Payton Parker took a step closer.

Liam Bowes shoved him to the side. "You *know* what he means, Parker. Don't push it." He stepped in between Parker and the old man. Past the men standing before her, Maria saw Prudence Vanderman on the ground, her hands tied behind her back. Prudence looked to be in a state of shock, staring wide-eyed at Maria.

Pushing his Mexican sombrero up on his forehead, Liam Bowes stooped down, gesturing a nod toward Prudence as he spoke to Maria. "She's told us who she is . . . now who are you?"

Maria hesitated, stalling, wondering exactly what Prudence Vanderman might have said. "I . . . I do not know this woman . . . who is she?"

"Don't get cagey on us, lady." Bowes leaned closer, his expression tight and serious. "She's one of the Vandermans. Who are you?"

"Oh." Maria let out a breath. "I am no one of any importance."

"It's no use, Maria," Prudence said in a shaky, hurried

voice. "I told them who you are. That you're my travel secretary. I'm afraid they already know everything about—"

"Shut up, lady!" Bowes looked back at Maria. "I want to hear from you."

Travel secretary? Maria stared at her. Why had Prudence told them that? Didn't this woman realize what the name Vanderman might mean to men such as these? But what was done was done, Maria thought. "It is true, I am her travel companion . . . her secretary."

"She's a damn liar," Payton Parker said, stepping closer once more. "Look how she's dressed—look how she dogged that train down."

"So, what are you saying, Parker? She's an engineer? For the railroad?" Bowes shot him a scowl. The other men had gathered closer now, a couple of them wounded and bandaged. A ripple of tired, muffled laughter moved through them.

Payton Parker's face reddened. "I'm saying she's lying. Maybe they both are." He swung a dark glance to Prudence Vanderman, then back to Maria. "All they'll do is slow us down, whoever they are. Shoot them and leave them here."

Behind him, his brother Leo and a couple of others nodded, agreeing with him. "See?" Parker continued, "we all know it's the truth. We've got enough problems, once those soldiers get regrouped and come up after us. Shoot these two, and let's get on out of here." As he spoke, he turned, making sure the other men heard him, wanting to get their support.

"Are you giving orders to my men?" The low voice of Major Zell startled the men like a clap of thunder. They stepped aside as he moved in. "Because if you *are* in charge, you may need to take *this* from me." A slicing sound of metal across metal swished through the air. Zell's cavalry saber streaked from its scabbard, and before Payton Parker could move away, the point of the long blade lifted his chin and held it high.

A gasp rose from the other men. Leo Parker's hand went to his pistol butt, then froze under the harsh gaze of Liam Bowes, whose hand had moved quicker and came up with his own pistol cocked and pointed. "Turn it loose, Leo," Bowes warned. "Your brother started it. Let's see how he finishes it."

Zell stared into Payton's eyes, the saber out at arm's length, the tip twisting slowly. Beads of cold sweat stood out on Payton Parker's forehead as a tense silence passed. "Oh? You don't want it?" Zell's voice spoke low and calm, yet menacing. "Well . . . perhaps I was mistaken." Zell shrugged his free shoulder. "Perhaps you'd like for me to say what we will or will not do here? Is that it?" The tip of the saber pressed a bit, coaxing an answer.

Parker tried to swallow down the tight, dry knot in his throat before speaking, but the tip of the blade wouldn't allow it. "I . . . I'm only trying to look out for us, Major, sir."

"Indeed . . . and well you should be, after your pitiful attempt at keeping watch for us back there." Zell's nostrils flared; his gloved hand tightened on the handle of the saber. "I've lost men because of you and your brother, Parker. The only good thing to come from this day is me running this blade upward through your brain!"

"Major Zell, sir"—Liam Bowes spoke, rising to his feet, his voice low and steady—"we can't spare a man right now. We need to keep moving. Let me deal with him after we cross the border. Please, sir . . . if you will."

Maria watched silently from the ground, taking it all in, remembering faces, names, getting a feel for her captors. Zell, the leader, trembling, his rage ready to boil over out of control. This man Bowes, moving in, calming Zell, taking charge in a subtle way. And these other two, one ready to die on the tip of a saber, the other ready to peel his pistol out and die with him. She glanced at the others, two of them ready to make a play. The way she saw it, they were on the Parkers' side. There was division here. She took close and careful note of it. Her head throbbed with each beat of her pulse. She had to think past the pain and keep her mind clear.

"Very well." Zell collected himself, eased down, and let out a tense breath. His saber lowered from Payton Parker's chin and drifted down to his belly. "But only because, as Mr. Bowes says, we can't afford to lose another man on this mission." His eyes moved from Payton to his brother Leo, then back. "But if either of you fail to carry out whatever task you're assigned, I will post your head on a stick and let it bake in the sun. I will not tolerate any man—"

As Zell spoke, his own words seemed to spark his rage once more; his voice grew stronger and stronger until Liam Bowes's voice broke in. "They know that, sir. Now we need to carry on. Deliver this load and get our gold." He stared with his pistol still cocked and pointed, only lowering it slightly when Zell let the saber slump in his hand and Leo Parker let his gun hand relax on his pistol butt.

Maria watched. Who had this man, Bowes, been pointing his pistol at near the end? she wondered. At first he'd trained it on Leo Parker, but at the last moment as Zell started out of control again, she wasn't sure. Across from her, she gazed at Prudence Vanderman, who sat transfixed, staring at the men before them. Prudence no longer seemed to be in shock. In fact, seeing a different look on the woman's face now, Maria wondered what sort of change had come over her. Prudence's eyes glistened and seemed to be drawn with keen interest on something that had been said.

"Here ya go, ma'am." Old man Dirkson stood, lifting Maria to her feet as the others eased down a bit and milled in place for a lingering second before drifting away to their horses. "Let's get you two women together and get ya into the wagon with me. We've got a hard push ahead of us." He pulled Maria forward by the rope around her tied hands.

"Where are you taking us?" Maria hesitated, resisting as the old man dragged her forward.

"You're heading for the border with us." He pulled harder. Maria stumbled forward one halting step at a time until they stood beside the loaded wagon. When he'd pushed Maria upward onto the wagon seat and walked over to get Prudence, Maria looked at the wagon reins and thought about snatching them up with her tied hands and making a run for it. But how far would she get in this heavy tandem wagon? And even if she got away, what about Prudence Vanderman? No, Maria would have to wait, go along with things until she saw a chance for both of them to make a break.

When old man Dirkson came back, leading Prudence by her shoulder, he saw the look on Maria's face and he chuckled, glancing at the reins, then back to Maria. "You're a thinker, you are." He winked at Maria. "I'll have to keep a close eye on you." He hefted Prudence up into the wooden seat beside Maria.

Once more Maria looked at the beckoning reins as old man Dirkson stepped around the wagon to the driver's side. With a grunt, he climbed up and righted himself on the seat. He grinned, taking up the reins. Then before moving forward, he pulled on the reins and called out to the mules in a low voice, coaxing them back a step. Again, he winked at Maria, close beside him.

"Just a little precaution I always take with a valuable

load," he said. Leaning forward with the mules backed up close, he bent down, taking a thick steel pin from inside his dusty coat. For a second he was down between the front of the wagon and the mules' sweaty rumps. He dropped the pin in the rear of the wagon tongue, securing it to the team, then came back up and settled onto the seat.

"Good thing you didn't try something foolish, little lady," he said to Maria as he slapped the reins and the four mules jolted forward against the weight of the wagon. "There's some here who would just as soon put a bullet in your head as look at you."

Little lady . . . God, how she hated that name! But she gazed ahead into the falling darkness and said nothing, watching the other riders move out in a single file along a thin elk trail leading upward to the high rock pass toward the border.

"If you gals will just do as you're told, it'll make things a lot easier on yas." He slapped the reins again, harder this time, the mules settling into their heavy load with their sweat-streaked shoulders thrust forward. "The major's a fair man . . . 'less you get him riled."

"I understand the situation. We are hostages, to be used in case the army gets too close." Maria turned facing him, studying his bearded face as he gazed ahead. "But what becomes of us once we are across the border?"

"See? You *are* a thinker." Old man Dirkson grinned without facing her. "We'll most likely set you free somewhere around Canyon Diablo. From there it'll be up to you to find your way back."

"This woman is not capable of withstanding such a trip." She glanced at Prudence Vanderman beside her. Prudence was sitting loose and wobbling in the wooden seat, her hands tied behind her.

"Well, with a name like Vanderman, I don't reckon it'll be long before word gets back to town. Her daddy'll have everybody and their brother out looking for her. Just be glad we ain't holding her for ransom . . . that could be worth a lot, you know."

Maria sat silent for a second. Why hadn't they already decided to do just that? It made sense, if all these men were after was fast money. She turned her gaze to Prudence. "Look at her. You should at least tie her hands in front of her as you did mine. She cannot balance herself this way." Maria lowered her voice a bit. "After all . . . we are only helpless women."

"Helpless? *Ha!* Not you. I saw what you did at the train. Hadn't been for you butting in, that train would've caught them soldiers before they ever got unloaded." They rode on in silence for a moment, old man Dirkson seeming to consider something. Then he looked across Maria at Prudence Vanderman. "Soon as we get a chance, we'll pull over and retie her hands in front of her."

"That would be decent of you." As Maria spoke, her eyes slid down to the pistol butt sticking up from the holster on his hip. *No. Too risky right now.* Besides, she still had the small derringer pistol in the well of her boot, thanks to one of the old miners aboard the train.

Dirkson slapped the reins again. "Meanwhile, you just settle down, and don't do something stupid. There's Mexican gold waiting for me and the rest at the end of this trip. We won't let you or anybody else foul things up."

"I give you my word that I will do nothing stupid." Maria sat back and felt Prudence Vanderman lean against her side.

"I . . . I'm so cold," Prudence said with a tremor in her voice. Prudence's face bobbed gently on Maria's shoulder.

"Try to get some rest," Maria whispered. "We will come

out of this all right." Maria raised her tied hands and looped
her arms around Prudence. She pressed her cheek against
Prudence's head lying on her shoulder. "Be brave, my
friend. I will not leave you."

"Thank you . . . you are so kind. I'm sorry we didn't get
along very well on the train. I must have seemed such a
spoiled and terrible person."

"Ssssh, please rest, regain your strength. We are in this
thing together. All that matters is that we survive."

"Yes . . . you're right. We must survive."

Maria pressed Prudence against her; and for a moment
they moved along in silence amid the creak of wooden
wagon and leather tracing, the mules handling the load now,
their breathing deep and steady. And after a moment, Maria
thought Prudence had fallen to sleep, until Prudence lifted
her face slightly and spoke in a guarded whisper close to
Maria's ear. "Do I keep hearing someone mention gold?"

Sergeant Baines stood at attention amid the low, crackling
flames of the campfire, even though young Lieutenant Howell had ordered him to stand at ease. Black powder soot
streaked down the sergeant's broad cheek beneath his right
eye. He'd given the lieutenant the worst of the news—seven
dead and four wounded among their ranks. He'd also re-
ported on the dead engineer and the oiler found shot alongside the tracks. When the lieutenant had asked how in the
blue-hell a ragged band of Mexican bandits could have in-
flicted such severe damage, the sergeant had braced himself
and replied, "Begging the lieutenant's pardon . . . this was
not Mexican bandits, sir."

Lieutenant Howell stared at him.

"No, sir," Sergeant Baines went on to say, slightly shaking his head. "I've fought my share of Mexican bandits, sir.

These men are Americans. If you'll permit me to speculate, this is an old band of Confederate raiders called the Border Dogs . . . led by Major Martin Zell." He lifted a bushy eyebrow. "Have you ever heard of Major Zell, sir? He fought the battle at Peach Orchard. At Little Roundtop. He's tricky. If we stay right on his trail, he'll lead us into a trap."

"Zell has been dead for years, Sergeant." Lieutenant Howell ran a dirty hand back across his sweaty, thinning hair, dismissing Sergeant Baines's idea. "He died in Virginia, in an insane asylum, under heavy guard, if my memory serves. I've already sent a rider back to the fort, informing the colonel of what's happened here. We have a bandit problem, Sergeant, nothing else. These are the same ones who hit our shipment of rifles and light field armaments."

"Yes, sir." Sergeant Baines tightened his jaw to keep from saying any more. This was his first mission under Howell's command. He'd known little about how to deal with this young lieutenant, but he'd been learning throughout the day. Whatever foolish order this man gave, it was Baines's job to change it, but to do so in a way that still made it seem like it was the lieutenant's idea. "Then I stand ready to carry out whatever orders you issue, sir."

"Good." The lieutenant let out a breath. "Let's have no rumors spreading about some dead Confederate major, or how tricky he might be. It's bad for morale. We'll have our hands full as it is, once word gets to the proper sources about Jameson Vanderman's daughter being taken hostage."

"That we will indeed, sir." Sergeant Baines glanced around at the troops where they stood gathered near their horses ten yards away. "I've instructed the men to step carefully should we run into these thieves tonight. They are all aware of the hostage situation."

"Damn it." The lieutenant lifted his hat and adjusted it on

his head. "See, these bandits are smart enough to know we won't take a chance on hurting those hostages in the darkness. Whether they know who Miss Vanderman is or not doesn't matter. They realize we're at a disadvantage here." He glanced around, then back to Sergeant Baines. "Have you any idea who the other woman might be?"

"According to one of the miners, sir, the other woman got on alone, three stops back. He said she was carrying only a small spindle and a rifle. Said when the trouble started, she kept her head and got them all off the train, just in time."

"A rifle, eh?"

"Yes, sir. We found it in the wreckage of the engine. The Border Dogs . . . that is, the bandits, got to her before we did.

The lieutenant's eyes flared a bit. "No more talk about Border Dogs, Sergeant. I hope I've made myself clear on that?"

"Yes, sir, *very* clear . . . sorry, sir." Sergeant Baines gazed straight ahead into the surrounding darkness. "She also has a pistol, sir—this other woman."

"A pistol?"

"Yes, sir. One of the miners said he gave it to her right before they left the train. Said she shoved it down in her boot."

The lieutenant winced. "That's all we need right now . . . some unidentified terror-stricken female, out there with a loaded gun."

"Begging your pardon, Lieutenant. But from what we've seen and heard of her . . . I'd hardly describe her as terror-stricken. Whoever she is, we can thank her that we didn't lose more men than we did back there." Sergeant Baines hesitated a second, then added, "The fact is, sir, I've heard of a young woman who fits her description. There's a

Ranger up in the high desert territory who rides with a tough little Spanish woman named—"

Lieutenant Howell cut him off. "Sergeant Baines, I appreciate that you've had vast experience in this barbaric land with all of its colorful people. But for now, let's stick to the facts and the crisis at hand. We'll be moving out of here in an hour. Get your men rested and fed quick time."

"But, sir, I would be lax in my duty if I didn't bring it to your attention—"

"That will be all, Sergeant."

"Yes, sir." Sergeant Baines fell back a step, then turned; and before walking away, he said in a lowered tone, "But if that is her, sir, the woman I'm talking about . . . we'd be wise to allow for her in whatever plans we make."

"Her safety and the safety of Miss Vanderman is foremost in my mind, Sergeant. Of course, that goes without saying."

"Yes, sir, but that's not what I mean. I mean we should allow for what action she might initiate . . . on her own."

"For crying out loud, Sergeant. She's a hostage! A woman! What can she possibly be up to on her own?"

"If that's the Ranger's woman, Maria, sir, I would start thinking of her right now as more than just a hostage."

"Oh? How then should I think of her?"

"Well . . . if it's her, sir, we'd best start thinking of her as our inside resource. She's on the job, sir. To her this is just another day's work."

Lieutenant Howell looked at him with a fixed gaze of authority. "That will be all, Sergeant Baines!"

"Yes, sir!" Baines snapped a salute and walked away across the campsite to where the men milled near their horses and ate strips of jerked beef, washing it down with tepid water from their canteens. "All right, men, make it snappy. Boots and saddles in an hour."

A groan went up among the men. The corporal stepped
forward, his blue shirt and galluses covered with dust. "Any
luck convincing him we're not up against a gang of Mexican thugs here?"

"None at all, Donnely. His report back to the fort says
these are Mexicans . . . so they are Mexicans." He shook his
head and looked over the tired, sweaty men. "There will be
no more talk about the Border Dogs. The lieutenant has in-
formed me that they do not exist."

"Jesus!" Corporal Donnely slapped dust from his leg with
his hat brim. "Somebody needs to enlighten him as to how
many young officers have been shot in the back while leading a charge."

Sergeant Baines glared at him. "I'll hear no more talk like
that from you, Corporal." He caught a glance of the men
nodding in agreement with Donnely. "You're here to follow
orders, not make threats against our commanding officer."

"Don't high-horse me, Baines." Donnely stepped forward, bristling. "I saw how you covered for his stupidity.
Only a bloody fool would have brought that train out of the
buttes into full view and stopped it there. We were sitting
ducks! He'll get these new men killed before this is over!"

"Lower your voice, Corporal," Sergeant Baines hissed,
stepping closer to him until they stood almost nose to nose.
"For now, he's in command." His voice lowered even more,
softening a bit. "Don't you think I see how ignorant this
young man is? If our men are to make it out of here alive, it
will be because you and I pay attention to orders and make
the best of them. Show your stripes, man. We both know
who and what we're dealing with out there. So what if the
lieutenant doesn't agree? You buck up now . . . we've got to
cover one another's arse here."

Corporal Donnely relaxed, letting out a tense breath. "It's

been a long day, Sergeant Baines . . . tell me what you want from us." He gestured a dusty gloved hand, taking in the tired, dirty troopers.

"There now, that's more like it." Sergeant Baines offered a thin smile. "I want you to keep at least a half dozen men scouting ahead of the lieutenant at all times, so he won't know whether we're on their trail or not—chances are he'll fall asleep in the saddle." Baines glanced across the campfire to where Lieutenant Howell had stood only a moment earlier. "Keep him thinking we're right behind them . . . but swing us around on the flatlands, get us a good twenty miles away from them by morning."

"But if we let them get away, what about the hostages?"

"We're not going to let them get away. I fought Zell at Peach Orchard and Tucker's Point while our lieutenant was still hanging from a warm teat. I know what Zell will do if we get too close during the night. We haven't seen his entire force. He's got more men posted along the high trail, waiting for us. You can bet on it. With hostages, he knows he's got the advantage. We've got to avoid him. He'll leave the high pass come morning—he's got to. It's the only way for his men to make it across the border with a heavy wagon. We'll be there waiting for him—whether the lieutenant knows it or not."

Corporal Donnely nodded, then returned the sergeant's smile. "He'll throw a bleeding fit if he finds out what we've done."

"That's quite all right. At least he'll still be alive to throw it. Now have these men ready to move out in less than one hour. This night doesn't end until the sun comes up."

Chapter 5

Ever since Prudence Vanderman had whispered the question about the gold into Maria's ear, Maria had been puzzled by it. She'd thought about it all night as the wagon lumbered upward along the high pass trail. The meaning in Prudence's question had been hard to understand. Had Prudence asked in a way so as to offer some sort of suggestion? Was she implying that if gold was involved, it might provide a solution to their dilemma? Or, as Maria had asked herself over and over, had there been a trace of honest, old-fashioned greed in there somewhere? *Nonsense . . .*

If there was a message there, it was certainly mixed, Maria thought. What possible interest could a woman like Prudence Vanderman have in gold, especially at a time like this? Her father had all the riches of the world to begin with. Besides, young ladies like Prudence would consider it poor taste to mention something so irrelevant as gold or any other monetary gain. The question had been strange, to say the least.

Twice during the night, old man Dirkson had stopped the wagon long enough for the two women to relieve themselves as he stood back a few feet, looking the other way. At the first stop, he'd taken time to untie Prudence Vanderman's hands from behind her back and retie them in front of her. When she and Maria moved behind a low mesquite bush, Maria had spoken to her in a pointed tone just barely above a whisper. "Why were you asking about the gold?" Then she watched Prudence's eyes in the pale moonlight and waited for an answer.

Prudence saw the strange look on Maria's face. "Why I . . . I must have been speaking out of my head. This is hardly the kind of situation I'm accustomed to." She stood and adjusted her torn dress about her waist. "Goodness, you act as if I've done something wrong."

There was something deceptive, almost playful in Prudence's response, and as she turned to walk back toward the wagon, Maria caught her forearm with her tied hands and spoke in a harsh whisper near her ear. "Listen to me! If you are thinking of playing some sort of game with these people, don't do it. I'm warning you. You are not wise to the ways of men such as these—"

"Oh?" Prudence whispered in reply. "If I'm the daughter of a wealthy man, then I must be some sort of idiot? Is that what you're thinking? That I'm worthless?"

"You gals doing all right over there?" Old man Dirkson asked in a quiet tone from a few yards away. "Gonna have to get moving here."

"*Sí* . . . we will be right there." Maria turned back to Prudence Vanderman. "No, I do not think you an idiot. But the only way we'll get out of this is if you keep your mouth shut and stay out of my way. Do not try something foolish on your own. Do you understand?"

But Prudence didn't answer. Instead, she turned and walked through the darkness, Maria staring hard after her.

As they rode on, Maria noticed more men joining them from behind at different intervals until she calculated the number of men to be well over twenty. Old man Dirkson noticed the tight silence between the two women. When they stopped once more at the peak of the high pass trail, and the old man let them move away to the other side of a rock spill, Maria started right in as if the conversation had never stopped. "Have you noticed how many more men have joined us? No, you haven't. This is a small army! Nothing you have ever done in your life has prepared you to deal with these men. One wrong move and we will both be dead." Maria hissed her words beneath her breath, her dark eyes glistening in the moonlight.

Prudence pushed Maria back a step. "I'm a learned woman. Don't treat me as if I'm a child. Would you be acting this way if I were some buffalo-smelling plains woman? Some sunburnt prairie flower in scuffed riding boots?" She glared at Maria. "Of course you wouldn't."

Maria lunged forward and grabbed Prudence by the bodice of her dusty dress. "But you are not one of those kind of women. So leave this to me! I know what I'm doing. Our lives are in my hands."

"Hurry it up over there," old man Dirkson called out. In the dim moonlight, Maria saw three more men move down from the cover of rocks and join the others. These men knew their business, she thought, as the black silhouettes moved quietly forward.

"In one moment, please," Prudence replied. She jutted her face close to Maria's, a different woman it seemed, standing her ground. "When it comes to my life, I'll decide whose hands I leave it in. Take your dirty fingers off my dress, or I'll break them. *Comprende, mi amigo?*" Her voice was different now, her mannerisms different, even the expression in her eyes—nothing about Prudence Vanderman was the same.

Maria stepped back, a bit stunned. She studied the face

before her in the moonlight as if seeing it for the first time, and in doing so a revelation became clear in her mind. After a second's pause, she asked in a low, level voice, "Lady . . . who are you? This time tell me the truth."

"You gals get buttoned and tucked, or I'll have to come get yas." The old man chuckled. "Don't know if my old heart could stand it."

Prudence half turned from Maria for a second, seeming to consider whether or not to answer her. But as Maria grabbed her once more by the bodice of her dress, she grasped Maria's forearm and leaned close to her face. "The truth? Okay, the truth! My name *is* Prudence, but it's not Vanderman. I'm Prudence Cordell, from Mama Bristol's Pearl Palace in New Orleans. If you think you've handled more of these kind of men than I have, you better think again, sister." She swung Maria's hand away, moved off a few feet around the rock spill, then turned and looked back. Maria hadn't moved an inch. "Well, can you trust me now? Or must I first learn how to spit, and say howdy partner?"

Once more they rode on. Maria thought hard all night, working it all out in her mind as the wagon bumped along the rocky trail. When morning came in a thin silver reef across the far horizon, old man Dirkson reached over and shook Maria by her knee. "Psst, wake up now, we're heading down."

Maria jerked her knee away from him. "I am not asleep. Keep your hands to yourself."

The old man grinned. "If everybody done that, this world wouldn't be near its size." Dirkson stopped the wagon, set the brake, and wrapped the reins around the metal railing beside the wooden seat. He stood, stretching his back while the rest of the men stepped down from their horses and moved forward on foot, as quiet as ghosts.

"You gals will have to excuse me while I join the men for a few minutes." He looked down at them, then raised a finger. "Oh, I nearly forgot." He leaned way down, pulled the steel pin from the rear of the wagon tongue, and stood up and winked, jiggling it in his gloved hand. "Wouldn't want you two to get restless and try to run away."

"I gave you my word that I would do nothing stupid," Maria said, looking away from him.

"That you did, yes, ma'am." Old man Dirkson grunted, stepping down onto the rocky ground. "It don't hurt to remind you though."

"Where are we?" Prudence asked, stirring, then running a hand across her disheveled hair.

"We are at the top of the high pass." Maria looked all around in the grainy light. "From here we go downward and pick up the border crossing into Mexico. If there is trouble with the army, we will find it down there on the flatlands."

As Maria spoke, she looked ahead to where Liam Bowes and Major Zell had stopped beside a large rock. They stood and dusted their trousers as old man Dirkson walked up to them. Now the three men gazed out across the flatlands far below as they talked back and forth.

"Mr. Bowes and I agree," Zell said, raising binoculars to his eyes and scanning the wide stretch of flatlands at the bottom of the narrow rocky trail. "They're down there waiting. The lieutenant anticipated us and swung his men wide around the flatlands. What say you, old man?"

Old man Dirkson scratched his beard. "He didn't look that smart to me . . . but he never rode into any of our traps back along the trail. They must not have been following us all night." He paused, considering it, then nodded. "Yep, they're down there, sure enough. We'll have our hands full crossing the wagon."

"Indeed . . ." Zell lowered the binoculars, still gazing out, thinking. "I must be careful not to underestimate our young Yankee lieutenant. He appears to be a bit of a tactician. He realizes we have but one way out of here to the border, and that we'd never outrun him with this heavy wagon." Zell considered things for a second. "But he can't possibly know our true strength. If we keep the wagon up here, he'll eventually have to come up for it. That means he'll have to risk harm coming to the women."

"Shall I prepare the men to make a run for it on horseback, Major?" Bowes asked.

"Yes, they'll have to charge through and take their chances, I'm afraid. But send down only the same number we had when we hit the train. The rest will stay up here with us to guard the hostages and the wagon for the time being." As an afterthought, Major Zell added, "Make sure the Parker brothers stay up here with us."

"Then we're going to abandon the ammunition when the time comes?" Bowes asked with a puzzled expression. "Lose what we've got coming in gold?"

"No, of course not. That would destroy our credibility with the *federales*." Zell let out a long breath, and turned to look toward Maria and Prudence Vanderman. "There is something distasteful about us keeping hostages. We must release them as soon as we get shed of these soldiers."

"But you have to admit, sir," Bowes said, "having them along has sure given the lieutenant second thoughts about rushing us."

"True," Zell said, "but I take no pride in it. We are men of honor . . . we have lived by it, and so we must die by it if need be. We are soldiers, gentlemen, let's not forget that." He gazed away in contemplation, then asked, "How many kegs of black powder do you suppose we have on the wagon?"

Old man Dirkson squinted. "I'd say seven, maybe eight kegs. Are you thinking what I think you are? Lure him up here and blow his men all to hell?"

"Indeed." Zell gave a dark smile. "I think it's time we shuffle the deck and redeal . . . find out what our young lieutenant knows about the holy art of poker."

As Zell had turned to Bowes and Dirkson, Prudence stared at their backs and spoke to Maria in a hushed tone. "Now that we are alone, let's make some plans on getting away from this bunch of murderers."

"Uh-uh." Maria shook her head. "Before we make plans of any sort, you tell me . . . why you are traveling as Prudence Vanderman?"

"Damn it. I hope this wasn't a mistake, telling you the truth. But it's a fact—you weren't about to rely on sweet little Prudence Vanderman, now, were you?" Before Maria could answer, Prudence chuckled under her breath. "Of course you weren't." Then she sighed and turned her gaze to Maria. "Look . . . you said yourself, we've got to pull together to survive. If you must know, I impersonate Prudence Vanderman all the time. I have for the last four years, after seeing a picture of her in *Harper's.* Not only do we have the same first name, we could actually pass for sisters! Anytime I travel, I use the Vanderman name—a bill comes, I simply sign her name and forget about it. Her father has so much money, it goes unnoticed, and she travels so much he seldom knows where she's at." She smiled. "You can't imagine the difference it makes."

"Yes, I can imagine. But you have deceived me. How can we—"

"Cut the crap, sister. What if I'd told you to begin with?

Would you not have pushed me from the train anyway? No, I don't think it would have mattered. Besides"—she patted herself up under an arm—"I have a little something here that Prudence never would have carried."

"Oh?" Maria looked at her.

"Yes. I have a straight razor in a leather case up here under my arm—call it a trick of the trade." She smiled. "Does it open any possibilities for you?"

Maria eased a bit and managed a thin smile herself. "Then we have a two-shot pistol, a straight razor . . . and a choker when we need one."

"A choker?"

"*Sí*, to strangle one of them with, if we must." Maria moved her tied hands over onto Prudence's lap. "Loosen this rope for me. Not too much . . . just enough for me to shed it when the time comes."

"Sure, right, a *choker*. Why didn't I think of that?"

"Perhaps because you have been too busy thinking of the gold these men will have once they cross the border?"

"All right, I'm guilty. But I figure if we're crossing the border anyway, we might as well come back with something to show for it . . . *if* we come back at all."

"I plan on coming back." Maria's voice sounded resolved as she wiggled her hands a bit in the loosened rope, then reached over and took Prudence's tied hands onto her lap. "There is a man waiting for me in Humbly. Believe me, I *am* coming home to him."

PART 2

Chapter 6

Three days had passed by the time the Ranger and Sheriff Boyd Tackett rode into town, leading the string of dusty sweat-soaked horses behind them. Between them, Willis Durant rode with his head lowered, his hands cuffed atop the saddle horn. Yet when the voice of a townsman called out, "There's one of them bastards, let's get him hung!" Durant's dark eyes lifted up for just a second, sharp and alert, scanning the town, then lowered again and disappeared beneath the shadow of his dusty hat brim.

Faces pressed forward from doorways. The man who cried out scuttled along the boardwalk toward other men who stood milling near the livery barn, one of them impatient, with a coil of rope resting on his shoulder. The small group of men grew close together and headed toward Tackett and the Ranger in a determined stride.

"I hope your townsfolk understand my policy regarding prisoners," the Ranger said to Tackett in a low tone. "Looks like we might have a little problem here."

"Dang it all," Tackett hissed, watching the men come toward them. He gigged his horse forward a step, then drew it to a quick halt quarterwise, stopping it in the street between the Ranger and the coming townsmen. "Now listen up, you men," he said to them. "We're hot and tired and been out on the flats for over a week. Unless you're headed out to lasso a jackrabbit, you better tote the rope back to where you got it."

"Guess what jackrabbit we've got in mind." the man with the rope on his shoulder said, jiggling it in his hands. "We'll take that black rabbit right there beside you, Sheriff." Behind him the others nodded and grumbled their support. Some of them leaned to one side, looking past the sheriff, past Durant and the Ranger, toward the dead bodies across the saddles.

"Put it out of your heads," Tackett said, sawing his horse back and forth in front of them. "You elected me to sheriff this town, and that's what I'm doing—now get on away before somebody gets their skull cracked."

As Tackett spoke to the crowd, Durant lifted a glance at the Ranger and said under his breath, "Makes you wish you'd shot me straight up, don't it?"

The Ranger just looked at him, then stepped his white barb up beside Tackett, leading the string of fly-ridden corpses. He called down to the men in the street, "While you boys aren't too busy, take these bodies off our hands." His gaze singled on the man with the rope on his shoulder. "You there, with your big mouth, you look like a person who can stand the smell long enough to get these bodies under ground." He leaned down and held the lead rope toward the man.

The man backed up a step, his hands coming up chest high. "Uh-uh! Not me. I'm a rail agent, not a grave digger. We came to hang that snake." His finger pointed up at Durant.

"Oh . . ." The Ranger looked down as if considering it. Then he looked back at him and said, "So, you're only wanting to hang ole Durant here. You won't be handling his earthly remains afterward?"

"Well I—" The man's words stopped short. He strained his eyes toward Durant in the sun's glare. "Durant? You mean that's—?" Again his words ran out on him.

"Yep, it's Willis Durant," the Ranger said. He feigned a surprised expression. "I figured you knew who it was . . . coming on with your rope and all."

"Well, no, I just saw he was a—" He stopped again and looked around at the men behind him, then back to the Ranger, avoiding the cold stare from Durant, but giving a nervous shrug. "I mean, hell, you can't blame me, can you?"

"Not yet, I can't." The Ranger stared at him, his eyes cutting like sharpened steel.

The man collected himself, looking less sure, but still determined. "Well . . . it don't matter who he is, I suppose. The man robbed our bank. We're going to jerk a knot in his neck. Ain't that right, boys?" He flashed a glance around to the others, then added, "Don't try to stop us, Ranger. We mean business here."

"In that case," the Ranger said as he backed his white barb a step, opening a gap between him and Tackett, leaving Durant and the string of corpse-draped horses alone on the hot dusty street, "get to hanging him then."

"Huh?" The man looked surprised.

"That's right," the Ranger said. "You heard me. I'm turning him over to you *personally*." He pointed a gloved finger down at the man's face. "Now get busy hanging him. Don't mess up though. You've all heard of Willis Durant—he'll be down your shirt like a rattlesnake."

Tackett saw what the Ranger was doing, and he stopped his horse wide of the crowd and sat with his hand on his pistol butt. Durant raised his sweaty face and stared at them from beneath his lowered hat brim. The men stood back, leaving the man in front alone now, the rope looking heavy on his shoulder, his face running freely with sweat. After a pause, Tackett said to him in a lowered tone, "Why don't you get back to the rail office where you belong, Herschel? The longer you stand there, the worse you're gonna look."

Taking one last shot at saving face before the other townsmen, Herschel the rail clerk swallowed back the dryness in his throat and said, "He robbed our bank, Sheriff. I can't just stand by and—"

"Hang him then and quit talking about it," the Ranger dared, cutting him off.

"Easy there." Tackett raised a hand toward the Ranger as if holding him back. "Herschel, go on now. You're just getting in deeper." Two men behind Herschel eased farther back, then turned and moved away, glancing over their shoulders. Others seeing them leave started giving it serious thought themselves. They rubbed their jaws and winced, shooting one another dubious glances.

"What's it gonna be, Herschel?" The Ranger glared down at him now, his hand going to the butt of his big pistol. "You gonna hang this man on your own, or am I gonna come down there and pistol whip you into doing it?"

"Huh? Now just a minute! Lord!" Herschel muttered, completely stunned.

"That's right," the Ranger said. "You said you was going to hang him. I hate a proud-stepping peckerwood who can't finish what he starts out to do." The crowd thinned more, the men quickly moving away, not facing one another.

"Sheriff, for God's sakes! You know me! I'm a law-abiding man. Are you going to let him do this?" His eyes widened, seeing the Ranger rise as if to step down from his saddle. He pulled the rope off his shoulder and flung it away. "See . . .

I ain't no hangman!" He backed a nervous step. "Do something, Tackett!"

"Can't help you, Herschel," Tackett said, shaking his head. "I warned you. That's all I can do." He turned to the Ranger. "Don't whip him as bad as you did that last poor devil. You knocked his eye out of its socket."

"The hell kind of town is this turning into?" Herschel blurted, then broke backward into a run, turning to hurry off along the dusty street, raising more dust in his wake. "Wait till Donahue hears about it. He won't stand for it!" he called over his shoulder.

The Ranger settled back down into his saddle. "Who's Donahue?"

Tackett ran a hand across his sweaty brow. "Don't you remember? He's the one we butted heads with back when you was looking for Montana Red. You shot half his line crew."

"Aw yeah, him." The Ranger pulled the string of horses forward, heeling the white barb off toward the jail. "What's his stake in all this?"

"Nothing, except he has a lot of money in the bank." Tackett led Durant behind him.

"Well," the Ranger said over his shoulder, "we got his money back for him. You'd think that would be enough."

"Yeah, you'd think," Tackett said. "But Donahue likes for everybody to know he has a hand in running this town. If he can do something to make himself look good, you can bet he will."

"See why I don't like working in town?" The Ranger nudged his white barb forward—"Come on, Black-eye"—toward the hitch rail outside the sheriff's office, pulling the worn out string of horses behind him.

*   *   *

Once they had put Willis Durant inside a cell and taken off his handcuffs, Tackett stayed at the office while the Ranger led their tired horses to the livery barn. At the barn, the Ranger turned the other horses over to a young man who stood scratching his shaggy head, looking at the bodies across the saddles. "What am I supposed to do with this mess?" he asked, slapping away flies.

"Get them off and into the ground," the Ranger replied as he dropped the saddle from his white barb and moved it into a vacant stall. "The sheriff's office will pay you a dollar a head to bury them."

"But I don't want to handle them."

"Then you've got a problem. It's going to be hard taking care of the horses with dead men on their backs." He reached down, took up a handful of clean straw, and began wiping the white barb down with it.

"Shit," the young man grumbled. He took the lead rope and led the horses through the barn toward the back doors.

The Ranger speculated that after cooling down his horse, watering and graining it, then boarding it here in a good clean stall, he would get himself a warm bath, a hot meal, and tonight, a good night's rest in a feather bed. With a little luck and no bad weather, he'd head out come daylight tomorrow, ride the twenty miles, and meet Maria in Humbly when she rolled in on the afternoon train.

But an hour later, when he'd finished with his horse and walked to the sheriff's office, he spotted the small crowd gathered on the boardwalk and knew this was going to be a long day. Three dusty horses that hadn't been there before now stood hitched to the rail. Walking past the horses, he looked at the marking on one of their hips—the Flying Cross brand. Running a gloved hand across the mark, he adjusted his pistol in his holster and stepped up onto the boardwalk. Townsmen parted to the side, looking him up and down, a sharp defiant gleam in all their eyes.

Here goes . . . He hesitated only for a second, long enough to hear the raised voice from inside the office. Then he swung the door open and stepped inside.

"You and I don't need to have trouble over this, Tackett," the Ranger heard an angry voice say. Even from behind, he recognized the broad-shouldered man as Donahue, as he leaned over Tackett's desk, his big hands spread atop it. "This is all that blasted Ranger's doings!"

Two Flying Cross cowhands stood near Durant's cell. They spotted the Ranger, and one of them said to Donahue in a cautious tone, "Uh, boss . . ."

But Donahue ignored him until the Ranger slammed the wooden door behind himself. Startled, Donahue spun around toward the sound and stood staring at the Ranger from eight feet away. Durant watched from his cell as the Ranger took a step forward, his thumb hooked on his holster. "We figured you'd be here, Donahue," the Ranger said. "Just didn't think it would be so soon."

"You stay out of this, Ranger," Donahue boomed. "This is a town matter . . . between the sheriff and me."

"Once I hear my name spoken, I count myself in the game, Donahue. Now just to keep this short and to the point"—he let his glance slide across the other two men, then back to Donahue—"anybody makes a move to lynch Willis Durant, I'll put a bullet in the most painful spot you can imagine."

"You've got no jurisdiction in this, Ranger!" Donahue's face swelled red, his fists clenched at his side.

"Neither do you," the Ranger said. As he spoke, his hand came up slow and easy with his pistol in it. He leveled it at the two cowhands and gestured them away from Durant's cell. "You boys make me nervous standing that close to the prisoner." They looked to Donahue for instruction, but before he could offer it, the hammer on the Ranger's pistol cocked. They moved away and across the office with their hands chest high.

"Easy now," one of them said. "We just follow orders here."

"Good," the Ranger said, "because I'm ordering you out of here in the next two seconds."

"Go on, boys," Donahue said, seeing the seriousness in the Ranger's eyes. "I'll be along in a minute."

When they'd shuffled past the door and closed it behind themselves, Donahue started in again. "Listen to me good, both of you." His finger swung from the Ranger to Tackett, then settled on Durant, who stood with his hands on the bars. "That thieving darky is going to hang . . . one way or another. I don't give a damn about his bad reputation! I can't afford to have every saddle tramp in the territory thinking they can rob my bank and get nothing but a slap on the hands."

"Ever seen the inside of the territorial prison?" the Ranger asked, then continued before Donahue could answer. "It ain't exactly a slap on the hands."

"You know what I mean," Donahue said, his voice tight with anger.

"Yes, I do." The Ranger moved in between Donahue and Durant's cell. "What you mean is, the people of this town expect you to act a certain way, and you don't want to disappoint them. But you're going to this time. I don't hold with lynching a man. If he hangs, it'll be because a judge says so—not because you want to look tough for everybody."

Donahue fumed. "Oh? It so happens that Judge Gant is a

personal friend of mine. We'll see how this goes, once he gets here."

"Fair enough. But nothing happens until then." The Ranger slipped his pistol down into his holster. Donahue was just blowing hot air, he thought, going from threats about taking the law into his own hands to boasting about his political connections.

Donahue stepped toward the door, looking away from the Ranger, toward Tackett. "And as for you, Sheriff, there's an election in three months. Don't get too comfortable in that chair."

"I've never been too comfortable in it anyway," Tackett replied curtly. The door slammed hard behind Donahue, raising a stir of dust. Tackett smiled, leaning back in his chair. "That wasn't so bad, now was it?"

The Ranger stepped over to the dusty window and looked out. Donahue and his cowhands had stepped off the boardwalk and were now headed for the saloon across the street. Behind them, the small following of townsmen hurried along, like smaller dogs following the leader. "We'll see what happens once they all get liquored up," he said. Before turning back to Tackett, the Ranger noticed a slender young man hurrying from the telegraph office with a piece of paper fluttering in his hand. "Think Donahue will let it lay for now? Or will he get stoked up again . . . make one more run at us just for good measure?"

"Naw, Donahue will stay in line now, so long as we keep out of sight. Don't want to go around reminding him of how he didn't get his way."

"I planned on heading out come morning," the Ranger said. "Will you be all right here?"

"Sure. The judge will be here in a couple of days." Tackett folded his hands behind his neck. "Me and Durant will just sit tight here. I've got a part-time deputy I'll call in—the kid that works at the livery barn. He'll relieve me long enough to fetch vittles and water."

They turned toward the door as it swung open and the telegraph clerk came in with an excited look on his face. "I saw what's going on out there, Sheriff," he said, out of breath. "And I'm afraid I've got more bad news for you." He pushed the piece of paper across Tackett's desk.

"All right, Robert." Tackett snatched the paper. "This better really be something, you busting in here this way."

The Ranger stepped closer. "What is it?"

"Dang it all . . ." Tackett words trailed off as his eyes read across the message.

"It just came in, Sheriff. But you can see it's two days late out of Humbly—they have the awfulest time keeping their lines up." The clerk stepped to the side.

"What is it, Tackett?" The Ranger asked intently again, seeing the expression on Tackett's face darken.

Tackett whispered something under his breath and turned his gaze to the Ranger. "Sam, this don't necessarily mean the worst has happened—"

"Let me see that." The Ranger grabbed the paper from his hand, glanced at the clerk, then read it. His shoulders slumped, a dark expression moving over his face like a coming storm cloud.

Tackett spoke quickly. "You know as well as I do how telegraph clerks can screw things up. This might all be a mistake."

The young clerk huffed and rubbed his toe across the dusty floor. "It's not a mistake, Sheriff. I checked it out right away with a telegraph to the army post. It's been sent everywhere, hoping somebody might spot these Mexican bandits before they do something else. Jameson Vanderman already knows about it all the way in New York. He's posted a reward for the return of his daughter."

From his cell, Willis Durant's eyes snapped to the clerk. "Did you say Mexican bandits?" But the clerk ignored him. Durant tightened his grip on the bars, a strange, knowing gleam coming into his dark eyes. "Ranger, listen to me!" He raised his voice, but still no one turned to him. His jaw stiffened.

"They've got Maria," the Ranger whispered under his breath, then glanced out through the dusty window and across the broad distant horizon.

"Wait, Sam!" Tackett stood and stepped around the desk. "Don't jump to conclusions here. Maria might not have been on the train. The message doesn't give her name . . . just Prudence Vanderman's!"

"She was on board, Tackett. You can bet on it."

Chapter 7

It took the Ranger no more than a half hour to prepare himself for the trek across the desert flatlands. While he laid out his shooting gear on Tackett's desk, checking and cleaning it, Tackett had gone to the livery barn to get the white barb and a spare horse for him. "I think you're making a mistake not taking me along with ya," Tackett had said after a few minutes of bickering about it. But the Ranger had only stared at him, until Tackett finally gave up and left, shaking his head and grumbling under his breath.

Now, with Tackett out of the office, Durant paced in the small jail cell like a trapped mountain cat, his dark eyes gleaming from a face full of sweat. "Ranger, you've got to hear me out." He stopped and gripped the bars. "You wanted to know about the men who killed my family . . . now I'm trying to tell you!"

The Ranger only glanced over, snapping his pistol back together, spinning the cylinder and holding it up close to his ear. He clicked it six times, listening to the sound of it, making sure the action was smooth and clean. "Durant, you didn't want to talk about it before when I had time to listen. So now you can save your breath." He holstered the pistol and picked up the big Swiss rifle, running a hand along the barrel. "We'll pick up where we left off once I get back."

"If you don't listen to what I'm saying, you might not get back at all." Willis Durant rattled the bars in his hands, his face pressed to them. "You're making a big mistake not taking me with you. These men are not Mexican bandits! These are the men I've been after all this time. You think I would lie about something like this?"

The Ranger looked up with a thin, tense smile, trying to keep his concern for Maria in check. "Well, let's look at it. You're facing a long time in prison on one hand, or a lynching party on the other." He paused and seemed to consider it for a second. Then he said, "Yeah, I can see where you might be tempted to bend the truth a bit." He slid a cartridge into the rifle chamber and snapped it shut. "But you're Tackett's problem now . . . I'm headed out." He slipped the rifle into its leather scabbard and leaned it against the side of the battered desk.

"Damn it, Ranger! Have you ever heard of the Border Dogs?" Durant glared at him from between the bars.

The Ranger stopped and looked back at him. A persistent conviction in the man's voice bore attending. "Yes, I've heard of them . . . an old Southern cavalry regiment left over from the war. A fellow by the name of Martin Zell used to be their leader. What about them?"

"This is them, Ranger! This is the men you'll be after. You've got to believe me!"

"Oh?" The Ranger just watched him, listening.

"Yes. They're still in business," Durant said in an urgent voice. "Zell is *still* their leader. Folks think he's dead, that he's been dead for years—but he's not! Him and his Border Dogs are the ones who robbed that army train a few weeks back. They pass themselves off as Mexican bandits. Took enough small arms and light cannon to start a war if they wanted to. They run guns to the Mexican *federales*." Durant's hands tightened once more on the iron bars. "You've got to take my word on this!"

Major Martin Zell . . . The Ranger ran the name through his mind, studying the seriousness in Durant's voice and expression. "A Southern cavalry regiment, huh?" He saw no waver in those dark eyes staring back into his. "All right, Durant, let's say I believe you . . . now what?"

"You've got to take me with you." Durant's voice leveled, full of resolve. He stood tense, waiting, afraid he already knew the answer, but having to ask it just the same.

"You're out of your mind, Durant."

At this point it made no difference who these men were. Bandits or cavalry, they had Maria. That was all he knew. He'd learn soon enough whom he was up against, somewhere out there along the border. The Ranger let go of a breath and picked his gray sombrero up off the desk.

"No! Please! Listen to me!" Durant stretched an arm out through the bars. "You asked about the men who killed my family. They're riding with Zell! Their names are Payton and Leo Parker. The Parker brothers . . . surely you've heard of them. I know where they're headed, where they hide out. I've got to catch them there, or I'll never get another chance at them! This is the break I've been praying for! For God sakes, Ranger—"

"I've heard of the Parker brothers. They're a couple of murdering snakes." The Ranger looked at him and adjusted his sombrero onto his head. He picked up the rifle and swung it under his arm. "Sorry, Durant." He turned and walked to the dusty window. Outside, Tackett led the two horses up to the rail and tossed their reins around it.

"You'll never find these men on your own!" Durant shouted from his cell. "Take me with you! You've got to, if you ever want to see your woman alive!"

The Ranger strode out the door and closed it behind him, then stepped off the boardwalk to the hitch rail. Tackett nodded toward the office. "What's Durant carrying on about?"

"It's quite a story," the Ranger said. He pushed up the brim of his sombrero and took a moment to tell Tackett the gist of it. Then, reaching out and tying his rifle scabbard to the spare horse's saddle, he added, "If any of it's true, he might get a little frisky on you before long. Better keep a close eye turned on him."

"Of course I will. But what if it's all true? I've heard of Martin Zell over the years. What if he is out there . . . still alive?"

"Maybe it's true, maybe it's not," the Ranger said. "Either way, I've got no time to lose figuring it out." He turned to the horses.

"Dang it, Sam. Are you sure you don't want me riding along with ya? There's no telling what you're apt to run into out there."

"I'm sure." The Ranger made a check of the spare horse's saddle, snugging the cinch tight. He would ride the spare horse, giving the white barb a chance to rest. "I'd say you've got plenty to do right here."

Tackett looked around the dirt street and off toward the saloon, where two of the Flying Cross cowhands stood leaning against the front wall with half-filled beer mugs in their hands. "All right then. Don't worry about nothing here. Just go on out there and get Maria."

"I plan to," the Ranger said, taking the reins and stepping up into the saddle.

Tackett watched the Ranger ride away until he passed the last building on the dusty street and turned out of sight onto the trail leading out to the sand flats. Before going back into his office, Tackett glanced once again at the saloon and saw that one of the cowhands had gone inside and came back with Donahue at his side. All three of them gazed after the Ranger's drifting wake of dust, then turned their eyes to Tackett as he opened the door to his office and stepped inside.

When Tackett closed the door, he expected Durant to be standing at the cell bars, ready to start in, giving him the same story he'd given the Ranger. But Durant had moved away from the bars and sat slumped on the edge of a hard wooden bed, his broad shoulders slumped in an air of defeat. Tackett eyed him curiously as he moved over to his desk and laid his hat down. "What's the matter . . . you've already run out of steam?"

"Yeah." Durant raised his face for a second, then lowered it, speaking down to the floor. "I know when I'm whipped, Sheriff. Just keep Donahue and his cowboys from hanging me before the judge gets here. That's all I ask."

"There'll be no lynching, Durant. You can believe that."

"I believe it, Sheriff." Durant stood up, a calmness about him, his arms hanging loose at his sides. His dark eyes moved across the floor, up the wall of the cell, and out through the bars to the dusty front window, where beyond it in the far distance past Donahue and his cowhands and the few townsmen who had come to join them stood the black scalloped shadows of the high badlands.

Durant continued sitting on the edge of the hard bed for the next few minutes, standing up every now and then to keep an eye on the growing number of men across the street. The young man from the livery barn had relieved Tackett, and Tackett had slipped out the small door in the rear of the building. "I hate sneaking down alleys just to go get a bite to eat," Tackett had said before leaving. He'd shot a glance at Durant sitting with his face lowered, and he added to the young man, "Stay on your toes, Donald. Do a good job, we'll see about getting you a deputy badge next time."

Donald, the livery helper, had only nodded, a solemn expression on his dirt-streaked face; but no sooner had Tackett closed the door when the young man's face spread wide in a grin. "Hear that?" He leaned back in Tackett's chair. "And they say a man can't get ahead these days."

"Yeah, kid, you're doing all right for yourself." Durant stood, glancing across the room out through the dusty window to the gathering crowd across the street. The rail clerk had reappeared now, the coiled rope back up on his shoulder. "Suppose Tackett trusts you enough to take me to the jake? I haven't been all day."

"Well, I'm sure he does." Donald folded his hands behind his shaggy head. "But I ain't going to. I know all about you, Willis Durant. I ain't taking no chances."

Durant shrugged and cast another glance out through the window. "If you're scared, I understand," he said. Across the street, Donahue and the rail clerk stood talking and gesturing between themselves, Donahue nodding his big head. The rest of the men nodded in agreement. "But I need to go pretty bad."

"Scared? Hell, I ain't scared. I just ain't stupid either." He grinned.

"Then suit yourself." Durant unbuttoned his trousers and dropped them to his knees. "You'll have a hell of a mess to clean up here." He started to squat down beside the wooden bed.

"Whoa now!" Donald snapped to his feet. "You can't do something like that!"

Durant stood up. "I told you I have go really bad."

"But damn it—!" Donald turned a half circle, looking for

advice from somewhere, his hand scratching his head. "Can't you wait? Just till he gets back?"

"If I could, I would, kid. Think I want to do this?" He half squatted again. "I've got no choice."

"Just hold on now!" Donald snatched the handcuffs from atop the desk, turned them in his hands, not sure what to do.

"I hold my hands out," Durant said. "You reach through and cuff them. It's that simple."

"I know it," Donald said, puffing his chest a bit, moving over to the cell. "Just don't try nothing on me, I'm warning ya."

"I won't." Durant raised his trousers, fastened them, and moved forward with his wrists out together, catching a glimpse of the cell key hanging from the young man's belt. "But hurry, kid." He bounced on his toes, tense and straining.

"I'm hurrying as quick as I can." Donald opened the cuffs and reached in through the bars with them. "Give me your hands."

"All right." Durant moved a step forward, letting the kid take him by his right wrist and reach toward it with the open handcuff.

Then, just as Donald was about to snap the cuff on his wrist, Durant jerked his right arm back, pulling Donald's wrist right into position, and seeing the cuff slap shut around it. "Damn it!" Donald jerked his cuffed hand back, but Durant had him. Catching him by the other wrist, Durant pulled him forward and in a flash of movement snatched the open cuff from Donald's hand and snapped it around his other wrist.

"Jesus! What the—?"

Donald's words stopped short as Durant yanked him forward against the bars, the young man's forehead sounding out a low, muffled ring on the thick iron. "Bad move, kid." He let him slide down until Donald's cuffed hands stopped at the iron cross-bracing and left him hanging there, knocked cold.

Durant moved quickly, reaching through the bars, taking the large brass key ring from Donald's belt, and hurrying to the cell door. Across the street, Donahue and the others seemed to be gathering nerve, milling closer together. Getting ready to make a move, Durant thought, casting a nervous glance through the window as he moved to the rifle rack on the wall. He took down a Winchester repeater and hurried to the desk.

Rummaging through the desk drawers, he snatched a box of cartridges, cracked the box open on the edge of the desk, ad loaded the rifle. Brass cartridges spilled onto the floor. His eyes searched for a pistol but found none; and when he shot another quick glance out through the window, he saw that Donahue had moved off the boardwalk, the others in line behind him.

In the back, the rear door creaked. He moved to it and flattened himself against the wall beside it as it came open. "Dang it, Donald," Tackett said, stepping inside, fanning the door shut. "Looks like I was wrong about Donahue. We might have some trouble coming—" He snapped to a halt, seeing Donald hanging limp from the bars. When he spun around with his hand on his pistol, Durant stepped forward, jamming the rifle barrel against his chest.

"Easy, Tackett. Don't make me kill you." Durant reached out with one hand, keeping the rifle in place, and, brushing Tackett's gun hand away from the pistol, lifted it from the holster and righted it in his hand, cocking it.

"Is he dead?" Tackett gestured toward Donald slumped against the bars.

"No." Durant shoved the pistol into his waistband, reached out and lifted Tackett's holster belt with the long row of cartridges in it, then slung it over his shoulder. "I just knocked him out."

"That's good." Tackett spoke in a clipped tone through clenched jaws. " 'Cause I'm going to break his dang fool neck when he wakes up." He looked down at the rifle barrel against his chest, then back up to Durant. "Now what about me?"

"In the cell," Durant commanded. "Hurry, we've got company coming."

"Uh-uh." Tackett stood firm and shook his head. "I won't be found locked in my own jail—a laughingstock."

"Suit yourself." Durant pulled the rifle back, taking it in both hands now, cocking the butt back to one side. "I hate doing this, Sheriff."

"No, you don't, you danged-on account son of a—" Tackett managed to get part of his words out a split second before the rifle butt snapped forward and slammed across his jaw.

Outside in the street, Donahue and his cowhands moved forward to the sheriff's office, a small throng of townsmen following close behind them. When Donahue stepped onto the boardwalk and turned to speak to the others before going inside, he did not see Willis Durant lurking in the alley twenty yards away, watching them. Durant had raced out the back door, down the ally, and back alongside the mercantile store. He crouched now and waited, listening to Donahue tell the townsmen how this was their town and how the sheriff had no right to deny them justice.

Then, as Donahue turned and proceeded inside the sheriff's office, Durant made his move. He sped across the dirt street and back toward the hitch rail, even as the townsmen pressed themselves past the door behind Donahue. With the pistol out and cocked in his hand, he dropped down among the three horses standing at the rail and freed their reins, holding on to a big grule stallion as it stamped and snorted and laid its ears back. "Easy, boy," he whispered, calming the big horse.

Behind him on the boardwalk, a woman standing in a doorway gasped and threw a hand to her mouth. But she fell silent as Durant's eyes flashed her a warning glance. Durant heard the men yelling from inside the office across the street. He swung up atop the big grule and turned it, giving it heel; and as it bolted down the street, he fired two shots in the air, scattering the other horses ahead of him in a spray of dust.

Chapter 8

Lieutenant Howell knew better than to question good fortune, yet a couple of things had kept him puzzled ever since the Mexicans had made their desperate charge out of the high pass the day before. First, how in the world had his troops managed to get around in front of the bandits and catch them as they came down from the high rock pass; second, how in the *hell* had the bandits gotten up into the rock pass in the first place? They'd followed the bandit's trail all night, yet come daylight when Sergeant Baines had awakened him in his saddle, they were at the mouth of the mountain trail, awaiting the Mexicans, who were now coming down toward them!

He ran a hand across his sweaty forehead. Well . . . call it blind luck, divine intervention, whatever. Thank God he hadn't lost any more men—only two wounded, another one down with heat stroke. And although most of the Mexicans had charged through his line yesterday and lit out for the border, the wagon load of ammunition and the two women hostages were still up there, somewhere above him on the rocky trail.

He had to admit these bandits were a lot more professional than he'd expected, the way they came charging down out of the rock land. Sergeant Baines's line of defense had seemed powerless to stop them. It was almost as if the sergeant had let them through. But as it turned out that might have been for the best. Now the bandits were divided. There could be no more than four or five of them left holding the wagon and the hostages.

Lieutenant Howell had let them sweat for a full day and night, not wanting to make any sudden moves that would endanger the women's lives. But now it was time to mop up, go back to the fort, and report this mission accomplished. The few remaining bandits up there would offer little resistance. Prudence Vanderman was as good as saved. He was certain of it.

He let out a breath. While losing Prudence Vanderman was the sort of thing that could ruin his career, saving her could make him a general someday, he thought, smiling to himself. Let's face it, the military might be run by brass and blue wool, but it was most certainly financed by top hats and cigars. He knew that much.

"Sergeant Baines." Lieutenant Howell called out to him from ten yards away. "Get your men into position . . . prepare to attack immediately."

"What? Sir?" Sergeant Baines came from behind a large boulder, his hands spread. He couldn't believe it. They had Zell's men broken up now, having tactically let a large part of them charge through and make a run for the border. He had no idea how many were still up there. This was the time to wait, not attack! Baines and his men had a strong position here. Didn't this fool realize his voice could be heard high up into the rocks? Baines squinted in that direction, then back to the lieutenant.

"You have my order, Sergeant. We've spent as much time here as we can afford." Howell swung onto his saddle.

For God sakes . . . Stunned, Sergeant Baines looked

around at the troopers posted beside him on one side of the
trail, their horses picketed off out of the line of fire. They returned his gaze, looking equally bewildered.

"That's it, he's dead!" Corporal Donnely jerked away
from a boulder, jacking a round into his rifle chamber. "I'm
gonna put one bullet right between—"

"As you were, Corporal!" Sergeant Baines yelled as he
shoved him back.

"But, Baines! You can't allow him to pull out now! This
is pure madness!"

"I'm not allowing him . . . or you, or anybody else," he
said as he swung a hard gaze around at the others, "to jeopardize my men or this mission. For the last time, is that clear,
Donnely?"

"I fail to see how shooting this jack-legged worthless
bast—"

Sergeant Baines snatched him by his sweaty shirt and
yanked him forward. "Careful, boy. You're one heartbeat
away from going home wrapped in pine." A hammer cocked
beneath Donnely's chin, Donnely felt the warm steel barrel
push against the soft flesh. Baines had made sure the other
soldiers didn't see the pistol, pulling Donnely in chest to
chest against him.

Baines's voice dropped to a hoarse whisper. "Listen to
me, you down-rank peckerwood! I've got my hands full
here without you getting these men all worked into a lather.
My job is to handle this shave-tail lieutenant . . . your job is
to handle these men while I do it. The next time you fail to
back me up, there won't be enough of your shirt left for me
to grab." He lowered the barrel an inch. "Now nod your
ragged head and say, Yes, Sergeant Baines, I agree."

"Yes-Sergeant-I-agree." Corporal Donnely's head bobbed
as if on a loose spring.

"Now stick tight here, Corporal. This will only take me a minute." Sergeant Baines stepped back in a way that kept his pistol hidden from the rest of the troops.

"What exactly is the hold-up? Did you not hear my order, Sergeant?" Lieutenant Howell asked, speaking down to Baines as he came walking up to him. Lieutenant Howell's horse fidgeted, stepping high-hoofed in place. Baines caught it by the bridle, settling it.

"Indeed I did, sir . . . as did all the Border Dog—I mean the bandits up in the rocks, I'm certain."

The lieutenant's face reddened a bit, but before he could respond, Sergeant Baines added quickly, "And I have to say, sir, I only wish I'd have come up with this same idea hours ago."

The lieutenant looked puzzled. "Oh? You do?"

"Aye, sir, that I do." Baines smiled and winked. "Make them think we're going to attack, eh? Get their guard up facing us while we slip a couple of men up wide around them and find out just exactly how many we have left up there?" He pushed up his sweat-stained campaign hat. "Yes, sir, I agree one hundred percent."

The lieutenant sat quiet for moment, a contemplative expression on his sweaty face. "Then what are we waiting for?"

"Not a thing, sir. Just thought it best to stall a few moments, let them sweat. Right, sir?"

Again a contemplative gaze. "Yes, Sergeant, exactly. Now carry on."

"Oh, one thing, sir." Baines stopped short as he turned. "Since I have so many new men, I'm sure you'll want an old hand like me to be one of the men scouting?"

"Yes, of course. That goes without saying." The lieutenant waved him back with a gloved hand. "Now let's get it done, shall we?"

Sergeant Baines moved to the men behind the boulder, where he squatted down and they drew around him. "Listen up, lads, the lieutenant has decided to move with caution— a damned good idea, I might add." He shot Corporal Donnely a glance, then went on to explain. "I'll take two men with me and do a little recognizance up there. Corporal Donnely will be in charge here until I return."

When Baines finished talking, he pointed a gloved finger. "You two troopers come with me. The rest of you pass the word down the line for everybody to hold fast to this position no matter what, unless the corporal says otherwise."

As the men moved away and Sergeant Baines stood up dusting his trousers, Corporal Donnely gave him a questioning gaze. "This wasn't his idea . . . it was yours, wasn't it?"

"It makes no difference whose idea it was. Ideas come from all directions." He stared at Donnely through cold gray eyes. "Are you back on my side?"

Donnely nodded. "Yeah, I'm with you . . . but I see how it's going to be. You'll keep on covering his worthless arse, won't you?"

"Until the saints step down from the sky, Corporal. Indeed I will. I'll cover his, you'll cover mine, the men will cover yours, and may the good Lord cover us all." He managed a weary smile and winked. "That's been the way of the soldier since time eternal."

"That doesn't make it *right*."

"And that doesn't make it *wrong*. We've got two women up there, Corporal . . . they need us to come get them. What say we do that and forget all this grab-arse? Those men who broke through yesterday might not be crossing the border at all. They might very well be coming back, to hit us from behind."

"Then why have they waited so long?"

"Because they could be bringing back more men with them."

"Jesus." Corporal Donnely let out a breath, thinking about the grim possibility. "Yes, you're right, they could be. Don't worry, I'll hold things together down here. But one thing I've got to know . . . would you have shot me?"

Baines's smile dropped like a flag to half-mast. "Buck me again if you truly want to know." He turned and walked toward the horses.

"Fair enough. But I'm telling you now, Sergeant, I'll follow your orders here, and when we get back to the fort, I'm requesting a transfer."

Baines looked over his shoulder, the smile coming back to him now. "*When* we get back, Corporal?" He shook his dusty head. "Never say *when* while the *if* is still in question."

It was hot in the afternoon when Sergeant Baines and the two men had belly crawled from rock to rock, higher and higher for the past hour. He'd deliberately chosen two brand-new recruits to go with him. These men were young, frightened, and would follow whatever order he gave as long as it didn't put them out front in a shooting situation.

"This is as far as you two go," Baines whispered over his shoulder. "Keep your heads down and stay put here."

"For how long, Sergeant?"

Baines looked into red-rimmed eyes, mantled by dusty hat brims. "Until hell freezes, lads."

The two young men looked at one another with uncertainty as Sergeant Baines slid forward toward a sheer rock wall towering above the steep sloping land surrounding them. "I hope you know what he meant by that, Dubbs," one whispered to the other, "because I sure don't."

"Yeah, I understand. He's saying use common sense—be ready for anything."

"Well, since you know what he wants, I'll just do like you say, all right?" He fidgeted with the rifle in his hands. "You've been soldiering a month longer than me anyway."

"All right then. Just stay down and stay quiet like he told us to. We'll be fine."

Ahead of them, Sergeant Baines rose up at the base of the rock wall and slipped into the black shadow of a crevice. Inside the darkness, he laid his rifle on the ground, took off his shirt, and began a hand-over-hand climb as the crevice grew wider. When his arms could no longer stretch across the width of the jagged opening, he reached out with his foot onto a narrow ledge and stepped out on it, struggling upward finger-hold by toe-hold until he scooted his weight over the edge and flattened himself on the ground.

Baines unsnapped his holster flap, took out his pistol, checked it, then crawled across the hot flat summit for twenty yards. At the other edge, he peered down through the spiny branches of a low juniper clinging to the cusp of rocky soil. Saints preserve us, he thought. On a wide spot in the dusty trail, he counted seven men strewn out around the loaded wagon. In the rocks a few feet above them, he counted four more in a high guard position.

The tandem wagon had been uncoupled and pulled apart. The ammunition crates had been moved into the front wagon, the one still hitched to the mules. In the second wagon, six kegs of black powder had been drawn into a cluster with a long wick hanging down from the center of them. Rocks had been piled up around the kegs. A doubled length of rope stretched from the rear of the wagon to a stand of rock, holding it in place. In the first wagon, sat the two women, their hands tied, the one in the ragged dress wiping a forearm across her face. Beside her, the dark-haired woman looked up and along the high edge, her eyes moving past him, then back down. *Had she seen him?* Baines ducked back instinctively. In front of the wagon, he'd seen the craggy face of Major Martin Zell.

It had been many years, but Baines remembered that face. Time had blown its aging breath across the man—his shoulders a bit thinner now—yet the fiery aura of Major Zell was no less bold or intense than the day Baines had watched Zell's Confederates overrun the Union position at Peach Orchard. Baines leaned farther back from the edge and closed his eyes for a second. He'd been right about it being Major Zell, and he'd been right about there being more men up here than the lieutenant had anticipated. This had been a trap waiting for them, a disaster in the making.

In the wagon below, Maria had caught a glimpse of someone high up on the rocky edge, seventy feet above them. She leaned a bit forward and spoke to Zell loud enough for whoever was up there to hear. "These soldiers are not fools. They will not ride in here blindly and be blown apart."

Zell turned and looked at her, wondering what had caused her to say such a thing. Then he raised his face slowly and scanned the edge of the rocky crest above the trail as Maria continued. "And they will know you are turning back and taking the high trail north while the rest of your men come back and attack from below."

Zell didn't answer. Instead, he spoke to Bowes as he scanned the high ridge. "Mr. Bowes, didn't you send Payton and Leo Parker to stand guard on the high point?"

"That I did, sir." Bowes scanned the ridge with him. "They should have been up there an hour ago."

"Then I must assume they have the summit secured," Zell said. He turned to Maria. "I have never shot a woman . . . please don't provoke me into doing so."

Beside him, old man Dirkson hurried back from checking on the mules and with a grunt raised himself up into the wagon seat. "I'll get this wagon turned and out of here, Major. Don't worry about these womenfolk. I'll see to it they cause no trouble." He jerked the wagon brake loose and turned the wagon around in the narrow trail, glancing harshly at Maria as he tugged back hard on one rein and slapped the mules' backs with the other. "Don't test him, little lady. Zell ain't the sort of man you can bicker with."

Atop the rock summit, Sergeant Baines heard Zell's words and moved back farther from the edge. There were two men up here? He glanced all around. Then where were they? Well, wherever they were, they hadn't seen him crossing the summit. He'd made it this far, and thanks to the woman in the wagon, he now had an idea what the lieutenant could expect when he brought the troops up into the rocky pass. Zell intended to move the wagon load of ammunition off across the high rock land, let the soldiers attack him from below, then light the wick and cut the rope holding the wagon load of black powder kegs as he pulled his men back.

This was a smart move on Zell's part. Baines took a deep breath. If the lieutenant fell for it, there would soon be dead soldiers all over the hillside. Baines wasn't about to let that happen. He eased back to the edge of the cliff and looked down as the old man coaxed the mules forward, pulling the heavily loaded wagon up onto a rough path leading off the

narrow trail. Baines saw the dark-haired woman shoot a
guarded glance up in his direction as the wagon pulled away.

Okay, here goes . . . Baines shoved his pistol back down
in his holster and snapped the holster shut. Then he slipped
over the edge, caught a toe-hold in the wall of rock and
slowly started down.

At the bottom of the rocky trail, Lieutenant Howell
stepped his horse back and forth, getting restless. It had been
over an hour, with no word from Sergeant Baines and his
two men. When Howell saw a thin sheet of dust drift above
the rocks a hundred yards up the slope, he turned his horse
and called out to Donnely. "Corporal, prepare your men to
advance." The rise of dust meant the bandits were moving
out. He wasn't about to lose them now.

"But, sir—!"

Corporal Donnely had started to protest, but Lieutenant
Howell cut him off. "Corporal, you have my order! Move
quickly!"

At the first sound of men and horses moving upward across
the rocks, Zell got down from his saddle and stood in the
trail. He looked back at the wagon load of black powder
twenty yards behind him and then at his riflemen. One man
had stayed back with the wagon, a lit cigar in one hand and
a knife in the other. "Ready, men. Here they come," Zell
called out to the men who'd taken position among the cover
of rocks and deadfall.

Above the wagon, Sergeant Baines inched downward,
hugging inside a dark crevice, keeping an eye on the man
behind the wagon. A trickle of loose sand spilled from beneath Baines's boot heels. He prayed the man below wouldn't
see it. "Let them press us back, men," Zell said in a lowered

voice. "Make them think we're giving them the high ground. Prepare to fall away on both sides."

As the first sound of sporadic rifle shots came exploding up from Howell's troops, Sergeant Baines had made it to the ground and leaped into rock cover ten feet behind the man at the wagon. By the time Howell's attack had reached full pitch, and rifle shots sliced through the air like angry hornets, Baines had crawled forward on his belly with his pistol out. He hugged the ground four feet behind the man at the wagon when Zell turned and called, "Light the fuse! Cut the rope! Barnes!"

Twenty yards down the slope, Lieutenant Howell leaped out of his saddle under a barrage of rifle fire. The men had spread out along either side of the trail, down from their saddles and taking cover where they could. "My God, Corporal! How many are up there?" Howell ducked down as he shouted. Bullets whined overhead.

"We might've known by now, sir, had we waited to hear from Sergeant Baines!"

Lieutenant Howell ignored him. "Press upward, men!" But as he stood to wave the men forward, a volley of fire sent him ducking back down. "Gads, man! They do not fight like a gang of ruffians!"

"No, sir," Corporal Donnely said in a tight voice, reloading his rifle, "they most certainly do not."

A young private came sliding in beside them beneath a hail of bullets. "Corporal, back there, riders coming!" His breath heaved in his chest.

Donnely looked behind them at the rising dust across the flatlands below. From within the swirl of dust, he saw the men coming forward abreast, twenty or more of them, their horses closing fast. "Oh, my Lord."

Zell had seen the riders as well and moved his horse off

to the side of the trail behind the cover of a tall rock. "Prepare to move back, men!" He turned, calling back the wagon, "Cut the rope and let it go—!" But his words stopped short, seeing the body lying on the ground beside the wagon. "What the hades?"

Behind Barnes's body on the ground, Baines stood holding the knife and the cigar. Zell saw him cut the fuse short, stick the tip of the glowing cigar to it, then run, leaping over the edge of the rock trail and rolling down into a bed of jagged rocks.

"Take cover!" Zell leaped as he screamed, seeing the fuse sizzle up the side the powder keg.

For a second, the whole slope of sand and rock seemed to lift off the earth and hang suspended. Then it fell with a bone-jarring thud as a heavy rain of rock and splintered wood showered down on Major Zell, his men, and the soldiers on the rocky slope below. Horses screamed and tumbled, blown sideways off their hooves, red ribbons of blood spurting away as broken rocks bored through them. Dust shot up, then balled downward in a gray-gold swirl of heat and debris, like lightning from within a blackened cave.

"My God!" a cowering soldier cried out. Baines heard him as he scrambled wide of Zell's men and downward through a shower of sand and hot swirling air. He stumbled, falling over rock, and running on as he rose to his feet. A rifle shot glanced past his head as one of the soldiers recovered from the blast and rose up to fire.

"Don't shoot!" Corporal Donnely cried out. "It's the sarge!" As he yelled, he looked back on the flatlands, seeing the other group of Zell's men closing fast, their weapons coming up, blossoming fire from their muzzles. Now bullets spun in from below, ricocheting and slicing the air around the pinned soldiers. "To the rear, men! Turn and fire!"

Sergeant Baines hit the ground beside the stunned lieutenant, snatching his rifle from his hand. He rose to his knee and fired at the coming riders as they veered and made their way into the rocky slope, keeping to one side out of Zell's riflemen's line of fire. Above the soldiers, Zell and his riflemen had recovered from the blast and began firing down on the helpless soldiers. Baines turned and fired back.

"Sergeant, we're trapped here!" Lieutenant Howell drew himself into a tight ball against the rock behind him.

"So it appears, sir." Baines fired steadily, first in one direction, then the other.

"We've got to push upward!" Donnely yelled above the heavy rifle fire. "Our only chance is to push them up the trail and get ourselves better cover."

"What trail? There is no more trail!" Baines shouted.

Donnely glanced over his shoulder to where the dust began to settle. The blast had brought down tons of broken rock into the narrow opening, turning the trail into a high wall of jagged rock. "Sweet Jesus!" He turned and continued firing.

"All we can do is swing hard to the side." Baines waved a dusty, blood-streaked hand. "We've got to get deeper between them. Make them fire on one another!"

Lieutenant Howell spoke in a trembling voice. "These . . . these men. They are not bandits at all, Sergeant! They are a seasoned military body!"

"Yes, sir, I believe you're right." Baines reached over and tore open an ammunition pouch on the lieutenant's belt. He hurried, reloading the rifle.

"Then we must . . . we must . . ." The lieutenant stammered, then stalled. "What *must* we do, Sergeant?"

Sergeant Baines pulled his holster open, snatched his pistol, and jammed it into the lieutenant's gloved hand. "We must fight, sir. Or we will die here."

*   *   *

Above the melee, around a higher turn in the rock land, the old man and the two women had felt the wagon quake and rattle with the hard jar of the explosion. Without stopping, Dirkson settled the spooked mules and slapped the reins to them, the wagon rocking and bouncing along the rough, narrow trail. "The major will be joining us real soon," he said, looking back over his shoulder. For a moment, the rifle fire ceased.

"I think you are mistaken," said Maria, looking back as well. Then she looked into the old man's weathered face, adding, "That explosion was too high up in the trail. Something went wrong. I think the pass is now blocked."

Old man Dirkson chuckled, but there was a slight nervousness to it. "You don't know the major, ma'am. Those kind of mistakes never happen."

Maria only nodded, recalling the glimpse she'd caught of the face above the ridge line. It was time she made a move. She glanced at Prudence Cordell, letting Prudence see her eyes gesture toward her boot. Prudence nodded; she understood. "So you think the major will let us go pretty soon?" she asked, just to draw the old man's attention while Maria made a move for the small pistol in her boot well.

"Well," old man Dirkson said, "I think if everything has gone as planned . . ."

His words trailed off as the Parker brothers, along with Delbert and McCord, moved their horses up into sight on the trail before them with their rifles raised and aimed. "Hold it right there, old man," Peyton Parker said, a dark smile on his face. "You look a little tired. We'll just take this load over from here."

Not now . . . Maria eased her tied hands away from her boot well and sat watching them. Prudence Cordell's hand drifted down from under her arm.

"The hell are you doing, Parker?" Old man Dirkson rose halfway from his seat, the reins hanging in his hand. "Bowes told you to keep watch on top of that—"

Payton Parker's rifle bucked in a spurt of fire. Dirkson flipped backward over the seat, bounced off an ammunition crate, and rolled to the ground while the echo of the shot resounded along a steep upthrust of boulders. "Now then, business aside, ladies," Payton said as his brother Leo grabbed the mules' harness to keep them from bolting forward, "we'll be traveling together a long ways over some rough ground . . . might as well get to know one another, don't you think?" His eyes moved across Prudence's torn dress, then settled on Maria.

"If you touch either of us, I will kill you," Maria said, her voice hard with resolve. Delbert and McCord laughed; but Payton Parker was taken aback at the level of conviction he saw in her eyes. He managed a tight smile. "Well now, excuse me. But I supposed you young ladies might welcome a change from that ole buzzard." He nodded toward Dirkson on the ground, his blood turning to a dark paste on his dusty chest.

"We better go ahead and kill 'em, Payton, while we got the chance. Women are bad luck on a deal like this." McCord rose in his stirrups, his rifle ready to level on Maria. She felt her hands drift instinctively toward her boot.

"Ease up, McCord," said Delbert. It might be bad luck having women along, but it's worse luck to kill one."

"Where'd you ever hear that? Payton wanted to shoot them both the other night. I say it would've been best all around." McCord let the rifle ease down in his hands. Maria let her hands creep up from near her boot. Behind them, around the distant turn in the trail, the sound of rifle fire started up again.

"Shut up, both of yas!" Payton Parker stepped his horse away from the wagon, facing the two riders. "I've changed my mind. We're keeping them with us till we get to old Mex. If they're good enough for Zell, they're good enough for us. Only difference is, we ain't letting them go once we get there." He turned and grinned at Prudence Cordell. "I know a couple ole *padrons* who'd give all the gold in their teeth to own themselves a couple of honeys like these . . . especially if one of 'em is Miss Prudence Vanderman."

"What will Zell do, once he catches up to you?" Maria asked, but only to try to find out what had happened on the trail below.

"I don't think the ole major is going to be catching up to us for a long, long time." Payton Parker smiled again. "He's got half a mountainside twix us and him right now . . . and a few Union soldiers to boot."

"Then the pass was closed by the explosion?" Maria looked confused, hoping to find out anything she could.

Payton gestured for Delbert to step over and take the reins to the wagon. "What's it to you, ma'am? You've got no place else to be right now."

Delbert settled onto the wooden seat and chuckled. "Maybe she's just one of those kind of people who enjoy discussing current events." He grinned across broken teeth. "Now that I'm here, you gals feel free to discuss whatever comes to mind."

Payton took the reins to Delbert's horse. "Pay no attention to him, ladies. Pretty women gets Delbert's blood racing, and it all leaves his head—if you get my drift." He winked and pulled back from the wagon.

Delbert slapped the reins to the mules, and the wagon pulled forward with a jolt. Prudence Cordell leaned slightly to the side and looked back at the old man's body lying limp

and still on the rocky ground. When she turned, she saw
Maria's dark eyes looking at her. "Be ready when we get to
the flatland," Maria whispered beneath the creak of wagon
and the strain of leather tracing. Prudence Cordell only nodded, knowing that both of them saw the same thing in these
four men. For now, these men were joking, teasing, postur-
ing like schoolboys. But their manner could turn ugly in the
quickness of a breath.

As soon as the wagon had ambled upward and out of sight
in a stirring wake of dust, the two young soldiers who'd
waited on the mountainside for Sergeant Baines came staggering forward, their rifles hanging from their hands. "Lord
have mercy," one said through his labored breath, stopping
to look down at the old man's body. "Maybe we should have
stayed put like the sergeant said."

The other soldier lifted his dusty hat brim and ran a hand
across his sweaty brow. "Damn it, Elerby. He didn't mean
for us to stay there whilst they blew the whole mountain out
from under us." From the rocky slope behind them, rifle fire
swelled above the screams of dying men and horses. He bent
down and rolled the old man's head to one side then the
other. "Suppose this one was a hostage too?"

"I don't know. But he must not be one of the bandits, or
they wouldn't have shot him, huh?"

"Reckon him and the women were getting away?"

"Beats me." Dubbs, who had bent down, jerked his hand
back when a groan escaped from the old man's lips. "Jesus,
Elerby! He's still alive!" He jerked back from the body as if
seeing the old man risen from death.

"He is?" Elerby took a cautious step closer, reaching out
with his rifle at arms length and tapping the barrel against
the old man's shoulder.

Old man Dirkson's eyes flickered, then drifted across them and closed again. "Help, me . . ." he gasped.

The two young soldiers stared at one another wide-eyed, their mouths gaping. Then Elerby shook his head as if to get it working again. "I think we better get out of here, Dubbs."

"We can't leave him—he's still alive!" Dubbs bent down slowly, cocking his head in curiosity, looking at the bullet hole in the old man's chest. "I never seen nothing like this close up. Give me your canteen. Let's see if he'll drink."

"What's wrong with your canteen?" Elerby took a half step back, his hand shielding the canteen at his waist.

"Nothing." Dubbs leaned over and propped the old man's dusty head up on his knee. "You said you'd do like I told you to . . . so give it here. He ain't diseased, he's just shot, for God sakes."

"Help, me . . ." Dirkson's voice rattled low and weak from deep inside the bleeding chest. His hand rose slightly, then fell back in the dirt.

"All right then . . . here." Elerby winced and handed his canteen to Dubbs. "What're we gonna do with him if he lives? We're cut off up here. There's no telling who's gonna win that fracas back there." Rifle fire still rolled along the edge of the rocky slope.

"I don't know what we'll do. Get him out of the sun, I reckon. Take cover till we see what's what." He poured a trickle of water into Dirkson's mouth. It went down, then part of it surged back up in a racking cough. "Easy now," he said, taking the canteen from Dirkson's lips.

The drifting eyes came to rest on Dubbs's face as the old man settled and finally breathed a steady breath. "Who . . . are you?" His voice was broken and weak.

"We're soldiers with the United States Army," Dubbs said, reaching up with his free hand, taking the yellow ban-

danna from around his neck, and wiping it across the old
man's forehead. "You just take it slow and easy . . . we're
not gonna let them do nothing else to you. You're under our
protection now."

"Soldiers, huh?" Dirkson's eyes drifted across the two of
them as Elerby moved in closer.

"Yes, sir. We're at your service," Elerby said, eying his
canteen, seeing the fresh streak of blood on it.

Old man Dirkson coughed again, a deep, racking spasm,
and let himself slump on Dubbs's knee. "That . . . figures,"
he said.

Chapter 9

Willis Durant had made it a point to ride out of town in the opposite direction the Ranger had taken. He would hit the higher rocky terrain where his tracks would be harder to follow. There was a hidden trail up there where he could cut back and catch up to the Ranger. He'd used it many times in the past, back when a posse had been on his heels. He hoped this would be the last time he had to use it—the last time he had to look over his shoulder to see if the law was gaining on him.

It was ironic that he should be out here now, after settling down and putting this life behind him. Riding the outlaw trail was no kind of life. He'd come to realize that years ago. But there was no point in dwelling on his circumstance. Last year his past had come back to haunt him, the day the Parker brothers rode into his front yard. He'd needed money and had done one small job with them. But that was all it took to reopen doors he'd closed years ago. One small mistake, and this is where it had brought him.

He checked the big stallion at the top of a rocky pass and gazed back on the flatlands below him. Well, no matter, he thought, his dark eyes moving along the horizon across the miles of sand and scrub mesquite brush. Nothing was going to keep him from setting things right with the Parkers. After that, it made little difference to him if he lived or died. There was no sign of Tackett and a posse. Not yet. But he knew they would be coming. Turning the big grule back to the narrow rocky trail, he gave it heel and pushed forward.

By nightfall he'd covered the long stretch across the high rocky land and brought his horse onto the trail the Ranger had taken. The Ranger had a good head start on him, but tonight he would close the gap between them. Durant wouldn't stop to rest. He would walk and lead the horse, resting it as much as possible. As for himself, he needed no rest. All he needed was to finish the job he'd set out to do. Come morning, he would spot the Ranger and stay away from him until he found a way to take him by surprise.

He didn't want to kill the Ranger; he only wanted to get the drop on him, long enough to make the man listen to reason. Their interests were now the same. The Ranger wanted the woman back alive, and Durant wanted his revenge. Surely, the two of them could work together.

As first light streaked gray and grainy in the east, Durant came upon the Ranger's tracks and followed them upward off the flatlands and into a clearing among a stretch of towering rocks. When he saw where the trail was leading, Durant backed off, staying shy of the clearing and easing his horse into the rocks above it. He got out of his saddle and looked down at the campsite below from within the cover of rocks.

The Ranger was no fool. Durant wasn't about to underestimate the man. He watched for a full ten minutes until satisfied that the campsite was safe to enter. This was the Ranger's trail, but evidently the Ranger had taken an earlier start. He would descend into the abandoned campsite, pick up the Ranger's tracks, and follow them. He walked down, leading the horse by its reins.

But the Ranger had heard the soft clop of hooves a half hour before, coming up the trail. He'd hurried and cleared the campsite and moved his horses off into cover. Then he'd taken cover himself. He waited. And now his patience had paid off. He watched Durant move past him on the narrow trail into the campsite. Then, breaking the deep silence of the land, the Ranger rose up in a dark shadow of rock and said in a level tone, "Over here, Durant. Take it nice and easy."

Durant's first instinct was to turn, drawing the pistol from his waist. But when he did so, he saw no sign of the Ranger, only the dark morning shadows between a split in a wall of rock. "This isn't what it looks like, Ranger," Durant said, his eyes searching. "I wasn't hunting you to kill you. If I had been, you'd never known it. I came to join you. You need my help whether you know it or not." He waited for an answer, scanning the dark shadows in the rocks. "Well, what's your answer?"

From out of nowhere a pair of handcuffs flashed in the morning light and landed at his feet. He spun, looking around. "Put them on Durant . . . you're under arrest."

"For Christ sakes, man!" Durant looked around again. A shot resounded from within a dark shadow. Durant saw the muzzle flash. A bullet thumped into the hard ground between his boots. "Next shot's going to hit about waist high," the Ranger said. "Drop the pistol. Pick up the cuffs and put them on."

Durant knew where to shoot into that blackened crevice now. But he didn't want to. He bent down, still staring into the sliver of darkness, laid his pistol in the dirt, and picked up the cuffs. He straightened up and snapped one on his wrist, then the other. Holding up his cuffed hands, he called out, "There, damn it. I'm cuffed. If I wasn't here to join you, there's no way I would have stood here and done this." He jiggled the cuffs. "I would have died first."

"It's not too late yet if you make a wrong move." The Ranger stepped out of the darkness as if appearing out of thin air. "I'm getting tired of seeing you on the long end of my rifle, Durant. How'd you pull it off? Is Tackett all right?"

"I had to crack his jaw for him. But he'll mend. He was too hardheaded to get in a cell."

"Can you blame him?"

"Naw, I suppose not." Durant let out a breath. "I didn't want to hit him though. I had no choice. Donahue and his boys were stoked up and headed for the jail right then."

The Ranger stepped in closer, looked at the cuffs on Durant's wrists, then picked up Tackett's pistol without taking his eyes off the man. "So you took his Navy Colt, I see." He turned it in his hand and wiped it on his shirt. "He won't forget this."

"I know." Durant slumped with his cuffed hands dangling before him. "But I had to catch up to you, Ranger. Can't you understand?"

"I understand this," the Ranger said, circling behind him, taking him by the collar and pulling him backward toward his horse. "If you meant to go with me, I reckon you succeeded. There's no time to take you back to town. But as soon as Tackett catches up, you're his prisoner."

"Then let's get on the trail," Durant said, his dark eyes unwavering as he stared at the Ranger.

The Ranger held the reins to Durant's horse as Durant stepped up onto the saddle. "Make no mistake, Durant. You get in my way while I'm hunting these men, I'll kill you graveyard dead. Fair enough?"

Durant settled in his saddle, his cuffed wrists resting on the saddle horn. "Fair enough," he said. "All I want is to catch up with Martin Zell and kill the men who murdered my family. After that, I'm ready for whatever follows."

The Ranger stood for a moment, looking up at him in the morning sunlight. "You really are convinced this is Zell's cavalry."

"I'm betting my life on it," Durant said.

"That you are." The Ranger thought for a second. He'd never met a man more sure of anything. If Durant was right, and he knew where these men were going, the Ranger needed his help. But if Durant was lying, if this was a trick of some sort . . . well, he'd know soon enough.

They moved on steadily, without stopping, the Ranger in the lead with Durant behind him, his horse on the short lead rope with the Ranger's spare horse. By noon they had reached the far northern end of the high pass that would zigzag south over rocky land until it took them above the stretch of sandy badlands leading to the border. When they'd stepped down to rest the horses out of the searing sunlight in the shade of an upthrust of jagged rock, the Ranger looked out and down at the narrow switchback trails below them. In the distance where the flatland rolled out of sight on the earth's curve, a drifting rise of dust stood slantwise and high in the air. They were getting close.

"If there's anything else you need to tell me about what happened to your family, now's the time to get it said, Durant."

Behind him, Durant had dropped down onto a rock and ran his cuffed hands across his dusty face. "What do you mean? I told you everything."

"Everything except why these Parker brothers were at your place to begin with."

"I told you. I knew them from the old days." His voice

sounded tight and closed, the way it had when the Ranger
mentioned his family the day he'd taken him prisoner.

"There's more to it, Durant. There always is." The Ranger
continued to gaze out across the heated land below.

A silence passed, then he finally heard Durant say in a
hollow tone behind him, "Okay, Ranger. You want it all?
Here it is. Leo Parker came to me. Said him and his brother
had a way to make some quick money rounding horses
down below the border. But they needed a third man, a
wrangler. I was broke and took the job."

"Rustling horses, huh?"

"No. Not the way I saw it. You know how it is with those
big Mexican spreads. Any wild mustangs in the region they
figure belongs to them. We cut out forty head or so and
drove them to Zell's encampment. That's how I know it's
Martin Zell, and why I know where he's headed. They were
planning to rob an army train then. I heard some of it from
Leo."

The Ranger only nodded, listening.

"After we sold them the horses, I took my share of the
money and cut back home—never did trust Payton Parker.
Him and Leo got drunk and lost their part of the money
playing poker. They came looking for me at my place, but I
wasn't home. The rest . . . ? Well, I've already told you the
rest."

The Ranger shook his head slowly without turning to Durant. If this was true, and he had no reason to think otherwise
now, Durant had brought all this trouble on himself when he
opened his home to the killers of his wife and child. There
was a lot the Ranger could have said right then, but he chose
not to. Instead, he turned and walked back beside the white
barb. He took a canteen, uncapped it, drank, and handed it
down to Durant. When Durant had swished a mouthful and

spit it out, he looked up at the Ranger. "So there. See why I didn't want to talk about it?"

"Yeah, I see." The Ranger brought the canteen back to the white barb and looped it over the saddle horn. He raised each of the white barb's hooves in turn, checking them as he ran his gloved hand across the frogs while the big horse shook out its damp mane. Then the Ranger straightened, looked at Durant, and said, "Let's get going. It's not getting any cooler out here."

They rode for the next hour, picking their way in and out of narrow crevices along the rim of the high rocky trail, until the Ranger caught the flash of sunlight off metal. He slowed the barb and drew it back into a shadow, forcing Durant's horse and the spare horse behind him. "What is it?" Durant asked in a lowered voice.

"Rifle flash, I think," the Ranger said. And they sat silent until both of them saw it at the edge of a cliff thirty yards ahead. The flash came from the barrel of Private Dubbs's rifle as he and Elerby struggled up from among the rocks, holding the old man between them.

"Don't shoot," Dubbs called out, seeing the Ranger step his horse out of the shadows toward them with a big pistol already out of its holster. "We're United States Army . . . got a wounded man here."

The Ranger eased down, holstered his pistol, and stepped from his saddle, letting go of the lead rope. Durant got down as well and held the lead rope and the reins to both their horses. "Stay put," the Ranger said to him as he moved forward, looking past the soldiers and scanning the edge of the cliff and the rocky land below. Before he could ask them anything, Dubbs said in a panting voice, "We were scouting . . . got cut off from our sergeant. You wouldn't believe what's happened ten miles back." He gestured with his rifle barrel. "We were hunting down the Mexicans that robbed our train. They held this man hostage . . . then they shot him."

"We know about the train," the Ranger said, moving in, taking over for Elerby. "Here, I've got him." Elerby's breath heaved as he turned the old man loose and dropped onto a knee, using his rifle for support.

"You knew?" Dubbs struggled the last few feet to the shade where Durant stood watching, taking a canteen down from his saddle horn.

"Yep. I reckon the whole country knows by now," the Ranger said. He saw old man Dirkson's cloudy eyes glimpse his badge as they lay back against a rock. "A hostage, huh?" The Ranger spread the old man's dusty shirt open and looked at the bloodstained bandage on his chest, the worst of it high and to the right, more of a shoulder wound, he thought. "Looks like you did a good job attending to him." The Ranger looked into the old man's eyes, searching for something there. "Lucky for you, it missed your lung. You're going to be all right."

"Yeah," old man Dirkson said, his voice low and breathy. "These soldiers hadn't happened along . . . I'd be dead by now." His eyes searched the Ranger's in return.

Then the Ranger stepped back and turned to Dubbs as Durant came forward and leaned in with the canteen. "What about the other two hostages? The two women?" the Ranger asked.

"They've taken the women with them," Dubbs said, slumping onto the ground in the sliver of black shade. "Four bandits are guarding them on a wagon . . . the rest are back there, beneath the high pass . . . fighting our troops."

Elerby had struggled to his feet and managed to drag himself over into the shade and collapsed against a rock. He took off his hat and let it drop. We've walked over ten miles . . . looking for a way to join our men." He shook his damp head. "There's no way down . . ."

"What about the main trail?" The Ranger looked back and forth between the two tired soldiers.

"It's gone," Dubbs said.

"Gone?"

Dubbs took a deep breath and told the Ranger and Durant everything that had happened since the train robbery. As he spoke, the Ranger glanced at the old man now and then, each time seeing the cloudy eyes look away from him. When Dubbs finished and slumped back against the rock beside Elerby, the Ranger slid a glance to Durant. Durant gave him a knowing nod, gesturing his eyes to the old man. The Ranger turned his gaze to the two soldiers. "These are not Mexicans, you know."

All the while as Dubbs had spoken, giving him the details, the Ranger kept getting a different picture of things. *Three hostages escaping with a wagon load of ammunition? The two women with their hands still tied? Uh-uh.* He wasn't buying it.

"They're not?" Elerby looked confused.

But Dubbs rubbed the sweat from his forehead. "Our sergeant didn't think so either. He thinks they're an old confederate bunch operating below the border."

The Ranger snapped a look at Durant now and held his eyes for a second. Then he turned to the old man. "Where were you headed?"

"What?" Old man Dirkson's eyes looked sharper now, not nearly so drained and exhausted as before.

"The train . . . where were you headed on it?" The Ranger watched his eyes closely, seeing the old man stall for a second, working things out.

"Oh. El Paso, I reckon." He managed a stiff shrug. "I've got kin there, somewhere." He winced, scooting himself up a bit against the rock. "Didn't really have any place in mind . . ."

"I bet you didn't." The Ranger stared at him, a thin, knowing smile on his face, then lifting his pistol from his holster and letting it hang down his dusty thigh. The soldier's eyes widened. "Sir?" Elerby said. But the Ranger didn't answer. The soldiers straightened, looking at the Ranger with grave curiosity. The old man only stiffened and returned the Ranger's piercing stare.

"Listen *real* close," the Ranger said to Dirkson, as if the others were no longer there. "I'm going to tell you what my interest is in all this. Then you tell me what you think would be the best thing for me to do." He stepped in closer, his gloved thumb over the hammer of his pistol. "Fair enough?"

Old man Dirkson studied the Ranger's eyes, then nodded, letting out a raspy breath. "I'll advise you the best I can . . . provided your interest and mine ain't too far apart." He narrowed his gaze beneath bushy eyebrows and waited.

Dubbs and Elerby looked puzzled. Noticing the cuffs on Durant's wrists for the first time, Dubbs pointed a dusty finger and said, "What's going on here? Is this man a prisoner?"

"It's a long story, young man," the Ranger said, his eyes fixed on the old man on the ground. He stepped back, took the key from inside his vest, then unlocked Durant's handcuffs and let them fall. "We don't have time to explain it."

Durant rubbed his wrists, looked at the Ranger, and said, "How about a rifle, Ranger, and that pistol you took from me?"

"Don't push it, Durant," the Ranger said. "I'm uncuffing

you so you can handle your reins better. We're going into harder country from here."

"But I was telling the truth. You just saw that." He nodded at the old man, then looked back at the Ranger, taking a short step toward him.

The Ranger stood firm, his thumb going back across the hammer of his big pistol. "You might have been right about it not being Mexicans. But don't start thinking that makes us partners."

The two soldiers just stared at one another. On the ground, old man Dirkson managed to spit and run a dusty hand across his mouth.

PART 3

Chapter 10

When the two soldiers had rested, they headed out with the Ranger, Durant, and the old man, back to the steep path the wagon had taken toward the flatlands. But instead of staying on the high trail, the five of them had cut diagonally down the rough sloping land in single file, leading the horses across jagged rock and loose sandy ground that shifted and spilled away beneath their hooves. More than once Elerby had tried to stop and catch his breath, but each time, the Ranger had coaxed him on. Yet when the old man stopped and swayed in place for a second, the Ranger called them all to a halt.

"Let's take a breather here." The Ranger took the old man by his forearm and moved him to a slice of shade. Elerby and Dubbs looked at one another, sweat pouring down their faces. They still did not understand the conversation that had taken place between the old man and the Ranger back on the high pass trail, and they still didn't understand what was going on between the Ranger and Durant. But Durant realized why the Ranger didn't want these two to know the old man was one of Zell's riders. The soldier's duty would be to arrest the old man. The Ranger needed the old man to show him where the wagon was headed—all the way into Mexico if need be.

They all rested in the shade and fanned themselves with their dusty hats until after a few moments the Ranger stood up with old man Dirkson beside him and waved them ahead.

They moved on, struggling for the next hour around a wide belly of steep rock, the horses shying away from the edge. At the other side where the slope grew less harsh, they moved down along the path the wagon had taken, and in another half hour stood at the more gentle slope of sandy soil reaching out into a broad basin. The Ranger stopped with old man Dirkson beside him and let his eyes follow the wagon ruts into the distant, wavering heat. "This is where we leave you, troopers," he said, turning to Elerby and Dubbs.

"What do we do now?" Elerby looked lost, gazing across the endless swirl of sand and heat.

"Stay right along the bottom here," the Ranger said, pointing east. "You should hook up with your troops a few miles back. If they're where you said they were, they should be moving this way."

"If there's any of them left," Elerby said.

"There will be. The main thing Zell's after is the wagon. Once he saw he was cut off from it, I expect he moved his men along these buttes until he found a way up. He's somewhere back behind us right now, I'd say, following these wagon tracks. If your lieutenant is any leader at all, he's headed this way to cut him off."

"Our lieutenant isn't much of anything," Dubbs said. "Our sergeant is the only one seems to know what's going on. Hadn't been for him, we all would have died at the train crash."

"Yeah?" The Ranger thought for a second, then said, "When you get back with your outfit, report to your sergeant first. Tell him what I'm up to out here. Be sure and tell him

I have this man with me." He gestured a gloved hand toward the old man standing beside him. "Will you do that for me?"

"Yeah, but what's the—?"

"Your sergeant will understand," the Ranger said, cutting Elerby off. "Now you two get moving. Zell's close behind us. Don't get yourselves caught out here."

"We won't." Dubbs turned to Elerby and pulled him by his shirtsleeve. "Come on, you heard him. Let's move out."

The Ranger, Durant, and old man Dirkson stood in silence beside the horses, watching until the soldiers had moved off thirty yards. Then the Ranger turned to the old man. "You take my spare horse. Just remember . . . you try cutting back to Zell, I'll put a bullet in the back of your head."

"Just a minute!" Durant stepped in. "We can't take a chance like that! For God sakes, Ranger!"

"Shut up, Durant, or you'll be back in wrist irons. I've got no time to stand here and argue." The Ranger stepped up into his stirrup and swung over onto his saddle. Hot wind pushed in from across the sand flats and lifted the brim of his sombrero. He tugged it down snug on his head. "Let's hope the army gets here and meets Zell's men coming down. If not, we'll have our hands full front and rear." He shot a glance at the old man as Durant handed him the reins to his horse and took control of his own big grule.

"Don't worry about me, Ranger," Dirkson said. "All I want is to get my hands on the turn-coat dry-gulching sons-abitches that shot me. As for the women, you're welcome to them. They'll both tell ya, I treated them as right as I could." He struggled up into the saddle grunting, the pain in his shoulder causing him to bend forward before righting himself and letting out a tortured breath.

"All the same," the Ranger said, his big pistol flagging

the old man and Durant forward, "I'll feel better with both of you riding in front of me."

They pushed on, following the wagon tracks. When they were a mile or more away from the base of the jagged hills, they glanced back into the wavering heat at the distant sound of a rifle shot. "Sounds like the two soldiers might've found the troops," the Ranger said, raising his sombrero for a moment. Then he lowered it against the hot wind and stinging sand, and heeled the white barb forward.

Back at the base of the hills, Elerby and Dubbs had flattened themselves on the hot ground, shouting and waving their arms at the two forward scouts riding toward them. "Feldman! Don't shoot! It's us! Dubbs and Elerby!"

The two scouts stopped their horses, leaped out of their saddles, and took aim from within their own rise of dust. "Hold it," one said to the other, hearing Dubbs's voice. He lowered his rifle an inch and called out to the pair of waving arms, "Stand up, keep your hands high."

"You got it, Feldman," Dubbs cried out, both panting and chuckling, struggling up from the hot sand. "Lord, are we glad to see you."

"Leave that weapon where it lays," the scout called out to them as Elerby picked up his rifle, struggling to his feet.

"Why? You see it's us," Elerby called out. "You won't believe all we've been through. We got—"

Dubbs reached over with his boot and kicked the rifle from his hand. "Shut up, Elerby. Now do like he says. You want to get shot by our own men?" He turned to Feldman and the other scout and added, "He's just tired . . . the sun's got to him. Look, our hands are up." He wiggled his dirty fingers.

"My goodness, Dubbs, we all thought you two were

dead," the scout said, finally recognizing him. "Sergeant Baines said he figured the blast killed yas."

"Well, it didn't." Dubbs let his hands down. "We figured the same thing happened to Baines. But I see it didn't." As he spoke, he saw Sergeant Baines come racing forward on a dusty bay.

"Uh-oh, Casey. Now you're in for it," Feldman said in a lowered tone to the trooper beside him.

"Who fired that shot?" Sergeant Baines came down from his horse as it jolted to a halt. He stomped forward, his rifle in his gloved right hand, a dirty bloodstained bandage wrapped around his bare left hand.

The two scouts shot one another a glance. Then Feldman stepped forward. "Look, Sergeant, it's Elerby and Dubbs."

"I see who it is. Who fired that shot?"

Private Casey stepped forward, a worried look on his face. "I did, sir."

"Don't sir me, you cracker-neck, bo-shanked, pecker-wood. You want to get us all killed?" He snatched Casey's rifle from his hand and slammed it against Feldman's chest. Feldman caught it, staggering back a step. "I gave you an order . . . no firing down here. They heard that shot halfway from here to hell."

He glared into Casey's face from an inch away, his big teeth bared like a growling dog. Finally, he stepped back. "Now you get your sorry arse back with the others before I lose a boot up ya." Casey turned with his horse's reins in his hands, but Baines snatched them from him. "You walk back. I need this horse for a soldier."

"Sergeant Baines, I—" Feldman started to speak, but the sergeant snatched his reins from him as well.

"You too, Feldman! For letting him do it. Get out of my sight, boy, before I have to write a sad letter to your mama."

While Feldman stepped away quick-time behind Casey, carrying both of their rifles, Baines turned to Elerby and Dubbs. Before he could say anything, Dubbs cut in. "I told them Elerby was addled by the sun, Sergeant . . . but he isn't. I just didn't want him saying anything until we talked to you first."

"Good lad." A faint smile spread across the sergeant's parched lips. "Now talk to me." He handed them both the reins to the horses as he spoke.

"Well, it's just like you thought. These aren't Mexicans we're up against—"

"We already know that, Dubbs. Tell me what happened up there. I know you made it to the high trail and back after I closed off the pass."

"You did that?" Dubbs looked at him, stopping for a second as they started leading their horses back along the base of the hills.

"I did. Now what about the wagon? Talk to me, trooper."

On their way to join the others, Dubbs told him about the wagon, the old man—the third hostage as he put it—and how the four men had left him for dead in the middle of the trail. Then he told him how they'd taken the old man with them and met the Ranger and his black prisoner along the high trail and left them a mile back where the wagon tracks led off toward the border.

"The dark-haired woman is some kin to the Ranger or something, I think," Dubbs added when he'd finished. "Anyhow, the Ranger seemed to think the old man could lead him to her." He left his hat and scratched his dirty head. "He said to tell you before we tell anybody else. Does any of this make any sense to you, Sergeant?"

Baines nodded, thinking about it. "Aye, lad, more than you can know." He stopped and looked at both of them.

"You've both done well, considering this was your first time scouting. Now I want you both to report to Corporal Donnely while I move forward and keep an eye on the trail. Tell him to hurry . . . Zell and his men will be coming down any time."

"But shouldn't one of us stay with you?"

"No, Dubbs. I'll be fine. The lieutenant is badly wounded, so don't tell him anything—especially about the old man from the wagon. Hurry now, lads, and tell no one what you've told me except Corporal Donnely himself. I left him in command."

"Yes, Sergeant, right away." Dubbs and Elerby stepped up into their stirrups. "Anything else?"

"Yes, Dubbs, one more thing." Baines swung onto this saddle. "I believe you have what it takes in this man's army. Tell Donnely I've made you acting corporal until we get things settled here. Then we'll see about getting you some permanent stripes."

"Right! Thank you, Sergeant Baines." Dubbs beamed and flashed a salute with his dirty hand. "You heard the sergeant," he said to Elerby, swinging his horse around, "let's get it done."

Sergeant Baines kicked his horse out along the base of the hillside while the two soldiers headed in the opposite direction. By the time he'd reached the point where the wagon tracks led down from the high trail, Dubbs and Elerby had made it back to the ranks, passing the two scouts on foot, and joining the tired, ragged troops who'd stood down to rest their horses in a wide rise of dust.

They moved past a spot where three dusty soldiers had carried Lieutenant Howell and laid him back against a turn of broken rock rising from the sand. The three stood gathered around him, one of them kneeling and pouring a trickle of water onto a yellow bandanna.

"Who goes there? Huh? Who goes there?" Lieutenant Howell babbled, half out of his head, rising slightly as Dubbs and Elerby rode past toward Corporal Donnely at the center of the men. They glanced over and saw the crazed look on the lieutenant's pale, drawn face. He called out to them. "I didn't make it, boys. Hear me? Go on, save yourselves." A long peal of pained, choking laughter came from his parched lips. "Oh, God, how it hurts! It hurts . . . it hurts . . ." His hand clutched tight at the blood-soaked bandage down low on his stomach.

Elerby grimaced. "I can't stand hearing this."

"Buck up," Dubbs said. "You'll stand worse than this if you soldier long enough." He heeled his horse the few remaining yards to Corporal Donnely, Elerby following.

"Where's the scouts? Damn it. Where's Baines?" Corporal Donnely stood up and met them, tying a strip of gauze around the calf of his bloody leg. He looked the horses up and down, then at the two grimy soldiers. "You two are supposed to be dead." He looked past them. "Where the hell is Baines?"

"We made it, Corporal," Dubbs said, sweeping off his hat and running a hand across his wet, dirty head. "Sergeant Baines went the other way to the bottom of the trail. He sent us back to report and bring the troops forward."

"Then report, Private. And let's get moving." Donnely looked them up and down again.

Dubbs took one step forward, leveling his shoulders. "First off, I'm not a private anymore. . . ."

Sergeant Baines had taken position, moving his horse back forty feet from the mouth of the trail. Behind the cusp of a low rise of sand, he laid the big army bay down on its side amid a sparse stand of mesquite brush, and laid his hat over its eyes. The horse tensed and thrashed its legs, then settled as he soothed it with a gloved hand. He took off his ammunition belt, laid it up on the horse's side, and laid his rifle beside it.

To the east he saw the rising column of dust as Donnely moved his men forward. Straight ahead and up the rocky trail, he saw the first sign of Zell's men—two front scouts edging their horses down, staying close to a stretch of high boulders against the afternoon sun. "That's it, boys, come to Papa," Baines whispered, taking the yellow bandanna from around his neck and tying it around his sweaty forehead.

He raised himself slightly, blew a breath on the rear rifle sights, dusting them off, then crouched down and watched as a half dozen of Zell's men scattered across the rocky slope, forming a ragged skirmish line for the others to slip through. But to the east, he saw some of Donnely's soldiers slipping upward themselves, scattering into the rocks and advancing along the steep slope while the main body of soldiers moved along the base of the hills. *Aye, you're learning, Corporal . . .*

Now pull out away from the hillside and take position, he thought. He watched the two main bodies of men moving toward one another. But he realized that Donnely had no way of knowing Zell's men would be coming down onto the sand flats at the same time as the soldiers would reach the trail. He would fix that from here.

Baines leaned into the rifle butt, raised it an inch from the horse's side, and locked it to his cheek, the length of his right thumb running firm beneath his right cheekbone. He cocked the hammer, took aim, let a smooth breath in, then out, watching the sights drift on his target with each beat of his pulse. And at the end of his exhale, he cut his breath off, felt the rifle settle dead still in his hand, and squeezed the trigger.

Here we go. Thirty yards up the steep trail through the rise of gray rifle smoke, Baines saw his target stand up and stiffen atop a round boulder. Then, as the other men scrambled for deeper cover, he watched his target melt down the side of the boulder like candle wax.

"Where did it come from?" Bowes shouted, sliding down between two of the men who'd jerked behind a rock at the sound of Baines's rifle shot.

"Out of the flats," one of the men said, rising enough to send a shot toward the stand of mesquite brush.

"Damn it!" Bowes heard the sound of rifle fire now, coming at them from the east. "Here they come. And they've posted scouts out there . . . between us and the wagon. Hold them back, men," he added before turning and dashing across the sandy ground.

"No problem," one of the men replied.

Bowes cut across the trail and stooped low as another round from Baines's rifle nipped up a clump of dirt at his feet. He ducked off the trail behind a high rock, snatching his horse's reins from one of the men's hands. "How is he?" he asked, looking down at Zell.

"He'll do," a voice said.

"Yes, I'm fit as ever," Zell said in a strained voice, his chest covered with dried blood. "Any sign of the wagon?"

"No, sir. The wagon must have made it through. But the soldiers have moved right along the flatlands with us. They've got sharpshooters out there. The rest are charging, hitting us on our left flank."

Sharpshooters . . . ? Zell listened for a second, discerning Baines's single rifle shots from within the dissonance of fire coming from the east. "There's only one man out there, Mr. Bowes. We must break through here . . . get to the wagon . . . or we'll be stuck in these rocks for a long time."

"Yes, sir." Bowes started to turn, but then he hesitated. "Are you able to ride, sir?"

"Prepare the men, Mr. Bowes. Whoever is out there is the same man who blew up the pass. He knows his business. Get past him before he gathers the rest of them to him."

But even as Zell spoke, out on the sand flats Baines saw the soldiers riding headlong for the mouth of the trail. He took aim on Corporal Donnely's horse, then moved his sights ahead of it and lower to the ground as Donnely raced forward. Then Baines squeezed off the shot and saw Donnely's horse veer away from the spray of stinging dust at its hooves.

Jesus! Donnely struggled with his reins, righting the horse and catching a glimpse of Baines as he rose up amid a hail of bullets, waving his rifle, yelling at the top of his lungs. *What the . . . ?* Donnely saw the sergeant duck out of sight; but he'd gotten the signal. "Turn, men!" he bellowed, cutting his bay into the onrush of confused men and veering horses. Then, seeing Donnely wave them out toward the sand flats as he cut away and swung wide of the trail ahead, the whole column broke to the left and followed.

Zell's men, positioned above them among the rocks, fired down as they moved out onto the sand flats. Baines rose up again amid a hail of fire from the trail and waved them into line across the mouth of the trail. Donnely got the message, hearing the heavy fire behind him. Over a long, low rise, he slowed his horse, coming out of his saddle, turning to wave the troops in, and sending them sidelong into a wide horse-shoe position around the mouth of the trail, thirty yards out.

"It's about damn time!" Baines yelled to him, then

dropped down as a bullet kicked up dust along the cusp of sand in front of his horse lying prone before him.

"Damn his stripe-legged, blue belly hide," Bowes said, slamming a hand against the rock in front of him. "He's pulled them out to him. Now we're buttonholed for certain." He raised a cupped hand to his cheek and called out along the slope, "Hold your fire, men."

"Well, hell," said the man beside him, turning his head and spitting tobacco juice. "We're still going through, ain't we?"

"I see no other way to go," Bowes said, slumping beside him. "Only now, it's going to cost us." He looked at the men alongside him with a grave expression. "One thing's for sure. They know they've not been fighting a bunch of common bandits." The grave expression shifted a bit into a weary trace of a smile. Now that both sides had ceased firing, a tense silence fell about them, disturbed only by the whir of hot wind off the flatlands.

The nearest man grinned. "Well, *gracias, mi amigo!*" He jerked the wide Mexican sombrero from his head and spun it out across the rock. "By God . . . at least I can like what I am." He looked around. "What about you, Chance Edwards? You're an old delta rat just like me. You gonna get shed of that funny hat and die a southern boy?"

"Dead's dead," the other man replied. "I take no honor in it, however it falls." He grinned. "But I vow, I'll live to eat the pig that shits itself out on your grave."

Bowes looked from one to the other of the dirt-marked faces. "Good men, all of you," he said. "Hold tight here until I see what the major wants us to do."

"Tell him it's no hurry on our account," one of them said as Bowes moved away from the rock. "We'll hold them off here for as long as you say."

Chapter 11

"When we get out of this, Sergeant, I'm definitely going to buy you a beer," Corporal Donnely said, lying beside Baines on the warm ground. Crawling through the sand had loosened the bandage on his leg. He adjusted it now, leaning against the bullet-riddled body of Baines's horse.

"Careful what you say, Corporal, I'll hold you to it." Baines looked along the semicircle firing line ten yards in front of them, then at the long shadows of evening drawing across the land. "How's the leg?"

"Stiff, painful, but otherwise okay. The bullet went through clean enough." He kneaded the tender flesh above the wound as he spoke. "The lieutenant is still having a terrible time, talking out of his head. Thinks we're fighting the devil and his demons up there."

Baines chuckled under his breath. "He's not so far off, from what I've seen of them." He tipped back a sip of warm water from his canteen and handed it to Donnely, still gazing out across the quiet land. "If the lieutenant stays out of his head long enough, we'll mop up out here and win him a citation." He offered a tired, wry smile. "See? As it turns out, you didn't have to shoot him after all."

Donnely looked ashamed. "I don't know what made me

say those things. Now that it looks like the lieutenant might not make it, I feel like a complete ass."

"Aw, don't worry about him. He's a young man. He'll be fine. You hear of how these gut shots always kill a man, but it's not always so. He's hit low, nothing vital, or he'd already be dead."

"I hope you're right."

"You hope?" Baines looked at him, again with a wry smile. "I'm always right, Corporal . . . that's my job."

For the past three hours, Zell's men had poured rifle fire down on them from behind rock cover—softening them up, Baines had called it—now, for the past twenty minutes, not a shot had been fired.

"Then what's Zell's next move?" Donnely asked, capping the canteen and laying it beside Baines. "You really think he'll rush our line in the dark? Coming down out of those rocks, he's apt to lose every horse he's got. He'd have to be crazy."

"Not crazy, Donnely . . . just desperate. What's he got to lose? We've fought him to a stalemate. He knows most of our horses are dead. If his men get down to the flatlands, we've left them thirty yards to spread out over. I had to give him that much to keep our men out from under his rifles. They'll come down hard, but most of them will try to spread wide of this firing line."

"Then we'll push our circle forward?" Donnely asked, seeing the grave consequences in his mind. He felt relieved when the sergeant said, "No, it'll cost us too many men and what few horses we have left. We'll stick it out here in the sand, behind these dead animals. Make Zell pay dearly for every foot of ground they cross."

"But some of them are bound to get past us."

"Aye, they will . . . but we will have done what I set out

to do. I meant to hold him here as long as I could. We've kept him off that Ranger's back. By now the Ranger has a good start toward the wagon."

"This isn't going to look very good on our report when we get back to headquarters."

"Damn the report. I've never seen a report yet that can't say what I want it to, eh?" He chuckled. "The long march out is to prepare for the battle. The long march home is to prepare for the paperwork. I believe it was Napoleon who said that."

Donnely raised an eyebrow. "I think you just made that up."

Baines shrugged. "The main thing here has always been the hostages. Capturing the wagon would have been a fine feather in the lieutenant's hat, but the lives of those women are more important. The Ranger will get to them now. And I'll finish up our little waltz with Major Martin Zell."

"You mean . . . ?"

"That's right, Corporal. When they charge through our line, I'm going with them. You'll lead the men back to the fort. We've got many wounded who'll need tending. There won't be much left of Zell's men after this charge. They'll be no threat around here for a while."

"But I can't go back and tell a blatant lie. They'll want to know what happened to you."

"Then don't lie. Just forget I said any of this. If I'm not here after they hit our line . . ." Baines let his words trail, then he added, "I expect the next time I see you, you'll be a sergeant yourself, after taking charge here, defeating Zell's men. Think about it." He studied Donnely's eyes in the gathering darkness.

Donnely did think about it for a second. Then he let out a

breath and nodded. "All right then. I don't remember a word you've said."

Baines reached over with his gloved hand and patted Donnely on the forearm. "I knew I could make a soldier of you, given enough time."

"Ha." Donnely shoved his hand away. "I was born soldiering, Baines, and you know it."

They sat in silence for a moment, then Donnely said in a quiet tone, "We've got only nine horses left. I could bring Little Randy over here for you. He's not the biggest, but he's fast . . . as strong as any horse we've got."

"Naw, it's not necessary. You'll need every horse you have. It'll look bad for cavalry men to return on foot. I'll pick up a horse from one of Zell's men." Baines reached down and drew a dagger from the well of his boot. "I've always been good at night work." He ran a thumb along the edge of the blade, turned the big knife in his hand, and laid it on his lap. He looked around in the grainy falling light, judging it. "You best get on back to the line now. They'll be coming down in ten minutes or so."

"Yeah. I suppose you're right."

Baines looked at him, then glanced toward the endless land bathed in the red glow of fading sunlight. "This is that time of silence every fighting man comes to know," Baines said in a soft tone, "when a voice inside him asks why he's here, and he realizes that he could turn at this second and flee the coming battle." He let out a weary breath. "I've felt it at some point before every fight. It has a hard pull on a man."

"Yes, I know the feeling," Donnely said. "Have you got enough water?"

"Enough."

"Ammunition?"

"Plenty." Baines patted his cartridge case with his gloved hand.

"Well." Donnely sucked a tooth, searching for something more to say. He could think of nothing. He half turned, hesitating before leaving. "You sure you don't want Little Randy? He's saddled, ready to go."

"Get on out of here, Corporal. Take good care of the men."

In the thin, dark light of a quarter moon, the riders moved down from the rocks as quiet as ghosts, save for the slight click now and then of a hoof against rock. They gathered and formed abreast, then sat in silence ten yards above the spill of the trail onto the sand flats. Major Zell and Liam Bowes wove their horses forward through their ranks until they sat at the front, three yards ahead of them. Zell drew his long saber, slowly, quietly, then turned in his saddle as Bowes stepped his horse down the last few yards.

Zell whispered back to the men with his saber raised, "At the sound of fire . . ." He held his words suspended until at the base of the trail, a shot from Bowes's rifle exploded. *"Charge!"* Zell's saber flashed in the grainy darkness as he kicked his horse forward.

"Steady, men," Corporal Donnely called out along the line, holding their fire. He rose slightly behind the body of one of the dead horses and crouched, watching the blossoms of gunfire blink in the darkness. He wanted Zell's men to ride deep into the curve of the firing line. But Zell would have none of it. Ahead of the soldiers, a growing wedge of gunfire came forward, yet the wedge was spreading out.

Zell's men knew what their major wanted from them. A half dozen riders came forward, spreading out behind Zell and Bowes, the others swinging wide of the half circle, not yet seeing the soldiers' muzzle flash. Donnely held their fire until shots began whistling past him and thumping into the dead horses along the front of his line. Some of them were already inside the half circle. He would take what he could get. These men would charge straight through, the others would circle behind, firing on the troops as they made a dash past them.

"Fire!" Donnely yelled as he dropped onto one knee, bringing his own rifle into play as his firing line exploded around the oncoming riders. Zell's men in the rear spread wider now, coming around from outside the half circle, seeing the muzzles flash and firing on them as they went. Every other soldier in the firing line turned with the riders, giving them a hard hail of bullets as their dark shadows streaked across the sand.

At the center of the half circle skirmish line, Donnely fired his rifle empty at the onrush of man and horse coming at him in the darkness. From both sides, the soldiers poured it on Zell and his riders, Zell's return fire lessening now as his men and their horses tumbled forward in a spray of sand and blood. Horses bellowed and whinnied, their pitiful pleas drowned beneath the roar of rifles.

Donnely raised his army Colt, firing it, then dropped down, snatching a spare rifle from the ground beside him. Still Zell's riders came, hard and fast, through the gantlet of fire. Donnely saw the dark shadows approach, fifteen yards, then ten, the horses' hooves jarring the ground. *Too close!* He held his fire, knowing these last few would be charging over them any second.

And so they did. Zell and Bowes held their fire, only a couple of men still with them now. They needed the darkness as they broke over the line. Both their horses went up at the same time, going high over the dark forms before them. One soldier stood up and fired, and before Donnely could reach out and pull him down, a hissing sound swept across him as Zell and Bowes's horses came over them and touched down, moving on without missing a beat.

Donnely rose on his knee and fired at the backs of the fleeing riders. Beside him, the soldier who'd just fired stood screaming, his chest split wide and deep from shoulder to hip by Zell's long saber. "Oh, God, Rodney!" another soldier screamed, running to him.

Fifty yards farther out on the sand flats, Sergeant Baines lay flat on his stomach, seeing and hearing the rise and fall of battle. He had shed his rifle now, carrying only his pistol in his holster and the big knife from his boot well. Ahead of him, the sound of hooves thundering across sand came closer, and the sound of a man whimpering in pain. The firing back along the line had wound down now. Baines strained his eyes in the darkness until he could make out the black forms moving across the pale dark sand. He moved sidelong, crawling on his belly, to where the riders' path would lead past him.

Zell and Bowes slowed their horses to a halt and listened behind them for any sound of coming soldiers. They heard none. "Are you hit, Mr. Bowes?"

"Nothing serious, sir. How are you holding up?"

"Fit," Zell said; yet his voice sounded strained, weak. From both sides, riders came in out of the greater darkness and formed around them. "How many men have we left," Zell asked, trying to make out the faces.

"Four here, sir," said a voice, moving closer from the side.

"Five here, sir . . . but three badly wounded," another voice called out in the darkness.

"One coming in here," another voice said, this one moving up behind where Baines lay flat on the ground. Baines turned on the sand toward the single rider. Here was the horse he needed, along with whatever else the man carried on it.

"Then let's move out, men," Bowes said. "Keep spread out in a single file. I'll take the rear and cover us. We won't stop until we've crossed the border and headed to Diablo Canyon. The old man will meet us there. Any wounded who needs attention, drop out to the left. I'll stop for you as I come by."

The single rider's horse moved closer as the riders formed up and turned away. At no more than ten feet from the other riders, Baines came up with the big knife, swept over the horse's rump and behind the man as the horse sidestepped beneath the new weight on its back. The horse nickered as Baines's arm went around the man's face and drew it back against him, the blade of the knife going in between his ribs and searching upward into his heart.

The horse nickered again when Baines eased the body down off its side and let it drop to the sand. "What's wrong with that animal?" a voice asked from ten feet away, blinded by the darkness. "Is he hit?"

"No"—Baines spoke in low tight tone—"just spooked a little. He's fine."

"Then keep him quiet," Bowes said. "Come on, get in front of me."

Baines looked around in the darkness, then rode past Bowes and fell into the slow-moving line. He would have to slip away the first chance he got and follow at a safe distance. He knew what he needed to know. *Diablo Canyon.* That's where they were headed.

Chapter 12

When Willis Durant awoke in the night from a restless sleep, he saw the Ranger sitting beside the low fire with a cup of Duttwieler tea in his hand. Durant wiped a hand across his face, sitting up on his blanket. "Figure I'll make a move on you if you doze off, Ranger?"

"If I did, you'd be hog-tied right now, Durant. This Mexican ground just ain't made to sleep on," he said, slapping a hand down on the blanket.

Durant's eyes flashed around in the low glow of firelight. "Where's the old man?"

"He's gone," the Ranger said in a quiet voice.

"Gone?" Durant looked at him as the Ranger raised the cup to his lips. Calm, seeming to be in no hurry—the Ranger's demeanor threw him for a moment. "You mean you let him get away?"

The Ranger lifted his eyes over to the empty blanket on the ground, then back to Durant. "Yep. About a half hour ago." The Ranger rose up with the cup in his hand and slung the last drops out on the ground. "Don't get the wrong idea, Durant. This doesn't change anything between you and me. I don't need him or you either to show me how to follow wagon tracks. I just let him get out in front of us. We're close to where those men are taking the wagon, ain't we?"

Durant sighed. "Yeah, we are. But you're going have to give me something to shoot with, Ranger. If you don't, all we're gonna do is die once we catch up to them."

The Ranger gave a slight smile. "I've given it lots of thought, Durant. So far you've been straight with me. But I can't trust you when it comes to meeting up with these men. You've said yourself, you don't care what happens to you so long as you kill the Parker boys. That makes you too dangerous for me to trust. You'd risk the women's lives if they got between and your revenge."

Durant thought about it and realized the Ranger was right. He replied with a straight face, shaking his head, "No, I want the Parker brothers, but I wouldn't get careless with the hostages' lives."

"It's not a chance I can afford to take, Durant. If you did, I'd have to kill you. You got careless before. That's what got you into this mess. You let the Parkers into your family's lives and it got them killed. Now it's eating you up. I don't think it's all that important whether they kill you or you kill them. Either way, I figure you'd call it justice."

Durant didn't answer for a moment. When he finally spoke, he'd dismissed the subject. "So . . . what do you want to do now?"

"We'll lag back a few more minutes, then follow the old man. He won't waste time following the tracks. He knows where the wagon is headed. He'll go straight to it."

Durant only nodded.

The Ranger stepped over and looked through the thin light of a quarter moon onto the dark flatlands forty feet below them. They'd made their camp up on the first level clearing in case Zell and his men should get past the soldiers early and come riding this way in the night. When old man Dirkson had slipped over and eased the horse away from the other two, the Ranger had lain feigning sleep, watching carefully from beneath the lowered brim of his sombrero.

Dirkson had at first gone to the white barb, but the barb shied back and lowered its ears, having none of it. Then the old man had moved to the Ranger's spare. Before he'd left, the Ranger watched him venture toward them, leading the horse. For a moment, he could tell the old man thought about making a move for the rifle lying alongside the Ranger. Had he reached for it, the Ranger would have had to kill him, flat out. But then the old man must have thought better of it. He turned, led the horse away from the camp, and moved along the rocky ledge. The Ranger had lain still and listened, hearing the soft click of hooves moving across the rocky ground.

"He stayed high up for a good ways," the Ranger said, turning to Durant. "Figured we'd go straight down and look for his tracks. That would take up our time."

"How do you know he didn't cut back and join Zell? That would make sense, wouldn't it?"

"He knows we'll catch up to him pretty soon. Whatever he's going to do, he knows he's got to do it quick. He won't waste time looking for Zell out there among all the army troops when he knows where the wagon's headed."

Durant checked the cinch on his horse's saddle, then dropped the stirrup. "He's pretty spry for an old bull with a hole through his shoulder."

"I expect he's been fighting and scratching like this his whole life," the Ranger said. "Nothing more dangerous than an old fighting man still looking to carve out a place for himself."

The Ranger stood with his rifle in his hand, watching Durant lead both the horses over to him. He handed the Ranger the reins to the barb. "An outlaw's just an outlaw, far as I'm concerned." The Ranger took the reins and ran a hand down the white barb's muzzle. "But it always pays to try and know why a man does what he does." He paused, considering something. "I get a feeling this was going to be his last big move—his retirement job, so to speak."

Durant stepped up into his saddle. "Oh? What gives ya that notion?"

"Just a hunch," the Ranger said. "Maybe something I saw in his eyes, no different from what I've been seeing in yours." He stepped up atop the white barb and righted it toward the thin path leading around the rocky ledge. "Something tells me this is the last thing he has to do in life. He'd rather die getting it done than to live letting it go."

"Maybe it's your own eyes you see this in, Ranger," Durant said.

"Yeah, maybe it is." The Ranger glanced at him, then looked away, getting a picture of Maria out there somewhere in the hands of killers. Durant saw the hollow look in the Ranger's eyes as they turned their horses and put them forward on the narrow path.

The only light burning in the little Mexican town of San Çarlos came through the dusty window of the crumbling adobe cantina. Payton Parker, his brother Leo, and McCord eased their horses along the rutted street, past a sleeping hog that only raised its dirty head and grunted, then dropped back in its bed of dust as the three riders moved on. A goat bleated somewhere in the darkness, and they heard its small hooves click away deeper into the velvet night.

"I bet ole Delbert's got one of the women pinned and poked by now," McCord said, pushing up his battered hat brim as they edged over to a hitch rail outside the cantina.

"Hell, maybe both of them." They got down and spun their reins.

Payton Parker looked around in the darkness, then stretched his back. "Well . . . he can pin and poke all he wants. When we get back, it's our turn."

Leo Parker looked embarrassed. "That's no way to talk, Payton. Those women ain't done us no wrong."

"Wrong?" Payton shook his head. "What's wrong got to do with it? I'm just talking about us getting what's coming to us. They're women, we're men. It's only natural we're going to do what men do, huh?" He jostled his crotch, nudging Leo with his elbow. "They'd think there's something wrong with us if we didn't."

"That's right," McCord said. "They're wondering why we haven't already. They might even think we don't like them."

Leo looked back and forth between them as they walked toward the open door of the cantina. "She said she'd kill you if you laid a hand on her. I believe she meant it."

"Leo, Leo." Payton shook his head, threw an arm across his brother's shoulder, and chuckled. "They all say that. But they never mean it. It's just a woman's way . . . but deep down, they're wanting it just as much as we do, maybe more. You and me are gonna have a long talk once this is all over."

"Still, I don't like it," Leo said. "They're served their purpose. Now we oughta let them go."

"Their purpose?" Payton and McCord laughed as they walked into the cantina and across to a bar made of boards spread between two wooden barrels. Payton raised his voice a bit to the old man behind the bar. "Juan, *hola, mi amigo!* Bet you'd just about given us up."

"For three nights I have kept this place open, waiting to

hear something." His voice was wary, agitated. "Where is Bowes? Always he comes with you, no?"

"Oh . . ." Payton Parker took his time, looking around the filthy cantina. "Not this time. Bowes and Zell got caught up in a little problem. They sent us three to handle the deal."

There were only two men in the cantina. One was the owner, Juan Verdere. The other man was Juan's partner and bodyguard, a Frenchman named Paschal. He stood at the far end of the bar with a double-barrel shotgun lying along the rough boards. The fingers of his dirty gloves were worn off back to the second knuckle, his fingers grimy, the same color as the stained leather. One hand lay near the shotgun, the other hand rested around a wooden cup of wine.

Paschal chuckled, saying in a thick, gravelly voice, "We have heard of Zell's problem—and it is no little problem either. He is holding two women hostage, one is the daughter of a very wealthy man. Maybe we wait and deal with Zell, after his problem is solved, eh?"

The three had spread along the bar, and as they spoke, Juan slid three wooden cups forward and placed a bottle of mescal before them. Payton Parker bowed his head over the bottle, then turned his face sidelong, looking at Paschal. "You know, every time I see you, Frenchy, I get this real strong urge to start shooting holes in your head." He spread a tight, harsh smile. "Why is that, you think?"

Paschal shrugged. "Who can say?" His right hand drifted up onto the grip of the shotgun, his grimy fingers tapping it lightly. "Perhaps it's because you are tired of this life and would like me to send you on to the next?"

Payton Parker's hand moved down from the edge of the bar. Juan Verdere glanced back and forth with nervous eyes. "Enough. You have come to do business . . . let us do it."

"That's what I say." Payton, still smiling, raised his right hand forming it into a pistol, and clicked his thumb up and down at Paschal, squinting one eye. Then he turned to Juan. "We've got everything your *federales* want—except we're a little short on the kegs of powder."

"How short?" Juan stared at him.

"Just a dab. We'll adjust the price down. The main thing is, we got to get settled up tonight." He shot a glance at Paschal, then back to Juan. "If you know about the problem, then you also know we've got to make some quick moves here. The wagon's out near Diablo Canyon."

"And our finder's fee? Zell always pays me and Paschal first." He tapped a finger straight down on the bar. "Then we tell the *federales* where to find you."

"Ordinarily that would be the way," Payton Parker said. "But this ain't ordinarily. You send them pepper-poppers on out, they pay us, and we'll pay you afterward." He reached over, took the bottle of mescal from McCord's hand and threw back a drink. He let out a hiss, holding Juan's suspicious gaze.

"No, no, no." Paschal wagged a finger, taking up the shotgun and moving closer along the bar, his big belly bouncing beneath his loose, ragged shirt. "I see you have been sleeping too long with your head on a cold rock. We get all that is coming to us," he said as he rubbed his grimy thumb and finger together in the universal symbol of greed, "or you can take your wagon back and try selling it to Jameson Vanderman. Perhaps he will be glad to—"

"Please, Frenchy, don't come no closer." Payton Parker cut him off with a raised hand. "The air's bad enough here already." He looked back at Juan Verdere. "That how you feel? Because if it is, we're gone. You can tell the *federales* you blew the deal, got them the guns . . . but can't get them no ammo. They'll get a big kick out of that, won't they?"

A tense silence passed as Juan Verdere wrestled the deal in his mind. Payton Parker let out a breath, snatched the bottle from the bar, and said, "Well, boys, let's go. I see we've got no business here."

"No, wait!" Juan Verdere cocked his head to the side. "We will do it your way, just this once." He raised a long finger for emphasis. "But Paschal and I will go with you. The *federales* are camped not far from here. We will go to them and take them with us. Paschal and I will be there when they give you the gold. This is the only way, *sí* "

"Since you don't trust us, yeah, I suppose that'll work." He looked at Leo and McCord and winked. "But I have to admit, our feelings are hurt." He turned to Paschal. "If you're coming along, stay aways behind us, Frenchy . . . you'll spook the horses."

"You joke and have your fun," Paschal said, falling in behind them as they turned toward the door. "But if you are not careful, someday I will raise you up on a sharp stick and watch you wiggle."

"Oh? Planning a dinner party?"

Outside, as the three of them waited for Paschal and Juan Verdere to go around back and get their horses, Leo said to his brother Payton in a hushed voice, "You shouldn't fool around with that ole Frenchman none. When he trapped fur up in the Rockies, they say he once got snowed in and et—"

"—Et an Indian's leg," Payton said, impatient, finishing Leo's words for him. He brushed it away. "Yeah, I heard all that. What's it suppose to do, scare me?" He glanced at McCord, then back to his brother. "Hell . . . that ain't nothing for a Frenchy. They all eat stuff you scrape off a mossy log. That don't make him a bad man." He raised his voice to Paschal as the big man lumbered back around the cantina, leading his horse. "Hey, Frenchy? Where does a man have to go around here to get a good Ute steak . . . maybe a side of baked Pawnee rib bones?"

"You keep it up with me, Parker . . ." Paschal let his guttural warning trail off. He stopped and grunted, rolling up into his saddle. Beside him Juan Verdere stepped up into his saddle and heeled his horse forward, taking the lead.

Payton Parker grinned. "Boy, I would *dearly* love a good deep roasted leg of—"

"That's enough," McCord hissed. "We've got plenty to worry about, getting this deal settled." He turned and swung onto his horse in behind Juan Verdere. Leo and Payton did the same. Paschal held his horse back, waiting for a second, then brought up the rear.

Payton chuckled, looking at Juan ahead of them and Paschal behind. Then he turned to McCord and Leo. "Relax, boys, you'll soon be sipping fancy wine and farting in clean bedsheets. We're about to be rich. *Rich!* Do you hear me?" He reached over to Leo and yanked his hat down over his eyes. "Not only that, boys, we got the rest of the night with them warm-blooded women—get caught up on our natural urges. Whooie!" He kicked his horse out ahead of them.

Leo grinned, pushed up his hat brim, and spurred his horse forward into the darkness. "Payton, you ain't got a lick of sense. You never did have."

Chapter 13

Maria had tried to keep track of time ever since Payton, Leo, and McCord rode off into the darkness. With these three men gone, she knew there would be no better time for her and Prudence to make their getaway. Yet things weren't working out for them. Before the men had left, leaving Delbert alone to guard them and the wagon, Maria had heard one of the men tell the other that it would be a three-hour ride to where they were going and back. How long had that been—an hour and a half, two hours ago? When she'd heard it, she looked at Prudence sitting beside her. A knowing glance passed between them.

But before leaving, Payton Parker had stepped up into the wagon and checked the rope tied around the women's wrists. "Nice try," he said, finding they had worked their ropes loose. "One more little trick like this, and I'll put a bullet through your heads. I hate a conniving woman."

He'd shoved both of the women out of the wagon onto the hard, sandy ground, loosened their ropes the rest of the way, and retied them. "Better keep close watch on them," Payton said to Delbert, coldly staring at Maria. "I don't think these young ladies are enjoying our company."

"They ain't going nowhere, Payton," Delbert said. "You know me. I might play around with them a little, but I'll have both eyes open all the while. They won't try nothing stupid, will you, girls?" He gave Maria and Prudence a nasty grin. They only stared back at him blankly.

"Play around all you want, but they better be here when I get back." Payton managed a grin himself, his eyes sweeping across the women. "And there better be enough left for the rest of us. Once we get this deal settled, we'll feel like a little celebrating."

When Payton Parker and the other two rode away, Maria and Prudence lay tied to a wagon wheel, the rope tight around their wrists, their hands above their heads. It was important that Delbert make the first move on them, Maria thought, otherwise he might see through their intentions. But so far he hadn't even come close. He stayed a few feet away near the low licking flames of the campfire, watching them.

For all his bold talk in the presence of his friends, now that they were alone, Delbert seemed uncertain of himself, almost as shy as a schoolboy. Maria watched him cast guarded glances in their direction. *What was wrong with this imbecile . . . ?* When he saw the women return his gaze, he would look down and shake his head, rubbing a stick back and forth in the glowing embers, snickering under his breath in tune to some lewd fantasy inside his mind.

Maria let out a breath, exasperated. They had to do something soon. She shot Prudence a troubled look and shrugged.

"I don't know about you," Prudence said in a whisper, "but I'm not going to sit here all night. Let's make a move."

"No, wait—" Maria saw Prudence lean a bit forward against her tied wrists.

But before Maria could stop her, Prudence spoke out toward the campfire in a raised voice, "Hey, you, Delbert.

Come here. I want to tell you something. Something important."

But Delbert only cocked his head to one side and pointed a finger at his chest, grinning. "Yes, *you*, Delbert. Come over here. What's the matter? I won't bite you." Prudence's tone of voice made it sound like a dare.

Maria sat quiet and tense, hoping Prudence knew what she was doing. "Yeah? What?" Delbert stood up, pitched the stick to the ground, and walked over to them, stopping four feet back, cautious. "I'm listening."

"I . . . I need to go over into the bushes."

Chuckling, he said, "That's it? That's what's so important? You need to go relieve yourself?" He shook his head and turned to walk away. "Not a chance in hell," he said, still chuckling under his breath. "I know a trick when I see one."

"No. Wait. Please!" Prudence rushed her words. "It's not funny, Delbert—it's no trick. I need to go, real bad." She shot Maria an unreadable glance, then added to Delbert, "I *do* have something important to tell you . . . something *very* important! It's . . . It's about her."

"Yeah?" Delbert stopped and turned back to them. "What about her?"

There was a slight pause, then Prudence said, "She's planning to kill you . . . and get away." She nodded toward Maria.

Maria's brow rose. *What was this?*

Delbert moved toward them once more. He lay a hand on the pistol at his hip. "You don't say?" He looked from one to the other. "And just how does she suppose she'll do that?" His chuckling tone changed, his grin gone now.

"I have to relieve myself," Prudence said in a clipped tone. "Then I'll tell you."

"I don't think so," Delbert said. He lifted the pistol from his holster and cocked it, aiming it at Prudence. Maria held her breath. "You tell me whatever you've got to tell me," he hissed, stooping down a bit closer. "If I like what I hear, then you can go do your business. That's all the deal you get."

"Prudence . . . ?' Maria's voice came low, cautioning. She saw something coming. She didn't know what it was, but she didn't like it. Maria didn't like making a move of any kind while their hands were still bound.

Delbert's eyes leveled harshly on Maria. "Shut up! If she's got something to say, let her say it. I'm in charge here!" He turned to Prudence. "Go on, get it said."

"But, if I do . . ." Prudence hesitated with an innocent wide-eyed expression ". . . can I trust you to do what you said?"

"Honey, you've got no choice." Delbert's grin returned, even stronger now that she'd awakened a sense of power in him.

"All right, then." Prudence shot Maria a dubious glance, Maria's eyes telling her to keep her mouth shut. But Prudence ignored her, let out a sigh of submission, and said to Delbert in a shaky voice, "She's armed. She has a gun. I saw it."

"What?" Delbert jerked back a step. His pistol swung toward Maria. Maria looked stunned.

"It's true," Prudence said. "She meant to kill you with it the first chance she got." She nodded. "Look in her boot."

Santa Madre! No! You fool! Don't do this . . . But it was too late. Maria slumped against the wagon wheel.

"Is that so?" Delbert stooped down, moving carefully toward Maria's boot, as if it were a snake. "Let's just take a little look here."

What could she do? Maria thought about burying her boot

in his face as he leaned in to run a hand down her boot well. But that was too risky. It was doubtful that she could kick him unconscious from this position—even if she did, then what? She lay staring at him as he moved with the small pistol in his hand and shoved his big .45 down into his holster. Whatever Prudence had in mind, it better be good.

"Well, well." Delbert chuckled, bouncing the pistol on the palm of his hand. "Ain't this just slicker than socks on a rooster?" Then his smile faded, looking down at Maria. His hand tightened on the small pistol. "I oughta empty both shots in ya, you sneaking, rotten—"

"Delbert, I have to go really bad," Prudence whined.

"What?" Delbert turned his gaze to her.

"You know . . . our deal? I told you what she was up to. Now let me go to the bushes. You said you would."

"Oh . . ." He scratched his head up under his hat brim. "You're not going to try to make a run for it, are ya?"

Prudence shot Maria a quick glance, then said to Delbert with urgency, "No, I'm not. Would I have told you about the pistol if I was going to? Jesus, Delbert! Come on, please!"

"Well . . . all right, but you can't go alone. I'll have to be with you."

"I don't care—just hurry!"

"Damn it." Delbert shoved the small pistol into his shirt pocket, stepped around beside Prudence, and began untying her hands from the wagon wheel. "This is why I hate traveling with women. Every five miles you've got to stop and—"

"Come on, Delbert. I have a nice surprise for you if you hurry. I promise." Her voice sounded playful within her urgency.

"Really? No fooling?" He lifted her to her feet, and his

eyes widened. "Then let's get going." He jerked her close to him. "I like nice surprises."

She pressed him away from her. "First things first, Delbert." Shooting Maria a glance, Prudence turned back to him with a coy expression, moving off into the darkness. Delbert stumbled along behind her. She added, "I keep hearing you boys mention all this gold you're going to get. Just how much gold are we talking about?"

You fool . . . Maria listened and watched as the two of them disappeared out of the circle of firelight. She jerked against the rope around her wrists, doing her best to loosen it. From across the campsite, out the scrub brush, she heard Prudence's muffled laughter, then the sound of Delbert's hushed voice. She tugged harder at her rope, but it held tight. If whatever plan Prudence had in mind didn't work, they would be in far worse trouble than they were before. The small pistol had been their ace in the hole. Now it was gone.

Inside the cover of rock and dry brush, Prudence heard Delbert say behind her, "Why are you so interested in the gold? From what I understand your family has more money than—"

"Forget the gold." Prudence turned suddenly and pressed herself against him. "There's more important things than money." She fumbled with his belt buckle, up on tiptoe, her breath warm against his ear. "Delbert, don't you realize how frightened I am by all this? Don't you realize I will do anything you want me to do . . . *anything* at all?"

"Easy, lady." Delbert stepped back while she pressed against him, moving too fast for him to argue. He let out a nervous chuckle. "Thought you had to—"

"No, I was just saying that, to get you out here . . . alone." Her words were rushed and breathless. He felt his gun belt fall away, Prudence's hands all over him now, seeming to be everywhere at once. No woman had ever acted this way with him. "Anything, Delbert, anything that pleases you." Her mouth moved warm and wet, nuzzling his sweaty throat. *Jesus . . . !* He reached for her hands, needing to slow her down a bit. But he was leaning farther back, sinking, her body moving against him in ways that pushed him down onto the sandy ground.

"Oh, Lord . . ." Delbert groaned. She was atop him now, his trousers down halfway to his knees, his body starting to respond. "Aw-yeah! Aw-yeah . . ."

Her hands moved beneath her dress, and he felt her warmth press down on him. She leaned forward over him, her face close to his, one hand still down there, stroking, squeezing him. "Oh, my, Delbert . . . you are *so* ready for me," she whispered. And as she held him tight in her left hand, her right hand crawled out like a spider across the sand and closed around a rock the size of a grapefruit.

She rose over him, his rough hands tight on her breasts, his body rising and falling to the rhythm of her hand tight around him. "Oh, do it . . . do it now!" Delbert moaned, his eyes squeezed shut.

Prudence brought the rock around in one vicious sidelong swipe that caught Delbert on the temple, his head twisting to one side. Beneath her, his body fell limp, and she rose and stood looking down at him for a second, shivering. *Should she hit him again? No. This was enough.* He wasn't dead, but he would be out for a while. She swallowed her nausea, dropped the rock, and ran her hands up and down her dirty dress, cleaning them both of something unseen.

Hurrying, she gathered his big pistol and the small derringer he'd taken from Maria's boot. Then Prudence calmed herself, took a few deep breaths, slipped her hand inside her dress, and took out the razor from its small leather sheath under her arm. With the opened razor in her hand, she walked back toward the glow of firelight.

Maria had noticed there were no more hushed sound of voices coming from the bushes. She lay still, her senses searching the darkness. Another minute passed, then she heard the soft rustle of footsteps through the brush. A dark figure stepped into the outer glow of flickering light, and when Maria saw it was Prudence, she let out a sigh of relief. Prudence held Delbert's .45 in one hand and a straight razor in her other. "Quickly," Maria called out in a hushed tone. "We must hurry and get out of here. They will be back soon."

But Prudence took her time. She stopped near the fire, laid the big pistol on the ground, and looked down at the razor in her hand. She wiped her thumb and finger along the glistening blade. "We're all right now," she said, stooping down and wiping her fingers back and forth on the ground. "Delbert is no longer a problem."

Maria jerked against her tied wrists. "Come on, Prudence! Untie me!"

Prudence moved toward her in what seemed to be a trancelike state, folding the straight razor and placing it inside her dress under her arm. "I killed him, you know," she said, lying in a matter-of-fact voice as she pulled and tugged, untying Maria's wrists.

"Yes, I thought as much . . . now hurry!"

As Maria felt the rope give, she pulled her hands free and rubbed her wrists, then rushed over near the fire and picked up Delbert's pistol. She checked it, saying, "We have no time to unhitch the mules. We'll take the wagon until we get away from here." She hurried over to where Delbert's horse

stood hitched to a low scrub juniper, still saddled, a rifle butt
sticking up from the scabbard. She untied the horse and led
it back to the wagon as Prudence stepped up into the seat.
Maria looked up at her as Prudence settled onto the seat.

"You had me worried," Maria said. "For a moment, I
thought you were only making a play for the gold."

Prudence flipped her hair, shaking it out. "Well, I have to
admit, the gold would be nice, but . . ." She let her words
trail, staring down at Maria. Then she changed the subject.
"So, now we're free. Where does this put us?"

"Now we get away. We have a fighting chance," Maria
said.

"They'll simply follow our wagon tracks, won't they?"
Prudence adjusted the torn shoulder of her dress. "We can't
outrun them. If we do, how will we live out there? We have
no food, no water."

"But they do," Maria said, nodding in the direction the
three men had taken. "We must take what they have." She
hitched Delbert's horse to the rear of the wagon, then
walked to the front and pitched the rifle up to Prudence.
Catching it, Prudence looked the rifle over as if seeing one
for the first time.

"How in the world do you hope to take their food and
water?"

"I have a plan," Maria answered. She looked up through
the darkness at the crest of the tall rocks surrounding their
clearing. "Once we leave the wagon, we will circle back on
the mules and be at the one place where they won't expect
us . . . up there." She gestured into the darkness.

Prudence looked up and along the dark high ridge line.
Then she shook her head. "No, I don't like it. I say we take
the horse and a mule and beat a path out of here as quick as
we can. With a little luck we'll find water along the way."

Luck . . . ? Maria didn't respond. Instead, she stepped up into the wagon beside Prudence and said, "That was a foolish thing you did back there with Delbert. You gave up our pistol and put my life on the line." She unwound the reins, pulled back hard on the brake level, and released it.

"Yes, but you are alive. It worked, didn't it?" Prudence gave her a sharp glance and brushed a hand up and down the dusty sleeve of her dress. She shook out her hair once more and ran her fingers through it.

"You had no way of knowing it would work," Maria snapped. "It was a dangerous, foolish gamble. Don't do something like that again."

"Oh? I couldn't see any other way." Prudence shrugged. "What were we going to do . . . let the opportunity get past us? Sit here, helpless?"

"I have lived most of my life in this land," Maria said, "and I have never been helpless."

"And I have never had to ask someone's permission to save my own life," Prudence snapped back at her. "We're free. What are we waiting for?" She looked away from Maria, dismissing the subject.

Maria had no more responses for her. What Prudence said was true. Regardless of how risky it had been, Prudence had taken the gamble and won. But she could not trust this woman again, Maria thought, slapping the traces to the mules. Prudence Cordell was a bold, self-determined woman—that much they had in common. But she had done nothing to instill trust between them, including lying about who she was the moment they'd met.

The animals lunged forward against the heavy load, then righted themselves onto the thin trail. Prudence Cordell was a user, interested only in herself and her personal well-being. But then, what could she expect, Maria thought, knowing where this woman came from and how she'd made her living.

She glanced at Prudence, looking her up and down as the animals struggled forward with the heavy load. From now on, she would keep a closer eye on this woman. Maria would not abandon her—that was unthinkable. But from now on, Maria would have to be more careful. Now that she'd had a close look at Prudence's true nature, she must not put herself in a position where Prudence's actions would jeopardize both their lives.

The mules pressed on slowly and steadily. Prudence moved about restlessly on the wooden wagon seat and looked over her shoulder. "At this rate we might just as well get off and walk. Can't you make these mules go a little faster?"

"No, not in the dark, on this kind of ground. It would be foolish to push them." Once more she looked Prudence Cordell up and down. "How did you kill him without getting blood on your dress?"

"Who said I was wearing a dress?" A silence passed, then Prudence spoke in a low, confident tone. "I'm very good at what I do." Her eyes met Maria's. "It's all about staying alive, isn't it? Wouldn't you have done the same?" When Maria didn't answer, Prudence added, "Well, if you wouldn't have . . . then maybe you're not as tough as you think." She gazed off into the darkness and absently rubbed her hands together in her lap.

Chapter 14

When the Parkers, McCord, Juan Verdere, and Paschal rode into the *federale* camp, a guard met them and escorted them to a stocky captain named Marsos Gravia, who had been sleeping on the hard ground beneath a cottonwood tree. Gravia awoke agitated, having already waited far too long for Zell to bring the ammunition. He rolled up from a dirty, rumpled blanket and smoothed a hand down the front of his wrinkled tunic, turning from the men long enough to put on his hat.

When the captain turned back and faced them, Payton Parker had stepped forward closer than the others. He grinned at the captain and said in an offhand manner, "Hate to wake you from your beauty sleep, but we need to get settled up on this ammo deal."

The captain looked around at his aide and said, "Who the hell is this *hombre*? Why did you bring these men to me without first waking me?"

"But he rides with Juan Verdere. They say it is most urgent they met with you—"

"Don't get your drawers in a knot, Capi-tan," Payton Parker cut in. "Me and my partners don't stand on too many formalities."

The captain's face grew tight, enraged. But he needed the

ammunition, and he kept himself in check and wiped a hand over his face. "If you have the ammunition as promised, then let's settle up and be on our way." He looked from Payton Parker to Juan and Paschal. "Why is this so different than all the times before? I have never had to wait this long on Major Zell. Where is he?"

Once again, before Juan Verdere or Paschal could answer, Payton Parker cut in, "Zell is what you call *indisposed* at the moment. But it don't matter. He sent us. So if ya want your bullets, hike your galluses and get a move on. We ain't got all night."

The captain glared at him, stunned with outrage.

McCord winced, seeing the harsh way Payton Parker was conducting himself with this officer. Juan looked at the captain with an apologetic shrug. "Very well," the captain said, keeping himself in check. "We have the gold. All that remains is for us to—"

Again cutting him off, Payton Parker let out a short laugh. "All right then. I like you better than I thought I would, Capitan."

"I hope you know who you're fooling with here," McCord whispered to Payton Parker as the captain turned and walked toward the horses, waving his men in with him.

"Can't you see, they're eating out of our hands?" Payton whispered back to him. "Let met handle these boys. They like it when you down-talk 'em."

They all left the camp, and when they'd ridden a few miles out through the rugged rock-patched land, the captain had drawn Juan Verdere and Paschal up beside him at the head of his nine-man column. Ahead of them by twenty yards, Payton, Leo, and McCord rode on in the darkness, barely distinguishable in the pale moonlight.

"I do not like doing business this way," the *federale* cap-

tain said to Juan Verdere and Paschal. He took a furtive look
at his troops behind him, then across his horse's rump where
the heavy saddlebags carrying thirty thousand in gold coin
lay. "What do we know about these Parkers? Why is Zell
himself not here? This could be some sort of trick, eh?"

"If it is a trick, *mon ami,*" Paschal said, "it is not of our
making. I can only apologize for this insolent pig and ask
you not to judge us on his behavior. We are on your side,
Captain Gravia, as always."

"You better be," the captain said, kicking his horse forward ahead of them. He rode in beside Payton Parker with a
hand on his pistol. "How much farther is it."

Payton Parker spit and waited a second before answering.
Then he said, "A couple miles, more or less. You can ride
that far without falling off your horse, can't ya?" He snickered, spit again, then added, "Don't worry, we ain't out to
double-cross the Mexican army, right, boys?" He grinned at
Leo and McCord in the pale moonlight. They only nodded,
McCord wishing Payton wouldn't act so cocky with these
men. So far things were going their way. He didn't want
Payton Parker blowing the deal by pushing too hard.

"Of course, if that gold is getting too heavy for yas," a
smug Payton Parker said to the captain, "we'll be glad to
take it now . . . save you the trouble."

"You have a smart *gringo* mouth," the *federale* captain
huffed, then let his horse stay back a few steps.

"Why don't you quit aggravating everybody, Payton,"
McCord said as the captain fell back out of sight. "Why
make things hard on us? We're about to get everything we
want here."

"I can't help it," Payton chuckled. "It just does me good
to know we've out-foxed everybody—Zell, Bowes, the

whole damn bunch of them. Don't that make you want to jump up and down?"

"No," McCord said. "It makes me want to keep my mouth shut and see this thing through. It's all about the gold for me. I didn't do it just to see if I could out-fox somebody."

"Yeah? Well, that's the kind of humble thinking that'll keep you from ever amounting to anything," Payton Parker said. "Me and Leo here have slicked our share of folks the past year or two. Nothing humble about us, right, brother?"

"Come on, Payton," Leo said in a hushed tone. "Keep your voice down. Somebody will hear ya back there."

"Shit." Payton adjusted his hat brim and gazed ahead into the darkness.

"He's right, Payton," McCord said. "This is serious stuff."

"Naw, he ain't right." Payton looked over at McCord. "I'll tell ya what's wrong with my brother. He's been scared for the past year, thinking there's a big Negro hunting us down." He laughed and moved his horse ahead of them a few steps.

"What's he talking about?" McCord looked at Leo.

"Nothing," Leo said with a curt nod. "Mind your own business." They rode on the last mile and a half to the camp-site.

Sitting on the ground with a wet handkerchief pressed to his shattered jaw, Delbert looked up as the men rode in and circled about him. He saw Payton Parker and the others crane upward in their saddles and look all around the glowing circle of fire. "My God, Delbert, where's the wagon? Where's the women?"

But Delbert's crushed cheek kept him from raising his voice. He mumbled something as he rose to his feet. Payton Parker saw the *federales* fan out around the campsite, suspicious, searching the darkness for some sort of trap. "Take it easy now, Capi-tan," he called out. "We've got a minor setback here!" His eyes flashed to Paschal and Juan Verdere. "Juan! Frenchy! Tell them everything's okay!"

"But we are not *okay,*" Paschal hissed, moving his horse in close to Payton, his hand raising the rifle from his lap and cocking the hammer. "Where is dogs ammunition?" Around the campsite, rifles cocked in unison.

"Delbert, boy! For God sakes, what's happened?" Payton Parker's once confident voice now sounded high and shaky.

McCord had jumped down from his saddle and run over to Delbert. Raising him to his feet, he called out to Payton Parker, "Damn it, Payton! You can see what's happened . . . them woman have busted his jaw all to hell and took off!" He looped Delbert's arm across his shoulder and struggled with him, bringing him over for the captain to see. "They can't have gone far, Captain. Let's not lose our heads. You want that ammunition—help us get after them."

The captain looked skeptical. Leo Parker moved his horse closer to him. "It ain't no trick, Captain. I swear it ain't. Payton didn't mean nothing, needling you the way he did. Help us find that wagon and let's get this straightened out."

Payton Parker tried to get a word in. "What he's saying is—"

"Shut up, Payton," Leo snapped. "You've said too much already."

Payton clenched his jaw. "Damn it then! Sit here all night if you want to . . . I'm going after them." He sawed his reins and straightened his horse out behind the wagon tracks.

The captain fell his horse among three of his men. He reached back, unfastened and saddlebags full of gold coin, hefted them off his horse's rump, and let them fall to the ground with a heavy thud. "You three men stay here. Guard

these with your lives." He stood up in his stirrups, looked at
Juan Verdere and Paschal, threw a suspicious glance at Mc-
Cord and Leo Parker, then called out to his troops, "The rest
of you follow me. We must have that ammunition."

Maria and Prudence hurried to lead the wagon off into a slip
of brush alongside the trail. As soon as they'd unhitched the
mules, keeping one to ride and shooing the others away,
Maria pulled a four-pound keg of black powder from beneath the canvas tarpaulin and trotted back to the horse with
it under her arm. "We'll need this," she said, passing Prudence, who stood tying a short rope around the mule's muzzle. "Hurry! Please!"

"I *am* hurrying," Prudence snapped. "Surely, you don't
plan on using that stuff. It's too dangerous."

"*Sí*, of course we will use it. When the time comes, we
will make a bomb of it."

"Do you know anything about it? Have you ever made a
bomb before?"

No, but only because I have never had to." She gave Prudence a determined look and led the horse from behind the
wagon up to her. "And you have obviously never made a
bridle before." She brushed Prudence's hand aside, took the
rope from the mule's muzzle, and hastily fashioned it into a
one-rein bridle. "This will do. The mule knows more about
walking a high trail than we do. Just use this to keep him
going."

Prudence looked at the bridle, then nodded. "Okay, I see
what you mean." Maria held the mule while Prudence
slipped up onto its knobby back. Prudence reached down
and took the rope from her. "Don't worry, I catch on quick."

"Good." Maria replied as she stepped up onto the horse.

"Now we go high into the rocks and head back. By the time they find the wagon, we will be in position to fight."

"Fight—?" Prudence's voice stopped short. "You said we would take what water and food we need from them."

"That is true . . . and they will not let us without putting up a fight." She turned her horse, the small powder keg laying in her lap. "We are going to do whatever we must to stay alive." She reached out and slapped a hand on the mule's rump and sent it forward.

They moved upward into the cover of rocks. When the animals picked up an elk trace in the pale moonlight, they followed it back overlooking the wider trail sixty feet below them. Less than two miles down the trail, they heard the sound of horses moving along the lower trail, and Maria stopped the horse and caught the mule's rope bridle as it plugged forward. They sat in silence for a moment. When the horses moved away toward the wagon, Maria whispered, "They have brought the others with them. We must hurry now. It will take them a little while to find the wagon and come back with it."

"Hurry? On this trail?"

"As much as possible, yes." Maria pulled the mule forward alongside her, then slapped it hard, feeling it jerk forward as Prudence cursed under her breath. They moved on along the narrow rocky trace, darkness engulfing them as they passed in and out of crevices in upthrusts of rocks, brush, and thorns that scratched Prudence's naked legs. When they reached a point on the trail where they could see the faint glow of firelight in the distance below them, Maria stopped once more, this time letting out a breath as if giving thanks. "Now we go to work," she said.

In the campsite below, Delbert still sat in the circle of light with a wet rag to his swollen jaw. Dark blood had dried down the side of his throat, and he glared back at the three *federales* who kept their eyes on him. The saddlebags of gold lay between two of them in the dirt. "The hell are y'all looking at," Delbert snapped to them in a weak, slurred voice. "I suppose the same thing ain't happened to every one of ya sometime or other? No woman ever busted you in the jaw with a rock?"

One of the soldiers looked at the other two and whispered something in Spanish. Muffled laughter stirred among them. "That's it, laugh, go ahead," Delbert said, "deny it if you want to. I ain't ashamed. It's happened to me every single galdamned time I ever tried fooling around with a woman . . . that's why I don't, not very often anyways." He grimaced as a sharp pain ran down the length of his throbbing jaw.

Sixty feet above them in the darkness, Maria's eyes moved from Delbert, to the saddlebags and the soldiers, then back to Prudence beside her. She whispered, "So, you killed him, eh? Cut his throat?"

"All right, I lied." Prudence hissed. "I wanted you to think I was tough. So what? It got us freed, didn't it?"

Maria looked down at Delbert and saw the canteen of water as he poured some of it onto the rag in his hand. She looked back at the soldiers, and at their horses standing beside them, also with canteens hanging from their saddle horns.

"So you boys are afraid I'll waylay ya and make out of here with the gold?" Delbert asked, pressing the rag to his cheek. "Well, don't worry . . . I ain't in no shape to pick those bags up, let alone ride off with them."

Maria whispered to Prudence without raising her eyes from the campsite, "So there it is, the gold they have been waiting for."

"Where?" Prudence craned for a better look, her voice

going a bit higher in excitement; but Maria caught her shoulder and pulled her back.

"Shh, they will hear you," Maria whispered. "We have to hurry before the others return." She rolled the small keg between them, turned onto her side, and judged the weight of it by hefting it up on her palm.

"How will you make a fuse?" Prudence asked, her voice a whisper now.

"Perhaps I will not need a fuse." Maria looked back down at the low flickering flames in the middle of the campsite, hefting the three-pound keg in her palm, judging the distance and the odds of tossing it down into the fire.

Prudence looked at the soldiers below, then over to Delbert close to the fire. "Oh, my. Poor ole Delbert," she whispered. But her eyes widened in fear as she added, "What if you miss?"

"Then we will have to make a run for it. I only have four rounds in the rifle and five in the pistol. Not nearly enough."

Prudence slumped and shook her head. "Then let's slip away and make a run for it, before it's too late—take our chances on finding water."

"No. Here we have only a small chance, but out there without water we have no chance at all." She rose onto her knees and hefted the small keg in both hands. "Go hold the animals. And get ready."

Chapter 15

The Ranger and Durant had stopped for a few moments, resting their tired horses alongside the thin trail when the sound of the explosion rolled in through the darkness. They both turned toward it at once, catching the flicker of light that flashed pale gold on the horizon. "Did you see that?" Durant asked, already reaching for his reins as he scrambled to his feet, dusting the seat of his trousers.

"Yep, I saw it. Let's go," the Ranger replied, rising at the same time.

Durant turned his horse beside the Ranger. "What do you make of it? Do you think it's Zell's men. Or the Parkers?"

"I don't know," the Ranger said. "But it looks like somebody just dealt out a wild card. We're going to play it." He gigged the white barb forward.

Earlier, less than two miles ahead, old man Dirkson had met up with Zell, Bowes, and the others. He'd come upon them riding slumped in his saddle, his shoulder wound broken open, bleeding down his chest. When Zell's men had dressed his wound and propped him against a rock, the old man drank from a canteen of tepid water and told them in a labored voice how the Parkers had shot him and taken the wagon and the women hostages.

He'd just finished telling Zell about the Ranger and the black man, and how he had escaped from them in the night, when the explosion rumbled and flashed upward from the distant canyon. The men swung toward the sound of it, then looked at Zell, Dirkson, and the shadowy riders gathered in the darkness behind them.

"That came from Diablo Canyon," Bowes said.

"Indeed it did," Zell replied, studying the darkness for a long moment after the echoes of the explosion had faded. "Who would have done such a thing, and why?" He turned to old man Dirkson. "What condition were the hostages in when the Parkers took them?"

"Same as before, Major. The dark-haired one was cocky as ever. The Vanderman woman was worn out from the road, but otherwise all right."

"I see . . ." Zell sat quiet for a second longer, Bowes beside him getting restless, keeping his eyes turned to the spot from where the explosion had come. When Zell spoke again, he said, "No Ranger loses a wounded prisoner—unless he wanted it to happen. If this Ranger is who I think he is, we may have our hands full."

He looked down at Dirkson, saw him struggle up to his feet with Bowes's help, and lean against his horse's side. "I'm going with you, Major. No need in discussing it."

Zell nodded, getting into his saddle, Bowes and the others following suit. One man stayed on the ground long enough to help Dirkson up onto his horse, then he turned and mounted. "We'll swing wide to the left and come in above the canyon," Zell said. "It will take us a few minutes longer, but we'll keep whoever's there pressed beneath us. Let's hope he and the Parkers have already come upon one another."

Bowes watched Zell raise an arm in the air and motion the

men forward. "Are you going to be able to keep up?" Bowes asked the old man, sidling near him as the others moved past them on the trail.

"Damned right I am. Just watch me." Dirkson's voice sounded weak, but determined. "I want to be there when we catch up to McCord and the Parker's. I owe them for this bullet in the chest."

"Then let's ride," Bowes said, and he reached out and slapped the old man's horse on its sweaty rump, sending it forward.

"Hurry!" Maria called over her shoulder in the darkness. The two women slid the last few feet down the steep slope through the dust and loose rock, until they both rolled forward into the campsite.

"My God," Prudence gasped, seeing what was left of Delbert splattered on the side of the canyon wall. The spot where the campfire had been was now nothing but a charred crater in the sandy ground. Tied within the shelter of a rock crevice, the soldiers' horses whinnied and shied, pulling at their reins. Dust still billowed in thick choking clouds. Maria jerked the reins free, then held them firm, settling the horses and leading them out. The horses resisted, still rearing slightly and sidestepping in fear. A few yards away, the bodies of the *federales* lay broken and twisted. One of them moaned, his bleeding hand clawing forward in the sand toward the dust-covered saddlebags.

"Sorry," Maria said, reaching down with her free hand and dragging the saddlebags back from his reach. He raised his torn face a few inches off the ground, turned his eyes up at her, pleading something under his breath, then his face dropped down into the dirt. Maria looked around and spotted a dust-covered canteen. She pulled the horse forward to it, snatched it up by its strap, and swung it over her shoulder. "Look for more water," she called out to Prudence. The horses had settled a bit, but they were still blowing and whinnying under their breath.

Prudence hurried, coughing in the thick dust, fanning her hands about her face. She found another canteen near one of the soldiers' bodies and slipped the strap over her shoulder. A pistol also lay in the dirt. She picked it up, shook it free of dust, and tried cocking the trigger. *Damn it!* It was jammed. But she shoved it down the front of her torn dress anyway.

"Help me with these, quickly," Maria called out to Prudence, dragging the saddlebags across the dirt.

"You bet," Prudence said, her eyes glowing at the prospect of so much gold in one spot at arm's length.

"Hold on to these." Maria handed her the reins to the horses. When Prudence took them and steadied herself against the horses bobbing their heads and resisting her, Maria hefted the saddlebags up with both hands and managed to sling them across one of the horse's back. She tightened the bags down with saddle ties, then moved around to Prudence and took the three sets of reins from her hand. "Mount up! We must get out of here!"

Prudence coughed and fanned, struggling up into a saddle while the horse shied a step sideways. Maria swung up onto the back of the horse with the saddlebags across its rump, tightly holding the reins to the third horse. "Do not stop until we have reached the flatland," she called out. "It will be daylight soon. Hurry, please! You must keep up with me!"

Eyeing the saddlebags full of gold as Maria spun the horse toward the trail, Prudence said, "Don't worry, sister. I'm right behind you!" Together they batted their heels to the horses' sides and shot out through the dust into the thinning night.

                    *   *   *

A thousand yards behind them, McCord called over to Leo
Parker as they raced their horses forward, "What could it
have been? It sounded like a cannon shot!"

"I don't know, damn it to hell! If Delbert screwed something up, I'll kill him!" He slapped the reins across his horse
as they plunged ahead in the darkness. Paschal, Juan
Verdere, and the *federales* rode hard, keeping up with them.
Before they'd heard the explosion, they had found the
wagon where the women had left it in the brush alongside
the trail.

Captain Gravia had ordered two men to unsaddle their
horses and hitch them to the wagon to pull it back to the
campsite. They had just started doing so as the captain and
the others reeled in their saddles, seeing the flash of light
from the direction of the campsite. "You two stay here and
finish!" Captain Gravia had called out. "The rest of you follow me!"

As the two men finished hitching the horses to the wagon
and had started to climb up into the wagon seat, they
stopped at the metallic sound of a hammer cocking, and
slowly turned toward it. One of them carefully placed a hand
on the pistol butt at his side, looking all around, searching
the darkness.

From within the darker shadows of mesquite brush, the
voice of Sergeant Baines said in a low, level tone, "Don't
even think about it. You're covered. Step down and raise
your hands."

But the two soldiers would have none of it. One yelled out
to the other, and both of them reached for their pistols. Two
shots from Baines's army Colt exploded in the darkness.
One soldier fell back against the side of the wagon and
crumpled to the ground; the other soldier sank straight down

on his knees, rocked sideways, then collapsed, pitching over sidelong into the dust.

"Damn foolish young troopers," Baines said, speaking down to the dead hollow eyes, leading his horse out of the dark shadow. "You needn't have done that. I only came for the wagon."

He tied his horse to the rear of the wagon, looked down again at the dead *federale* soldiers, and shook his head. He dragged the bodies away into the brush and picked up their caps. He dusted them against his leg and placed them on the mesquite bush marking the spot. Then he wiped his hands together and jumped into the wagon.

In a moment, the horses had pulled the wagon out of sight, higher up along a trail into the towering rocky land. At a point where the trail forked, Baines stopped the wagon and heard creaking leather and the sound of hoof against stone. Silently, he climbed down from the wooden seat and crouched beside the wagon, his army Colt drawn and cocked.

When the sound came again from the thinning darkness, Baines caught a shadowed glimpse of a horse moving toward him. "Don't shoot," cried the voice from atop the horse, the man's hands up chest high, his face blacked out beneath the wide hat brim. "I'm unarmed . . . coming in."

"Stop right there. Who are you?" Baines asked, searching the darkness behind the rider, but seeing nothing there. In the east, pale silver-gray light mantled the horizon. Morning was coming fast.

"I'm Willis Durant," the voice said. "I'm not one of Zell's men. Are you?"

Sergeant Baines considered the question for a second. Whoever this man was, he'd just taken a big chance, identifying himself that way. All right, Baines thought, maybe it was time to take a chance himself. The rider had stopped when Baines told him to. Now Baines glanced around one more time, crouched farther down, ready for anything, and replied, "Sergeant Baines, United States Army."

"So you're Baines," the voice said. "We heard about you from two soldiers—Elerby and Dubbs. We're sure glad it's you out here." Willis Durant mentioned the soldiers by name, hoping it would settle the sergeant.

Baines thought about it. The man had said we. Not *I*, but *we*. Twice. "Who's with you?" Baines asked, searching the shadows.

"I'm traveling with a Ranger. Don't get spooked, but he's behind you."

Baines jerked a glance over his shoulder, his finger ready on the trigger. He could see only black shadows among the rocks. "All right then, let's hear from you," Baines said.

"I'm back here, Sergeant Baines," the Ranger said, nothing but a quiet voice from somewhere in the darkness. "I'm Ranger Sam Burrack. We're after the same thing out here. I came to get the hostages. Let's all move easy, show who we are at the same time. Does that sound fair to you?"

Before Baines could reply, something small landed at his feet with a clinking metal sound; he looked down at the Ranger's badge and let out a breath. "Sounds fair enough," he said, running a moist hand across his damp forehead. He straightened and stepped out from the shadow of the wagon, his pistol still in his hand, but away from his side, pointed down.

"One of those hostages is Maria, the woman I've heard about—she rides with you, right?" Baines watched as the Ranger moved forward a step, out of the blackness, his big pistol pointed at the ground, his duster open and loose, the outline of his battered sombrero standing tall in the morning light.

"You're right, Baines," the Ranger said.

"I knew it," Baines said under his breath. He'd kept his thumb over the hammer of his Colt, but now he let it down, relaxing his grip. "I tried telling my lieutenant . . . couldn't make him understand. All he can see is what a feather it would be in his hat, saving Prudence Vanderman. I'm ready to do whatever it takes to bring down Zell. Tell me what you want done."

"I appreciate it," the Ranger said. "Sergeant, you've done a good job tracking these men. But you can go on back to your company now. I'll take it from here."

"Not on your life, Ranger. If it's all the same, I plan on riding this thing till it's over. Zell doesn't know it, but he and I have some old unfinished business. We go all the way back to Peach Orchard." Baines reached down, picked up the Ranger's badge, and handed it back to him.

"I see. So it's more than just the hostages to you." The Ranger took the badge, wiping it on his duster and pinning it on his chest. He offered a thin smile. "I figured you'd want to finish this out for your own reasons." He nodded at Willias Durant as Durant stepped forward, leading his horse. "The man behind you is my prisoner. He broke from jail, and now he's after the Parker Brothers for killing his family."

Baines turned and looked Willis Durant up and down.

"Looks like we're all three in the same game for different reasons," the Ranger said. As he spoke, he reached behind his back, took out Tackett's pistol, and after checking it, he pitched it to Durant.

Durant caught the pistol, looking surprised. "But you said—"

The Ranger cut him off. "I know what I said before. I

changed my mind. We're close to the heart of this thing now. You want the gun or not?"

Durant spread a tight smile. He checked the pistol himself, rolled the cylinder down his forearm, tested the action, then shoved it down in his belt. "Ready when you are, Ranger."

"It'll be full daylight soon," the Ranger said. "I figure the first ones we'll deal with will be Zell and his bunch, come sun up. Any problem with that, Durant?"

"No." Durant shook his head slowly. "I'll back whatever play you make . . . until it comes to the Parkers. Fair enough?"

The Ranger nodded, looking back and forth between them. "Let's move then," he said, "and get this thing settled."

Chapter 16

Not knowing how far ahead of them McCord and the Parker brothers had gotten in the darkness, Paschal sidled his horse close to Juan Verdere, took Verdere's horse by its bridle, and checked both their horses down. "Let go! What are you doing?" Verdere wrestled with the reins, but Paschal held the bridle firm.

"It is a terrible mistake to go into the canyon with those men," Paschal said. "Stay back with me. I trust none of them."

"But what about our pay? What about Gravia and his men?"

"We wait and see," Paschal said in a firm tone. "Too many things are going wrong. Let them straighten this out . . . then we will see where we stand."

Juan Verdere sat his horse still, the two of them seeing the last of Gravia's men follow the others into the black mouth of the canyon. "Yes, Paschal, I think you are right. There is more at stake now than us getting our money."

At the campsite, Payton Parker looked around wild-eyed, yanking his reins back hard, his horse lowering almost down on its haunches. "Jesus H. Christ!" he shouted to Leo and McCord. "Look at this place!" Behind them, the sound of Gravia and his men thundered in along the canyon trail.

Charred and smoldering bits of wood from the exploded campfire still glowed among the rocks surrounding them.

"Those women? They did this?" McCord looked around at the grizzly sight of Delbert's body plastered to the canyon wall. "My God, look at Delbert!" Gravia came in ten yards behind them, raising a hand, cautioning his four remaining men.

"To hell with Delbert," Payton Parker said, stepping down from his saddle, McCord and Leo doing the same. "Where's the damn gold?"

"They blowed up the gold?" Leo looked bewildered. "Why would anybody blow up sacks of gold?"

"Hell, no! They didn't blow it up! They took it, you squirrel-eyed idiot!" Payton raged. "No wonder Pa always said he wished he'd pitched you in the wood stove!"

"I never heard Pa say—"

"Just shut up, Leo!" Payton rubbed his hands on his face and shook his head in thought.

"What now?" McCord stepped close to Payton Parker, nodding toward Gravia and his four men. They'd dismounted and came walking forward now, their weapons up and ready. "This is going to take some tall explaining," McCord whispered.

"I ain't explaining a damn thing," Payton said, reaching out and grabbing Leo by his forearm, pulling him around to face the *federales*. "Keep close now . . . pay attention here."

"I am through with you and your games, *gringo*," Marsos Gravia said. "Where is the gold, you fool?"

"As you can see, it ain't here right at the moment." Payton Parker spread a hand, making a sweeping gesture. "You tell me where it's at."

Gravia thought about the wagon load of ammunition back along the trail, wondering if this was all some sort of trick.

"We have the ammunition. You better pray nothing has happened to it when we get back there."

That's not my problem right now, Capi-tan, that's yours," Payton said. "My problem is that we brought you the ammunition, just like we said we would—now where's our pay? We ain't leaving without some gold."

"Jesus, Payton," McCord whispered, "don't push it. We're outnumbered here."

"We brought you the gold," Gravia said to Parker, his voice getting more and more testy. "I do not know what craziness has caused you to lose it." Marsos Gravia looked around in the darkness, past his four men, and back along the empty trail behind them. "Where is Juan Verdere and the Frenchman?" He sounded suspicious.

"Beats the blue hell out of me," Payton said. "Don't suppose this is all their doing?"

"No." Gravia turned and faced him, his hand tight around his big pistol. "I think it is all you . . . you and these two *gringo* fools with you. So what do we do now?"

Payton gave a wild, crazy grin. "Boys, there ain't but one thing left to do now."

Marsos Gravia saw the pistol coming up out of Payton Parker's holster, Payton's horse jumping to the side as if knowing what was happening. Gravia cocked his own pistol on the upswing, moving fast. But not fast enough. Payton's first shot hit him in the forehead, spraying blood and brain matter on the four men behind him as Gravia slammed backward into them. The men responded, but not from a good position, as their dead leader was in their way.

McCord and Leo fired fast and kept on firing, most of their rounds hitting the young soldiers before they could make a stand. Payton Parker yelled and fired, moving forward, taking a graze across his forearm, but not slowing down until his pistol was empty and the soldiers were down in the dirt. Smoke rose and hovered above them.

In a second, it was over. In the ringing silence that followed, while Payton Parker reloaded his pistol, one of the soldiers looked up from the dirt and moaned, stretching a hand toward Payton's boot. *"Merced, señor . . . por favor, merced!"*

Payton chuckled, jerking his boot back away from the soldier's bloody hand. "What's that, huh? What? Oh . . . well, to hell with you and your mama too." He spun the pistol on his finger, caught it, cocked it, and fired one round straight down into the soldier's face.

"You didn't have to act like that, Payton," Leo said. "He was only asking for mercy—he was dying anyway."

Payton shrugged and grinned at Leo. "So? Then what harm did I do?"

They stood looking at the dead on the ground. "Well, boys," Payton said after a moment's pause, "we might not do everything just right, but when it comes down to it, damned if we ain't the awfulest killers there ever was." He laughed and spit, running a hand across his mouth.

"This wasn't right, us having to do this, Payton," Leo said. "I don't see nothing funny about it."

"Well . . . that's how you are, brother. You say the same thing every damn time we kill somebody. I swear, I don't know what's wrong with you." Payton shook his head, walking back to his horse.

McCord let out a breath, shoved his pistol into his holster, and said, "So, it looks like we're screwed to the wall on this deal, huh?"

"Naw, we just got to get that wagon and take it on in somewhere. The *federales* will still want it. We'll just have to be careful how we handle it."

"Let's get back to the wagon then, before something else goes wrong," McCord said. He'd already made up his mind—once he got what was coming to him—he was through with Payton Parker. He never wanted either one of these sons-a-bitches near him again. He started to step up into his stirrup, but Payton caught his arm and stopped him.

"Hold on, McCord, ain't you learned nothing from all this? That wagon ain't back there where we left it."

"What are you saying?" McCord turned to him.

"Can't you figure it out?" Payton grinned. "What do you suppose happened to Verdere and that stinking Paschal?"

McCord shrugged, looking confused. He had no idea.

"They cut out on us. They went back and got that wagon." Payton tapped a finger to his head. "Use your brain a little. They seen what was abut to happen. They've got that wagon and gone with it."

"Then let's get after them." McCord sounded impatient. "They can't be far off."

"In the dark?" Payton chuckled. "You never want to hunt a Frenchman in the dark. We move toward San Carlos. That's where they're headed. There's no place else they can go. We'll pick up the wagon tracks on the flatland and ease right up on them in broad daylight."

"Yeah, and what if you're wrong? What if the wagon's still setting back there right now?"

"Have I been wrong yet?" Payton said with his hand resting on the pistol in his holster, a strange tight smile on his face.

McCord just looked at him. "No, so far you've done one hell of a job."

Above them on the edge of the canyon wall, Juan Verdere and Paschal had found the horse and the mule the women had left behind. They'd heard the gunfire and crept forward, peering down into darkness. With no firelight in the camp-site below, all they saw was the flash of the final round as Payton Parker put a bullet in the young soldier's face.

"See?" Paschal whispered as they stepped back from the edge and to their horses. "With men like these, you must always count on their treachery. They are animals."

"*Sí,*" Juan Verdere said. "But now we are on the spot. When the *federales* come and see what happened to the soldiers, we are the ones they will hang."

"Perhaps not . . . not if we get the gold and take it back to them and explain what has happened out here. There is only one place for the women to go. They are headed to San Carlos."

The two women pushed the horses hard and fast, too fast for the rocky flatland in the darkness. As they descended onto a long stretch of flatland, they'd heard the sound of pistol fire in the distance behind them. They slowed for only a second, looking back into the murky dawn. Prudence asked, "Who could they be shooting at?"

"I don't know, but they will soon be on our trail." She batted her heels to the horse's sides. They pushed the horses even harder.

In the gray hour before first light, Maria saw the glow of a lamp from the distant town of San Carlos and made for it, Prudence following close behind until her horse slowed all at once and whinnied, taking off sideways, walking wrong on its right front hoof. Maria had heard the animal cry out; she circled wide and came back as Prudence got down from her saddle, cursing under her breath.

"I don't know what happened to this thing," Prudence said. She bent and struggled to raise the horse's hoof, the horse whinnying, resisting her. "Stand still, damn it!"

"Drop the saddle and come on," Maria said, jumping down and leading her horse over to Prudence. "The horse is spent."

Without waiting for Prudence to make a move, Maria reached under the horse's belly, loosened the cinch, and shoved the saddle from its back. She stripped its bit and bridle and dropped them. The horse turned, blowing its breath, and limped off sideways.

"Are you going to shoot it?" Prudence asked, running a hand across her dusty, matted hair.

"No. We do not have time, and they will hear the shot. Get on my horse. We'll have to ride double."

Prudence stepped up, eyeing the saddlebags across the horse's rump, and looked down at Maria. "Here, take these," Maria said, handing her the reins. She saw a strange look come into Prudence's eyes for just a second as Prudence seemed to brace herself in the saddle. *Was she ready to bolt away?* Maria quickly got up behind her on the saddle and reached around and took the reins. Prudence settled, as if having given something a second thought and resolved it.

"Are you ready?" Maria asked. Yet even as she spoke, she kicked the horse forward. "We cannot make it across the sand flats and to the town before daylight. We must hide this gold somewhere out here."

"You're out of your mind," Prudence shouted over her shoulder above the hoofbeats of the horse. "We've got our hands on it—you want to take a chance on losing it?"

"The gold means nothing! It is only extra weight. We must hide it. It might become a bargaining chip to save our lives." The horse pounded on beneath them toward San Carlos on the distant horizon. A mile farther ahead, Maria reined the horse down near a dry wash running alongside them. In the east, the first sliver of golden sunlight pierced the purple sky. "Hold the horse," Maria said, loosening the ties on the saddlebags before jumping down.

"Where will you hide it?" Prudence looked all around.

"In the wash, beneath the cottonwood stump." Maria pointed out the jagged dead stump, and hefted the saddle-bags off the horse and onto her shoulder, bowing under the weight.

"You'll need help," Prudence said.

"No . . . stay with the horse."

She struggled with the saddlebags and hurried over the edge of the dry wash, sliding down the few feet to where the brittle dead roots of the cottonwood stump reached out of the sandy soil like the talons of some otherworld beast. She scratched and scraped, her breath heaving in her chest. As she dug out a place in the soil behind the stump roots, she looked all around the bottom of the dry wash, catching sight of a flat rock standing three feet high back against the op-posite bank.

"How is it going?" Prudence shouted.

"I'm almost done," Maria called back to her. She hurried, shoving some of the dirt back beneath the stump roots, then smoothed her hand back and forth across the dirt. Glancing up the wash and making sure Prudence didn't see her, Maria hefted the saddlebags once more, moved across the bed of the dry wash, and dropped them beside the rock.

Maria pulled the flat rock out from the wall, put the sad-dlebags behind it and shoved the rock into place. She smoothed her footprints out with her hand as she backed across the wash.

"Are you sure this is a good idea?" Prudence asked as Maria came from the edge of the dry wash, dusting off her hands.

"I am sure of it." She gazed toward the tiny glow of light

from the town of San Carlos. "We must rest our horse as much as possible. Get down. We will walk a mile and ride a mile from here in."

"But it didn't take the men over three hours last night. Why will it take us so long?"

"Once the sun gets overhead, you will understand how a three-hour ride turns into an all-day ordeal. The heat on the sand flats can kill you as surely as a bullet," Maria said.

"It can't be that far," Prudence said, stepping down. "We can see it from here."

"This land will fool you. It may look close, but we will be lucky to reach it by the time the noon sun is boiling overhead. We cannot afford to spend this horse."

They moved forward on foot, pulling the tired horse by its reins, both of them heaving difficulty on the rocky, sandy terrain.

Chapter 17

The Ranger and Sergeant Baines lay behind the cover of rock at the edge of Diablo Canyon, the morning silence surrounding them like an open grave. Beneath them on the floor of the canyon, the new campfire glowed in the gray dawn amid the bodies of the dead *federales*. Forty yards across, on the other side of the canyon, Durant lay in hiding, Tackett's pistol in his belt, which was filled with ammunition.

On his way across the canyon, Willis Durant had stopped long enough to gather brush and some scraps of dried wood. He'd built the campfire and moved on, taking note of the soldiers' bodies on the ground and the body of Delbert, so smeared against the rock wall that it appeared he had been put there by some sort of large stamping device.

Now the Ranger, Baines the soldier, and Willis Durant the prisoner waited as sunlight spread in long stripes, like ribbons of gold spun out from the far edge of morning. Baines craned his neck, looked out across the canyon, and said to the Ranger as he settled back beside him, "You seem awfully sure you can trust that man Durant."

"Yep, I trust him." The Ranger looked up from running his bandanna along the barrel of his big Swiss rifle. "I knew him years ago. He got off on the wrong foot for a while, got in some trouble, and paid his time. He settled down after that. Then this thing happened to his family. His only interest now is the Parker brothers, plain and simple. He knows his odds at getting them are a lot better without me breathing down his neck. Willis Durant hasn't come this far to stop now, not until he's played out his string." The Ranger smiled. "He gave his word."

Baines started to say something about the word of a prisoner, but then he thought better of it, and gazed out across Diablo Canyon once more. He said, "I was no more than a young civilian the first time I ever saw this place. After hearing its name so much all my life, I found myself a bit disappointed when I first laid eyes on it."

"Yeah, it's not much more than a hole in the earth," the Ranger said.

"Aye, but aptly named, nevertheless. Devil's Canyon . . ." Baines said, his words trailing, thinking about it. He looked at the fire and the dead bodies scattered about on the canyon floor. "Those poor bastards. Devil's Canyon sure had its claws around them last night, I'd say."

The Ranger just looked at him, shook out the bandanna, and tied it back around his neck. He laid the big rifle across his lap and rested a gloved hand on it. Suddenly, he cocked his head. "I heard something," he said, his voice going quiet.

"Zell." Baines whispered the name under his breath as if uttering a curse.

"They've seen the wagon and the glow of the fire . . . they'll have to come check it out," the Ranger whispered in reply. "He's probably sending a man forward. Get ready."

Baines stared along the thin trail into the canyon, sitting as still as stone until he caught the faintest sound of a horse picking its way slowly below them. They waited, the Ranger casting a quick glance across to where he knew Willis Durant lay in hiding. When he looked back at Sergeant Baines, Baines held up two fingers without turning to him.

The Ranger nodded, then watched as Baines slipped a long knife from his boot well, lowered himself down onto his belly, and crawled away along the rocky edge.

Back at the mouth of the canyon, Zell, Bowes, and old man Dirkson sat atop their horses, gazing at the empty wagon and past it into the shadows of Diablo Canyon as sunlight lit slantwise across its eastern edge. Zell pressed a hand to the wound in his chest. Behind them, the other men waited, some of them wounded and sitting stooped in their saddles. His men needed water and food. The horses needed sustenance as well—even the strongest of the lot stood staggering in place, their manes hanging limp and wet against their necks.

When nearly a full hour had passed since his two best scouts rode forward, Zell looked back at his men, then to Bowes and the old man beside him. "They're dead," Zell whispered. "I can feel it."

Old man Dirkson spat, his mouth dry and cottony. "The Parkers, you suppose?"

"No. It's the Ranger you told us about. The Parkers couldn't get the drop on them this way—with no gunshots and no noise of any kind."

"Say the word, Major." Liam Bowes spoke in a lowered voice. "I'll take some men around the edge of the canyon and flush him out." He watched Zell struggle with the pain in his chest, his hand clasped against it for a second.

Then Zell collected himself. "No. This Ranger will not allow himself to be flushed out. He has our ammunition stashed somewhere, and he's not alone. This is his way of sending us a message. He's saying whatever we want, we'll have to take it from him here and now."

"There were three sets of hoofprints back at the wagon tracks," old man Dirkson said. "One will be the black feller. Who do you figure the other ones are?"

"Haven't the slightest idea," Zell said. "And it doesn't matter." He looked back once more at his men, then to Liam Bowes. "The Ranger has no intention of us getting our hands on the ammunition. He'll destroy it first."

"But it's just three men, Major," Dirkson said. "Surely to God we can handle three men."

"It's not the numbers that count this time. It's their position," Zell said. "Three good men in Diablo Canyon are worth twenty men on level ground, especially when those three men hold the ammunition—the object of the hunt. The Ranger knows that. He's no fool."

"We don't know for sure he'll destroy the ammunition, Major," Dirkson said.

"I know it. It's the very thing I would do in his situation. He knows we don't have the women . . . knows we have nothing to bargain with. He's ready to fight it out with us right here, so he can go on to more important business. He wants the two women—wants them bad." Zell winced, thinking about it, looking all around at the rough land. "Damn Diablo Canyon. And damn the Parkers. They've caused all of this. We never had a problem until those two joined our cause."

Their cause . . . Liam Bowes had been wondering about their cause lately . . . and the more men he watched die, the more he wondered. He shook the thought from his mind, let out a breath, then straightened himself in his saddle and adjusted his hat brim down tight on his head. "We're going to lose some more men here, sir. We're down to thirteen, counting ourselves."

"I'm fully aware of our situation, Mr. Bowes," Zell said,

again clutching his hand to his chest wound. He coughed in pain under his breath. "But this fight can't be avoided."

Bowes looked him up and down, seeing how the wound had taken a terrible toll on him. "Then if you'll excuse me, sir, I'll prepare the men to make a charge."

"Yes, you do that, Mr. Bowes. Prepare three squads; one on either side of the canyon, and one straight up the middle. We'll make a fast sweep and see what we're dealing with."

"Lord, Major," old man Dirkson said. "Can't we figure out something else? I was counting on this to be my last go-round. Planned on getting me a place with a porch on it."

"So did I, old man," Zell said. "You were right about one thing. This might well be your last go-round. Our losses will be strong."

"Damn it all." Old man Dirkson drew a rifle from his saddle scabbard, checked it, and laid it across his lap. "I'd hate dying in Mexico. You know what I mean?"

"I know what you mean." Zell looked at him. "Feel free to pick which squad you'll ride in with. Mr. Bowes and I will lead the assault up the middle, of course."

"Then that's all the picking I need." The old man grinned and dropped his horse back a step and waited as Liam Bowes prepared the men to attack.

Back among the group, Liam Bowes explained what Zell was asking them to do. As he spoke, he noticed they cast guarded glances back and forth to one another. Finally, the young southerner Chance Edwards took a step forward and said in a quiet tone, "This is not the best thing to do, is it, Bowes?"

Bowes looked away, then back to him. "No, it's not. Major Zell is hurt bad—maybe dying. He's losing the ability to make sound decisions."

"I knew it," Chance said in a tone of remorse. "Nobody takes a bullet that deep in the chest and lives through it."

Bowes continued. "As far as I'm concerned, this campaign stopped the moment we found this empty wagon. If the Ranger is sending any message at all, he's telling us that from here on in, we'll be fighting for no good reason. I agree with the major—we'll never see the ammunition unless it explodes in our faces."

"Then for God sakes, Bowes," Chance said, "relieve the man of his command and take over."

The others nodded in agreement.

"I can't do that, gentlemen. I swore an oath of allegiance to Zell long before most of you joined us. As long as he can give an order, I'll obey it. Any of you who want out, don't tell me about it. Just don't show up when we hit the canyon. Nobody will hold it against you."

"This is crazy, Bowes," Chance Edwards said. "Don't put us in a spot like this. We've all been good soldiers."

"Yes, you have, no one can say otherwise. But this is the best I can offer you," Bowes replied. He looked around at the haggard, dusty faces, then raised his voice slightly. "Squads, separate—prepare to attack."

As the men stepped up into their saddles, drew their rifles, and checked them, they looked to Chance Edwards. "What do you think, Chance?" one of them asked. "Are you going through with this?"

"Yeah, I'll give it one last try. After that, who knows? It all depends on who's left standing once the smoke settles." He pulled his horse sidelong, the four-man squad behind him doing the same.

A mile ahead of them, halfway up the canyon wall above the burned-out campsite, the Ranger sat in a crevice of rock with the big Swiss rifle laid out in front of him. He'd taken the tripod from his saddlebag and attached it to the rifle barrel. From here, no one on the canyon floor could get to him. He could hold here for as long as his bullets lasted. He looked at the bullets on the rock beside him. Six for a reload, and six in the rifle. It would have to do.

On his right, near the edge of the canyon, Willis Durant lay prone behind a stand of mesquite, down in a shallow pit he'd scraped out for himself. From there, Durant could fire across the flatland or down into the canyon itself. On the Ranger's left, Sergeant Baines had taken a position behind a deadfall of dried cottonwood. His field of fire was the same as Durant's, but beneath him, back into the crevice where the three *federales* had reined their horses earlier. The ammunition now sat stacked out of sight and ready for use.

When the Ranger heard the first sound of the thundering hooves coming from the far end of the canyon, he crouched behind the butt of the big rifle, worked it back forth on the swivel, scanning through the scope, and waited. The first shot he heard came from Durant's side of the canyon, then from Baines as two of Zell's small squads rode forward, sweeping the edges of the canyon.

Below him on the canyon floor, the Ranger sighted the first rider coming into range. He was a long ways back, but just where the Ranger wanted to make his shot. The big rifle exploded, slamming into the Ranger's shoulder and sending the man and his horse upward as the he flew from his saddle with the reins still tight in his hand. The horse rolled sidelong into Zell, sending Zell into a swerve as the Ranger leveled his rifle scope on him. The shot went past Zell, missing him by an inch, taking down another horse and rider in a spray of dust and loose rock.

"Lord God!" Old man Dirkson yelled, seeing the damage caused by the big rifle. He also swerved as Zell sidled into him. Bowes, beside him, dropped his horse back, coming down from his saddle as his horse reared. He scrambled behind the cover of a broken boulder on the canyon floor. The Ranger had recocked and he fired another round, sending a rider backward from his saddle and into the rider behind him. From either side of the canyon's edge, Durant and Baines fired in rapid succession.

As soon as the Ranger's shot hit the rider and sent him out of his saddle, Bowes bolted from his cover. He sprang to the middle of the canyon floor to where Zell wobbled in his saddle, his horse spinning, spooked and with no direction. While the Ranger recocked, Bowes snatched Zell from his saddle and hurried with him back to the cover of rock.

"He ain't even letting us within range!" Dirkson shouted, grabbing Zell, pulling him down beside him. Bowes fell to the ground, snatching up his rifle, rolling onto his side, and firing a round up toward the Ranger's rifle smoke.

"Of course he's not," Bowes said. "Would you if you were in his position?" Bowes shot fell short by twenty yards, the bullet whining off a large rock.

"Damn it, I reckon not." Old man Dirkson jerked down on his hat brim and checked his pistol.

"Didn't you see he had the big rifle with him?" Bowes shouted at Dirkson above the sound of rifle fire erupting from both sides of the canyon. "You were with him! Didn't you see it?"

"No! Hell, no! I didn't see it! All I saw was an ordinary repeater rifle in his saddle boot. How was I to know about this?"

"We're pinned here," Bowes called out. He turned to Zell beside him, whose breath labored, the wound in his chest reopened and bleeding heavily. "Major, can you hear me?"

Zell swung his eyes to Bowes, and Bowes saw the trickle

of blood dribble from his lips. "Attack," Zell said in a shallow voice. Bowes and old man Dirkson gave each other a guarded glance and lay still behind the broken boulder.

The Ranger held his fire, hearing the sound of shots from either side of the canyon edge still going on. He knew from the start that Durant and Baines would take a hard hit, each of them outnumbered four to one if Zell did what Baines said he would, and split his force into three squads. Now it looked like Baines had been right.

Up on the right edge, Durant looked out from his position, and through the tangle of mesquite, he saw two men lying dead in the sand beneath a drifting rise of dust. Beyond them, the other two men had felled their horses on the flatland and had taken cover behind them. They fired on him, but their shots were only kicking up sand.

Okay . . . I don't have all day to fool with these two. Durant scooted out of his shallow scraping still beneath the cover of brush. With pistol in hand, he belly-crawled backward a few feet until he reached the crest of a slight drop in the silty soil. Once behind it, looking along its sandy edge, he saw it snake off and turn back toward the two men. *Good enough . . .* He wasn't going to wait around here and let the Parker brothers get away. He would circle around these men, taking his chances. He had nothing to lose.

Along the left edge of the canyon, Baines had fired his rifle empty. One of the four men went down, and two others had raced away, emptying the rifles around him, sand stinging his face as they rode off out of sight. One remained now, down behind a rock twenty feet from him. Baines checked his pistol and waited. When the man rose, firing his rifle, Baines remained still, tense, waiting for just the right second, counting each shot of the rifle.

When the last shot was fired, and Baines jumped up and

aimed, he caught a glimpse of the man disappearing out of sight, running away from him. Only when Baines dropped back down to the ground did he feel the warm blood spreading over his chest. Only then did he feel the deep, searing pain high up in his ribs . . . the numbness closing in around it.

Uh-uh, not yet . . . Now that the pain had come upon him, he didn't want it to leave. Once the pain was gone, he knew he would be gone with it. *No! Not now!* He shook his head clear, and turned to crawl over the edge of the canyon wall. He wasn't about to die . . . not yet, not until his job was finished.

From his cover behind the broken rock, Bowes saw the big sergeant coming down the eastern wall of the canyon. He managed to rise and fire a shot, then drop back down in time to hear the Ranger's bullet whistle overhead. Bowes's rifle shot kicked up a spray of dust near Baines's boot as he dove across the sand beyond the campfire, crawling around into the crevice where the crates and kegs of ammunition lay in the shade.

Damn the blood. Sergeant Baines staggered to his feet in the cover of the rock crevice. His hand was wet and slick when he raised it from his chest to look at it. *What's a little blood more or less,* he said to himself, stripping the yellow cavalry bandanna from his neck, shaking the dust from it, and pressing it against the wound. He needed only a few more minutes here—surely any merciful, right-thinking God would give him that.

Baines staggered to the small open keg of gunpowder, hefted it up under his arm, and spread a stream of it from the pile of ammunition to the outer edge of the crevice where dust-filled, rays of slanted sunlight seemed to dance there among the dead. "I'm done in, Ranger," he called up toward the Ranger's position. "You and the black man get out of here."

The Ranger heard him and called down. "We won't leave you, Baines. How bad are you hit?"

"Take my word for it"—Baines's voice faltered—"I won't be leaving here."

"No. I'm coming down, Baines. Cover me if you can."

Bowes and the old man heard them calling back and forth to one another and got ready to fire. Zell had managed to collect himself and pulled himself up beside Bowes. They listened intently.

"Don't try it, Ranger," Sergeant Baines called out. "My fight will end here. You go on—get the women."

The Ranger called down, hearing Baines's voice grow weaker, more shallow, "Are you sure about this, Sergeant?"

"Go!" Baines called out. Then he collapsed against the rock crevice wall, the keg under his arm, spilling powder onto his boots.

From their cover, Bowes and old man Dirkson glanced out toward the campfire. When they jerked back, Bowes looked past Zell and said to the old man, "See those bodies?"

"Yeah, *federales,*" the old man replied. "And that looks like Delbert dripping down the wall."

"Think the Parkers managed to make the switch? Got the gold and got out with it?" Bowes stared across Zell and into Dirkson's eyes.

Old man Dirkson shot a glance up along both edges of the canyon, hearing no more gunfire. "That's possible, I reckon."

"What do you think? We could back out of here and get on their trail."

Old man Dirkson let out a breath, raising his eyebrows. "It beats sitting here."

They both looked at Zell. "Major," Bowes asked, "what do you think? We might have one more play for the gold."

Zell managed to chuckle low in his shattered chest. He wheezed and said in a broken voice, "The only thing worse . . . than me dying here without the gold . . . is for me to die with it at my fingertips."

"Then we stay, sir," Bowes said with finality.

Old man Dirkson slumped, dejected, against the rock.

"No," Zell said just above a whisper. "You two go on . . . find the gold. I'll hold this position."

"No, sir, we'll all three—"

"That is an order, Mr. Bowes." Zell's voice found some strength. He sat up straighter against the rock. He reached over and clasped Bowes' arm. "We've had . . . a bold run at it. They never beat the Border Dogs."

"But, Major, sir—"

"He's right," old man Dirkson cut in. "He's told you what he wants. Don't deny him, for God sakes!"

"Listen to . . . the old man," Zell said, a faint smile moving across his lips. "Get out of here, Mr. Bowes."

Bowes swallowed back the dryness in his throat, looked at Dirkson and nodded.

Above the canyon on the right, Durant stood up with a bloody knife hanging from his hand. At his feet, the man's boot quivered for a second, then went slack in the sand. The horse had stood up on its own in a drift of dust, and Durant caught its reins and settled it. He looked across the ground at the other body twenty yards away, the horse beside it now up from the ground, still shaking out its mane and poking its muzzle down near the blood on the man's lifeless chest. Dust drifted in long sheets.

He led the horse over, picked up the reins to the other

horse, and led them both to the edge of the canyon. Looking down at its far end, Durant saw the two men move back from behind the cover of rock, out of pistol range. There was a rifle on one of the horses behind him, but Durant saw no point in wasting bullets he would need later. Besides, those two men were backing out. They'd had enough. He looked across the canyon and saw the wake of dust left by two horses moving in a hurry, believing it to be all that was left of Zell's men.

Looking toward the other end of the canyon, Durant saw the Ranger coming up from his perch among the rocks, the big rifle held out to his side, headed to where Durant knew the white barb and the other horse stood waiting. On the canyon floor beneath the Ranger, Durant saw Baines leaning against the edge of the crevice. He saw the dark blood spreading on Baines's chest and the small open keg of powder under his arm.

Baines looked up, saw Durant, and motioned him away. Durant hesitated for a second, and Baines raised his arm and shooed him away once more. *One hard old soldier . . .* This time Durant raised his arm in reply, waved it once above his head, and stepped back from the edge. Well, Durant thought, he'd done what he promised the Ranger he'd do. Now he had business of his own to attend to. He stepped up into the saddle, swung the horse around and kicked it out across the flatlands, leading his spare horse by its reins. The Ranger would just have to understand.

Bowes and old man Dirkson had made it back forty yards along the canyon floor when they came upon their milling horses, having moved back as soon as they'd shed themselves of their riders in the hail of rifle fire. Once atop their horses, they rode fast along the rocky narrowing trail until they came upon Chance Edwards and the two riders with him, who had just rounded down along the east edge of the canyon. "There you are, you sons a bitches," Dirkson yelled out to them. His hand went to the pistol at his waist as he and Bowes reined their horses down. "For two cents I'd blow your damn heads off!"

"Stand down, old man!" Bowes shouted, seeing that Chance Edwards and the other two were ready for whatever Dirkson had to offer. "These men did their job. They swept their side of the canyon."

"That's right, we did," Chance Edwards said, glaring at the old man. "It ain't like we had the numbers we use to, you know. I lost a good man up their to that damn Yankee soldier." He spat and looked around. "Where's the major? He didn't make it?"

"No, he's back there," Bowes said. He gestured a nod back into Diablo Canyon. "He sent us out. Did any of you happen to see what's lying in there?"

"I got a look over the edge," Chance Edwards said. He nodded and added, "Saw three dead *federales*. You thinking what I'm thinking? Maybe the Parkers pulled it off?"

"It's a strong possibility," Bowes replied, "strong enough that I'd like to catch them and find out." He gave Chance Edwards a questioning look.

Chance offered a tight smile, looked around at the other two, and asked, "Odell? Tommy? What do y'all think? Feel like checking out the Parkers? See if we can come up with some gold out of all this?"

"My arm's shot plumb to hell," Tommy Neville said, "but it's only my left one." He took a deep breath, let it out, and straightened in his saddle. "Yeah, I say let's get to it."

"Me too," said Odell Sweeny. "Gold or no gold, I'd like

to put both my thumbs in Payton Parker's eyes and see what squirts out. We owe that much to the major."

"So, there you have it," Chance said, turning back to Liam Bowes with a tired smile on his face. "Looks like the Border Dogs ain't finished yet. You're in charge, Mr. Bowes . . . tell us what you want done."

As they turned their horses back along the trail leading up on the west side of Diablo Canyon, old man Dirkson sidled up near Chance Edwards. "I shouldn't have said what I said awhile ago. Reckon I was just testy about all that's gone wrong. Hope you've taken no offense."

"I did," Chance said, "but I'm over it. We're all back together, same as always. You can call one offense a slip of the tongue." He looked hard at Dirkson. "But call the next one suicide, old man."

They moved single file in the heat of the morning sun, each man going over his weaponry, checking pistols, rifles, cleaning and reloading them as they rode on up toward the flatlands and on into the wavering heat toward the town of San Carlos.

Zell had seen the Ranger move up along the canyon wall and out of sight. That had been a few minutes ago; and now Zell gathered his failing strength and looked down in his lap at his personal belongings. An old photograph of the woman he'd married back before the great civil conflict lay in his bloodstained hand. He glanced at a faded letter she'd written him years ago, telling him of a son he would never see.

After a moment of silence, Zell put the picture and the letter back inside his bloody shirt, looked up at the swirling sunlight and out across the sky. Then he rose to his feet, brushed dust from his shoulder, and stepped forward, calling out in a resolved tone, "Major Martin Zell, sir. Whoever you are . . . I trust you've waited a long time for this occasion?"

Sergeant Baines didn't answer, not from this far away. He knew his breath would fail him. Instead, he stepped from the edge of the crevice and offered a weary salute. Zell moved forward, a bloody hand on the pistol butt in his waist belt. Instead of returning Baines's salute, Zell waved it away with a weak hand. His voice faltered as he said, "I take it you're the one . . . who has hounded me ever since my raid on the train?"

"Aye, Major, that would be me . . . Baines, sir. First Sergeant Baines, United States Army."

"I see." Zell looked around at the dead *federales,* gathering his breath. "Then I was mistaken to think a young lieutenant could have maneuvered so well. I should have known."

Baines only nodded, the keg of powder under his arm causing him to bow slightly, the dark circle of blood on his chest widening, a trickle of it running down his thick forearm.

Zell looked at the small powder keg, the line of powder leading back and around into the rock crevice. "And the ammunition? I take it you have it in there?" Before Baines could answer, Zell added, "What a pity. Had my men only known . . ." His words trailed off. Then he added, "But of course, you never would have given it up."

"You knew it was there, Major," Baines said. After a moment's pause he added, "And you knew I wouldn't give it up."

"Perhaps," Zell said. "They were good men, my Border Dogs. Hard fighters every last one." He looked at the low flames in the short licking fire. "What about the Ranger? What was his stake? The women?"

"It doesn't matter," Baines said. He staggered a step, but caught himself.

"No . . . it doesn't." Zell drew his pistol from his waist. "What about you, Sergeant? How far back do we go?"

"All the way back to Peach Orchard," Baines said. "You owe me for two kid brothers . . . and a lot of good troopers." He righted his footing a bit and stared at Zell through weak yet determined eyes.

"A pity about your brothers, Sergeant." Zell sounded sincere. He cocked the hammer on his pistol, pointing it downward. Blood ran from his open wound, across the top of his hand, dripping from the pistol barrel into the dirt. "We all lost someone . . ." His free hand went to his chest, pain racking him for a second, until he gathered himself. "Now we shall both die as all good soldiers must." He staggered, raising the cocked pistol toward Baines across the low flames. "Ready, Sergeant?"

"Aye, sir." Baines struggled, raising the keg from under his arm. He stepped forward to heave it into the flames, but then faltered and rocked back a step, the keg coming down onto the ground beside him.

Zell clenched a bloody hand to his chest wound, uncocked the pistol, and shoved it back down into his waist belt. "Here, Sergeant," he said, everything about him starting to tilt and swirl as he moved in halting steps around the low licking fire, "let me give you a hand. . . ."

On the western edge of the canyon, moving farther away, the old man said to Chance Edwards and the others behind him, "Don't look back. It's the way the major wanted it." Ahead of him, Liam Bowes rode on without so much as a glance backward when the sound of the explosion trembled the ground beneath their horses' hooves. In the distance, a wall of dust stood high, drifting on the horizon.

In front of that wake of dust, the Ranger gave the white barb his boot heels, moving fast now. He had also heard the explosion, and looked back for only a second, long enough to see the five riders move up from the canyon trail.

A mile to the left of the Ranger and a thousand yards behind him, Willis Durant saw the Ranger's dust as he rode farther away from him, around a long stretch of low buttes that would end near the town of San Carlos.

PART 4

PART 4

Chapter 18

The sun stood high overhead, scorching hot, torturing the desert floor. Heat wavered in an angry swirl by the time the women reached the outskirts of San Carlos. The horse trudged behind Maria as she pulled it by its reins. Prudence staggered along beside her, having torn away a long section of her dress and fashioned it about her head for protection from the scalding white rays of sunlight. Their last canteen of water lay empty a mile back in the sand.

"We can stop for a moment, can't we? We're this close. We've made it, haven't we?" Prudence asked, her voice sounding thick and parched. She swayed to one side but caught herself, righting her steps. Ahead of them, San Carlos stood as a black streak of wavering mass in an otherwise stark and endless furnace of sand, mesquite, cactus, and broken boulders that lay strewn about as if tossed there by the careless hand of the Devil.

"*Sí* . . . we will make it." Maria gasped a lungful of dry hot air, struggling on, her legs determined yet drained, her trousers burning against her skin, her shirt dried to her back and stained white from her sweat. "But we cannot stop here. The desert is full of the bones . . . of those who stopped for one last rest." Her words were coming out jumbled, she knew. She shook her head and motioned Prudence forward. "Can't stop—"

"Turn the horse loose," Prudence said, seeing Maria struggle with the worn-out animal. "He's slowing us down."

"No. He stays with us." She stared ahead into the shimmering heat.

"But . . . he's not going to make it." Even as Prudence spoke, she felt herself sway over against the horse, the animal wavering itself until Maria jerked on the reins and righted it forward.

With her free hand, Maria caught Prudence's arm without stopping and pulled her forward. "He is going to make it. Soon he will smell the water . . . it will draw him in."

Prudence whispered under her breath, a mindless, failing curse that seemed to cost her what little strength she had left. She seemed to grow smaller with each faltering step, as if sinking step after step down into the burning sand. Then, after a moment, the white heat above her no longer pressed her down. Indeed, the heat seemed to draw her upward now, weightless and free, above the desert floor and into a cooling breeze somewhere high up, in a softer body of air.

"*Santa Madre,*" Maria said.

Prudence heard Maria's voice, but it seemed to come from a long ways off, as if through a thin, watery veil. From some distant place, Prudence seemed to argue with her. She'd asked Maria earlier why they couldn't find shade among a strip of low buttes or in a dry wash along the trail. Maria had said they could not stop because the Parkers would catch up to them. Well . . . maybe that was so, Prudence thought, catching glimpses of the sandy ground drifting past her face, below her now as she moved forward without effort. But now look at them.

Maria pressed on, the horse struggling harder now with Prudence lying across its back. Yard by precious yard, she willed herself toward the wobbling black thread of San Carlos, seeing it grow and take shape. When she felt the staggering horse grow less heavy behind her, she glanced back and saw its muzzle had lifted slightly into the hot breeze. Behind them, their tracks snaked backward into the heat as if having led them out of some fiery netherworld that lay consumed and dead·in the vanished distance.

When a few blank minutes had passed, she found the horse had taken the lead somehow, its legs trembling and unsure, yet finding within itself some instinct stronger than its exhausted muscle and sinew. Maria staggered along behind it now, her hand entwined in its tail, the horse blowing its breath deep and steady. She heard a voice call out in Spanish through the unstable floating world before her, and as she tried calling back to the voice, she realized her hand had slipped free from the horse's tail, and her face lay hot against the sand. The horse moved on without her.

"Get her up. We must hurry," a voice said in Spanish. Maria heard them talking and wanted to tell them never mind about her, that she was all right, that they should see to her companion and the horse, that she herself would just lie here for a second and catch her breath and be along in a moment or two . . .

No . . . ! Maria found the strength to shake her head clear and look up into the eyes of the old woman and the young boy bending down to her. She struggled up onto an elbow and assisted herself as they raised her to her feet. The young boy tried to cradle her back into his arms, to carry her, but she told him in Spanish that she could walk. Maria looped an arm across his shoulders and staggered forward with him, seeing the old woman move ahead of them and take up the horse's reins as the animal moved forward step after halted step to the adobe wall of the town well.

"San Carlos . . ." Maria whispered the words to herself.

"*Sí,* San Carlos," the young boy said. *"Facil, facil."* He held her arm around his narrow shoulders and led her to the sparse shade of an ancient sourwood tree whose branches stretched above its own black shadows on the sandy dirt street. "For now you must rest, *sí?*"

Once beneath the tree, Maria looked up, then all around, seeing the old woman slide Prudence down off the horse's back and into the arms of an old man who came forward out of a crumbling adobe. The horse stopped and stood spraddle-legged, shoving its muzzle deep into the run-off trough from the well.

"Sí, facil," Maria said in a hollow voice, feeling her mind start to clear itself. "I will rest for now . . ." A hand came from somewhere in the heat with a dripping water gourd. She raised it, cupping it with both hands, and poured it back onto her forehead, catching part of it with her open mouth as it washed down her dusty face. She lowered it for a second, spat out a short stream, then sipped a mouthful and looked back into the sweltering inferno.

They rested in the shelter of the small adobe. Maria had poured water over her head, took off her clothes, and then poured water down her body. She stood naked except for the thin serape she held around herself and looked down at where Prudence lay on a pallet of straw. "You must try to gain your strength. We are still in danger."

"How long—?" Prudence looked around in confusion at the adobe walls, and at a lank and scraggly chicken that pecked on the dirt floor near her. "How long have we been here?" Prudence looked down at herself, seeing her dress had been removed, and that she was naked and glistening with beads of water where Maria had squeezed out a large sponge and washed her down, cooling her skin.

"Not long," Maria said, "perhaps an hour. Can you sit up? If you can, you must. The Parkers will be coming soon."

Prudence sat up, addled for a second as she shook her head, and ran a hand through her damp hair. "What . . . what if they don't make it across the desert? We almost didn't."

"They will make it. We were down to only one horse, and very little water. They will be better prepared. Believe me, they will be here, even if they wait out the hottest part of the day and come in this evening." As she spoke, she reached down among Prudence's clothing on the dirt floor, picked up the straight razor in its leather case, looked at it, and pitched in onto the straw pallet beside her.

"Then, can't we also wait and make a run for it tonight? I mean, if it's that much easier at night . . ." Prudence rose farther from the pallet, having to take it slow, her head swimming a bit.

"And go where?" Maria lowered the thin serape to her waist and tied it, her bare breasts still beaded with water, mixed with fresh perspiration. She'd had the young boy bring the rifle from her saddle scabbard, and now she reached down and picked it up from the dirt floor and checked it.

"Anywhere," Prudence said, her voice sounding a little stronger, "somewhere where there's law—protection, soldiers or something."

"There are only a few small towns like this for the next

two hundred miles . . . and they can offer us no protection. The boy said there is a *federale* camp not far from here. But they will be looking for us also once they hear what happened. Don't forget, it is their gold we took last night." She jacked a round into the rifle chamber and cradled it in her arms. With her free hand she gathered her wet hair back. "We will make a stand here and fight."

"Fight them?" Prudence staggered to her feet and stepped naked off the straw pallet onto the dirt floor. "What chance do we have against three armed gunmen, not to mention the others who were with them!"

"We *will* fight them. We have no other choice."

"Like hell we don't have a choice. We've got their gold! You said yourself last night, it might become our bargaining chip. Let's deal our way out of this."

"You cannot trust men like these. This Payton Parker is an animal, and a stupid animal at that." Maria moved over to her own clothes lying on the floor, where she'd stepped out of them. "Of course we will use the gold to bargain our way out of this. But we will have to fight them to even be in that position. If they overtake us, they will try to torture us—beat the gold out of us. From here on, we must deal only from a position of strength."

Prudence thought about it, picking up her tattered dress and slipping it on. "Will these people help us? I mean, they have so far."

"No. We cannot ask them to risk their lives for us. I have spoken to the old woman and the boy. No one here even has a gun except for the old man. He has an old flintlock rifle. It would only get him killed. There is a Frenchman and a cantina owner who both carry pistols, but the boy said no one has seen either of them since last night. They rode out with some *gringos,* the boy said." Maria stared at Prudence, pulling up her trousers and hitching them around her waist, the rifle still cradled in her arm. "What does that tell you about them?"

"Jesus." Prudence looked out through the open door of the adobe, then back to Maria. "Just our luck. They're connected to the Parkers."

"*Sí*, that is what I think." Maria handed Prudence the rifle. Prudence looked at it, turning it in her hands as Maria slipped into her shirt, leaving most of it unbuttoned, shoving the tails down into her trousers. "I think we still have a long day ahead of us." She took the rifle back from Prudence. "Come on, let's take a look at our options." Together they stepped out into the heat of the afternoon.

Three miles out on the sand flats, Payton Parker sat slumped against the dirt bank of a narrow dry wash, a thin slice of shade mantling him and his brother Leo. They watched, squinting against the sun's glare as McCord walked his horse toward them, followed by the Frenchman, Paschal. "Now this ought to be real interesting," Payton said to Leo. He spat and ran a dusty hand across his mouth.

Leo stood up, dusting the seat of his trousers as the two men walked up, but Payton stayed seated in the shadow of the dry wash bank, looking up from beneath his hat brim, first at McCord, then at Paschal. "I thought I smelt something rotten on the wind," Payton Parker said. "How long have you been flanking us, Frenchy?"

Paschal bristled at the insult, then calmed himself and said, "Ever since first light, off and on." He squatted down with a deep grunt and let his tired horse's reins drape over his thick knee. "If you had been paying attention, you would have seen what Juan and I have seen behind you. You have riders behind you, you know."

"Well . . ." Payton Parker sneered a bit. "I reckon you've seen more than us—scooting back and forth all over this desert. Looking for some stray Injun to eat, more than likely. Where is ole Juan? I'd kinda like to see him, maybe shoot a couple pounds of fat off his greasy arse."

"Who's behind us?" McCord asked, shooting Payton Parker a sharp glance.

"A black man to the west"—Paschal pointed a grimy gloved hand in that direction—"and back there, a lawman, a Ranger maybe, or else a bounty hunter."

"A black fellow?" Leo Parker looked spooked. He rubbed his sweaty throat and stared off into the wavering sand flats.

"That is right, a black man, leading a spare horse." Paschal squinted, eyeing Leo Parker, seeing it had frightened him. "There was much shooting from Diablo Canyon, then a loud explosion."

"We heard all that, Frenchy," Payton Parker said. "Tell us something we don't know." He looked away along the dry wash and chuckled under his breath, shaking his head.

"You heard him Payton," Leo said, "a *black* man, it's bound to be Durant—"

"Shut up, Leo. Don't soil yourself out here. Frenchy smells bad enough." Payton looked back at Paschal. "Now look what you've done. Leo's been seeing a big Negro after him in his sleep for the past year. What about this lawman? What did he look like? A tall sombrero? Riding a white horse, had one black-circled eye?"

Before Paschal could answer, McCord cut in, asking Leo, "Did you just say, Durant? *Willis* Durant?"

"Yeah, he said Durant," Payton Parker answered before Leo got the chance. "What of it?"

"I *know* Willis Durant, from years back. He's one mean

son of a bitch. Why's he following us?" McCord looked concerned.

"It's none of your business why he's following us," Payton Parker said. "All you need to do is back my play here. Once we get the gold from those women, you can look that big Africano up and ask him, since you know him and all." He turned back to Paschal. "Now what about this lawman?"

"Yes, he wears a gray sombrero," Paschal said, "but I could see no circle around his eye."

"Not *his* eye, you slug-sucking idiot . . . his horse's." Payton Parker shook his head in disgust.

"I did not see his horse's eyes either. But if you stay here much longer, you will see for yourself. He is not that far behind you."

"Oh . . ." Payton nodded, standing and slapping dust from his trousers. "So, out of the goodness of your heart you decided you best come warn us, huh?"

"No. I came because we must get together on this thing for any one of us to ever come out ahead. Juan Verdere has gone on to the *federale* camp. He is telling them what happened and bringing them to San Carlos." Paschal waited, seeing Payton Parker work it over in his mind. "The women lost one of their horses. I saw where they were down to one set of hoofprints. If they have the gold with them, we will find them lying dead somewhere in the sand."

"But that ain't what you think, is it, Frenchy? You figure they've hid it out here somewhere? Figure we'd never find it on our own?" Payton Parker winked. "Boy, that's some powerful figuring for a Frenchman in this kind of heat."

"That is what I think, yes," Paschal said, ignoring Payton's insults. "I think you do not know this desert the way I do. You need my help. Tell me if I am mistaken, eh?" He puffed out his broad chest with a confident look on his face.

"I bet this's gonna hurt your feelings, Frenchy," Payton said, raising his pistol from his holster. "But you are more wrong at this minute than you've ever been in your whole frog-licking life."

Paschal's eyes opened wide as Payton Parker cocked his pistol and pointed toward his large stomach.

"Hold it, Payton!" McCord called out, seeing Payton had every intention of pulling the trigger. "What if he's right? What if they did bury the gold out here somewhere? He does know this place better than us!"

"Aw hell, McCord, I've never known a woman in my life smart enough to dig a hole, let alone put something in it and cover it back up." He shook his head and leveled the cocked pistol on Paschal's stomach. "Naw, I really do want to shoot some holes in this tub of guts."

"Come on now, Payton," Leo said, "them women were smart enough to get away . . . to take the gold, blow ole Delbert into dust. Maybe McCord's right. What have we got to lose, taking Paschal with us? You can't just keep shooting everybody!"

"Well, now, who says I can't?" Payton spread a dark smile at Leo, a muscle twitching in his tight jaw. "Just 'cause you're my brother, Leo, don't think you get a right to start telling me—"

McCord cut in. "If the women have the gold with them, you can always kill this man after we get it. For God sakes, Payton, let's do this thing right and get it done. We've got Willis Durant, a lawman, and Lord knows how many of Zell's men on our trail. Don't start shooting—not out here!"

Payton made a sucking sound between his teeth, let out a breath, and settled himself. He wiped his free hand across his face. "All right then, Frenchy. I won't shoot you right now. But you get on that horse and keep your stinking arse downwind from me. If them women have that gold with them, I'll have to kill ya . . . you can understand that, can't you?"

Paschal just stared at him, lifted his horse's reins, and stepped up into the saddle. "I only understand that we need to hurry. After we get the gold, we will see which of us ends up dead." .

Chapter 19

The Ranger saw the back of the lone horse above the edge of the dry wash. It stood in the narrow wash, scraping its hoof at the outcropping of spindly roots from the cotton-wood stump. At first the Ranger thought it might be Willis Durant's horse; but when he'd gotten down from his saddle amid the hoofprints alongside the trail, he saw the smaller footprints and realized these were made by a woman. Could it be Maria? He bent down with his reins in his hand and touched his gloved fingers to the footprints in the sand, as if touching them alone would tell him something.

When he arose, the sound of a low groan came from the dry wash. With his saddle rifle in his hand, the Ranger moved closer to the wash, leading his white barb behind him. The sound came again, and he crouched on the edge of the dry wash and looked down into it, the lone horse only tossing its head up at him for a glance, then lowering once more to its business of scraping at the cottonwood roots. Across the wash, the Ranger saw the Mexican lying against the flat rock on the other bank.

"Por favor, señor," Juan Verdere said in a weak voice, one hand against the deep gash across his stomach. His other hand, bloody and gritty with red-stained sand, reached up

toward the Ranger, then fell to the ground. "Please, *señor . . .* water, *por favor.*"

"Un momento." The Ranger stood up and looked all around before leading the white barb down into the wash and lifting the canteen from his saddle horn. He looked more closely at the bleeding wound on the Mexican's stomach as he handed the canteen down to him. "Who did this to you?" the Ranger asked, glancing all around once more as Juan Verdere raised the canteen with a trembling hand and drank from it.

Verdere struggled up a bit, a pained look on his face, adjusting his back against the rock. "My *compañero . . .* he did this to me." Verdere's voice was strained, weak and fading. Beneath him, blood had spread like a dark shadow on the floor of the dry wash. "He betrayed me."

"Some partner," the Ranger said, bending down beside him now.

"Can you believe it, *señor?*" Juan Verdere struggled to speak. "For years . . . we have been together . . . now he does this to me."

"You're tied in with the men I'm tracking, aren't you?" The Ranger reached out and raised Verdere's hand from the bleeding wound as he spoke.

"Sí . . . if you are after the Parkers." Verdere looked into the Ranger's eyes. "They caused all of this." He gestured around him with his bloody hand.

"Where are the women?"

"I do not know . . . San Carlos perhaps, if the Parkers have not killed them already." Verdere lifted the canteen from his bloody chest and took another drink.

"How much farther is it to San Carlos?" the Ranger asked.

"In this heat . . . three hours." Verdere's eyes moved up

across the white barb, then back to the Ranger. "On a good horse, perhaps less."

"He's a strong horse . . . I cooled him out a little." The Ranger lifted the canteen from Verdere's hand and stood up.

"A little? Then he and you will die out there," Juan Verdere said.

"What about you? Are you going to make it?"

Juan Verdere shook his head slowly. "No . . . I am stabbed deep. I will die here."

"Then I've got to get going," the Ranger said.

"He would not . . . have done this, my *compañero* . . . if it were not for the gold."

"I understand," the Ranger said. "What's his name?"

"Paschal . . . he is a Frenchman. A big man. He will be with the Parkers . . . I think."

"What makes you think it?" The Ranger reached back as he spoke and looped the canteen on his saddle horn.

"Because . . . if I were him . . . that is where I would be." Verdere offered a tired, thin smile. "Gold does strange things to a man, eh?"

"Yep." The Ranger led the white barb over beside the other horse, lifted its reins and pulled it away from its scrapings. The horse looked fresh, streaked white with dried sweat but rested, having been cooling in the thin shade of the dry wash while its owner lay dying. He led it over to Verdere and looked down at him.

"Take him with you." Verdere raised a bloody hand toward the horse as if to stroke the animal one last time.

"Are you sure?"

"Better he goes with you." He nodded, then lowered his head, fresh blood rising on his stomach above the black coating of dried blood clinging to his shirt.

"*Gracias,*" the Ranger said in a lowered tone. He turned,

took the canteen down again, and pitched it over beside Juan
Verdere. Then he stepped up onto Verdere's horse and, leading the white barb, moved off along the dry wash to a step-
up onto the sand flats. Giving the horse his boots heels, he
rode off into the eddies of heat in the afternoon sun.

A mile across the scorched desert floor, Willis Durant had
moved up onto the low buttes for a quick look around at
whomever might be moving across the sand flats on the
other side. He found water for his two horses in a shallow
rock basin. Loosening their cinches, he stood them at the
basin's edge. While the horses drew water and blew themselves out, Durant topped off his single canteen and lay
down flat, looking back across the wavering endless stretch
of sand, rock, and scrub brush through a set of field lenses
he'd found in the saddlebags of his spare horse.

Durant spotted a low rise of dust and adjusted his lens on
it. Ahead of the rise, he saw the Ranger, riding at a strong
steady pace on another horse now, leading the white barb
behind him. Less than a mile behind the Ranger, he saw
what was left of Zell's men, and they too were coming on
hard, two of them splitting off ahead of the others, coming
his way. *Damn it!*

He saw what they were doing. They'd spotted the
Ranger's dust and sent two men out in front, over to the
buttes. These two men could make it if they pushed hard
enough. They could get around the Ranger and cut him off
as he looped wide to the right and headed on to San Carlos.
Durant lowered the field lens from his face and rubbed the
sun glare from his eyes. *Well . . . so what?* There was nothing he could do. The Ranger would have to find out for himself.

He stood up, moved back to the horses, and led them back

from the basin of water. *Damn it!* Drawing the horse's
cinches, he looked back over his shoulder and out past the
edge of the butte. Every minute he spent here was a minute
more in favor of the Parkers getting away. He caught a remembered glimpse of Payton Parker's laughing face, caught
a stronger, more painful memory of his wife and son lying
dead in the evening sunlight, a circle of buzzards high in the
air above them.

Don't do this. Don't think about it . . .

The heat pressed down on him, and he wiped a hand
across his face and shook his head, trying to clear the terrible scene from his mind. He saw himself standing there in
his yard, heard his own scream and the sound of his pistol as
he drew it and fired, sending one of the big grizzly birds
away in a batting of wings and a flurry of dust. He was too
close to the Parkers now—he couldn't let anything get in his
way. Yet . . . *damn it all!*

Durant snatched the rifle from the scabbard on the spare
horse and gathered both of the horses' reins and walked
them over to the edge of the butte. He levered a round up
into the rifle chamber, and without raising the rifle to his
shoulder, fired and levered, firing two more shots. *All right,*
he thought, *three shots should tell the Ranger something
was up.* Behind him, the horses had shied against their reins
at the sound of the rifle; they pulled back from the drift of
powder smoke on the air.

"That's all you get, Ranger," Durant whispered to himself. He stood watching for a moment without the field lens,
seeing the tiny dot at the head of the rising dust—the
Ranger—and seeing the dust of the two men coming on farther behind the Ranger, veering over, farther away from the
others. Durant turned, settled the horses, stepped up into the

stirrups of one of them, and heeled away, leading the other, his rifle still in his hand.

Down on the sand flats, the Ranger heard the three shots and brought his horses down in a spray of sand. He turned in a circle, gazing first toward the stretch of low buttes where the shots came from, then all around him. *Three shots in a row? Warning shots?* Sun glare kept him from seeing anything atop the buttes, but following them back he caught sight of the rising dust. Squinting, he saw the two riders swinging wide of him to his left, a long ways off yet working hard at getting past him on the sand flats. *Zell's men?* He'd bet they were.

His eyes went back to where he'd heard the shots. There was nothing more there, only a white glow of sunlight glistening like melting iron. *All right, those shots were definitely a signal,* he thought. He saw the two men moving around him now. That had to have been Willis Durant up there, telling him to watch his flank. Ahead of him, the Ranger saw where the trail moved off to his left toward the thin black line in the distance, shrouded by the shimmering waves of heat. That would be San Carlos. Those two men were circling him, trying to cut him off as he made the turn toward town.

The Ranger heeled the horse he was riding forward, the white barb jumping out with them, rested now without the Ranger's weight on its back. As he rode, he drew the white barb up alongside him, reached under the bedroll behind the saddle, and unfastened the leather case. Laying the rifle case across his lap, he took out the big Swiss rifle and fitted it together, one piece at a time—the barrel, the butt, the front stock, and last the brass-trimmed scope.

By the time he'd snapped the scope into place and reached over to hang the rifle case on the barb's saddle horn, the two riders had pushed nearer to the stretch of buttes, stopping near the turn in the trail toward town. They'd seen him fall in behind them now, his dust moving closer and closer until it had to dawn on them that he had taken up position. Now they had to make a plan, having already seen what the big rifle could do.

The Ranger took out his two last cartridges and put them into the rifle, then drew his horses down when he saw the riders' dust had stopped at the end of the stretch of buttes. He spun the horse in a quick circle, stirring up a flurry of dust, then walked them upwind a few yards. Stepping down, he looked back and saw the rest of Zell's men behind him, closing hard. He didn't have much time.

At the far end of the buttes, Tommy Neville and Odell Sweeny swung down from their horses and pulled them in behind the cover of a rock spill. "Damn it to hell," Tommy Neville said, rubbing his wounded arm. "We had him cold! Now he knows we're waiting on him." His eyes searched upward and back along the edge of the buttes. "Who was it up there warning him?"

"I don't know," Odell Sweeny said, coming down beside him, looking back toward the Ranger's swirl of dust. "But sit tight. He's got that big rifle. Bowes and the others will hit him from behind. He can't sit there forever. He's dead now, he just don't know it yet."

"Yeah, I hear ya," Tommy Neville said. "If they push him to us, we've got him. He can't shoot through rock. If he sits there, Bowes and them will eat him up." He pushed up his hat brim and relaxed. "It's about time something went our way."

"Kind of like a chess game right now," Odell Sweeny

said, grinning as he squinted into the wavering heat. "I'll just get our canteens and we'll—"

His voice stopped short at the sound of a pistol cocking behind them. "Real easy, boys," Willis Durant said, sitting atop his horse, the other horse standing beside him. "Empty your hands before you turn around."

"Says who?" Odell spoke without turning, his rifle tight in his right hand, a round already in the chamber. "I don't drop my gun for nobody." As he spoke, Sweeny's left hand inched to his belly, to where the .45 Colt sat high in his waist belt.

"You do now," Durant said, "one way or another."

"It's . . . it's that colored man!" Tommy Neville cried out, having caught a sidelong glimpse of Durant. "Listen, buddy," Tommy Neville added, talking fast while Sweeny's hand made its way around to the butt of the pistol, "it makes no sense, you dropping us this way. The old man said you was that Ranger's prisoner—said he wished he could have said something to you, let you know that we ain't that much different, you and us."

"That's right," Odell Sweeny joined in, his face still turned away from Durant, his hand ready to make a move with the pistol. "You're on the wrong side here. We get to town, we've got gold waiting to be had. Think about it, boy. What's that Ranger got for ya? Not much, I bet."

Durant took note of the man's hand moving out of sight, his left shoulder braced, ready to make a move. "Some things money can't buy," Durant said, his thumb lying tight across the cocked pistol hammer. "Now either swing 'em or drop 'em—I don't give a damn which."

From his position on the open sand flats, the Ranger had taken stock of his situation and had already made his decision when he heard the three pistol shots ring out almost as one from the far end of the buttes. With just two cartridges left, his only choice had been to take out two of the riders coming up behind him, then ride out hard and take his chances on the two men ahead of him when he got there. But those pistol shots had caught his attention. They could change everything for him.

The Ranger stayed kneeling, listening to the shots echo across the stretch of buttes, the big rifle cradled across his right arm, ready to bring it into play. He waited for a long, tense second until he heard three rifle shots in a row, coming from the same direction as the pistol fire. There it was, Willis Durant again, telling him something. The Ranger stood up, dusted his knee, and swung up onto his saddle, this time mounting the white barb, giving the other horse a breather.

He rode fast, stretching the barb out beneath him, the horse wanting to run even in the heat of the afternoon. When the Ranger reached the rock spill at the end of the low buttes, he expected to find Willis Durant. But Durant hadn't waited around for him to cross the mile or more of sand flats. Instead, the Ranger saw the two dead men, one lying across the rock where he'd fallen, the other stretched out on the ground, a pistol lying only inches from his hand. Their horses had been stripped of their saddles and bridles, and they milled about a few yards away, grazing on a single clump of pale, dry grass.

The Ranger got down from his saddle long enough to break down his big rifle, put it away, and walk over to the two bodies. He turned the one on the ground over with the toe of his boot and saw the large bullet hole in the man's forehead. The other body, lying back over the rock, stared through dead and hollow eyes into the blazing sun. A bullet hole in the chest had spread dark and thick, and blood ran down over the rock into the sand beneath it. One man shot in the head, the other man in the chest. That accounted for two of the pistol shots. But what about the third shot he'd heard?

In the distance, Durant's dust stood high and drifting. The Ranger looked at it for a second, then turned and looked back across the flats at what remained of Zell's men; three figures came into view, thin wavering ghosts from out of the stark white sunlight. Stepping back up into the saddle, he noticed the dark spot of blood on the sand less than fifteen feet away from the bodies. He moved his horses over to it.

That was the third shot—Willis Durant had been hit. The Ranger moved his horses along slowly, looking down at the ground at the next spot of blood ten feet away, then at another ten or more feet beyond it. However bad he'd been hit, the Ranger knew it made no difference to Willis Durant. He wouldn't stop until he either found the Parkers or fell dead from his saddle. "Come on, Blackeye," the Ranger said, heeling the white barb forward, leading the other horse by its reins. "See if we can find this man before he bleeds to death on us."

On the other side of the long stretch of buttes, a ten-man *federale* patrol had heard the shots and turned toward them, taking the same trail upward that Willis Durant had taken to the basin of water. From atop the low butte, the leader of the patrol looked down at the three riders moving across the sand flats below. The patrol had been sent out earlier when Captain Marsos Gravia and his men had not returned from last night's meeting with the men who had brought the ammunition.

Now the leader, a young captain who had not wanted to

head up the search party to begin with, turned to the others and said in Spanish, "These men come from the direction of Diablo Canyon. Surround them. We will take them back to camp for questioning. It will be better than spending the day out in this wretched heat."

A sergeant beside him said, "If these men are Border Dogs, part of the ones we have been buying rifles from, they will be hard to surround, and even harder to take in for questioning if they do not want to come."

"These are three *gringos,* Sergeant Gomez," the young captain said without facing him. "Are you saying ten of us are no match for these Border Dogs as you call them?"

"I am saying it would be wise of us to see what they have to say without making threats or giving them orders. They are some bold *hombres* . . . these men."

"Nonsense." The young captain sawed his reins back, turning his horse to the trail that twisted down the side of the low butte. "Follow me. I am not wasting time out here. They are going back with us. We will find out what has become of Marsos and his men."

On the sand flats, old man Dirkson was the first to see the patrol working their way down toward them. "Mr. Bowes, on our left. Looks like *federales.*"

Bowes, Dirkson, and Chance Edwards reined their horses down together and stopped them on the bare open land. When the young captain led the men at a fast trot across the sand, Chance Edwards cocked his head a bit and said to Dirkson beside him, "This fellow looks like something has him upset." He chuckled under his breath and added, "You still happen to have that scattergun under your bedroll?"

"Yeah, why?" Old man Dirkson spoke to Edwards, but kept his eyes pinned on the *federale* captain.

"Just something telling me this ole boy ain't going say

one word we'll want to hear." Chance Edwards let his hand drift to the pistol sitting high in his waist belt. He drummed his fingers idly on the pistol butt. "What about it, old man? Mind if I hang on to that scattergun awhile? I won't get it dirty."

"Uh-uh, I might want to hang on to it myself," the old man said, seeing both the haughty expression on the captain's face as he came forward, and the men behind him starting to spread out, riding abreast now and checking their horses down at a distance of fifty feet.

Liam Bowes sat silent, but moved his horse a step forward of Chance Edwards and the old man.

"Saludos, buenas tardes," old man Dirkson called out, raising his left hand, waving. Leaning back in his saddle a bit, his right hand went back behind him and slid the sawed-off ten-gauge shotgun from beneath his bedroll. "He's one pissed-off–looking peckerwood," the old man added under his breath, letting the shotgun hang down alongside his leg.

The butt of the shotgun had been cut off and shaped into a pistol grip, its double barrel no more than a foot long. His thumb went across the hammers and cocked them back. Hearing the shotgun cock, Liam Bowes said to the other two in a lowered voice, "Mark time, gentlemen, let's hear what the man has to say."

"They're spreading out, Mr. Bowes," old man Dirkson said, smiling at the *federales* as he whispered his words.

"I see it," Bowes said, his hand lying on the rifle across his lap. The *federales* moved closer, spreading into a semicircle, coming slow and steady. But at thirty feet, before they could get the three men surrounded, Liam Bowes called out to the young captain, "Hold your men right there."

They stopped, and the captain leaned over to the sergeant beside him for a second and spoke to him Spanish. Then the sergeant moved his horse a few feet closer and said, shrugging, "My captain only wants us to talk, *señor.*"

"That's close enough for talk." Liam Bowes moved his horse around sidelong to the *federales*. "What's on his mind?"

"Get ready," old man Dirkson whispered to Chance Edwards.

"I been ready," Chance Edwards replied. "What're you loaded with?"

"Nail heads, both barrels," the old man said without looking at him. "I'll take the honcho out, first thing, then work my way to the left."

"Got ya," Chance Edwards said, smiling to the *federales* as he spoke. "I've got the right half covered." He chuckled. "Not a lot of shade out here . . . gonna get awfully hot."

"Not as hot as where we're headed," old man Dirkson whispered, chuckling as well. Then his expression turned serious as he spat and ran a hand across his mouth.

"We come in search of a missing patrol," the *federale* sergeant said. "They have been missing since last night. Perhaps you have seen them?"

"Yes, we saw them," Liam Bowes replied.

"Oh . . ." The man turned and looked at the captain as if not expecting such an answer. The captain nodded him forward, and the man heeled his horse a step closer. "Tell me, *señor,* do you ride with Major Zell? Have you come with the ammunition?"

"Major Zell is dead, sir," Bowes said. "Had you been watching toward Devil's Canyon earlier you would have seen the ammunition gone up in smoke. We're all that's left of the Border Dogs."

"I see." The man gave Bowes a curious glance, then turned and spoke again with the captain in Spanish. When he turned back to Bowes, he looked apologetic. "It is too bad about that ammunition. My captain asks, if you are all that remains of the Border Dogs, what good will you be to us in the future?" He offered a cautious smile and shrugged again. "It is only a question, of course."

"Of course," Bowes said. "Does your captain not speak English, or is he just talking through you to annoy me?"

The sergeant squinted and smiled. His voice lowered a bit. "*Sí*, I think maybe he does it to annoy you. He is very upset about Captain Marsos and his men being missing. He does not like searching for them in this heat."

"I see." Bowes turned to old man Dirkson and said, "Tell this sergeant to inform his captain that I see no way in hell we'll be any good to him in the future." Bowes paused and moved his horse a bit to one side. "And tell him that the captain and the patrol he is searching for are lying back in Devil's Canyon, feeding the buzzards by now."

Old man Dirkson cackled, raising the shotgun into sight and propping it up on his thigh. "Mind if I tell him in German?"

"That is not necessary. He hears you," the sergeant said, raising a cautious hand, moving his horse back a few steps. "I think he wants you three to accompany us back to our camp. He has many questions, and it is far too hot to talk out here, no?" He fanned his grimy face and once more tried to offer a smile, this time the smile looking thin and troubled.

Old man Dirkson looked at Chance Edwards, winked and grinned, the shotgun tight in his hand. "Damned if this ain't the only way to go."

"Captain," Liam Bowes called out, all the polish and manner now gone from his voice. He bypassed the sergeant and stared across the thirty feet of wavering sand into the young captain's face. "I want you to take a good long look at us. Do we look like the kind of men who're going to do one damn thing just because you ask us to?"

Rifle bolts clicked, pistol hammers cocked, horses shied and blew and grumbled under their breath. The young captain flashed a look back and forth among his men. He sat erect and raised a hand, either to keep them back or send them forward. No one would ever know which, as the shotgun exploded in old man Dirkson's hand and a belch of smoke and a spray of sharp hot nail heads lifted the captain, his horse, and the horse and rider nearest him, sending them backward, twisting sidelong in a bloody red mist.

Chapter 20

The Ranger had heard the gun battle rage in the distance behind him, less than three miles back, he figured. But he pressed on without so much as a glance over his shoulder. He had followed Willis Durant's trail around the end of the buttes and on toward San Carlos, the town coming into better view now as long evening shadows stretched across the flats.

In the west the sun stood low, red and watery, its fiery mantle streaking the dome of the sky. He'd found no more blood on Durant's trail since the first few spots back near the bodies. Either Durant had stopped the flow, or else he'd bled himself out. Judging the steadiness of the hoofprints in the sand, Durant was holding his own. But for how long?

At an island of rock on his left where the hoofprints led into a spate of black shadows, the Ranger heard the low nicker of a horse. He moved closer and was about to call out Durant's name when Durant's voice spoke from within the darkness. "Stay back, Ranger. I don't need your help."

"How bad is it?" The Ranger did not stop, but he slowed the horses and let the white barb step sideways, the other horse shying a bit at the sound of Durant's voice.

"I'll do," Durant said. "Needed to cool these horses out for a second."

"All right," the Ranger said. Durant's voice sounded strong enough, but the Ranger still had his doubts. "I'll just come take a look at it."

A pistol cocked within the shadows. "I said stay back, Ranger."

"Can't do it, Durant," the Ranger said, moving the horses closer, fifteen feet, twelve, then ten. "We've both got more important business than to stand off out here against one another. If you shoot me, I swear I'll kill you. Then we both lose—the Parkers win." As the Ranger spoke, he stepped down from his stirrups and lifted his other canteen strap from around his saddle horn.

"If I hadn't wasted time on you," Durant said, the Ranger seeing his eyes glinting within the shadows now as he moved closer, "I'd be heading into San Carlos by now. Instead, I've caught a bullet in my side."

"I didn't ask you to waste time on me," the Ranger said, in the darkness with Durant now, seeing him slumped against a stand of rock. Durant's face was lined with long streaks of sweat.

"I know it, and I shouldn't have," Durant said. His left hand pressed a blood-soaked bandanna to his side. His right hand held Tackett's pistol up toward the Ranger, the hammer cocked, his thumb not too steady across the hammer.

"I wish you'd uncock it," the Ranger said, nodding at Tackett's pistol. "You're not looking real spry. I'd hate getting shot on a mishap."

"I . . . I can't," Durant said, his eyes moving to the pistol, then back to the Ranger.

"Easy then." The Ranger stepped to the side, out of the line of fire, reaching a gloved hand over, letting his thumb down in front of the hammer. "Just turn it loose."

Durant let it go and slumped farther down the rock. The

Ranger uncocked the pistol and shoved it into Durant's holster. "Let's see what you've got here." He lifted Durant's bloody hand away from the wound, then peeled the soaked bandanna from it. Turning Durant slightly, he looked at the long stain of dark blood down his hip. "You're lucky—it went clean through."

"Hell, I know that." Durant resisted the Ranger's hand; but the Ranger held firm and loosened the bandanna from around his neck with his free hand.

"Take it easy, Durant. The quicker we can get you patched up, the better." He hooked a finger in the hole on Durant's shirt, ripped it open, shook out the dusty bandanna, and pressed it to Durant's lower back. "Hold this right here for me."

Durant drew in a painful breath, reached a hand around, and pressed the bandanna against his back. "What was the shooting about back there?"

"Beats me," the Ranger said, ripping the back of Durant's shirt away, then tearing it into long strips for a bandage. "*Federales,* if I had to guess. They must've run into the body of the snake."

"The snake?" Durant eyed him as the Ranger wrapped the strips of cloth around his waist.

"Yeah, the snake. I figure Martin Zell didn't live through Diablo Canyon. He was the head of the snake. Once he died, the rest of the snake just crawled off with no direction— looking for a place to spend itself out and die. Sure sounded like they found it."

Durant drew a breath and held it while the Ranger tightened the bandage around him and tied it off. "There, that'll keep you from losing any more blood. I'm surprised you haven't bled yourself dry already."

"I won't die before I settle up with the Parkers. I swear it," Durant said in a solemn voice.

The Ranger reached down, picked up the canteen from the ground, uncapped it, and handed it to him. "I believe you, Willis Durant. You're the most hardheaded man I've seen in a while."

"Yeah, I suppose I am." Durant tipped back a drink of tepid water, wiped the back of his bloody hand across his mouth, and said, "Now let's get going."

"No, you sit down for a minute—give that wound a chance to clot up some." He saw Durant tense, and he added, "It'll be dark soon. We'll slip into San Carlos. Go on now, sit down."

Durant let out a breath and slid down the rock to his haunches, a hand against his bandaged side. "Don't think I'm going to pass out and let you leave here without me, Ranger. It's not going to happen."

"It never crossed my mind," the Ranger answered, lowering himself down on one knee, taking his big pistol from his holster and checking it as he spoke. "Since you haven't passed out by now, I expect you're not about to." He rolled the cylinder of the pistol down his forearm, clicked the action back and forth with his thumb, then let it rest across his knee. "There's no point in me trying to talk you out of it, I reckon."

"You'd be wasting your breath, Ranger."

The Ranger pushed up the brim of his dusty sombrero and shook his head. "Yep, I sure would be." He stood up, raising the big pistol. "Sorry, Durant." With a quick, hard swipe, he backhanded the barrel across Willis Durant's forehead. Durant's head jerked to the side and fell slack. He slumped farther down and fell over on his side. "I just can't risk it, the shape you're in."

The Ranger shoved the big pistol down in his holster, bent down to cap the canteen, and righted Durant back against the wall. He laid the canteen on Durant's chest and checked Durant's horses to see that their reins were well fastened around an edge of rock. Then he stepped up onto the white barb and turned it toward town.

In a stable built of broken adobe blocks, scrapes of sun-bleached wood, and covered by a ragged tarpaulin, Maria and Prudence stood looking out across the dirt street of San Carlos into the gray evening light. Maria ran a hand down the horse's side. "The horse is still tired, but he has rested now." Beside the horse, two desert burros stood crunching on grain, their nuzzles deep down in the wooden feed trough.

"Have you ever ridden one of these things?" Prudence asked, looking the burros over with a skeptical expression.

"Of course I have ridden burros . . . long before I ever rode a horse. In the mountain country they are favored over horses. We will be all right, you'll see."

"I'd feel better staying here," Prudence said.

"And so would I," Maria agreed. "I had hoped the Parkers would be crazy enough to ride in today, this afternoon, with the sun to their faces." She studied the shadows on the land outside of San Carlos, then turned back to Prudence with her rifle cradled in her arm. "But I was wrong. It will be dark soon. The Parkers knew we would see them a long ways off during the day . . . that is why they have waited. Tonight, with the darkness on their side, they will come. You can count on it."

"Then Payton's not as crazy as we thought," Prudence said. She too began searching the long shadows across the desert floor.

"He *is* as crazy as we thought," Maria said, "but even a raving lunatic knows to protect himself." She turned and stepped around to the burros. "Come, we must be out of here before they arrive. The boy, Hernando, will keep a lantern burning in the window throughout the night. He will brighten it when the Parkers ride in."

They drew the burros away from the feed trough and out through the back of the stable. Using the late evening shadows as cover, Maria led the way, her rifle ready in her arm, going from one darkened area to the next until they reached the blackened side of an abandoned hovel on the far outskirts of San Carlos. "We will sit here until it is fully dark." Maria nodded toward the string of jagged cliffs in the upreaching foothills a hundred yards north of town. "From up there we can watch Hernando's lantern. The terrain will be too rough for anyone to sneak up on us."

"I hope you know what you're doing," Prudence said.

"I know what I am doing. On higher ground, with this rifle and these pistols, we will be safe until morning."

"But then what?" Prudence looked around at the darkening land and hugged her arms across her bosom.

"Then, we see what tomorrow holds for us." Maria reached onto the back of one of the burros, took down a rolled-up blanket, shook it out, and threw it around Prudence's shoulders. "For now, we have food, water, ammunition, and most important, our freedom." She offered a firm smile. "We have come a long way since the train robbery."

A mile back in the falling darkness, on the other side of San Carlos, where the sand flats ended, the Parker brothers, McCord, and Paschal stepped down from their horses and stood gazing at the few pale lights that had begun to glow in dusty adobe windows. "The women are there all right," Payton Parker said to the others, pushing up his hat brim. "I can feel 'em."

"Then what are we waiting for?" asked Leo Parker. "Let's get in there and get them." He'd already turned to step back onto his horse when Payton caught his shirt-sleeve and yanked him back.

"Don't make me smack you, Leo," Payton said. "We're not charging in there half-cocked and get ourselves shot out of our saddles. Why do you suppose we've been hanging back the past couple hours?"

Leo looked confused. "Waiting for it to get dark?" he scratched his head up under his hat brim.

"Right. We're gonna wait till it's good and dark, then ease in and make our play. Jesus, Leo, don't make me say it again."

"Payton's right, Leo," McCord said. "Anybody can see us from two miles out in daylight. We'd have been sitting ducks for a rifle out here."

"Well, thank you, Mr. McCord," Payton said in a mock tone. He turned and lifted a canteen loop from around his saddle horn, uncapped it, and took a mouthful of tepid water. Then he spat it out with a sour expression. "This water's starting to taste like horse piss from a dirty jar. We don't get some whiskey pretty soon, I'm gonna shoot somebody just for the hell of it."

Paschal grunted. "I don't know about the rest of you, but I'm starting to get hungry."

Payton chuckled, giving the Frenchman a dark glance. "If you say that loud enough, Frenchy, there won't be an Injun left in the territory come morning."

Paschal seethed, his dark eyes turning away from the others as they laughed among themselves. "Stupid bastards," he cursed under his breath, stepping back to his saddlebags and taking out a moldy piece of jerked beef. Wiping it on his dirty trousers, he tore a bite off with his teeth.

After a moment, Payton Parker turned to him and said, "Don't get too comfortable on us, Frenchy. I need you to ride in and do a little scouting for us."

"Scouting?" Paschal spoke over a mouthful of stiff jerky. "But you just said a person with a rifle—"

"I know what I said. But it's dark now—dark enough you can get in there and find something out."

"Why me?"

"Because most these people know you, damn it! They're used to smelling you all over town. If they happen to see your stinking arse drifting around, they might not think nothing of it."

"I don't like it." Paschal shook his head, finishing off the jerked beef and wiping his hands on his shirt.

"I don't care if you like it," Payton said, cocking his head with a dark smile. His hand rested on his pistol butt. "You like it better than me putting a slug in your greasy face, don't ya?"

Paschal raised a hand chest high, easing Payton down. "What am I looking for?"

"All you need to do is see if the women's horse is there. They had to be riding one of the *federales'* horses. Look around for a Mexican army saddle—you can do that much, can't ya?" Payton wiggled a hand through the air. "Just sort of sneak in, then sneak out. If it looks like we might be here a little longer, bring us a bottle of something from ole Juan Verdere's cantina. Something he ain't got spiked with rat heads and lizard shit."

"Aw, that is what you really want, eh?" Paschal nodded. "You send me to pick up some whiskey."

"Well?" Payton spread his hands. "It beats having you here fouling the air for all of us."

"Maybe this is not a good idea," McCord offered.

"Don't you start your crap, McCord," Payton said, swinging toward him. "I brought you in with us because you're supposed to be some kind of real hard-nut . . . a big gun out of Texas. Ha! You ain't shown me shit. My aunt Bertha coulda done what you've done so far, and she's got a wooden leg."

Leo cut in, "Aunt Bertha ain't got no wood—"

"Shut up, Leo! It's just a saying!" Payton spun in a circle and stamped a foot in the sand. "Now damn it to hell, boys!" he screamed at them. "We're going in there directly! Get the women! Get the gold! *Kill* the women! *Take* the gold! Then we'll get ourselves out of this damn blast furnace and go somewhere and live like white men ought to!" His breath heaved. "But first!" He settled down and held up a dirty finger for emphasis. "*First!* I want me one damn good drink of whiskey." He turned his eyes from one to the other, each of them moving back a cautious step. "Does anybody else need to comment on that?"

Paschal saw the killing, red-rimmed stare focus on him. "I go now, Payton. I won't be long." He grunted, hefting his big body up onto the saddle, the horse steadying itself against his weight.

When he'd kicked the horse out onto the dusty trail, Payton Parker turned to Leo and McCord. "Now see? See how easy that was? He gets back, we'll have a little toot or two, and get down to business."

McCord and Leo nodded. Payton went to his horse and looped the canteen strap over the saddle horn. The horse nickered and shied a step. "Don't you start in on me too, fool," he said, jerking the horse's reins hard and pulling it over beside him as he gazed out through the falling darkness.

Chapter 21

Payton, Leo, and McCord restlessly waited in the dark for the Frenchman to return. "It must be after midnight," McCord said. "What if he decides to just skip on out of here? If the women have the gold with them, he could kill them, take the gold for himself, and go off doing whatever it is Frenchmen do when there's nobody around to stop them." McCord paced back and forth, drumming his fingers on his pistol butt. On the ground beside their horses, Payton and Leo looked up at him in the darkness.

"Damn it, McCord," Payton said. "If you're so ate up with the what-ifs, why don't you ride on out and see what's taking him?"

"Naw, damn it." McCord took a deep breath and settled himself. "Just getting edgy. Wishing we'd get this thing done before something else goes wrong."

"It's not going to, so shut up about it," Payton said. "You're spooking yourself. If you're not careful, you'll get as crazy as Leo here—always thinking there's a big Negro coming for him."

Leo shot him a dark glance. "Durant is back there, Payton. You heard Paschal say it. He saw him."

"Maybe he saw a big Negro, maybe he didn't," Payton responded. "Once you start believing that stinking idiot, you

open up all sorts of possibilities. Even if there was a big
Negro back there, that don't mean it's Durant."

McCord shook his head. "I don't know what you boys did
to Willis Durant, but if he really is on your backs, he won't
be easily stopped."

"Here we go again," Payton said. "I wish Willis Durant
really *was* dogging us, just so's I could show you both how
easy it is to blow his bushy head off." Payton chuckled
under his breath. "I swear, you're getting as finicky as
schoolmarms." He swung his gaze to McCord, seeing him
pacing again. "Sit down, McCord, you're getting on my
nerves! I'm wondering if there's room for you on our next
big job."

Next big job? McCord looked at Payton Parker, then at his
brother Leo. *Jesus.* . . . He sat down and pulled his hat low
over his eyes. If he got his gold and got away from these
two, he'd shoot them both if they ever came riding into sight
again.

They waited.

Another hour had passed before Paschal came back with
a tall bottle of rye shoved inside his dirty buckskin shirt.
"What the hell took you so long, Frenchy?"

"I had to go through a back window to get this whiskey,"
Paschal said, patting the bottle in his shirt.

"Well? What'd you find out for us?" Payton Parker
reached a hand, snapping his fingers toward the bottle before the big Frenchman had a chance to step down from his
saddle. Paschal grunted, pulled the bottle out and pitched it
into Payton Parker's hands.

"It is like you said. The horse is there—I saw it—and the
federale saddle in the stable." He swung his big body down
from the horse.

"Damn it, Frenchy," Payton Parker said, wiping the bottle

up and down his trouser leg. "Couldn't you carry this in your saddlebags? It's hot now and smells like it's been passed through a buzzard's belly." He pulled the cork and threw back a drink. "Anything else?" Payton wiped a hand across his moistened lips and took another drink, staring at Paschal.

"A boy who cleans up Juan Verdere's cantina said the women were there earlier, but they are gone now."

"That's a damn lie," Payton said, grinning. "There's no place to go from here . . . especially without a horse."

"The boy, Hernando, said they traded the horse for two desert burros." Paschal reached for the bottle of rye, but Payton passed it over to Leo.

"Ha, I bet." Payton spat and licked his lips. "Now wouldn't that be a pretty picture? Two women on donkeys, beating it out across the desert, with us right behind them? I hope to God you didn't believe any of this, Frenchy."

"No, of course I did not believe him." Leo finished taking a drink and started to hand the bottle to Paschal, but McCord slipped his hand in and took it just before it reached Paschal's grimy fingertips. Paschal fumed. "You asked me to find out what I could, so I did. There are burro prints leading out to the foothills north of town. I think the women are hiding up there somewhere."

"Hmmm . . ." Payton thought about it. McCord took a long drink from the bottle and finally passed it to Paschal. Paschal guzzled away until Payton snatched it from his lips. "Damn it! Don't drink the whole thing." He wiped his palm around on the tip of the bottle, inspected it, and shoved the cork back down its neck. "I don't suppose you saw your ole buddy Juan Verdere while you were there, huh?"

"No, I did not see him."

Payton Parker nodded. "He probably ain't back yet from telling the *federales* what happened out at Diablo Canyon."

"Most likely he is not," Paschal said, eyeing Payton, sensing something at work in Payton's voice.

"Bet he won't be for a hell of a long time, either," Payton said, winking, offering the Frenchman a nasty grin.

"What do you mean by that?" Paschal asked.

"Meaning . . . I bet you killed that ole fart and left him out there for buzzard bait." Payton Parker chuckled, looking around at Leo and McCord, then back to Paschal. "Come on now, Frenchy. Did you think I fell for that little story? You two never get that far apart. If he'd gone to the *federales* you would have been right beside him, stinking to high heaven."

"I think the whiskey has kicked you like a mule, Payton." Paschal shot a nervous glance at the other two, trying to smile and pass it off, but his smile lacked substance beneath a widening sheen of sweat. "You know that Juan Verdere was like a brother to me."

"Yeah, yeah . . ." Payton Parker brushed it away. Uncorking the bottle, he took another drink, let out a whiskey hiss, and said, "Why so worried, Frenchy? It ain't as if we're gonna tell anybody. Look at us, we're outlaws, Border Dogs, *desperados,* for chrissakes." He spread an arm and shrugged. "So what—you killed your old friend. More power to you is all I got to say."

"Then why are you asking me such a question—making such a big thing out of it?" Paschal looked worried, suspicious.

Payton let out a low belch. "It's just that if you'd kill your best friend for his part of the gold . . . where does that put Leo, McCord, and me? How do we know you won't do us in when the time comes?" He grinned. "We're a little concerned, especially ole McCord there. He's got some Injun blood in him, making him more than a little suspicious, right McCord?"

"That's right," McCord said, giving Paschal a dark stare. "Part Cherokee on my mama's side."

"Come on, *amigos,* we are all after the same thing here." Paschal said, sweating more as Leo and McCord drew closer. "What has gotten into you? What can I do to show you we are all friends? I will do it. Anything! Anything at all!"

"Now that's a frightening thought, Frenchy," Payton Parker said. "But now that you mention it—how well do you know those foothills north of town?"

"Like the back of my hand—" Paschal's words stopped short, realizing what Payton was about to demand of him. His big chin dropped. "Surely you are joking? You can't expect me to go up into those dark foothills, knowing they are armed and waiting! They will kill me!"

"That's only a possibility," Payton said. He patted the pistol on his hip. "If you don't do what I'm telling ya, this here is a sure thing, parly-voo . . . you stinking polecat son of a bitch? We ain't carrying your ornery hide on this job. You got to work for your share."

Paschal swallowed a dry knot in his throat. "Go alone? Where will you be?"

"We'll be down in San Carlos, keeping watch. Don't worry, we hear anything up there—see any muzzle flashes or whatever—we'll be in there like a streak of lightning. It'll be morning in a few hours. I got an idea how to flush them gals out, once you make sure where they are." He grinned and threw back another shot of whiskey.

Like two birds in a dark rock nest, the women huddled beneath blankets thrown around them and looked back toward

San Carlos, where the lantern glowed dim and steady through Hernando's adobe window. Hernando's grand-mother had taken it on herself to go out right after dark and wipe the window clean with a rag, in order for the women to see it more clearly.

"I don't see how we'll ever stand it up here all night," Prudence said. "I'm freezing already. It's colder here than it was on the sand flats at night. God, I hate this crazy land. Give me good ole New Orleans any time."

"We will manage," Maria said without turning to her. "If we get too cold, we will sleep between the burros. Their body heat will keep us warm." Her eyes stayed on the dim light in window. "I was in New Orleans once, for a week."

"Really? What did you think of it?" Prudence leaned toward her a little.

"It rained," Maria said.

"Oh . . ." A silence passed, then Prudence continued in a quiet tone, "But you got to see some of the sights, I'm sure."

"It rained every day for the entire week." Maria let out a tired breath, gathered the blanket around her, and after a pause said, "When you get back to New Orleans, you will have quite a story to tell all your friends."

"Shouldn't you say *if* instead of *when* I get back? You certainly sound optimistic."

"We have come this far. I have no intention of losing to the Parkers, do you?"

"No, of course not," Prudence said. She jiggled the big pistol on her lap and seemed to think about something for a second. "Where you hid the gold beneath the tree, do you think anyone could just happen by and find it?"

"You saw the sand flats," Maria said. "How many people do you suppose just *happen* by there?" She shook her head.

"No. The gold will be there a thousand years unless we tell something where to look."

"But behind the roots of a tree? What if a big rain washed away more of the bank?"

"I will tell you a secret," Maria said. "It is not behind the tree roots."

Prudence's eyes took on a sharpness, watching Maria gaze down at the soft glow of light from the window. "Then where is it?"

"It is behind a flat rock against the other bank of the dry wash," Maria said.

"Oh, really?" Prudence stared at her.

"I thought it was best you did not know in case the Parkers caught us before we crossed the flats. If they got their hands on us, you could not have told them something you did not know."

"And you thought if it came down to it, you could hold out, but not me?"

"Let me put it this way," Maria said. "We had the desert to cross. I did not know if you would make it or not. At the time I could not afford to take the chance."

"But you can now?"

"Now I can." Maria kept her gaze on the light from the window.

On the dark trail into San Carlos, Payton, Leo, and McCord came forward at a slow, steady pace, keeping their horses quiet. Paschal had cut away, upward across the hundred-yard stretch of ground between the town and the black jagged outline of the foothills to their right.

"Let that stinking bastard prowl around up there half the night," Payton said in a low voice. "We'll take it easy at Juan's cantina until we get this thing settled." They moved on through the darkness until they sidled over to the hitch rail. Leo and McCord stepped down outside the cantina doors.

"It's locked up tight," Leo said, getting to the doors first and shaking the latch in his hands.

Payton still sat atop his horse with the half empty bottle of rye in his hand. "So? Kick it in, idiot," he said. "It ain't like Juan Verdere's gonna sue us over it."

"All right then, I will." Leo raised a boot, sent the doors flying open in a spray of splinters and dust, and stepped inside, laughing. McCord turned and saw Payton still on his horse. "What about you? Ain't you coming in?"

"In a minute," Payton replied. "This town is far too quiet to suit me. First I'm gonna ride up to where Paschal said the boy lives." He gave an evil drunken grin. "Gonna introduce myself, so to speak." He backed his horse from the hitch rail and moved it forward along the dirt street.

Inside the cantina, McCord and Leo found the lamps hanging above the bar, lit them, and helped themselves to tepid beer and a fresh bottle of rye while Payton Parker rode up to the stable beside the adobe, where Paschal had told him the boy, Hernando, lived with his grandparents. "Well, now . . ." Payton whispered to himself, stepping down from his stirrups over to the lone horse that had been lying down in its stall. The horse stood and shook itself, nickering softly.

Payton walked around it in the darkness and ran his hand along the *federale* saddle lying across a stall rail. As he stood there, he noticed the glow of the lantern brighten across the ground behind the adobe. He looked at it for a second, threw back a drink from the bottle, and peered into the outer darkness toward the foothills. "I'll be damned." Then he corked the bottle, turned, and walked to the door of the adobe. This was going to be easier than he'd thought.

*   *   *

Above the sleeping town, Paschal moved higher up into the foothills, farther up than he thought the women would be hiding. He knew these steep, narrow paths, knew how to move along them as quiet as a ghost. The women would be concentrating more on the town below than on the darkness above them. He didn't like being up here, but now that he'd made it this far without somebody shooting at him, the rest would be easy.

But Paschal had news for Payton Parker—he wasn't about to flush these women out for him and the others. To hell with them. If he could take these women himself, he'd lead them higher up past the foothills and into the rocky passes of the distant mountains, familiar to him as the back of his hand. The Parkers would never find him and the women. Paschal could hold out up there and wait until the Parkers gave up. Then the gold would be his . . . he might even keep the women too. He smiled to himself, getting down from his horse, leading it downward now, cautiously taking his time.

Chapter 22

When Hernando and his grandparents heard the horse move past their adobe, they had looked out through the crack in the door and saw the dusty *gringo* ride by with a whiskey bottle in his hand. The old woman muttered and made the sign of the cross. Hernando and his grandfather, Ramon, looked at one another with worried eyes. Old Ramon nodded at his grandson. Hernando stepped quietly over to the window and raised the wick on the lantern. He looked out toward the black foothills, then went back to his grandparents.

They stood in silence, the three of them, listening, waiting, as people might when a predator of the wilds prowls their yard. After a moment, they held their breath at the sound of heavy boots crossing the narrow planks to their door; and when they heard the pounding on the rough wooden door, their eyes flashed across one another as if in dark finality, and they stood silent for a second longer.

Old Ramon had seen such men as this in the past. He knew if he did not open the door, the next sound would be the door ripping off its leather hinges. With a worried glance back at his wife, old Ramon moved to the door and slipped the bolt back with his trembling hand.

"Well, *buenas noches!*" Payton Parker roared. He barged

into the room, past old Ramon, catching him by his shirt and dragging him along behind him. Payton stopped at the window where the lantern glowed out toward the foothills. "Looky here, looky here! I bet that's the cleanest window this side of hell!"

Young Hernando had stepped in, his small fists balled at his sides. But with a sweeping backhand, Payton Parker sent the boy sprawling across a wooden table and into a short pile of dried brush and kindling stacked beside a small sooty fireplace. "A little of the old light-in-the-window trick, eh?" Payton chuckled. He slung the old grandfather to the dirt floor and kicked him away like an empty feed sack. He then turned back to the lantern and laughed. "Now ain't that the cleverest thing yet!"

The old grandmother stood back in terror, her serape drawn tight against her weathered bosom. "Where are they, folks? Don't make me mad at you!" Payton demanded.

Old Ramon lay gasping on the dirt floor, his bare feet scrambling to seek purchase, but finding none. *"Señor! Por favor!"* Hernando struggled up from beside the fireplace, a trickle of blood running from his lips, a red whelp throbbing on his cheek. "My grandparents did nothing to you! They are old and sick! Do not hurt them!"

"Ain't this sweet." Payton smiled a crooked, drunken sneer. He stepped over and kicked the old man in the ribs again, just hard enough to make him heave for air. When Hernando lunged at him, Payton caught him at arm's length by the throat and held him there, Hernando's bare feet kicking an inch above the dirt floor. The woman took a step forward, but stopped when Payton said, "Don't come at me, you damned old rag. I'll break this boy's neck . . . yours too."

"No! No!" The old woman shook her head. "Don't hurt

him . . . I beg of you! What do you want here? Do not hurt
him!"

"That's a little more hospitable," Payton said. He loosened his grip around the boy's throat, but kept him out at
arm's length. "I was beginning to think I wasn't welcome
here." He shook Hernando back and forth. "Now, where are
those two girlfriends of mine, old woman. Tell me before I
kill this little peckerwood."

The old woman turned slightly, pointing a trembling finger in the direction of the foothills. "Please do not hurt them,
señor. They are tired and scared—"

"Shut up now," Payton Parker said. "It's best to say no
more than you've been asked. I might yet decide to pump a
few bullet holes in you folks if you make me mad."

On the dirt floor, old Ramon clutched the wooden table
leg and with all his effort, managed to pull himself up.
"That's right, old man, get on up, show some manners here.
We've got us some talking to do. Then you're gonna go with
me. We've got to roust out everybody in this little buzzard's
nest and have us a nice town meeting over at Juan's cantina."

"Do not . . . do not hurt . . . the boy," the old man gasped.

"Oh, but I truly will," Payton Parker said. "I'll hurt him
really bad. Then you . . . then this old hen of yours if you
don't do like I say. *Com-pren-de?*"

"*Sí, por favor.* I understand."

From their dark perch in the foothills, Maria and Prudence
had seen the lantern grow brighter in the window. They'd sat
tense for a few minutes, watching and listening, until behind
them farther up among the loose rocks on a higher path, a
faint sound came down to them. Both women looked around
without saying a word and sat still as stone. When they

heard no more sound from above them, Maria looked back toward the adobe below. But her breath stopped in her throat when she saw the light in the window had gone out, the black of night lying flat and unbroken now as if the town of San Carlos had vanished.

"Santa Madre," Maria whispered, her hand tightening around her rifle stock.

"Oh, no," Prudence whispered. "They're there. They know we're up here."

"Be still," Maria said, her eyes darting behind them, upward into the darkness. Only silence came from up there. Maria turned back to Prudence and without a sound took her by the forearm and pulled her along, the two of them slipping across the rocky ground a few feet until they crawled behind an upthrust of rock.

Close to Prudence's ear, Maria said, "I must get down there and see what has happened to the boy and his family."

"We'll both go." Prudence replied, clutching Maria's forearm.

"No. You are free. Stay here, stay hidden." Maria's voice was little more than a faint breath in her ear. "No one can find you here if you stay quiet."

"What about you?" Prudence's voice was the same soft wisp of breath in reply.

"I will be all right. Lie still."

Maria crawled away to the burros, glancing back only once into the higher darkness. Perhaps it was a cat they'd heard up there. Perhaps it was nothing. This was not a place familiar to the Parkers, she thought, or else these people would have warned her. Besides, in the darkness, behind the rocks, all Prudence had to do was keep her wits about her— and she'd proven she knew how to do that.

Maria crept up between the burros, took the rope hobble

off the hooves of the one she'd ridden up the path, and with its reins in her hand, she moved it off to the path. She sliced a worried breath with each short, soft chop of its burlap-covered hooves on the loose rocks beneath them. At the bottom of the winding path, where the last turn spilled out onto the flatland between there and San Carlos a hundred yards away, Maria swung her leg over the burro and let it carry her through the night.

No sooner had she started out on the burro than Paschal, higher up above the women's dark campsite, raised his head and listened for the sound he'd heard earlier. He knew the atmosphere of the foothills at night, what sounds should be here and what sounds shouldn't. At night the foothills should be full of coyote and elk, and even wolves in search of prey—but not tonight, at least not on the path beneath him. Farther back he could hear the occasional brush of padded paw over rock, the quick breath of a bull elk, but not down there. All he heard down there had been the muffled click of a hoof and nothing more.

They were down there, those women. It was time he made his move. He slipped the knife from his dirty boot well and wiped it across his trouser leg. He would soon have them . . . them and the gold, and everything he'd ever dreamed of. If he got lucky, he might even get a chance to catch Payton Parker somewhere in the future . . . reach down below Payton's crotch with a good sharp skinning knife and lift him up on the tip of it. He smiled to himself, moving down into the darkness. That might be too much to hope for. He'd settle for the gold.

At the sound of the burro's breath in the surrounding stillness, Paschal inched forward until he laid a hand on the animal's neck and felt its skin quiver. *Only one . . .* He crouched close to the ground and slid his hand a back and forth gently, feeling for footprints in the dark the way the Indians of the high Northwest had taught him to do. But this loose rocky ground revealed nothing. He had started to work back up the path when close behind him he heard the faintest rustle of someone shifting in the darkness.

As soon as Prudence made the slightest move, she knew it had been a mistake. She froze and listened, but the sound of someone lurking a few feet away had stopped now. Had they moved away, or had they heard her and stopped, and now lay in wait for her? The burro made a blowing sound under its breath and scraped its burlap-covered hoof on the ground. Prudence relaxed. Maybe it had been the burro she'd heard all along.

Yes, that was it. She'd been too spooked. She needed to settle down a little. In the darkness she'd started to get up an inch when Paschal's big arm swung around her and pinned her to his broad chest. "Easy, *cheri,*" he whispered close to her ear. She felt cold steel edge press against her throat. Her breath caught in her chest. For a second it seemed her heart had stopped beating. "Where is your friend?" Paschal breathed in her ear, liking the smell of her and the way she had gone dead still at the touch of him against her. When she did not answer right away, he pressed the steel blade more firmly, felt her tremble, rigid against him.

"She . . . she left me," Prudence said, thinking fast, reaching for something inside herself—a trick, a lie, a plan, anything. "God, she left me here alone. Who are you? Are you one of them?"

Paschal waited for a second, considering. After all, there was only one burro. "One of them?" He chuckled, his big belly rolling against her back. "Perhaps I am . . . perhaps I am not. Where is the gold from the *federales*?" As he spoke, his voice rose above a whisper, and his knife hand eased down a bit.

"I . . . I think I know where she hid it. She didn't trust me. I think she wants to keep it for herself."

"I see." Paschal relaxed his grip around her, but still held her against his chest. "Which one are you? You are the Vanderman woman, eh?"

Prudence's voice sounded shaky, yet her mind clicked like a well-tuned clock. "Why, no . . . I'm not her. I'm . . . I'm the other one. I'm, uh, Maria . . . yes, Maria."

"The other one? Now that is so cute of you." He chuckled. "But you are not a good liar, *cheri.* The other woman is some sort of half-breed. I can tell by your voice who you are. Now do not lie to me again, or I will have to kill you. Do you understand? It would be terrible to kill a beautiful, rich woman."

"Yes, I understand. I'm sorry." Her voice still trembled, her mind still fast at work. "I'm just so frightened . . . all those horrible men, then her, the way she has treated me." She sobbed. "God, what will I do? Please don't kill me."

"Shhh, be quiet now." Paschal raised the knife from her throat, then sheathed it. "So, she has left you alone? She wants the gold to herself?"

"Yes . . . I think so." Prudence sniffled, collecting herself. "But . . . but I don't care about the gold. My father has enough gold to pave this desert. He would gladly give it to see me return home safely. I've tried to make people understand. Why won't anyone listen?"

"Hush now," Paschal said. "I am here. I am listening."

"You are?" Prudence sniffed again, her voice childlike.

"Yes, of course. You see?" He turned her facing him, the two of them only catching a shadowy image of one another. "I have not come to harm you, no, no." He shook his head.

"I have come to save you . . . from Payton Parker and the others."

Prudence rubbed her throat, Paschal's big hand still holding her shoulder. "But, the knife . . . ?"

"Ah yes, the knife. Well, how was I to know it was you? I had to be sure, didn't I?"

"I . . . I suppose so."

"But of course," he said and smiled. This was going to be too easy. "Now that I know it is you, you are safe. No one will harm you. You have my word as a gentleman."

"Thank God." Prudence let herself fall limp against him. "Then this is over? This whole horrible nightmare has ended?"

"Yes, put it out of your mind." He brushed a grimy hand down her tangled hair. "I have a horse waiting, right up there."

"You do . . . ?" Prudence turned her eyes up into the night along the outline of the black foothills.

"Yes, and I know a way out of here that leads back along the trail toward Diablo Canyon." He paused for a second, then added, "That is where she hid the gold, isn't it? You would recognize the spot?"

"Well, yes." Prudence touched a finger to her lips, thinking about it. "I'm certain I will once I see it." She lowered her finger. "What about the reward my father will pay you for bringing me home? It will make you rich."

"Yes," Paschal said and grinned, "but still, we cannot leave all that gold out there to go to waste, now can we? One can never have too much gold, now can one?" With a grimy thumb under her chin, Paschal raised her face to his and winked.

"Whatever you think is best." Prudence smiled and lowered her eyes. "I'm placing myself completely in your hands."

A few yards from San Carlos, Maria stepped down and tied the burro's reins around a low scrub pinyon in the shadow of an abandon shack. She moved forward in the darkness, crouched on foot, her rifle in her hand. At the window of the adobe where the lantern had burned earlier, she looked in but saw no one—only an overturned table and a pile of debris near the fireplace. Maria heard the soft sobbing of Hernando's grandmother, and after a moment when she'd heard no other voices, she pecked on the glass and stood back in the shadows, ready, her thumb across the rifle hammer.

When the window opened and the old woman put her head forward, Maria whispered to her, "It is me. Are you alone?"

"*Sí,* I am alone. Thank God you have returned . . . they have taken Ramon and Hernando," the woman cried, whispering in a trembling voice.

"What happened?" Maria asked, moving forward until she stood at the window and held the woman's hand in hers.

"I did a stupid thing," the old woman said. "I cleaned this old window, and the gringo saw it! They are killers, these madmen! They say they will kill everyone in San Carlos if you do not come down and surrender to them! They made me tell them where you were. I have been such a fool!"

"Don't blame yourself." Maria squeezed her hand, then turned it loose. "Where have they taken Hernando and your husband?"

To the cantina, with everyone else. They only leave me here because I am so old and cannot get away. But they will come back for me . . . I know they will. It will be daylight soon, and they will kill all of us!"

"Not if I can help it," Maria said. "Here, come with me." She reached in to help the old woman out through the window. "We will get you away from here."

"No," the old woman resisted. "How can I live if they kill my family?"

"You must have faith. Come quickly now." Maria pulled her forward. This time the woman spilled out into her arms. "There is a burro tied behind the old shack." Maria stood her on the ground. "Take it and go up into the foothills. Find Prudence and stay with her until this is over."

The old woman looked at her hesitantly and said, "But what about you? What are you going to do here?"

Maria's eyes turned away from her. "Do not worry about me. They want the gold. I will trade the gold for the lives of the people.

"But these men are animals," the old woman said. "They will kill you once they have this gold they are looking for. Do you give up your life for those you do not even know?"

"Only a fool gives up their life," Maria said. "To get my life, these men will have to take it from me. A lot can happen between here and where the gold is hidden." She tightened her grip on the rifle in her hand.

Chapter 23

Inside the cantina, the few townsfolk of San Carlos sat huddled together on the floor in a corner. They looked frightened and lost, yet they had said nothing about the two women who'd ridden into their town earlier, pursued like deer by a pack of wolves. They'd been awakened in the night and dragged from their homes by these angry, drunken men with guns. Most of the people were elderly, the young men of working age having left San Carlos when the mines in the foothills had played out three years earlier.

Leo Parker grinned, pointing his pistol into the midst of the huddled townsfolk at old Ramon, who lay on the floor like a bundle of rags. "Want me to drag him out here too, Payton? He ain't doing nothing there but taking up space."

From the darkened corner, the people watched as Payton Parker dragged Hernando by the short length of rope around his neck. The tip of a single-barrel shotgun lay against the base of Hernando's skull. Payton's hand lay around the shotgun stock, his thumb across the cocked hammer.

"Naw, Leo," Payton Parker said. "That ole peckerwood probably won't live till morning anyway." At the bar, Payton Parker slung the boy around beside him. "This boy is our best investment. Women get all blubbery over kids. They'll give up. You'll see, about the time we drop a couple of these old geezers' bodies out in the street . . . then tell 'em the next one is going to be little Hernando here." Payton laughed and looked at Hernando wide-eyed. *"Bang,"* he said, jiggling the shotgun and rope in his hand.

Leo had just lifted a mouthful of rye whiskey, but he lost it in a spray, seeing the frightened look on Hernando's face. "Damn it, Payton." Leo laughed, slapping a hand down on the bar, whiskey dribbling down his chin. "Now look what you made me do!"

McCord just watched, noticing that the more Leo Parker drank, the crazier he became, looking wild now, his eyes darting toward the people in the corner, his expression turning cold and malevolent. So here was the new Leo, McCord thought. All this time he'd been Payton's slow-witted brother. Now, seeing the depravity the whiskey conjured up from inside Leo, McCord began to realize why Payton kept him around. *Jesus*. . . . He wanted away from these men.

"What's the matter with you, McCord?" Leo still chuckled, casting an evil glare his way. "You losing your sense of humor?"

Sense of humor, in this . . . ? McCord fidgeted, looking over at the townsfolk in the corner. Nobody with even a low speck of decency left in them would do something like this. Was Payton serious about what he'd just said? Would he kill this kid for no reason? McCord raised a drink and placed the empty shot glass down. Yes, he believed so. "To tell the truth," McCord said, trying to get around Leo's question, "I'm wondering about Paschal. We shoulda heard something from him by now, don't you think?"

"Paschal? Lord have mercy, McCord," Payton said. "We've got what ya might call a stacked deck going for us here, and you're worried about hearing from a pig-licking Frenchman?"

McCord shrugged, pouring another drink into his shot glass. "I'm just asking, is all. It's coming on to morning . . . he's been up there an awful long time."

"Shiiit," Leo said, grumbling the word out beneath an ugly expression. His otherwise dull face had turned menacing now, his features sharp and evil, his eyes caged and cold. "You ain't got an idea what's going on here, do ya?" He swept his forearm around and knocked McCord's glass off the bar. "Drinking whiskey from a damn glass!" He snatched a bottle by its neck and slammed it down in front of him. "There! Turn it up like a man."

McCord bristled, but held himself in check. He wanted that gold badly enough that he could overlook some things for now. Leo was getting drunk, and wild as an bull elk. "Take it easy, Leo. We're all three friends here."

"Shiiit . . . " Leo Parker said again, staring at him long and hard. McCord held his ground, but felt the skin crawl on his neck, looking into those wild drunken eyes. "Friends? You ain't no friend. You're one more low, rotten, no good—"

Payton cut him off, laughing, reaching over with his free hand, and slapping Leo on his back. "All right, Leo! It's about damn time you woke up and got something moving through your veins. Now you're acting like your old self. Nothing like a little wild-eyed rye to get the blood pumping. Right, brother?"

"Yeah," Leo said, his eyes red-rimmed and boiling. "Want to tell him what we done to our last friend? That big Negro, Durant?" He swung around to Payton, then back to McCord. "Killed his woman, then his boy . . . would've killed his damn dog if he'd had one." He turned to the people huddled in their corner, drawing his pistol and cocking it, beading down on them one after another, one eye squinted shut.

"Pow, pow, pow!" he intoned with a savage grin, a string of saliva swinging from his lower lip. Chuckling low and ugly, he said, "I'm ready to do some killing, brother. Where you want me to start?"

Outside the rear window, above the heads of the people in the corner, Maria stood watching, her eyes only a sliver above the windowsill. When Leo had swung his pistol toward the townspeople, she'd dropped down, waited, then rose and looked back in, seeing the Parkers laugh, watching as Payton Parker tugged on the rope around Hernando's neck, the shotgun stiff and menacing against the back of his head.

Maria looked off to the purple-black horizon, where a thin silver promise of morning glowed on the rim of the earth. There was no time to go back into the hills and tell Prudence what was going on down here. Prudence was safe up there, and that meant something. Prudence was sharp and capable. She would see enough of the town from up high come daylight—enough to warn her to stay away. Maria crept away from the window, stood up in the darkness, and moved quietly back to the stable. She would wait until first light, then face these men alone . . . in the dirt street of San Carlos.

In the dim silence, Willis Durant lay slumped against the rock, his horse standing beside him. The horse had only twitched its ears and raised its muzzle toward the two riders as Liam Bowes and Chance Edwards moved past him less than twenty feet away. Perhaps it was the sound of the passing horses that had first caused Durant to drift back toward consciousness. But the riders were well past him and farther into the distance by the time Durant managed to shake his head and feel his senses draw slowly back into focus.

Once the gray veil began to lift from his mind, it took Durant a few more minutes to drag himself up the rock, find the horse's reins, loosen them, and hand-walk them back to the horse's muzzle. "Easy, boy," he said in a thick voice, trying to balance himself on unsteady legs.

He found the saddle horn with a weak hand, then found the stirrup with the toe of his boot. Struggling upward and spilling over onto the saddle, he ran a loose hand down to the holster on his hip, feeling for the pistol butt, making sure it was there. Then he turned the horse, sitting loose and slumped in his saddle, and put it forward into the dusk.

On the trail ahead of Willis Durant, Chance Edwards felt his wounded horse falter and sway to one side, and he slowed the animal down and ran his hand back along its bloody withers.

"He's done in," Chance said in a raspy voice, barely making it down from the saddle before the horse beneath him dropped over onto the sandy ground and whimpered in a failing voice. Chance staggered in place with a blood-soaked bandanna tied around his forehead. "I think I'm getting there myself."

"Give me your hand," Liam Bowes offered, his own voice weak and gasping. He reached a bloody gloved hand down to Chance Edwards.

Chance shook his head. "No, sir. I think . . . maybe this is as far as I go."

"Nonsense, man. We'll have none of that." Liam Bowes sidled his horse over and grabbed Chance by his shoulder and pulled up. "Get up here . . . we're going to make it to San Carlos . . . or die trying."

"Forget it, Bowes . . . I've had it."

"I said come on!"

Chance Edwards drew a deep breath and got with him, climbing up and clutching with his blood-slick arm as Liam

Bowes pulled. Once behind Bowes on the horse, Chance fell forward against Bowes's back and struggled to say, "Ride on, damn you to hell . . . how does a man quit this outfit?"

"A man doesn't," Bowes said, his heart hammering in his wounded chest, "till I say he does." They pressed on, the sound of the dying horse fading in the darkness until at length the night consumed it.

By the time they'd made it to the outskirts of San Carlos, the gloom had lifted, lightening to a grainy haze. When Liam Bowes saw the horses at the hitch rail outside the cantina, he nudged Chance Edwards, who lay still and quiet, slumped against his back. Bowes said in a whisper, "Roust up now . . . we're here."

"I . . . I can't get moving," Chance Edwards said.

"Yes you can . . . one last time, buck up." He poked Chance Edwards harder. "The Parkers are here."

Liam Bowes turned the tired horse onto a narrow path that led back between two small adobes. At the sight of the two men, a lank spotted dog had stood up from the ground where it had spent the night. The dog stretched, shook itself off, and stared at the two gray apparitions approaching it. It's hackles swelled as a low growl rumbled in its throat. But at the oncoming smell of death, and the aura and promise of more death to come, the dog shied back from the soft drop of the horses' hooves.

"Get out of here," Bowes hissed; the dog moved off and away with a low whine until it looked back at them once more from a safer distance, then finally it disappeared into the morning's glare.

In the thin alley, Bowes helped Chance Edwards to the ground. When he slid down beside him with the old man's sawed-off shotgun in one bloody hand, Bowes palmed the horse on its rump, sending it away. Together, the two men moved to the side of the adobe wall nearest them and leaned against it, gathering their strength.

"We had . . . a hell of a fine thing going till the Parkers came along," Chance Edwards panted. He pressed a hand to the wet bandanna around his wounded head, then lowered his hand and looked at it. "Never shoulda took 'em in."

"New men . . ." Bowes pulled off one bloody glove with his teeth and spat it to the ground. He nodded, looked at Chance Edwards, and added, "These ones coming up nowadays . . . there's no honor in them."

They stood in silence, looking up the dirt street toward the dim lights of the cantina where a jolt of drunken laughter rose above the sound of breaking glass. A moment later, a woman's voice called out, pleading in Spanish. Chance Edwards asked Liam Bowes, "Have we still got any interest in the gold?"

But Bowes didn't answer. Instead, he only looked at Chance Edwards and smiled grimly. Hefting the shotgun from the crook of his arm, he said, "Follow me, Mr. Edwards." On the dirt street, the first shaft of pale sunlight streamed in from the far horizon.

Chapter 24

Inside the cantina, McCord watched Leo move among the frightened townsfolk, kicking at them, swiping at them with his pistol barrel, and finally grabbing an old man by his thin shoulders and yanking him to his feet. The terrified townsfolk could only watch, ducking their heads and averting their eyes, the old women making the sign of the cross and whispering in prayer to the Virgin Mother.

"You'll do for starters, you old buzzard," Leo said, throwing the old man out of the corner onto the dirt floor, where two elderly women sat crying and supplicating beneath their breath. Payton Parker stood in the middle of the dirt floor, chewing on a burnt matchstick between his teeth. Hernando stood rigidly beside him, with the cocked shotgun still against his head. "For God sakes, Payton," McCord said, banging his empty whiskey bottle on the bar, "do something with him!"

"Why? He's doing pretty good on his own." Payton pulled Hernando around with him, facing McCord. "Leo's hard to stop once he gets wound up."

"He's gone crazy, Payton! He don't have to carry on this way. I'm here for the gold, not this."

"If you ain't happy, McCord, leave!" Payton rolled the burnt match to one corner of his mouth, staring at him through feral bloodshot eyes. "I dare you to." His free hand raised the pistol from his holster, cocking it. Beyond him, Leo stopped and turned also, his eyes a swirl of whiskey-fueled madness.

"Jesus, Payton!" McCord took a step along the bar, raising a hand. "I'm in this thing with you to the end. Don't get me wrong."

"Listen, McCord. Leo and me get a kick out of this stuff. If you don't like it, you never shoulda got in to start with."

"I didn't know—"

"You didn't know what?" Payton sneered. "Didn't know it was going to get a little bloody? Well, by God, it has. You should've thought about it first. That's one thing about life, McCord . . . what you don't know to start with, you damn sure learn before you're finished."

"Hell's fire, Payton," Leo said, wiping a hand across the seepage on his lips, "let's get on to the good part."

But Payton ignored him, still staring at McCord. He jerked Hernando across the dirt floor with him. "Look at this boy here, McCord! Look how scared he is! I'm going to kill him and he knows there ain't a damn thing he can do to stop it. There's a lot being said in this boy's eyes! Open them damned eyes, boy! Look at the last face you'll ever see."

"No, no, please, *señor!*"

Payton shook Hernando. The boy had squeezed his eyes shut, his lips trembling in silent prayer—a prayer his grandmother had taught him when he was no more than a baby and the shadows of a terrible dream lingered near him in the night.

Payton Parker stared at McCord, leaning toward him, the burnt match bobbing between his teeth. "I got you going, didn't I? You saying you were some kind of rootin'-tootin' big Texas killer? Wanted to run with *el desperados*? You mighta killed yourself a few ole boys, got yourself convinced you're some kind of bad-ass, blood-handed devil. But right here's where we are." Payton Parker jiggled the pistol in McCord's face.

McCord took another step back. "All right, Payton, easy. I'm with ya here."

"You ain't with us yet, but you better get there, damn quick. You better turn some blood, and you better say you love the taste of it. Border Dogs? Shit," he hissed. "Leo and me ain't nothing but straight up *murderers* . . . always was. Right, brother Leo?"

"As right as you can make it," Leo said.

Payton pointed his pistol toward the cowering people on the dirt floor. Leo stood among them with his pistol by his side, the old man's thin arm still clutched in his free hand like the plucked wing of some emaciated bird. "Now you best get your arse over there with him, McCord—grab yourself some hair and skin. Today the axe is down to the stump!"

"Here, take this thing," Leo said, snatching a woman from the dirt and pitching her to McCord as he dragged the old man along with him and headed for the door. "Let's go to work now."

They moved outside the cantina into the dirt street, walking a few feet toward the stable until they stood in plain sight of the foothills. McCord and Leo Parker held the two hostages against their chests, their eyes scanning the land in the growing streaks of early sunlight. Payton Parker stood between them, Hernando out beside him at arm's length at the tip of the shotgun barrel, his knees weak and trembling in his ragged peasant's trousers.

"Buenas dias, señoritas!" Payton Parker called out across the hundred-yard span of sandy soil. "We know

you're both out there. We've got some folks down here we're gonna start killing in about five seconds if you don't answer me! Ya hear? Better say howdy or something, pretty damned quick!"

He stood quiet, waiting and listening. Leo chuckled on his right, boring the pistol barrel against the old man's ear. McCord held the frail old woman against him, feeling sick as she quaked in his grasp, hearing the whispered plea in her chest quiver against his forearm. "You settle down, lady. Don't go pissing on me," he said close to her ear.

"Well, suit yourselves then, I reckon," Payton Parker called out when no reply came from the barren hillsides. He glanced at Leo and McCord. "Let's start with the old man first. Get set, Leo. Hold him out when you shoot him—make sure they can get a look at it. Then the woman, McCord. I'll save this boy for their dessert. What do you wanta bet me that they won't let things go that far?" He grinned and winked at McCord. McCord swallowed back the sick bile in his mouth.

"Well, you heard him, old-timer," Leo said. He held the old man out to his side, grinning, squinting one eye shut, making sport of it for a second. "Bet you never figured on going this way, huh?"

"Here we go, ladies," Payton called out to the hills. "Pay attention up there!" He looked back at Leo and started to nod.

"Wait!" Maria's voice called out to them from twenty yards up the dirt street. Sunlight mantled her from behind, the rifle butt standing propped against her hip. "Turn them loose. You will have your gold."

Payton Parker swung toward her first, squinting into the glare of sunlight. "Well, I'll be—" His words stopped short for a second until his mind caught up to his surprise. Then he smiled, facing her, drawing Hernando around beside him. "See, boys, it didn't even get started. I was damn sure right." He chuckled, saying to Maria, "Where's your friend, the Vanderman woman?"

"She is dead," Maria said in a flat tone. "A rattlesnake bit her. Let the people go. I'm the one you want."

"Rattlesnake bite . . ." Payton looked at the other two in wonder, then back at Maria. "Did you really think we'd believe something like that? Where is she?"

"She is gone. What is the difference where she is? You want the gold. I am the only one who can take you to it. Turn these people loose."

"Whoa now, little lady." Payton Parker drew Hernando closer to him. "You don't waltz in here telling everybody what to do. We might go ahead and kill a couple of these old birds just for the sake of principle—you making us ride all this way, killing ole Delbert and all." He nodded. "Yep, we'll go on—at least kill this old man anyway. What do you say, brother Leo?"

"Sounds good to me." Leo snickered.

"If you kill anyone, you will then have to kill me," Maria said in a matter-of-fact tone. "Kill me and you will never have the gold. I promise you."

"Aw, hell, little lady, you ain't about to—"

"Damn it, Payton!" McCord yelled. "Listen to her, *please*! She's not lying. If she'll take us to the gold, what more do we want? What the hell are we waiting for?"

Payton Parker turned an angry eye to McCord. "You keep your mouth shut, McCord. I call the play here. Leo, if he opens his mouth again, put a bullet in it!"

"Right, brother," Leo said. He pressed the old man down to ground, keeping a handful of his ragged shirt collar twisted in his hand. Leo moved his pistol back and forth,

from Maria farther up the street, to McCord a few feet away
from him. "I'll shoot anybody you want shot—just say the
word."

"You heard him, girlie." Payton laughed. "It's all up to me
whether you live or die."

Maria stood firm. She'd stepped out onto the street prepared for whatever outcome fate dealt her this morning.
She'd spent the final moments before dawn clearing her
mind, watching the first glow of sunlight spread upward
along the edge of the earth, as if this coming morning might
be her last. Was today a good day to die? But of course it
was . . .

She smiled to herself. Her nerves were surprisingly calm.
Her eyes and hands were steady. If her next act would be
that final point to where all other actions of her life had led
her, then so be it. She took a long breath and tested her grip
around the rifle stock, getting ready. The world before her
became small, a long tunnel she would now step into and vie
for her right of passage.

"You decide only one thing," she called out in a pointed
voice to Payton Parker, her eyes moving across each of the
three men. "Whether you want the gold . . . or whether we
kill one another here in the street. All other matters are out
of your hands."

"I like it," Leo Parker said. He slung the old man to the
side, the man scooting across the dirt as he came staggering
to his bare feet, then scurried out of sight.

"Go," McCord whispered in the old woman's ear, turning
her loose and shoving her out of the way. *Damn these idiots!*
If he ever got out of this mess, so help him God.

Payton Parker felt Hernando tug against the rope. "Where
you think you're going, fool? I ain't turning you loose. I'm
still gonna kill ya. I ain't never turned nobody loose in my

life." As Payton Parker spoke, he kept his eyes on Maria, the sunlight working to her advantage—but not that much, he thought. She'd still go down quick. To hell with the gold. *This* was what men lived and died for, wasn't it? Just this. He wasn't sure exactly what *this* was, but it wasn't about gold. It was something much larger than gold. It was . . . Hell, he had no idea. But it felt right to him. With his hand still holding the rope and the shotgun against Hernando's head, he leveled the pistol in his other hand toward Maria.

But as he looked at her now, behind her coming out of the golden glow, he saw two dark figures step into view, coming closer. He squinted. *Who the hell?* As if hearing his question, Liam Bowes called out in a voice as cool and hollow as the updraft from an open grave, "Good morning, Mr. Parker. Thought we'd missed you there for a minute."

Maria half spun, facing them sideways, seeing the two bloody men walking up the street behind her. Their eyes were glazed, appearing not to see her, or if seeing her, having no interest in her and her small problem of staying alive.

"Son of a bitch . . ." Payton whispered and looked at Liam Bowes and Chance Edwards for a tense second. But then he blinked, spat the burnt match from between his lips, grinned, and said to Leo and McCord, "Damn, boys, we might have us some trouble here."

From atop the roof of the cantina, the Ranger had hurried to the back of the building and started climbing down the second he saw Maria come walking along the middle of the dirt street. He'd crept into San Carlos under the cover of darkness, those few moments before dawn. Upon hearing the Parkers inside the cantina and seeing through a crack in the door the boy with the shotgun to his head and the people huddled into the corner, he'd pulled back, made his way around the cantina, climbed up, and taken position.

He knew better than to make a move until the Parkers were out in the open. So he'd waited and gritted his teeth. But once he'd heard them walk the people out into the street and heard Payton Parker call out to the foothills, he'd gotten the picture and aimed down from the cantina roof, ready to put a bullet through Payton's head as soon as he let go of the boy. Up in those foothills, Maria and the Vanderman woman were safe until he could end this thing. Or so he thought.

As his eye trained along the rifle barrel, Payton Parker's head moving back and forth in his sights, the Ranger had heard Maria's voice, seen her in the sunlight . . . and for a brief instant, he thought his mind had played a trick on him. But she was there all right—down there, on the street, one lone woman, armed and ready to stand off with these three killers. He had to get down to her. He had to shift the focus of these men away from her.

So he had hurried; and now as he rounded the dirt street and stopped at the corner of an alley, he looked in one direction at the Parkers and in the other direction at the two wounded men who'd stopped on the other side of Maria. Maria was now right in the midst of a killing zone. One of the men raised a stripped-down ten-gauge shotgun as he spoke, and the Ranger noted how they stood close, side by side, not spread out the way two would do if they entered a gun battle with any hope of coming out of it alive. As the one with the shotgun talked to Payton Parker, the Ranger stepped out in the middle of the street, drawing his big pistol from his holster.

"You better drop your guns right now, boys," the Ranger said, leveling the pistol, moving it back and forth. "This is gonna get awfully bloody in about a second or two."

Maria's eyes darted to the Ranger. *"Sam . . . ?"* She looked stunned.

"I'm here, Maria. This is your play. I'll back whatever move you make. You just call it."

She stood staring at him in disbelief, but collected herself quickly. She turned to the Parkers. "You heard him—it's over. Give it up. Let the boy go."

"Ha! Nothing's over!" Payton Parker shouted. He raised his voice to Liam Bowes and Chance Edwards. "You boys gonna drop your guns, like this woman and this damned Ranger lawdog told you to?"

"A Ranger?" Liam Bowes half turned toward him, the shotgun leveled in his bloody hands, still keeping an eye on the Parkers. "A Ranger, over here? In *Mejico,* where's there's no law to be found? You're the man with the big rifle?" Bowes managed to keep his voice strong in spite of his wounds and his loss of blood. "The one who butted heads with us at Diablo Canyon? Killed some men of ours?"

"I'm the one," the Ranger said.

"Good show, Ranger," Bowes said. "You should feel honored that the men you killed were among some of the finest—"

"Better kill him, Bowes," Payton Parker called out, stopping Liam Bowes from finishing his words. "We've got the gold . . . once the little lady takes us to it. You're in for a part share. Just get with me here."

"Turn the boy loose," Maria said to Payton Parker. "There is still time."

McCord stood rigid, his pistol drawn and cocked. Beside him, Leo Parker chuckled. But as Payton spoke, the Ranger noticed he had taken a couple of short steps back, pulling the Mexican boy with him. "Did you hear me, Bowes?" Payton

Parker said. "Let bygones be bygones. We're talking *gold* here."

"Gold?" Bowes mused, shooting Chance Edwards a glance. "But don't you see, Payton, we came here to kill you. What do we need with gold?" He started to level the shotgun back toward the Parkers.

"Don't do it," the Ranger warned Bowes, hoping beyond hope to keep this gun battle from raging—for the boy's sake, for Maria's sake. "Drop the gun . . . do it *now*."

Liam Bowes breathed deep, smiled sidelong at Chance Edwards, and said to the Ranger, "Do either of us look to you like men who have ever dropped a gun in our lives?"

Chapter 25

No! The boy! Wait . . . ! But the Ranger had no time to say the words as they spun through his mind. Liam Bowes turned from the Ranger as if he weren't there—a peaceful, trancelike stare on his face, the shotgun swinging toward Payton Parker. Maria saw it coming as Payton Parker backed away, dragging the boy. Bowes pulled the trigger, and a belch of fire and the loud exploding ring of nail heads spit forward through the morning air.

But Bowes staggered as he fired, the Ranger getting off a shot that caught him high in his shoulder and kicked him back a step. The shotgun went off to the side, the nail heads missing Payton Parker, but lifting Leo off the ground and slamming him backward, his pistol going off toward Maria. Maria dove headlong into the dirt street at the sound of the shot. A shot from her own rifle slammed into McCord's chest as he screamed above the melee, *"Wait!"* But even as he'd screamed, his pistol fired, hitting Chance Edwards.

"Leo! Damn it!" Payton yelled, firing with his pistol. Hernando was still at the tip of the shotgun barrel, being slung back and forth, his bare feet stirring up dust. "Do something, Leo!"

Leo pitched upward onto his knees like some demon risen back from its grave, his chest riddled with nail heads, his face a mask of torn pulpy flesh. *"Brooother!"* He screamed loud and long, firing his pistol blindly, one of his shots hitting Chance Edwards, spinning him against Liam Bowes, as Maria put another rifle shot into Leo's bloody chest. Payton moved sidelong now, dragging Hernando, moving behind Leo and back toward the cantina.

The Ranger tried taking aim on Payton Parker but couldn't risk hitting the boy. A shot from Liam Bowes's pistol careened past the Ranger's head. He ducked, spun, and fired, Bowes taking the round in his chest, flinging backward into Chance Edwards, the two of them seeming to be all that held one another up, bullets pounding them in place. Their bodies jerked in time to the sound of each shot from Maria's rifle, from the Ranger's pistol—two broken, twisted marionettes on strings held tight by the hands of a madman.

Payton fired from the door of the cantina, Leo facedown in the dirt street now. McCord was on his knees, his arms spread wide, his pistol down in the dirt, a long string of red saliva swinging from his open mouth. "Turn him loose, Payton!" Maria yelled. In the street, Bowes and Chance Edwards staggered back-to-back, Bowes with an arm behind him around Edwards, steadying them both.

"Like hell!" Payton screamed, then jerked the boy to one side and said, "You want him? Here he comes!" He pulled the trigger on the shotgun as Hernando begged in a frenzied jumble of words.

Maria winced, squeezing her eyes shut. "Noooo!"

The Ranger ran forward and crouched. Nothing would save the boy now. All he could do was make sure Payton fell dead behind him. But then the Ranger skidded to an abrupt halt as the shotgun in Payton's hand clicked on an empty chamber . . . and an eerie silence fell upon the bloody street. Even the plumes of rising dust seemed to stop in the air.

"Shitfire!" Payton said, breaking the deathly silence. His voice had gone flat and weak, looking at the empty shotgun in his hand. *Damn it . . . !* Why hadn't he checked it first? It was too late now. Hernando slumped straight down, his legs giving out beneath him. Payton turned him loose and ducked inside the cantina among the screaming townsfolk as a shot from Maria's rifle whined off the door frame in a spray of splinters.

"Out of my way!" Payton Parker shouted, waving his pistol, moving across the dirt floor as the old peasants scurried from beneath the rear window. He dove headlong, crashing through the glass, taking out frame and all, and rolled to his feet still running. The Ranger came through the door of the cantina, his big pistol cocked. He saw the broken window and turned, knowing full well that the man would head straightaway for the small stable at the end of the dirt street.

"Sam!" Maria held on to the door frame with her free hand, her rifle hanging limp. Dark blood spewed from her thigh with each beat of her pulse.

"Maria! You're hit!" He grabbed her as she fell forward against him, then lowered her to the dirt floor.

"No, Sam . . . go get him! He must not get away!" She clutched his forearm.

"You're bleeding bad. Hold on." He stripped her bandanna from around her neck, tore open her trouser leg, and pressed his thumb firmly against the flesh above the wound. The bleeding lessened. He turned to the townsfolk. "Bandages, please, hurry." He looked back at Maria. "You'll be all right . . . we just need to get a tourniquet around your leg."

Outside, the sound of a horse's hooves pounded away behind the cantina, headed toward the trail across the sand flats. "He is getting away, Sam."

"He's not getting very far," the Ranger said, thinking about Willis Durant out there somewhere, on his way here, maybe right outside the town by now, having heard all the gunfire. "Don't worry about Parker—he won't get very far. You're all that matters to me."

The Ranger stayed by her side, helping the women of San Carlos dress the gunshot wound until at length they found a way to let him know that he must either attend to Maria's wound himself or else get out of their way while they did it. One of the old women shook a weathered finger at him and pulled up a wooden stool for him to sit on. But no sooner had he sat down when Hernando's grandfather limped through the cantina door on a walking stick and told him that one of the men in the street was still alive.

"I really should go check on everybody," the Ranger said, looking a bit embarrassed, his sombrero in his hand. "I should have as soon as it was over."

"*Sí,*" Maria said. She smiled, glancing down as one of the women carefully laid strip upon strip of clean fresh bandages around her thigh. "It is not like you to let things go."

"I know," he said, taking a step to the door. "As soon as you're able, point out the spot were the Vanderman woman is hidden. I'll go get her."

The Vanderman woman . . . Maria nodded—she had a lot to tell him—and watched the Ranger move out onto the dirt street among the dead and dying. "These two are dead for certain," Hernando's grandfather said, jabbing his walking stick into Leo Parker's bloody ribs. He wobbled on his feet and Hernando grabbed him to keep him from falling. The old man spat a white foamy wad on Leo Parker's mangled face.

"Come, Grandfather, they are dead . . . let us forget

them," Hernando said, his face ashen, his eyes swollen and puffy from lack of sleep.

"Un momento." The grandfather turned and spat the same way on McCord, who lay at a twisted angle, one arm stretched out toward a pistol in the dirt. Flies had already moved in. They danced and buzzed above his bloody head. The spotted dog stood a foot away, lapping at the spill of dark blood puddled on the street.

As the Ranger, Hernando, and his grandfather walked to the bodies of Liam Bowes and Chance Edwards, who sat upright back-to-back in the dirt. Hernando's grandmother came leading both burros out from between two adobes. The old grandfather hurried to her, calling out her name. Hernando turned to the Ranger with a questioning look, and the Ranger said, "Go on, young man, see to your family."

With his big pistol reloaded in his hand, the Ranger walked on to Bowes and Edwards, seeing Bowes's bloody hand rise an inch on his lap and then fall over onto the dirt, palm up. The Ranger stepped around first to Chance Edwards, saw the large hole in the side of his forehead, then moved around to Liam Bowes and kicked the shotgun away from him. He got down on one knee in front of Bowes and looked into his eyes.

"Are you needing anything?" the Ranger asked.

"No, not a thing." Liam Bowes struggled with his words, shaking his head slowly. "Both Parkers . . . dead?"

"One is. The other soon will be," the Ranger said. "Are you sure I can't do something for you?"

"I'm sure." With much effort, Liam Bowes moved a bloody hand down his own length. "I daresay . . . I've taken more shots . . . than anyone I know."

The Ranger looked at the many wounds on his chest, his

shoulders, and his neck. "You've taken your share, that's for sure."

"So tell me, Ranger . . . what does a man . . . have to do . . . to die around here?" He spread a thin, wasted smile.

The Ranger didn't answer. Instead, he picked up the dusty battered hat from the dirt, shook it off, and placed in on Bowes's head. "I'll tell them to leave you be for a while."

Liam Bowes nodded and dropped his chin to his chest.

The Ranger stood and walked toward the cantina, waving back a few townsfolk who'd moved barefoot along the dirt street near Bowes and Edwards. "Stay back from him," the Ranger said. "He won't be but a minute."

"Ranger, *por favor*!" Hernando called out, waving him toward him and his grandparents beside the two burros. "Come listen. She says the other woman is gone!"

"It is true, she is not up there," the old grandmother confirmed as the Ranger walked up to them. Doing so, he caught a glimpse of Maria limping out of the cantina, a crutch under one arm. "I find the spot where Maria sent me." The old woman made the sign of the cross, then kissed her thumb. "But she is gone, and the body of Paschal the Frenchman is lying there, half naked. It is terrible! His throat, it is . . . it is . . ." She grimaced, running hr thumb beneath her chin.

The Ranger turned and looked at Maria as she came up to them. "There are things I must tell you all about her," Maria said. "First of all, she is not who you think she is. . . ."

"Oh? Then tell me out of the sun." The Ranger steadied her with a gloved hand on her forearm, and turned her back toward the cantina. "Am I going to have a problem keeping you off your feet for a few days?"

She managed a tired grin and shook her head. "No, but you must listen to me. . . ."

* * *

Even with the wound in his side, Willis Durant had taken the woman and her horse down in a spray of dust, leaping down on them like a mountain cat as they'd rounded a turn beneath a tall standing boulder. Perhaps she would have stopped for him anyway. But he couldn't risk it. He knew she was one of the women from the train. She had made her getaway, and for all he knew, she could have been hysterical—could have bolted away and left him afoot in the morning haze.

But now he had a horse beneath him. That was the main thing. He'd been walking long enough, his own horse having come up lame as he'd pressed it hard toward San Carlos the hour before dawn. This woman and her horse had come to him like a gift from the heavens. He'd held her against his chest for the past half hour, his arms around her, holding the reins, she in the saddle, he behind her, pushing the horse in the final stretch toward the sound of gunfire.

At the sight of the lone rider two hundred yards away headed in the opposite direction, Durant slowed the horse down and spun it around. Was that who he thought it was? "See! There goes Payton Parker!" She spoke fast. "I told you, don't go to San Carlos! Please!"

He hardly heard her as he focused on the lone rider, the man bowed forward in his saddle, moving fast, leaving a tall-standing sheet of dust behind him. *Jesus! It* is *him!* Payton Parker's face turned toward them, his hat brim stand-up-flat-in-the-air; even at this distance, Willis Durant recognized the face, the build, even the aura of Payton Parker. Judging from the way the man ducked his face forward at the sight of him and slapped the reins across the horse's sides, Durant knew Payton Parker had just recognized him as well.

"You're right, ma'am!" Durant turned the horse and batted his boots to its sides. "We're not headed to San Carlos. Hang on!"

Prudence braced herself against him, letting him take her closer to the gold, away from everything else. She knew Maria would have her hands full back there once daylight came. Had she not been snatched by the big Frenchman, a knife held to her throat, she would have stayed and waited for Maria to return. But that hadn't been the way it worked out.

Things had gotten out of hand, the light winking out in the adobe window—something had gone terribly wrong there. Then the big Frenchman came ready to cut her throat. *How dare that bastard,* she thought. Well . . . he'd learned a hard lesson there. She'd put the straight razor to him as soon as she got the chance, then taken his big strong horse, and headed out. She wasn't ashamed of it. In fact, she wondered if maybe Maria hadn't told her about the true spot where the gold lay buried as an added incentive to get out of there should things start going wrong for her. That was something she would always wonder about.

When this man had sprung down and taken her and the big horse to the ground, she'd thought for a second that the game was over. But here she was, still headed for the gold, almost as if it was meant for her to have it. She smiled, seeing Payton Parker ahead of them, their big horse gaining on him. *Run, you son of a bitch! But keep running in that same direction . . .*

Somewhere along the trail of dust and heat, Prudence lost all sense of time. By the time this man handed her the reins and raised the Frenchman's long rifle from its boot, the sun seemed to have leaped from its spot on the eastern horizon, standing white hot above them. "Keep it steady," Willis Durant said near her ear.

She nodded, feeling the stock of the rifle on her shoulder, his left arm coming up across her bosom, taking the front stock in hand. She felt the jolt of the explosion and felt the rifle rise off her shoulder, the horse pounding on beneath them. *Well, of course he'd missed. How could anyone make a shot like that?* she thought.

But as she squinted into the sun's glare, feeling Durant take the reins from her hands, she saw Payton Parker's horse sway in the distance, its bellowing brown wake twisting back and forth, then coming to an end altogether in one large puff of dust. In another second, the wake of dust had drifted, and she saw Payton Parker struggling on foot, scrambling upward on a sandy rise.

"You shot the horse! My God! How did you manage to—?" She turned in the saddle, looking up at Durant's face, his features shadowed beneath the brim of his hat, his beard wild and untrimmed and full of road dust. He slowed the big horse down, reached a hand forward past Prudence, and rubbed the horse's withers.

"I was aiming for the man," Willis Durant said.

She saw his eyes fixed resolutely on Payton Parker as he stopped the big horse altogether and got down from the saddle. "Climb down," he said. "We're going to walk for a spell."

Ahead of them, Payton Parker struggled upward. All he needed to do was get to cover somewhere—make a stand. Hell, Willis Durant wasn't going to kill him. He'd find himself a dark spot on this white blazing inferno and pick *el Negro's* eyes out. *No problem,* he thought, getting to the crest of the sandy rise. But then something hit him hot and hard at knee level from behind. "Christ!" he screamed, going down hard on the burning sand. Then he heard the explosion and knew what had happened. "Damn it all!" He twisted around in the sand, struggling up on one leg, his hand clasped around the gush of blood where his kneecap used to be. "Why, Willis? You son of a bitch!" He spread his free arm out as he yelled. "In the knee? You can do better than—"

His free arm jerked back, struck by a hot jolt of lead. He saw the puff of blue smoke and fell back from the impact just as he heard the explosion. "Well, shit!" He caught a glimpse of them walking toward him out there in the haze, leading a big horse. Frenchy's horse? That figured. Payton Parker rolled down into the dry wash on the other side of the sandy rise and lay there catching his breath, his arm bleeding freely down his side, his right kneecap all but missing.

Back on the trail, Prudence looked up into Durant's dark caged face. "You're torturing him? Why? For God sakes, man. Don't take him apart like this, one piece at a time! Either kill him or take him alive!

She reached out for Durant's arm as he lowered the rifle, gazing at the crest of the rise where Payton Parker had just seemed to sink into the ground. But Willis Durant jerked his arm away from Prudence's hand, staring straight ahead. "I prefer doing both," he said.

They walked on. Willis Durant loaded another round into the Frenchman's long rifle and cradled it in the crook of his arm. As they walked, Prudence asked Durant what could Payton Parker have done to make him want to torture him this way? "I mean, just kill him if you have to and get it over with," she said. "Why do this to him?"

"You wouldn't understand, ma'am." Durant looked at her, this young, wealthy, pale-skinned woman, whose father had raised her on silver-threaded cushions throughout her life. What did she know about pain and suffering? Yet, for some reason, by the time the two of them had reached the dead horse and started up the rise of sand, he had told her everything—spilled the whole story of his wife and son as if ridding himself of some terrible weight bearing down on his shoulders.

When he'd finished, they stopped at the crest of the sandy rise and looked down at the blood trail leading off along the dry wash, the wash itself looking familiar to her. "I know how ugly and wrong this all sounds to somebody like you, Miss Vanderman," Willis Durant said. "But you asked . . . and now you know."

At the floor of the dry wash, Durant hitched the big horse to a stand of brush in the shade of the dirt bank. He moved forward along the wash and said to Prudence, "Stay back here. He's still got some fight left in him."

"Then why are you walking straight into him? Do you want him to kill you? Is that what this is? You want to die? Will that make things right in your head? Will that take away the picture of your family lying dead in the dirt? Who killed them, Willis Durant? Him . . . or *you*?"

Willis Durant swung his intense, dark eyes to her, Prudence shying back a step from the heat of his stare. His nostrils flared; his shoulders seemed to rise like the hackles of some creature at bay. "Ma'am—" He bit on his words, trying to keep control of his boiling rage. "You best stay back here . . . you don't want to see this kind of killing." His hand went down to his boot well and came up with the knife blade glistening in the sunlight.

Chapter 26

The Ranger had ridden hard atop Leo Parker's big dun horse, leading McCord's horse and the white barb behind him. He'd spent the dun out, cut it loose, and rode the other spare until he reached the spot on the trail where another set of hoofprints had bored in from the right. He had been switching his saddle over to his white barb when he heard the sound of gunfire not too far ahead. But from here, the roll of the land cut his vision short a few hundred yards out. He heeled the white barb forward, bearing left up onto a higher pitch of land, hoping to get above the flats before the waver of noon heat began to swell and boil. Somewhere out there he hoped to see the woman, or Parker . . . or Willis Durant—perhaps all three before the day was over.

From along a higher level of sandy ridge line, the Ranger raised the big rifle and looked out through the scope, using it as a field lens, trying to spot someone out there from where the shots had come. In a blur, he saw only one lone figure riding beyond a dip in the land. He homed in on it and made out the wavering image of the old man—the last of Zell's riders—moving down out of sight. There was a deep dry wash down there, he thought, the one Maria had told him about, the place where she'd hidden the gold.

"Come on, Black-eye," he said to the white barb, "let's get around to where we can see something."

While the Ranger circled wide, gaining sight of the dry wash, on the belly of the wash old man Dirkson slipped down from his bloody saddle and fanned his horse away. He dropped to his knees, tightened the bloodstained bandanna around his hand, took the long pistol from his waist, and checked it. Then he moved along the wash, edging up, getting closer to the black man and the woman he'd seen go down in it only moments before. The woman had brought the man here to pick up the *federale* gold—no doubt about it.

When he heard a sound in the wash beneath him, Dirkson stopped, crouched behind a stand of rock, and waited. He heard the sound of boots moving on loose stone down the center of the wash. There they came, the big black man, a knife in one hand, a rifle in the other. *The Frenchman's rifle? It damned sure was!* Behind him, the woman struggled to keep up. Yep, they were headed for the gold—he'd bet on it. Old man Dirkson grinned to himself, pressing a hand against the wound in his chest. He still had some play left here. All he had to was bide his time. He stayed in the cover of rock, ten feet above them, watching. . . .

Willis Durant heard a sound ahead of him and turned around in the dry wash. He said over his shoulder in a low tone, "He's there. For the last time, ma'am . . . get on back out of the way."

Prudence stopped, looking all around at the rocky ground beneath their feet. She lifted her face at some rancid odor adrift on the air and said just above a whisper, "What's that smell?"

"Something's dead around there," Durant said. He looked down at Payton Parker's blood trail, stopped, and listened, then slowly stepped forward around the turn in the wash.

Five feet in front of him, the remains of Juan Verdere lay scattered on the rocky ground where the scavengers had left it. A small creature struggled with a piece of a bloody boot, dragging it backward into a dark hollow space beneath a rock.

Durant lifted his eyes up the wash, following Payton Parker's blood trail. "Come on out, Payton. You've got one good hand left. I know there's a gun in it. Get out here and use it."

Moving up behind him, Prudence looked around at the scraps of Juan Verdere and at the bloody smear where he had leaned back against a flat rock in the bank of the dry wash until the scavengers began their feast. Her eyes went across the wash to the standing stump of the cottonwood tree, recognizing it. Her eyes flashed back to the rock. *Was that it? The rock where Maria had hidden the saddlebags of gold? Yes! It had to be!*

"What do you say, Payton?" Durant called out. "Want to come out here? Do this like a man? Or sit in the rocks and bleed to death like a rat?"

A pistol shot exploded, kicking up sand and loose rock at Durant's feet. "You don't look too spry yourself, Willis," Payton Parker called out from the side of the wash. "You're still pissed off over Leo and me killing that Injun woman and her half-breed brat, I reckon? I don't know why—she wasn't all that much when we got down to it." He chuckled, low and ugly.

Willis Durant had spotted where the shot came from. He moved forward, crouching, following Payton's voice. Laying the rifle aside and gripping the long skinning knife tight in his hand, Durant crawled up onto the bank through brush and spilling sand.

Farther back in the wash, Prudence kicked a few bloody

scraps of clothes and bones out of her way and clawed around the edge of the flat rock with her hands, digging fervently like a dog. She scratched out a good hand-hold for herself, and with one foot against the bank, she pulled and grunted until the rock came forward and fell over onto the ground. "Sweet Jesus," she exhaled in a hushed tone, falling to her knees. There it was . . . the gold! The saddlebags had been pressed back against the sandy bank, but as she stared at them, the weight of the gold pulled them loose, and they fell over at her knees in a puff of dust.

Looking down at the saddlebags, she heard a raspy voice behind her say in a whisper, "One down . . . one to go." She jerked her head around. But all she saw was the glint of the pistol barrel as old man Dirkson swiped it around and hit her across the forehead.

Dirkson dropped down, hefted the saddlebags over his shoulder, and moved back up onto the edge of the bank. Once there, he crouched behind the cottonwood stump and waited with his pistol in his hand. He wasn't leaving here with this black man dogging his trail.

"No! Willis! For the love of God!" Payton Parker pleaded, loud and long, until his pleading turned into a long, loud scream. Old man Dirkson listened, winced, and let out a sigh of relief when the scream stopped short and silence fell across the dry wash. *There went Payton Parker,* Dirkson thought. *Good riddance.* He rose slightly, the saddlebags over his shoulder and his gun hand braced against the side of the stump.

Willis Durant staggered out of the brush, the skinning knife hanging from his bloody fingertips. His breath pounded in his chest. In the loose sandy bed of the dry wash, he dropped down to his knees and bowed his head to calm himself for a moment; then cupping his hands, he scooped up sand and wiped it up and down his forearms, cleansing himself of Payton Parker's blood. It was finished. He could suddenly breathe now, without the oppressive tightness that had clutched his chest these many months.

When he'd finished cleansing himself, he pitched the knife away, stood up, and took a deep breath. But just as he stood up, old man Dirkson above him took aim, now at less than twenty feet. When the shot went off, Durant only had time to flinch and duck his shoulders, the bullet whistling past his ear. He heard the rustling in the sandy dirt above him and turned to it, braced, his pistol already out and cocked. What the . . . ?

Old man Dirkson stood there with a strange, bemused smile on his face, the pistol hanging from his hand, the saddlebags draped heavily across his shoulder. Willis Durant suddenly saw him rock forward a step, catch himself, then topple forward like a downed tree, falling headlong, the saddlebags coming up off his shoulder as he landed facedown at Durant's feet. Dark arterial blood rose in a low braid from the hole in the back of the old man's neck. Durant stared down at it and saw the blood flow dwindle down and stop, as if a hand had just turned off a spigot.

Durant looked all around, hearing the echo of the shot from a long ways off. There was only one person could've fired that shot, from that far away. He scanned the endless land. Then he looked down at the saddlebags, seeing where one of the flaps had come open. He knelt and just stared, his pistol still in his hand. He didn't hear Prudence stumble and catch herself on the other bank as she moved up behind him. "It's . . . it's the gold," she said in a halting voice, a hand against the swollen whelp on her forehead.

"Yes . . . I see it is." Durant stayed down on his knees. After a pause, he shook his head slowly and said, "You can't imagine the things I would have done in the past just to get my hands on this."

As he spoke, Prudence moved forward closer behind him, her head clearing now, her hand lifting the bloody straight razor from up under her arm. "This gold is mine," she said.

"I stole for it"—Willis Durant went on, not hearing her— "I schemed for it. Killed for it . . . even went to prison for it."

"It belongs to me, and nobody else," Prudence said, opening the straight razor, moving closer to his broad back.

"And now," Durant said, still not hearing her, "I look at this, and I realize . . . it's nothing anymore."

Behind him, Prudence had started to reach out with her free hand, the razor drawn back, ready. But she stopped, waiting for a second. "I gave up on this," Durant said. "Because I found something better. Found a woman I loved . . . a woman who loved me. A son . . ." She saw his broad shoulders tremble as he stopped and shook his head again. "Now they're gone . . . and this falls into my lap." He let go of a long breath and sat back on his haunches, away from the saddlebags. "Well, it means nothing to me now." He glanced at her over his shoulder. "You take it, Miss Vanderman . . . not that you need it. But there's no sense it just lying out here."

He ran a palm across his watery eyes and turned the rest of the way around, seeing her, and the straight razor in her hand. She lowered the razor, closing it into its pearl casing as Durant looked up into her eyes, a curious expression on his dirty blood-streaked face. She smiled, seeming to let go of something inside herself. "You're right, there's no point in it lying out here. I'll take it." She smiled. "See that it gets a good home."

Durant looked down to the closed razor in her hand, then he lifted his eyes back up to hers. She saw the question there; and she bounced the razor on the palm of her hand and said,

"Oh, this?" She reached her free hand down to help lift him by his broad shoulders. "Come on," she said as he stood up. "I have a canteen on the horse. You look like you've been dragged through a slaughter house. Go wash your face." She placed the razor in his hand. "A shave wouldn't hurt either. We have a long ride ahead of us."

"We do?" Willis Durant just looked at her. "Miss Vanderman, I have no place in mind. You take the horse . . . you'll need it to get out of here."

"Nonsense . . . and my name is Prudence, not Miss Vanderman. Come along now." She took him by his shirtsleeve. "You're not leaving me alone in this hellhole, carrying these bags of gold. Do you think I'm a fool?"

Willis Durant drew his arm away. "Ma'am, it goes without saying, you and I are a long ways from one another . . ."

She smiled. "Oh, not as far as you might think, once you know more about me. But we can talk about that some other time, some other place . . . say, Mexico City?" She cocked her head to the side.

"Mexico City?" Willis Durant considered it, gazing off toward the northeast as if collecting his dark memories from the wavering heat in that direction.

"Leave them. Let them rest in peace," Prudence said. "There's nothing back there, nothing you can change."

"But . . ." Durant ran a hand across his dirty face, searching for something to say, something to justify keeping the bad memories alive.

"No," she said, "leave them behind. We always leave something behind." And she gazed off into the distance with him, but only for a moment. Then she turned with him, and together they picked up the saddlebags between them and walked back toward the horse.

*   *   *

Above the crest of the sandy rise, the Ranger watched the two of them ride up from the dry wash atop the big horse and head up the slope of sand, going west. He'd seen everything from up here through the small round circle of his rifle scope. He'd watched old man Dirkson stand up, taking aim on Willis Durant. *Now we're even, Durant,* he'd thought as the rifle butt slammed his shoulder and old man Dirkson pitched forward, out of the small circle of the scope. A moment later, he'd watched the woman move up behind Durant, the razor open in her hand. At that point he'd centered the scope on her too. But something had told him to wait. So he'd waited, then relaxed the rifle when he saw her move back a step and close the razor. *Willis, Willis . . . you hardheaded peckerwood.*

The Ranger smiled to himself. The rifle lay on his lap now as he saw the horse carry them out of sight across the roll of the land. Nothing remained but the rise of their dust; and the Ranger turned the white barb before they lifted back into sight on the next sandy rise. He didn't know what he would tell Sheriff Tackett when he saw him. Tackett sure loved that pistol Willis Durant was carrying.

But Tackett ought to realize that's how things go out here, he thought, heeling the white barb forward. "Come on, Black-eye." Raising a hand, he tightened down the brim of his tall gray sombrero against a hot gust of wind. *You lose something here, win something there . . . and in the end, all that's left is the last hoofprint in the drifting sand.* He'd get on back to Maria now, hear what else she had to say. He'd never admit it, but, God, he loved the sound of her voice. And he'd think of something to tell Tackett once they got back across the border. He wasn't sure what, but he'd think of a good story. Something would come to him. Something always did. . . .

Ralph Cotton

JUSTICE   19496-9

A powerful land baron uses his political influence to persuade local lawmen to release his son from a simple assault charge. The young man, however, is actually the leader of the notorious Half Moon Gang—a mad pack of killers with nothing to lose!

BORDER DOGS   19815-8

The legendary Arizona Ranger Sam Burrack is forced to make the most difficult decision of his life when his partner is captured by ex-Confederate renegades—The Border Dogs. His only ally is a wanted outlaw with blood on his hands...and a deadly debt to repay the Dogs.

BLOOD MONEY   20676-2

Bounty hunters have millions of reasons to catch J.T. Priest—but Marshal Hart needs only one. And he's sworn to bring the killer down...mano-a-mano.

DEVIL'S DUE   20394-1

The second book in Cotton's "Dead or Alive" series. *Los Pistoleros* were the most vicious gang of outlaws around—but Hart and Roth thought they had them under control...Until the jailbreak.